Hostage
Copyright © 2015 by Tfutza Publications
ISBN: 978-1-60091-353-2

Tfutza Publications
P.O.B. 50036
Beitar Illit 90500
Tel: 972-2-650-9400
Tfutza1@gmail.com

©All rights reserved. No part of this book may be reproduced or transmitted in any form or by any means (electronic, photocopying, recording or otherwise) without prior permission of the copyright holder or distributor.

First printed in Hebrew as: *Bat Arubah*
Cover Design: Aviad Ben-Simon
Translation: E. Perkal

Distributed by:
Israel Bookshop Publications
501 Prospect Street
Lakewood, NJ 08701
Tel: (732) 901-3009
Fax: (732) 901-4012
www.israelbookshoppublications.com
info@israelbookshoppublications.com

Printed in Israel

Distributed in Europe by:
Lehmanns
Unit E Viking Industrial Park
Rolling Mill Road,
Jarrow , Tyne & Wear NE32 3DP
44-191-430-0333

Distributed in Australia by:
Gold's Book & Gift Company
3- 13 William Street
Balaclava 3183
613-9527-8775

Distributed in S. Africa by:
Kollel Bookshop

Ivy Common
107 William Rd, Norwood
Johannesburg 2192
27-11-728-1822

Distributed in Israel by:
Shanky's
16 Petach Tikvah St.
Jerusalem
972-2-538-6936

CHAPTER 1

Moscow, 1987

Natalya Kolchik surveyed the room with a critical eye. The two beds, positioned on either side of the ornamental fireplace, were neatly covered with elaborately patterned comforters, and she carefully adjusted the matching throw cushions, before standing back to enjoy the overall effect. Beneath the picture window, the mahogany dresser was polished to a sheen, and a vase with freshly picked blossoms stood on its surface. The curtains had been laundered just the day before, and now they added a sense of luxury to the room, their velvet creases bound by burgundy ribbons, drawn back to let the pale sunlight filter into the room.

Despite her satisfaction with the results of her efforts, Natalya sighed. Would her guests be happy with their accommodations? The room was small, and she had intended to host just one of the girls there and the other in the adjoining room, but Katerina had insisted that the girls would prefer to stay together, adding that neither of them were accustomed to a high standard of living and that they would be more than happy with whatever they were offered. Nonetheless, Natalya shook her head ruefully, reflecting that the girls would doubtless not appreciate whatever they were given to its proper extent. The youth of that day of age knew little of the deprivation of their parents' generation; they had no idea what suffering meant.

Natalya forcefully returned her thoughts to the present, and to how eager she was for the girls to arrive. Despite, or perhaps because of, the opulence of her home and lifestyle, the void that was within her ached constantly to be filled. Aside from Katerina, bless her soul, no one was privy to her loneliness and yearning for company. Katerina was her closest friend in the world and probably the only person who came close to understanding how badly she sought solace. Thus, it had come as no surprise when Katerina suggested that her daughter should visit Natalya for the summer; and Natalya had gratefully seized onto the idea.

Fifteen-year-old Luba would soon be arriving, along with a friend, and Natalya could hardly wait. She was certain that the two girls would bring vitality, creativity, and renewal into her humdrum life, and she preferred not to dwell on the fact that the girls would only be temporary guests. At least while they were there she would be able to take her mind off her longing for her son, a child to dote on. Even though six years had passed since he had lost him, she still felt as if she were mourning him, even though on the outside, her life continued as before. But her emotions were frozen, and now she hoped that the visit of Katerina's daughter and her friend would break the ice and allow her to begin life anew.

After casting one final glance around the room, Natalya walked back down the corridor to the kitchen, to check that she had stocked up with enough fresh food. The refrigerator was full, with dairy products, fruits and vegetables, as well as other sundry items, and the cabinets were also bursting with dry goods. For a moment, Natalya savored the feeling of pleasure in giving to others, as well as her sense of accomplishment at having put everything together in time. Checking her watch, she saw that it was almost time to leave for the Metro station where she would meet the girls and bring them back to her home.

She reached the station with plenty of time to spare. The wait on the platform stirred memories of days long since passed, of all the times she had waited at the primitive train station in her childhood village for her friends to visit her. Most of her friends had been cultured city girls, and, to her bemusement, they had been eager to seize the opportunity to vacation in her simple village for a few weeks during the summer. They had spent hours playing in the turnip fields and then jumping in the hay, giggling when the strands got caught in their hair and enjoying the sense of liberation that only vast open expanses of countryside could provide them.

Natalya had delighted in their company, even though she was bemused as to why they seemed to prefer village life to the excitement she imagined was daily fare in the big cities. How she had envied them back then! With longing eyes, she would stare at their store-bought dresses and she dreamed of living in one of the tall, multi-story buildings that lined the teeming city streets. Yet, whenever she begged her parents to consider moving, she was swiftly rebuffed. "You don't know how lucky you are to live in the country," her father would tell her. "People starved in the cities during the war. And it's easier to keep out of sight of prying eyes…" But it was many years before Natalya understood his words.

Of all the many girls who had visited her in her country cottage, she had loved Katerina and Anya the best and had eagerly awaited their arrival. Oh, Anya… Why was she suddenly recalling that traitor who had brought such tragedy upon her? Nonetheless, Natalya couldn't deny that once upon a time, Anya had been her closest friend, the girl in whom she had confided her deepest secrets, the one to whom she had poured her heart out whenever she had needed a listening ear. How cruel she had been, to take something so beautiful and rip it to shreds! The anguish and feeling of betrayal was as acute today as it had been back then, making her occasional forays into the past painful, jarring experiences that she preferred to avoid.

Thankfully, she was jolted out of her reveries by the roar of an approaching train, and she watched the huge metal monster speed down the tracks, its bright lights like luminous eyes in the gloom of the station. A squeal of brakes heralded its arrival and a minute later, the doors opened and Natalya watched a sea of humanity spill onto the platform. Suddenly, she wondered how in the world she would succeed in identifying two unfamiliar teens. It had been five years since she had last seen Luba, and the child was now a young woman who could have changed immensely during that passage of time.

People in an array of colors and expressions brushed by, with everyone seemingly in a hurry. Natalya didn't spot even one vaguely familiar face, but luckily, Luba found her first.

"Natalya!" she called, waving vigorously to her mother's friend. "How nice of you to come and meet us!"

"Luba," she greeted the girl warmly. "I'm so thrilled to see you, and to be hosting you! I didn't know how in the world I'd find you here! How was your trip, girls?" she directed her question at both Luba and her companion.

"Longer than we thought it would be, but the scenery was very pleasant," Luba replied politely.

Natalya studied both girls, her gaze lingering slightly longer on Luba's friend. She had an interesting face with azure eyes that were somewhat sad and a small, firmly-set mouth. She waited for the girl to introduce herself, but her guest merely returned her gaze with an even stare and the faintest wisp of a smile.

"What's your name?" Natalya queried.

"Karina Levandrova. Thank you for inviting me along with Luba," the girl replied courteously.

"I hope you'll both enjoy yourself here," Natalya replied with a friendly smile. Karina's words somehow gave her such a good feeling, although she couldn't explain how or why. "So, girls, are we ready to go?" she asked brightly. The two friends nodded and began to drag their suitcases across the station. They had been travelling for over four hours, and when Natalya saw how tired the girls appeared from the trip, she decided to wait until later to engage them in conversation.

Two hours later, the girls had freshened up from their trip and joined Natalya in her opulent dining room for dinner. Natalya served the roast beef that she had prepared earlier in the afternoon, proudly inhaling the succulent smell of meat and rich gravy. Vegetables and legumes were served in matching porcelain dishes, and Natalya urged the girls to fill their plates.

"Thank you, Natalya," Karina sounded apologetic, "but I'm a vegetarian and don't touch meat."

"A vegetarian?" Natalya treated the girl to a horrified look. "But why? And who planted such a ridiculous idea in your head? What on earth do your parents say to that?"

"They don't have much of a choice," Karina explained. "Any meat, chicken, or even fish causes me terrible stomach pains and digestive problems. Several years ago, the doctor told my parents that it seemed that the only solution to my health issues was simply to go vegetarian. It wasn't easy, believe me!" the girl added.

"I've never heard of such a thing!" Natalya shook her head in disbelief as she replaced the platter of meat on the table. "Meat and chicken are such healthy foods. I don't see how a person can maintain good health without them, and especially a growing girl like you."

"Usually, you're right," Karina conceded. "But my case is one of the exceptions to the rule. I have a terribly weak stomach, and I suffer from even the slightest variation to my diet. I was miserable for years, and by the time the doctor reached his prognosis, I was willing to try just about anything, as long as it would make me feel better. And those were his orders."

"And it really works?" Natalya asked skeptically.

Karina shrugged. "I stopped losing weight, and I started feeling much better. Is there any better proof than that?"

Natalya stole a regretful look at the succulent slices of meat, and she felt a pang in her heart. "Luba, your mother didn't mention that your friend is vegetarian."

"I don't think she knows," Luba shrugged good-naturedly. "But don't worry, Natalya. It's really not such a big deal. Karina's fine just eating fruits and vegetables, and bread of course."

"That's right – it's really not a big deal," Karina agreed quickly. "I've stayed away from home several times in the past few years, and it's never posed any difficulty."

"Well, I have plenty of fruit and vegetables, and you can eat as much bread as you wish. But…" Natalya sighed. There was no way she could showcase her culinary skills when the most she could do was dice a salad. "Oh well, never mind."

Her disappointment was clearly evident, and Luba hastened to console her hostess. "Well, I'm looking forward to tasting your roast. It looks, and smells, amazing!" she exclaimed brightly.

Natalya smiled. "Enjoy your meal. I went to a lot of effort for you – both. At least one of you will be able to eat my food." As she spoke, she passed the dish of steamed vegetables over to Karina. "Please, help yourself."

Karina blushed as she eyed the dish suspiciously. "Um, was it cooked together with the meat?" she asked hesitantly.

"Of course! That's why it's so delicious! At least you'll get to enjoy a taste of what you're missing!"

"I wish," Karina sighed regretfully. "But if the vegetables were cooked together with the meat, then I can't eat them."

Natalya froze with the serving spoon in the air. "Really, now!" she said disapprovingly. "Don't you think that doctor of yours is going a little too far?"

"I did think so at first, but when I saw how effective the diet was, I stopped complaining," the girl replied. "I suffered so much for so many years that even swearing off some of my favorite foods was worth regaining my health. I'm used to it by now. And it's not as bad as it sounds."

Well, I'm not used to it, and I think it's terrible! Natalya complained mutely. If it were up to her, she would send this Karina Levandrova back home and tell Luba to invite a different friend to join them. The mere thought of cooking and enjoying her favorite dishes while her guest ate nothing but fruit and vegetables grated on her, but of course, she didn't say a word.

CHAPTER 2

It was late by the time they finally closed the door to their room. Karina collapsed onto her bed and sighed as she contemplated her suitcase, which she had yet to unpack. "I guess I'll do it tomorrow," she mumbled to nobody in particular.

"You look awfully pale," Luba observed as she changed into pajamas. "Are you feeling okay?"

"All that small talk with Natalya tires me out. I feel like I have to watch every single word that comes out of my mouth. It's exhausting."

"You know what?" Luba said suddenly. "We really didn't prepare for this properly. If we're supposed to be good friends, then we should know a lot more about each other."

"You're right. I should know a lot more about you, and about your friends too." Karina nodded wearily. "Natalya probably won't ask much about things – just superficial questions and stuff – but in case she does…"

"But what do we do now? You look so tired," Luba replied worriedly.

"I am tired. Exhausted, to be precise, But we can't go to sleep until you teach me everything significant that I need to know. This visit is way too important for us to mess up."

"But you're falling asleep," Luba argued, noting the gaping yawn that split Karina's face.

"I'll stay awake somehow, and you'll shake me if you need to," Karina said, only half-jokingly. "I have this feeling that Natalya will be right there waiting for us the moment we open the door in the morning," she added dryly.

"All right, if you insist," Luba said doubtfully, sitting up on her bed and staring straight into Karina's eyes. "Where should I start? Well, first there's my group of friends. There are five of us, and we hang out together most of the time. There are other cliques that are always competing with us."

"Competing?"

"To earn the top grades. It's academic, social, you name it."

"Do you think I need to know their names?"

"At least some of them."

Luba began listing names, with Karina repeating after her, trying to commit them to memory. Despite her fatigue, she forced herself to learn six names by heart, which she hoped would be enough for the next few days, at least.

"Before we leave the room tomorrow, maybe you should give me some more details," she said finally, before stretching out in bed and murmuring some foreign-sounding words that made Luba stare.

"What's all that about?" Luba asked, eyebrows raised.

Karina motioned to her friend that it wasn't important and then turned around to face the wall.

Natalya inspected the breakfast table with a stern eye, hoping that the girls would appreciate her efforts. She had to admit that the table was set far more elaborately than anyone would expect for a regular weekday, but Natalya still couldn't help herself – after all, how often did she have guests such as these?

Dmitri chuckled as he watched his wife. "Not good enough yet? You'd think you were hosting a contingent of international diplomats! Do you really think the girls need to eat breakfast on fine china?"

"Why not?" Karina retorted. "In my eyes, these girls *are* important guests, and I'm enjoying their visit immensely. I want them to enjoy it just as much. What's so wrong with that?"

"Nothing, I suppose," Dmitri replied. "Just don't let yourself get too attached to them, because I don't want it to be too difficult for you when they have to leave." His tone was unusually gentle.

Natalya froze; she hadn't thought that far, even once, but she quickly regained her composure. "It may be painful," she conceded, "but at least I'll have enjoyed every moment of our time together. They'll be spending nine weeks with us, and I'm determined to enjoy every second of the vacation."

"Even at the cost of the pain that's sure to follow?" Dmitri refused to yield so quickly.

This time, Natalya allowed herself to contemplate his question honestly, and her husband afforded her the time to think. "Yes," she finally replied. "Even at that cost." She just hoped she'd feel the same in nine weeks' time.

Dmitri left for work, leaving Natalya alone in the kitchen. Every few minutes, she walked down the corridor, almost as far as the door to the guest room where the girls were sleeping. When would they get up already? Natalya had never been renowned for her patience, and now it was wearing thin.

It's only seven-thirty, she reminded herself. *And they're on vacation. They're teenagers, and they're probably making the most of their oppor-*

tunity to sleep late. Nonetheless, Natalya felt her annoyance mounting. After all, she had taken the day off work in honor of her guests, meaning, in her eyes, that every moment she didn't spend with them was wasted.

It hadn't been a simple matter to be granted permission for a day's leave of absence, especially as she hadn't wanted to divulge the reason, sufficing with a vague excuse of "having something important to attend to."

Yenina had treated her to a disapproving stare in response. "You know that I can't just authorize a day off without a better explanation than that."

"Yenina, please. How many sick days have I taken in the last year – even several years?"

Yenina thought quickly and then nodded reluctantly. "You're right. Not one. I won't argue that point. But that's the way it should be. If you're healthy, there's no reason to take off work; and be happy that you are."

Natalya had lowered her voice until her boss had to strain to hear her. "And one more thing, Yenina: How many workers procure fictitious medical reports to allow them to take a day off here and there? Can you argue that?" Ultimately, Natalya knew that her winning card would be her husband's prominence which escorted her like a shadow wherever she went. Even Yenina couldn't be too stubborn, especially since her own husband had once benefited from Dmitri's generosity. Friends in high places were a rare and valued commodity, and Yenina was not about to alienate Natalya over a relatively minor matter.

Thus, eight o'clock the next morning found Natalya staring out of her kitchen window rather than sitting on a Moscow Metro train on her way to work. By the time the ornate grandfather clock chimed eight-fifteen, she was pacing the floor with gritted teeth, berating herself for not thinking to arrange a schedule with the girls the previous night. She had assumed that as responsible high school girls they would be up and about at an earthly hour, but this was impossible! How could they remain so oblivious to her impatience?

For the umpteenth time, she tiptoed down the corridor, pausing close enough to the girls' door to hear if they were up. This time, she wondered if she shouldn't simply knock sharply at the door and rouse them. Surely they would understand once she explained that she had taken the day off work especially for them?

Natalya stood quietly for a moment, and then she heard it – the sound of muted voices from the other side of the door. The girls were up! Assuming that it was only a matter of moments before they emerged, she hurried back to the kitchen where she set the kettle on the stovetop, and a few minutes later, three china cups filled with hot tea were placed on the breakfast table, complementing the beautiful spread of pastries and fruit.

Several minutes passed. The steam from the teacups dissipated, but there was still no sign of life.

Unable to restrain herself any longer, Natalya strode down the corridor until she was standing right outside the door to the guest room. The girls were still conversing quietly, but other than that, there was no sign of life. Without wasting another moment, Natalya lifted her hand and rapped firmly on the door.

The voices instantly died, and Natalya couldn't fathom what was going on. Why weren't they opening the door? Although her instincts screamed at her to stop, she heard herself knock again, even louder than the first time.

The door opened hesitantly, and Luba's face appeared in the crack between the door and wall.

"Is everything all right, girls? Don't you know what time it is?" Natalya demanded.

"What time?" Luba asked in astonishment.

"Half past eight! I admit that I forgot to tell you, but I took the day off of work especially so I could show you around the city. Breakfast was on the table over an hour ago already!"

"Oh, Natalya, we're terribly sorry!" Luba apologized profusely. "We didn't realize, and we were both so tired from the trip that we were just lazing in bed. We'll be up and out of here in a flash. I hope you're not upset with us. We didn't dream that you were waiting for us!"

"Well, now you know, so don't make me wait any longer!" Natalya forced a smile. The last thing she wanted was to appear impatient or bad-tempered, but on the other hand, Natalya felt that it was appropriate for the girls to feel at least somewhat obligated to her in return for opening her home to them.

Less than five minutes later, the girls entered the kitchen. Luba was smiling, but Karina's eyes were slightly downcast.

"How are you feeling? How did you sleep, girls?" Natalya asked warmly, eager to make amends for her impatient outburst. Once again, she felt the same inexplicable rush of compassion and tenderness at the sight of Karina's delicate features. Something about the girl touched a chord deep in her heart, even though she had no idea why that should be.

"We really feel terrible, Natalya," Karina repeated Luba's apology. "We didn't dream that you were waiting for us. If we had, we never would have delayed like that."

"Well, let's forget about all that now!" Natalya smiled broadly. "What matters is that you're both here with me now." Natalya herself couldn't explain why she felt compelled to make things up to Karina – after all, she was still upset at both girls. And yet, she felt immensely relieved to see Karina's anxious look fade as she took her seat at the table.

"Guess what?" she added brightly. "I arranged a VIP tour of the Red Square for today! What do you say to that?"

"Unbelievable!" Luba breathed, and Natalya was delighted to see Karina's eyes sparkle in excitement.

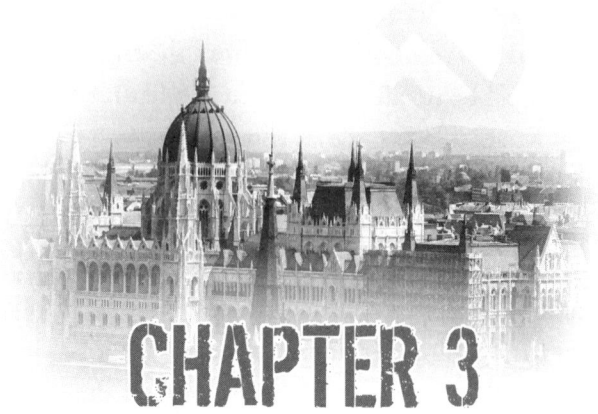

CHAPTER 3

Beyond the red stone wall, the tower soared gracefully to the heavens, and the girls, with Natalya, stood transfixed.

"Wow – it's stunning," Karina exclaimed, awed at the sight. "Now I understand why people make such a big deal out of the Kremlin. It's truly beautiful."

Natalya turned to Karina in surprise. "You mean you've never been here before?" she asked the girl. "This is your first time in Red Square?"

"Yes, my first time." Karina blushed and lowered her eyes.

"I'm astonished!" Natalya continued. "You never visited your own capital city? At your age? You don't even live that far away. Where did you go during vacations, then?"

Karina bit her lip. "We stayed mainly local and toured our own region. It never really worked out for us to travel major distances like this."

"Major distances? Four hours on the train isn't called major!" Natalya retorted.

"It was almost five hours," Luba corrected, coming to her friend's defense. "But you're forgetting Karina's health condition. Until recently, her mother was afraid to let her travel far, because she never knew how she'd feel. Only since she started her diet has her health improved enough for her to travel."

"Really?" Natalya asked suspiciously. "Is that the reason?"

Karina nodded, and her eyes shifted quickly back to the magnificent scenery.

Feeling slightly guilty for having made Karina uncomfortable with her questioning, Natalya changed the subject, hoping to restore the previously lighthearted atmosphere of their outing.

"Girls, did you notice the cypress trees behind the fortress?" she said, gesturing toward them.

"I guess someone wanted to give this place a bit of a humane touch," Karina blurted out, immediately regretting her words. "I mean, like… " she stammered, "something green, natural…"

"And what about all the gardens we just saw? Aren't they a beautiful touch of nature?" Natalya replied in annoyance.

"Oh, of course they are!" Karina said, hoping her enthusiasm sounded at least somewhat genuine. "All I meant is that, right here, it feels different. These high red walls, they're… colossal, formidable, almost frightening. I just thought that maybe the architect wanted to portray something softer," she ended lamely.

"Well, if you know anything about what lies behind those trees, then you'll look at things differently," Natalya noted dryly.

"The cemetery?" Luba asked knowledgeably.

"Exactly, Luba. Directly behind that row of tees are the tombs of all the great Communist leaders and the Premiers of the State. Further down is the mausoleum bearing the remains of Lenin; his body was embalmed and encased in black marble. Would you like to see it?"

Karina paled. "His actual body? I think I'll pass. Maybe we can visit something else instead?"

Natalya laughed. "Of course we can. We have plenty of time left to visit some of the museums in the area, and I'm sure you'll find the displays fascinating."

Karina nodded, inwardly berating herself for her slip. In the future, she would have to take greater care to sound a more positive note toward the symbols of Communist power. For the next three hours, she assiduously guarded her tongue, exclaiming in awe at the museum exhibits and feigning interest in the countless displays of the opulence of the Czarist era.

"Wow! These garments date back to the period of Ivan the Terrible!" Luba read from one sign.

"That's almost five hundred years ago," Karina noted.

"And just look at this coronation robe," Natalya pointed to the exhibit. "It was fashioned from the fur of three hundred animals!" She then showed them one of the robes of a Czarina, a dress embroidered with real gold thread and decorated with literally thousands of precious stones. All around them, hanging from the walls, were weapons dating back hundreds of years, swords and spears with ornamental handles studded with jewels and engraved with the names of their original owners.

"This is our history, the glory of our Russian nation!" Natalya told them proudly. Karina studied her hostess's glowing features, noting the pride in her sparkling eyes. Natalya truly believed every word she spoke – she was not merely repeating the lessons that had been indoctrinated in her.

"Why are you so proud of all this?" she couldn't help but protest. "While the Czars decorated themselves in gold and jewels, countless millions of ordinary Russians perished of hunger or disease."

"And that's why our Communist party rose to power!" Natalya replied with fervor. "We built the socialist present upon the ruins of our past, but our past and present draw from each other."

Karina nodded and bit her lip, forcing herself to keep her true opinions locked inside. She had spent most of her life on the other side of the Iron Curtain, and she was aware that she lacked the instinctive caution that even young children exercised when speaking about the realities of Russian government. Her mother wouldn't have blurted out that last sentence even if she were being held at gunpoint.

"Oh, we didn't visit the Alexander Gardens yet," Luba reminded them suddenly. "I was there once, years ago, but I hardly remember it anymore. Mother said that I shouldn't miss seeing it."

"Your mother is always right," Natalya smiled. "There are many beautiful parks in Moscow, but the Alexander Gardens is undeniably the most beautiful of them all." They exited the museum together, and the sudden contrast between the dim lighting inside and the brightness of the sun blinded them momentarily. They paused for several minutes and sat down on a park bench to relax.

"Luba," Natalya's features turned serious, but her eyes danced with uncharacteristic mischief as she spoke. "I hope you're like your mother, because I miss her so much! I often think back to the old days, and the good times we had together. We used to do all kinds of crazy things, until we got a bit older and wiser."

"What kind of things?" Karina inquired.

Natalya was surprised that it was Karina, and not Luba, who had posed the question. "Are you close with Luba's mother?" she asked. "Why are you interested?"

"I just like learning about the past," Karina replied smoothly. "And I love Luba's mother. She's wonderful, and she treats me almost like a daughter."

"Isn't your mother jealous?" Natalya couldn't deny the twinge of envy she felt in her heart. How she hoped that by the end of this visit, Luba and Karina would think similarly of her. Especially Karina.

There was something about Karina that, for all her idiosyncrasies, was unique, and Natalya was sure that she would never forget her.

"Jealous?" Karina burst out laughing. "Of course not! On the contrary, she's thrilled that Katerina likes me. It's such a good feeling to visit a friend and know that you're really welcome in her house."

"Do you visit often? How often?" Natalya's sudden display of curiosity astounded both girls, who exchanged surprised looks.

"Sometimes every day, sometimes every other day, and sometimes not at all. It depends on what's going on in my life – in our lives." Karina exchanged a glance with Luba. "You know how it is: we study for tests, do homework together, and sometimes just hang out."

"Luba, are you as funny as your mother? Your mother had a remarkable sense of humor," Natalya changed the subject abruptly.

"Oh, Luba's hilarious!" Karina replied instantly. "She definitely inherited her mother's sense of humor."

"Well, as they say, the apple doesn't fall far from the tree…" Natalya mused, her expression turning thoughtful. "You know what's interesting though, Karina? You also remind me very much of someone, though for the life of me I can't think why that should be."

Karina swiveled her head quickly, pretending to be riveted by the scenery. She felt the color draining from her face, and she was terrified that her hostess would notice the change in her demeanor.

"Who does Karina remind you of?" Luba asked curiously.

"Another old friend of mine. Your mother probably remembers her too."

"Really? I'll ask her. What's her name?"

Natalya grimaced. "Really, I shouldn't call her a friend at all. In fact, I would much rather forget about her existence entirely. I don't even know why Karina suddenly reminded me of her." She waved her hand dismissively, trying to clear the sudden tension in the air, and released a loud, hollow laugh. "Think nothing of it, Karina dear.

You're nothing like her at all. Maybe a slight physical resemblance, but the personality is totally different. Totally."

Karina kept her back turned to the other two, feeling terror clutching at her heart. Did Natalya sense her fear?

Natalya sensed something else entirely. "I'm sorry if I hurt you," she spoke softly, trying to smooth what she assumed were the girl's ruffled feathers. "I didn't mean it, and I'll be more careful in the future. Luba simply carried me back into the past which, unfortunately, occupies far too much of my thoughts when I'm alone – which is often. But now that the two of you are here, all I want to do is to enjoy myself and maximize every moment. Do you forgive me?"

Karina was tempted to explain that she hadn't been insulted at all, but she knew that she had to camouflage her fear somehow. She forced herself to meet Natalya's gaze and reply, "It's fine. Don't mind me."

"Of course I'll mind you!" Natalya exclaimed. "You're my guest, and I want you to be happy here! Come, girls, why don't we continue on to the Alexander Gardens, like Luba suggested? We'll look at the flowers and forget about this silly incident." Natalya stood up abruptly and began walking ahead rapidly with the girls trailing uncomfortably behind her, sharing disconsolate looks.

The Alexander Gardens ran parallel to the historic Kremlin wall. Between two red turrets, carpets of colorful flowers dazzled in the bright sunlight, yet the breathtaking beauty was insufficient to distract Karina, who couldn't seem to tear her eyes away from the blood-red wall.

"Do you see that segment of wall over there?" Karina interrupted the heavy silence that had fallen between them. "It's built differently from the rest."

Natalya and Luba turned to where Karina was pointing. "That's a remnant of the ancient fort that once stood here," Natalya explained. "The Kremlin was built upon its ruins."

"And what's that thin plume of smoke coming from behind the tower?" Luba asked.

"It's the Tomb of the Unknown Soldier," Natalya replied, "a memorial to all those who gave their lives for liberty and justice. Shall we continue?"

They paused again beside the giant sprinklers and gazed in awe at the statues of the dark horses.

"I've seen these countless times, but I'll never cease to be amazed by their magnificence and beauty," Natalya commented. "The horses are poised so naturally that they look like they could leap right over us!"

Karina pressed her lips into a thin line. She didn't like the statues at all, even though she loved horses. In her heart, she reflected how puny the horses really were, and that they were fashioned of nothing but stone.

CHAPTER 4

Moscow, 1976 (eleven years earlier…)

After alighting from her bus, Anya Krasnikov walked briskly down Lubyanka Street, wondering, as she had done so many times before, if she would ever cease to feel the mounting trepidation the closer she got to her place of work. Three years had passed since her transfer to an office in KGB Headquarters, and throughout those years, almost without fail, her heart had begun to pound as she approached the building.

Unlike other fears and phobias, familiarity with the object of fear had done nothing to dispel the fear itself. Rather, the opposite was likely true. As an "insider," Anya knew only too well that the fear of all Soviet comrades for the organization that spied on them – their thoughts, as well as their actions, was not misplaced. In fact, even those who had worked for the KGB for years, or decades, were not above suspicion, nor would they ever be in the future. It was common knowledge that many of the people rotting away in rat-infested cells in the basement of the huge building had once occupied offices on the upper floors. The transition from power to prison was usually swift and brutal, designed to instil abject terror not only in the new prisoner but also in all those privy to the events.

For her part, Anya preferred not to know too much about what went on beyond the four walls of her office. She had been hand-picked for her position when her new boss learned of her exceptional efficiency and dedication to her work, and although she had trembled inwardly when she was told of the new location of her workplace, she knew the option of refusing the transfer was non-existent.

Now, three years later, she had already been promoted several times, and was trusted with classified information, the details of which she was not even permitted to reveal to her husband. Merely flashing her badge at the security guard at the main entrance was sufficient to grant her swift and courteous entry, and today was no exception.

Anya headed straight for the elevator, deliberately refusing to so much as glance to her left, where the staircase down to the lower floors was located. The offices upstairs were modern and attractively furnished, giving no hint as to the nature of the below-ground-level floors of the building. Anya's own office boasted a view of the park across the street below, but she didn't even glance out of the window after entering, instead hanging up her coat and hat and immediately sitting down to work. Anya never started her workday with small talk or a cup of coffee, which was one of the qualities that had attracted her superiors' attention. She worked steadily, rarely lifting her eyes from the documents on her desk, to the extent that she sometimes thought of herself as a robot rather than a human being. But undeniably, her uncompromising work ethic had been the attribute that had led to her successive promotions.

"Anya, take a look at the communiqué I left on your desk. It's a coded message from Fyodorev," Maxim Fyodorev's personal secretary called from the doorway, before returning to her own office. Anya glanced around quickly more out of instinct than anything else – there was nobody other than her in the little room. Then, she unfolded the paper and scanned the contents.

The message was brief, a summons to a top-secret meeting at the end of the work day. The only information she gleaned was that the invitees were few, and that she was thus forbidden to mention the meeting to anyone else. Not that she would ever dream of saying anything to anyone. Throughout her years of working for the KGB, Anya had learned that the less said, the better. She reread the note to check that she had correctly memorized the details, and then ripped the paper to shreds which she dropped down the chute that led to the building's incinerator.

Returning to her desk, Anya could barely contain the smile that threatened to turn up the corners of her mouth. She was truly flattered to be among the select few invited to one of Fyodorev's meetings. It was well known that Fyodorev trusted nobody and that admission to his inner circle of employees was a hard-earned privilege.

On occasion, Anya wondered if Fyodorev was aware of her Jewish roots. Given that he was a virulent anti-Semite, she had reason to assume that he was not aware. Had she thought deeper into the matter, however, she might have reached a different, more frightening conclusion. How could a senior employee of the KGB not know about such a significant detail? Presumably, the notoriously efficient Fyodorev had simply made the cold calculation that he would exploit his Jewish employee as long as it was convenient for him to do so – but the moment it was no longer convenient, Anya would be dismissed, and not to an early or peaceful retirement.

That day was one of the longest that Anya remembered, with the impending meeting constantly on her mind even as she completed a myriad of unrelated tasks. Finally, at four o'clock, the hour she always ended her work day, she collected her files, locked them in the safe in the corner of the room, and headed downstairs in the elevator, along with the others who worked on her floor. Together, they exited the building and walked down the street to the bus stop, where Anya parted from her colleagues, politely wishing them a good evening.

"Aren't you going home?" Olga asked in surprise.

"I have a couple of errands to run first. I'll see you tomorrow." Smiling at her friend, she turned the corner and approached the building from the parallel street. Ten minutes later, she found herself back in Headquarters, about to enter the last room on the fourth floor.

The tense silence in the room informed her that they had been waiting for her before commencing the meeting. Anya strode briskly to the one empty seat and slipped silently into the chair. Fyodorev cleared his throat before beginning.

"During the last few years, we have succeeding in neutralizing the last of the religionists in Moscow and the environs. Through careful investigation and after intensive efforts, we exposed all the forbidden sects of learning and dispatched them to the penal colonies in the east, assuming, and reasonably so, that this would eliminate the problem. It appears that we were mistaken, however, as new groups have formed right under our noses here in the city center. Youths who until recently had no affiliation at all with any religious denomination have suddenly begun to show interest in the Talmud, and somehow they even managed to procure for themselves teachers."

"If we eliminated the last of the Talmudists several years ago, then where did the teachers crop up from?" asked Marsky, Fyodorev's deputy head of operations.

"That's a good question that still needs to be answered," Fyodorev agreed. "And there's much to learn from this omission, but we'll leave that for the next stage. The point right now is the present and the pressing need to begin an operation, which is why I convened this meeting. We have precisely one hour to formulate the basis of this operation, and I'd like to hear a basic outline from all of you. At the end of the meeting, we'll divide the tasks among us."

The heated discussion that followed left Anya unusually quiet while each of her colleagues jostled to have his own opinion accepted as the decisive voice in the debate. Finally, Fyodorev weighed in with his decision, and to the surprise of all present, he assigned Anya the task of overseeing the execution of the plan.

"I don't have the time right now to direct this project," he explained. "Comrade Krasnikov will devise the details of the strategy, coordinate all activities, and deal with any problems or issues that arise during the course of the operation. I'm delegating her full authority to do as she sees fit, and I hereby order you all to abide by her instructions."

With a final nod, Fyodorev rose and strode out of the conference room, leaving the others to wrap up the loose ends of the plan. From the ensuing silence in the room, Anya realized that the others were now awaiting her instructions, which she gave in her typically concise fashion. New agents were to be recruited to gather intelligence, by infiltrating the various groups in order to uncover their modus operandi and obtain the names of all their members. Most crucial of all was to identify the leaders of the groups, and only once they had done so, would the mass arrests take place.

When the meeting finally dispersed, Anya breathed a long sigh of relief. Throughout her long bus ride home, she mulled over the events of the afternoon, and she couldn't avoid the uncomfortable suspicion that Fyodorev had assigned precisely her the task of heading the operation in order to force her to display her loyalty to the KGB over any residual shred of attachment to her religion. Even though Anya felt no conflict of interest – after all, her parents, long since deceased, had told her nothing about Judaism other than that she was Jewish – she still preferred to push to the back of her mind the uncomfortable thought that she was about to bring disaster upon her co-religionists.

It was only later as she walked into her apartment that Anya grasped that, although no one had said so explicitly, she had just moved up a rank in the KGB.

CHAPTER 5

Anya was lost in a magical bedtime story when she noticed that her little one had already fallen asleep. Just a few minutes earlier, her daughter had asked an amusing question that had caused Anya's story to take an unexpected turn, and now, before even hearing the end of the latest instalment, Karina was fast asleep.

Anya had only discovered her talent for storytelling when her daughter graduated from infancy into childhood. Karina turned out to be an avid story-lover who refused to go to sleep without a story. At first, Anya had read to her from colorful picture books, but finding them lacking, she had begun telling her own stories.

Her first attempts were mostly tales drawn from old Russian folklore, but over time she became more creative and began crafting stories of her own. Usually, they were set in a faraway, sundrenched land. She still recalled the very first story she had told; it had centered around a little girl whose entire nation of captive slaves was set free after centuries of oppression, and it related how they had then journeyed to the distant land of their dreams. Other stories she told were variations on the same theme, with the picture of the faraway utopia a constant, until Anya became convinced that she must have heard a story about a fairy-tale land sometime in her youth, even though she had no conscious recollection of it.

Now Anya gazed at her sleeping daughter and softly stroked her cheek before leaving the room and closing the door behind her. As she walked into the kitchen, she noticed her husband had arrived home.

"Oh!" she exclaimed in surprise. "I didn't realize you were here already. When did you get back?"

"About ten minutes ago," Lev replied.

"Well, it's a good thing you stayed in the kitchen, otherwise I'd never have gotten Karina to sleep," Anya noted. "She finally fell asleep just now, so we can eat right away."

Lev seemed relaxed. "How was she today?"

"It was a rough day," Anya admitted. "I was late coming home from work, and when I finally got back, Karina threw a tantrum and wouldn't calm down for at least twenty minutes."

"You were home late?" Her husband was surprised. Ordinarily, Anya was as punctual as a Swiss watch, and he couldn't recall another instance when she had been delayed.

"It wasn't my fault. They asked me to stay late for a meeting, and they only told me about it this morning." Anya washed vegetables and diced a salad as she spoke while Lev pulled two small pots out of the refrigerator and placed them on the stovetop to warm.

"Aren't you going to ask me what the meeting was about?" Anya couldn't hide her smile.

"Will you tell me if I do?" he responded dryly.

Anya chuckled. "You know the rules, but it's so frustrating! Especially something like this…" Anya frowned, remembering the nature of the complex operation she had been ordered to head. "Well, there's no way I can tell you, and that's that. But what I can tell you is that it looks like I was just promoted."

Lev spun around in astonishment, his face breaking out into a grin. "Was that what the meeting was about?"

"Yes and no. I mean, like I said, I can't tell you what the meeting was about, but it became obvious from the way things went that I was promoted. Majorly. And I don't see any reason to keep that secret. Although," she continued in a quieter voice, "you probably shouldn't share the information with anyone, just in case."

"Of course. Just like I keep just about everything to myself, Anya, including the nature of your workplace and the name of your boss."

Anya sighed. "I know, it's complicated sometimes. For me probably even more than for you. But you know it's not my choice. I never really wanted this job; it just happened."

Lev washed his hands. "I know, but you're still better off wanting your job, because if they discover you don't care for it, you could place yourself in danger."

"I know."

She carried the salad bowl to the table and divided it into two portions. "I do want my job, Lev. Why shouldn't I?" Her words sounded hollow even to her own ears, and Lev nodded mutely in response. If it were up to him, he would pull his wife out of there and have her work in a dreary factory – anywhere but the KGB – but in Soviet Russia, no one cared for the opinions or aspirations of the individual. It was the collective good that took precedence, over everything.

They had barely finished their salad when she spoke again. "There's going to be a problem, though."

Lev wrinkled his brow. "What kind of problem?"

"My new duties will force me to stay late in the office. What will we do with Karina?"

Lev's appetite all but vanished. "You mean you'll have to work longer hours now?"

"Yes, and I'll have new responsibilities. That's all part of it."

"Really? I thought the opposite was normally true. Someone who gets promoted can usually reduce his hours," he pointed out, "and delegate more of his tasks to others."

"Not in the KGB," Anya grimaced. "Fyodorev won't excuse me from my regular duties, I'm sure of it – partly because this new operation is only supposed to last a few weeks. But at least my salary will increase, significantly."

"But what about Karina?"

Anya stared helplessly at her husband, wishing she had a solution to offer – but she had none. The increase in salary would be nice, but Karina needed a mother, not a higher standard of living. And, there was little hope of getting Fyodorev to understand that. The man wasn't even married – except to his job – and in his mind, children, and usually women, too, were nothing more than a nuisance.

"It's a huge problem," she repeated. "We need to find someone to look after her from four thirty, at least. I hope not later," she added doubtfully. "I really hope not."

"If only we had a choice in the matter," Lev muttered. "It's just not worth it."

Anya paused for a moment, hesitating before voicing her thoughts. "Lev... Maybe you could skip your afternoon courses for the next few weeks? It's just for a few weeks, most likely," she cajoled him. "If it ends up being longer than that, then I'll look for another solution."

Lev frowned. "No, I can't skip any of the courses," he replied sharply.

"Are you sure?" Anya persisted. "I mean... maybe you could find someone to replace you..." Her voice trailed off as she noticed the anger on her husband's features.

"You think that it's only the KGB that demands loyalty?" he exploded. "My job may not be vital for state security, but it's important, nonetheless. Even if I could find a replacement, the academy would probably be furious."

Anya realized that she had gone too far. "I'm sorry, Lev. It's just that I'm under terrible pressure, and I wasn't thinking straight. So, I suppose we'll have to send Karina to the special nursery for KGB workers. I really didn't want to send her there, but if there's no choice, there's no choice." She exhaled a miserable sigh.

"Out of the question!" Lev ruled. "We discussed this long ago, and we both agreed that we didn't like the strict atmosphere there. There has to be some other option."

"Like what?"

"Like a private babysitter. We can ask a neighbor to watch Karina until you get home. You'll be earning more, so we can afford to pay a babysitter."

Anya squirmed. "You mean Jenya Idelevitz?"

"Why not?" Lev replied. "She's a good-hearted woman, and what's more, she has a little girl Karina's age. Having a friend to play with will minimize the sting of not seeing you all day long."

"I don't know. I don't like the thought of leaving her for so many hours with Jenya. She's very critical of me, and she doesn't have to say it for me to know it."

Lev toyed with the remains on his plate. "It may not be pleasant for you, but it's the best solution for Karina, and she'll enjoy it there. Our primary consideration has to be Karina's welfare, don't you agree?"

Anya couldn't deny that, but neither could she deny her reluctance to approach her upstairs neighbor. However, there was really no other choice.

"All right, I'll speak to Jenya tonight," she conceded.

CHAPTER 6

Anya felt her muscles tense as she alighted from the bus. Her street was only four blocks away, but today, the walk felt impossibly long. She glanced at her watch and cringed. Twelve hours had passed since she had said goodbye to Karina that morning. For her, the hours had flown by, so busy had she been with the myriad aspects of the new operation. But for Karina, it wasn't so simple. A child of her age couldn't be expected to understand why her mother had to spend so much time away from her. Each additional hour alone must have stretched out interminably.

Worse still, Anya was late, much later than she had told Jenya she would be. She had promised her neighbor that she would pick up Karina no later than seven, but it was already long past that hour. Her heart ached as she thought of her precious little one. Somehow, the little girl would have to learn to cope with the long hours of separation, but she wished she could have spared her daughter the ordeal.

A few minutes later, she reached her building – only to hear hysterical cries emanating from within. She knew that cry; it was unmistakably Karina's. What could be wrong? Despite her pounding headache, she ran up the five flights of stairs and reached the landing breathless. What had happened to Karina? She wouldn't cry like that without good reason. Had she gotten hurt?

Anya knocked loudly on her neighbor's front door, and Jenya opened immediately with Karina in her arms. The girl was in the midst of a full-blown tantrum, kicking her babysitter and pulling her hair viciously.

"Karina! Karina!" Anya stretched out her arms to her daughter, and the little girl practically catapulted into the safety of her embrace. "There, there… Mamochka's here now. Calm… Shh…"

Pale-faced, Anya turned to her neighbor. "How long has she been like this? Did something happen?"

"Nothing happened," Jenya assured her. "She just wanted to go home, to her mother. If you had left me a number where I could reach you, I would have called you at work. She's been crying for ages."

Anya winced, but remained silent. She wasn't permitted to relay any work-related number to anyone, not even her husband. Once again, her child was paying the price of her job – but how would a phone call have helped, in any case? There was no chance she would have been given permission to leave work in order to attend to Karina.

As she stroked Karina's tear-streaked face, something suddenly occurred to her. "Where's Svetlana? I hoped the girls would play together…"

"They did, but only for the first half hour. Then, Karina started asking where you were, and when I told her you'd be back later, she started crying. The crying got worse until she refused to do anything but kick and scream."

"You mean she's been like this since five o'clock?" Anya gasped.

"On and off," Jenya admitted. "She fell asleep at one point, but only for twenty minutes or so, and when she woke up and saw that you still hadn't returned, she started up again."

"I'm so, so sorry, Jenya!" Anya apologized profusely. "It must have been really hard for you. I'm paying you double for today."

"It was hard for Karina too," Jenya sighed. "But you can't compensate her." There was definite reproof in her voice.

"I know," Anya replied miserably, lowering her eyes. "But at least it's only a temporary thing. Within a few weeks, I hope, I'll be back to my regular schedule."

Gathering Karina's little knapsack, Anya thanked her neighbor and wished her goodnight. Neither said a word about the next day, and Anya hoped that somehow, Karina would swiftly resign herself to the situation and not throw any more tantrums.

Later that evening, after Karina had collapsed into bed and succumbed without even asking for a story, Anya and Lev sat down to supper, though they ate little. After five minutes of playing with his fork, Lev rose from his chair and began pacing the kitchen like a caged lion. "This can't continue, Anya, even for a few weeks," he mumbled repeatedly.

"So cancel your course," she retorted.

Lev was silent for a moment, and then inhaled a long, deep breath followed by a sigh.

"You're not answering me," Anya attempted in a shaky voice.

"I can't."

"You can't what?"

"Cancel the course."

Anya felt her fury rising, and she could hear herself shouting at her husband that unlike her, he didn't work for the KGB, and that he had choices, whereas she had none. But then the voice of sanity spoke up. In Soviet Russia, nobody had choices. Orders were given, to be obeyed either willingly or not, but they were orders, not suggestions or options.

"So Karina will just have to get used to things, then," Anya concluded miserably. "It won't be easy for her, but kids adjust quickly, and she'll manage somehow, I suppose."

"Just like I did."

It was a strange comment, and Anya wrinkled her brow quizzically. "What do you mean?"

"You're forgetting that my mother used to work for the Kremlin. She came home at seven most days, and we barely saw her."

"Of course I didn't forget, Lev. She's the one who got me my first job in the Kremlin."

Lev continued pacing, shaking his head at the irony of it. "And to think that I was once excited that you'd gotten the job. How could I have been so foolish? It's not the place where I want my wife to be working, or the mother of my child."

"Well, at first, it wasn't so bad," Anya pointed out. "Until I was transferred to Lubyanka, things were much simpler."

"Yes, but even then you came home at four, not two, like with many other jobs. And now…" His voice trailed off and his eyes were distant. "You can't imagine what it's like for a kid not to see his mother until a few minutes before bedtime."

"It must have been awful," Anya replied softly. "Who looked after you?"

"When we were little, we had a babysitter, a classic babushka. When we got a little older, we took care of ourselves."

"Maybe I should look around for a babysitter who would agree to watch Karina here?" Anya mused.

Lev wrinkled his nose; he had no fond memories of his old babysitter. "What would Karina do here all by herself with no one but an old babushka for company? At least at the Idelevitzes, she has a friend."

"Well, you saw how long they enjoyed each other's company today. A grand total of thirty minutes," Anya retorted.

Lev finally quit pacing. "She'll just have to get used to it," he echoed his wife's previous statement. "I just hope that this assignment really ends up being only for a few weeks, and that Karina's suffering will be short-lived."

"If she gets used to it, she won't be suffering," Anya pointed out, finally taking her first bite of food.

"Hopefully," Lev conceded doubtfully, joining her at the table.

They ate in heavy silence, until Anya finally put her thoughts into words, telling her husband what had bothered her since sharing the news of her promotion. "I couldn't understand why you were taking this so hard until you mentioned your mother."

"And now you do understand?"

Instead of answering, she asked, "She was really never home during the day?"

Lev pressed his lips into a thin line. "Never. And when she did get home, she was exhausted and had no patience for us. Just like you were tonight. You didn't even tell Karina a bedtime story."

"It wasn't me. She was too tired for a story. She fell asleep the moment her head touched the pillow."

"Because she wasted all her energy crying at the Idelevitzes."

"It wasn't Jenya's fault. She did try."

"No one's at fault, Anya. No one."

No one, except the KGB.

CHAPTER 7

Fatigue became Anya's constant companion, and she wondered how it was possible to adjust to chronic exhaustion. It was already dark when she returned home each evening, and she dragged her feet wearily from the bus stop to her building, hoping that at least she wouldn't find Karina in the midst of another tantrum.

In fact, it took the little girl just three days to adjust to the new schedule. During those three days, she barely played with Svetlana, but by the beginning of the second week, she had ceased her protests entirely and spent the afternoons playing happily with her friend. To Anya's relief, Jenya was happy with the arrangement, and at work, Fyodorev was also pleased with the way things were progressing.

The agents Anya had hand-picked for the operation had succeeded in their tasks, and the groups they had uncovered were stormed. Thirty prisoners were now detained in subterranean cells in the KGB building, awaiting trial.

Anya was glad that she was spared the interrogation work. There were certain aspects of the job that were simply not for her, and Fyodorev, recognizing this, had appointed someone else to supervise the judicial stage.

The next day, Svetlana passed by Anya's office and stopped to murmur, "Fyodorev will be attending your meeting tomorrow afternoon, at three o'clock, instead of five."

Anya looked up sharply and narrowed her eyes. "Why? What happened?" Fyodorev never attended a meeting without good reason. He had made it clear that he trusted her implicitly and relied on her judgment. If he was planning on attending the meeting, he must have something important to share.

"Nothing happened, as far as I know," Fyodorev's secretary replied evenly. "But the operation is drawing to a close, and he wants to summarize the results and restore your previous work schedule."

A huge stone rolled off Anya's heart. Tomorrow, she would be going home at a normal hour! She could pick Karina up from the daycare center she attended and spend the late-afternoon hours with her, just like a normal mother. She knew Lev would share her relief, and Karina would be delighted.

That evening, the family celebrated together. Karina danced happily around the house, hugging herself in delight. "Mamochka is coming home! Mamochka is coming home!"

"Coming home?" Anya laughed. "But I didn't go anywhere!"

Karina looked at her with big, wide eyes, replying with words that were far too understanding for a child of her age. "Yes you did. Instead of coming to get me, you went to a bad, horrible place. But you're not going there anymore!"

Anya could barely contain her gasp. Who had told her little girl that she worked for the KGB? What would happen if she repeated those words outside the house?

Noticing his wife's horror, Lev smiled and hastened to reassure her. "Anya, calm down. Karina would think that any place you'd gone instead of getting her was a bad place. She didn't mean anything with her words – although, we'd better set her straight," he added. "After all, few people are blessed with such a wonderful employer as you are, my dear."

Anya raised her eyebrows, and then sighed. "If anyone hears her referring to my workplace as bad, they'll suspect me immediately."

Lev gazed curiously at her. "I understood that your position there was pretty secure."

"As secure as anything else in that building. They trust me more than most others, but the turnover rate there is still unbelievable."

She didn't have to say anything more; Lev knew exactly what she was referring to, but he tried to brush away the sudden aura of tension that had settled over the house. "Let's forget about that now and just celebrate!" he suggested brightly. "You've been working too hard, and you deserve a break, and Karina's so happy! What's that box you brought in with you?"

"A present for Karina," she replied. "It was a bit expensive, but with the bonus I got, we could easily afford it."

"And she deserves it," Lev added. "Let's give it to her together."

Karina unwrapped the box excitedly and stared in amazement at the life-like doll. "Can she talk? Can dollies talk?"

"This one can!" Anya smiled. Turning to her husband, she explained, "It's imported. I bought it at the Orbit Plaza."

Lev raised his eyebrows. "You don't usually go there. You always said you hated it."

Anya nodded. She did hate the feeling of unjust privilege – only government officials were permitted to shop at the Plaza, paying in American dollars for items that regular citizens could only dream of. But today, for Karina, she had made an exception.

"Would you like to invite Svetlana to play with your new doll?"

Anya suggested brightly to her daughter.

"No! Tomorrow, I'm playing only with you! We haven't played together in ages!" Karina reminded her.

They never did play the next day, however, although it wasn't because Anya arrived home late. At half past four, mother and daughter entered their building hand-in-hand, chatting excitedly about their plans for the rest of the afternoon as they walked up the stairs together.

Someone was standing outside their apartment, and when Anya realized who it was, she shrieked in delight. "Natalya! What are you doing here? It's been ages since we've seen each other." The two women embraced warmly, and Anya hurried to invite her inside.

"How many years has it been?" Natalya asked emotionally.

"Too many!" Anya replied. "I think the last time was when you came for my wedding! I don't think we've seen each other since then."

"No, we haven't," Natalya agreed. "What kind of friends are we?"

"It's not a matter of friendship; it's a matter of life. We both work long days, and we live so far away from each other…"

A short silence settled between them. "So you missed me?" Anya chuckled lightly.

"Sure I missed you. I always miss you. But this time, I need your help," Natalya said seriously.

"Of course – whatever I can do," Anya promised. "Let me just get you some tea, and cake first, and then you'll tell me all about it."

A few minutes later, the two friends were sitting side-by-side on the couch, with Karina playing on the floor nearby. Feeling guilty, Anya gave her daughter a weak smile, and resolved to make it up to her the next day. There was no choice – Natalya had made a special visit, and she had to devote herself to her old friend, even today.

Natalya looked unobtrusively around the house as they spoke, clearly impressed with her friend's standard of living. "I see the KGB pays its employees well," she remarked dryly.

Anya was tempted to respond that no salary could compensate for the difficult conditions, constant pressure, and sense of danger that pervaded the building on Lubyanka, but of course, she held her tongue. "My son was just hired to work for your employer," Natalya continued, finally introducing the topic that had brought her to the center of Moscow and her friend's house.

"Your son?" Anya countered in astonishment. "How old is he?"

"Nearly twenty. You're forgetting that I got married a full six years before you did."

"Yes, but it's not just the six years," Anya recalled. "I waited a full ten years before having a child. Karina is only four."

"It can't be easy, working such long hours with a young child," Natalya commented sympathetically. "At my stage of life, it's easier to invest more in my job, and I'm finally advancing somewhat."

"I'm glad to hear that," Anya said sincerely. "And hopefully your son will too, soon enough."

Natalya waved her hand dismissively. "I wish. It's not that simple. Unless," she paused, "one has *protektzia*."

Anya stared. "Oh," was all she said.

"The job my son has now only provides a paltry salary that barely covers starvation rations," Natalya continued. "But he's a very capable young man, even though he doesn't want to continue his studies in the university. He'd rather work than study, but he has an excellent head on his shoulders. I'm telling you, he can be of tremendous use to the regime."

Anya nodded. "I believe you."

"His current job isn't much more than cleaning and maintenance, and it's breaking his spirit."

"I hear you," Anya nodded again.

"So, could you put in a good word for him? I'm sure your word carries a lot of weight. I can see from your apartment that you're doing well, and I would so much appreciate you sharing your good fortune with me…" Natalya gazed at her friend hopefully. "Will you?"

"I'll do my best," Anya replied honestly. "Do you know what kind of job your son would prefer? What's he good at?"

"Security, clerical – anything like that. Anything more respectable than what he's doing now. Something with potential."

Anya thought fast. Throughout her years of employment, she had never once made a personal request on behalf of anyone, including herself. Who could she approach? Svetlana? Diamonov? Fyodorev himself? How would they react to her request? Swallowing her anxiety, she pasted a smile on her face. "I'll do my best, Natalya. I really will."

"I knew you would agree!" Natalya glowed happily. "I knew you valued our friendship too much to turn me away!"

Mention of their longtime friendship sent them plunging into a sea of happy memories, and the two women spent the next hours reminiscing nostalgically over their shared past. It was only when Natalya finally cast a regretful look at the clock and mentioned that she needed to be on her way if she wanted to arrive home before her husband that Anya realized that another day had passed without Karina enjoying her company.

CHAPTER 8

Anya thought long and hard about how to keep her promise to Natalya. In all likelihood, all appointments to the branch of the KGB for which she worked had to be approved by Fyodorev, which mean that to direct a request to anyone lower down in the hierarchy was probably a futile exercise. But to appeal to her boss himself... The very thought of it made a chill run up Anya's spine. Years of working for the man hadn't mitigated her fear of him, and although he had already promoted her several times, Anya still knew him as a dangerous snake who liked to keep those around him in a state of uncertainty as to his real feelings toward them.

Several days after her reunion with Natalya, Anya found herself needing to consult with Svetlana, Fyodorev's personal secretary, on a work-related matter. Fyodorev himself wasn't in his office, having gone to the Kremlin for an important meeting, and Anya decided to use the opportunity to seek Svetlana's advice.

"She's a very close friend, and I would really like to help her," she concluded, after outlining her dilemma. The silence that followed was so long that Anya began to doubt that Svetlana intended to reply at all.

"Do you think I should approach him?" Anya tried again, her voice barely above a whisper.

Svetlana looked up and met Anya's eyes for the first time. "Fyodorev doesn't appreciate these types of requests," she whispered back. "He can't stand political appointments."

"This isn't a political appointment," Anya protested, "just a favor to the son of a friend of mine."

"Yes, but Fyodorev isn't into doing people favors," Svetlana replied. "He does what he wants, when he wants, and how he wants. All for the sake of Mother Russia," she hastily qualified her statement. "Doing people favors isn't in the best interests of the State. I'm sure you understand that."

Anya nodded slowly. "Yes, I understand. Thank you, Svetlana. And, of course, you won't need to mention this conversation to anyone, right?"

"Right," Svetlana agreed quietly. There was no need to elaborate. Both of them knew all too well that it was unwise to make unnecessary enemies, as taking revenge was all-too easy in Soviet Russia.

Anya spent the next hour working by rote, her thoughts miles away. As much as she longed to help her friend, her instincts were screaming at her to drop the issue; yet her conscience plagued her. Finally, after realizing that she had read the same line on a communiqué six times without absorbing its contents, she gave up. Taking a deep breath, she rose and strode purposefully to Fyodorev's office, hoping that he had already returned from his meeting.

Her boss heard her out patiently — today, it seemed, he was in a good mood. "You're in luck," he announced when she finished. "Just this morning, a position opened up for a security guard at one of the entrances to the building. What's the boy's name? You say you know his mother?" Trying to conceal her astonishment at the cordial reception, Anya quickly relayed the necessary information to Fyodorev.

"Your personal acquaintance with his mother is an excellent endorsement, as far as I'm concerned. I'll make the arrangements, and I hope he'll be working here by tomorrow morning."

Anya thanked her boss and returned to her office, feeling a great sense of relief. Natalya would never know how hard it had been for her, but she didn't need the other woman's appreciation; she was simply glad that she had been able to help.

There was only an hour left to her workday, and after weeks of working until seven or even later, Anya appreciated each opportunity to leave early enough to pick up Karina from her preschool and spend time with her. Her thoughts far away, it took her a moment to realize that someone was standing at the door to her office, waiting for her to notice his presence. Anya looked up, and then stared in surprise at her visitor, Vladimir Sirkhov, the chief interrogator of a parallel department, whose name she knew only from their occasional encounters at interdepartmental meetings.

Sirkhov addressed her in a low, gravelly voice. "Comrade Krasnikov, I understand that you completed your special operation approximately two weeks ago?" It was a statement more than a question, but Anya nodded anyway. She felt her heart plummet to her toes; Sirkhov's opening did not bode well. "I am sorry to disappoint you, but it seems that there were learning groups that you failed to expose," he continued.

This time, Anya met his gaze evenly as she responded to the accusation. "What reason do you have for making such an assumption?"

"An interrogation that I conducted today revealed several interesting facts. Tell me, Comrade, did you ever think to investigate at the University?"

She returned an astonished look. "At the University? Why would we do that?"

Sirkhov's mouth turned up in a sneer. "I see it did not occur to you, although I cannot imagine why not. Nonetheless, it emerged that three of the teachers in the Talmud study groups we arrested are students at Moscow State University. What do you say about that, Comrade Krasnikov?"

"What am I supposed to say about that?"

"What happened to your famous intuition, Comrade Krasnikov?" Sirkhov replied, his tone mocking. "Three teachers who *just so happen* to be students at the same university doesn't tell us something?"

Anya thought fast, struggling simultaneously to regain her bearings. To the best of her knowledge, Sirkhov had no reason to want to discredit her, but that didn't mean that she could let down her guard. Far too many promotions were achieved by stepping on others in order to gain favor in the eyes of the management.

"In such a case," she answered, her tone steady despite her pounding heart, "it would be reasonable to assume that a group exists in the University itself."

"Brilliant!" Sirkhov applauded her scornfully. "The only thing that I don't understand is why you omitted to investigate the University at the outset. After all, a significant percentage of the students there are Jewish, and you should know that first-hand, seeing as your husband is employed there," he added pointedly.

Anya swallowed hard. There was clearly a great deal more to Sirkhov's words than met the eye. Did he suspect her, or perhaps her husband, of something? Of what?

"Very well," she replied slowly, forcing herself to meet the investigator's gaze, "in that case, we'll need to speak to Fyodorev, who I imagine will want to reinstate the operation."

"I've already spoken to him, and he requested that you stay late today, and for the rest of this week too. Your agents have also received notice. It's back to work!" he announced. Anya nodded, and a moment later, the interrogator was gone.

The disappointment hit hard, but there was no time to indulge in feelings just then. Her first priority was to make arrangements for Karina, and then she would have to devote all her attention to completing the operation to Fyodorev's satisfaction. If she failed again, there was no doubt that Sirkhov would alert her boss' attention to the fact, and there was no way that she could afford that to happen.

Quickly, she dialed Jenya Idelevitz's number, hoping desperately that she would find the woman at home. To her relief, her neighbor picked up at the second ring.

"Jenya, it's me, Anya. I'm terribly sorry, but I just found out that I need to stay late again today. I had no idea until literally a few minutes ago, which means that I wasn't able to make any arrangements for Karina, including picking her up from kindergarten," she explained.

"Can't you tell your boss that, and stay late tomorrow instead?" Jenya suggested, reluctant to return to her post as babysitter.

"I wish I could, but I really can't. Please believe me. None of this is up to me, but I can't get into the details." Anya was begging by now.

"I wish you would have told me earlier," Jenya complained. "That way, I could have arranged my schedule differently."

"I know, and I'm sorry. Jenya, I'll compensate you for it – whatever you ask."

"It's all right," Jenya relented. "You don't have to pay me extra. I was just venting. We both know how much I love your Karina, and that I wouldn't leave her without a place to go. It's enough that her mother is so busy all the time."

Anya bit her lip, swallowing the implicit insult, even though it wounded her deeply. She murmured a weak "thank you," and then hung up the phone, letting the anger, frustration, and helplessness wash over her like a huge wave.

Oh, how she hated her job sometimes! But there was no turning back. From the moment she had started work for the Kremlin, only to be transferred to the KGB, she had left any element of choice behind. True, the average Soviet citizen had precious little say over the form and content of his life, but working for the security services brought with it its own peculiar form of imprisonment.

Anya couldn't deny that there were advantages to her job, the salary chief among them. She enjoyed a standard of living far above the average, and she hadn't failed to notice the tinge of envy in Natalya's eyes as she silently absorbed the opulence of her Moscow apartment. And yet… was it worth it? Even her promotion was bitter-sweet, the price to pay for it being the longer working hours. Even when she felt that she simply couldn't go on – that Karina was suffering, that she was exhausted beyond her limits – refusal to execute her duties in a satisfactory manner was still out of the question.

Anya had influence. She had power, and prestige. She had even managed to secure Natalya's son a more desirable position at the KGB, but if the simple pleasures of life – enjoying quality time with her husband and daughter – were going to be denied to her, then what was it worth? And, moreover, if the added responsibilities that accompanied her higher rank in the KGB hierarchy only brought her more tension, more fear of failure, and more scrutiny by those only too eager to see her fall, then she knew with certainty that she would rather have remained a humble secretary all her life.

But it wasn't up to her. In Soviet Russia, one didn't own one's own life.

Suddenly, Anya glanced at the clock, and froze. She had just forty minutes left to complete her day's work and prepare for the coming meeting with her operations team. She wondered what her husband would say, if she were allowed to tell him of the new twist in her job. Maybe he even knew some of the students involved – if he did, he would certainly never voluntarily reveal the information, even to her.

How foolish of them, Anya thought to herself. *Instead of devoting themselves to their professional studies, they chose to gamble away their chances at pursuing a successful career, and now they're going to be paying the price for their stupidity.*

―⚜―

CHAPTER 9

Moscow, 1987

Luba opened her eyes to greet the bright rays of sunlight that streamed through the spotless windows. The intensity of the light informed her that it was already late in the morning, and she stretched out luxuriously in bed as she contemplated how delicious it was to get up late, with nary a care in the world. In fact, she was about to roll over and go back to sleep when she realized that Karina's bed was empty.

Assuming her friend would be back any second, Luba closed her eyes but didn't fall back asleep. When the minutes passed without a sign of Karina, she began to feel anxious. Where could she be? Grudgingly, Luba dragged herself out of bed and went to open the door to their room and peer down the corridor. Still no sign of Karina, and the apartment was silent. Dmitri and Natalya had presumably left for work hours ago already, but Karina couldn't have gone anywhere, surely? She didn't know her way around Moscow, so where was she?

Luba went back into the bedroom and hurriedly got dressed, before heading to the kitchen in search of her friend. Out of the corner of her eye, she spied something moving, and when she turned to see what it was, she finally spotted Karina, sitting in a small alcove with a book in her hands, swaying back and forth and oblivious to Luba's approach.

"Karina! What on earth are you doing?" Luba addressed her. "Why did you get up so early?"

In lieu of a reply, Karina made an ambiguous motion with her hand, but didn't utter a word.

"Is something wrong? Why aren't you talking?" Luba began to panic. There was so much about Karina that she didn't know, and it seemed that each successive day spent with the girl revealed new idiosyncrasies. What would be next? And, how on earth would she manage for another eight weeks like this?

Sensing that Luba was staring at her, Karina finally turned to face her and smiled encouragingly, motioning with her hand that she should be patient and wait for her to finish whatever it was she was doing. But why wouldn't she just say something? Karina's smile didn't have the intended result – instead, Luba felt herself becoming even more confused. The two of them were alone in the apartment, so why all the secrecy? And, if someone was listening to them via some hidden device that Karina had perhaps discovered, why did Karina look so pleased with herself?

"Can you please tell me what's going on with you?" Luba burst out, in frustration. "If you can't talk, then at least write something down! I'm going crazy with worry!"

Karina nodded emphatically, but returned her gaze to the little book in her hand. Meanwhile, Luba raced frantically to their room where she found a pen and paper which she handed to Karina.

"I'm praying, and I can't talk till I finish," Karina wrote. Luba read the note in disbelief. She spent the next ten minutes watching Karina in shocked silence, trying to figure out what she meant by "praying." At one point, Karina even got to her feet and stood, stock still, for what seemed like ages, until Luba began to fear that the ordeal would never end. Finally, Karina closed her little book and smiled at her friend. "I'm with you now."

"Why couldn't you talk?" Luba pounced on the girl.

"When I'm praying, I'm speaking to the Master of the world, so I can't interrupt our conversation to speak with anyone else," Karina explained, a smile playing at the corners of her mouth.

"You're a nutty religionist," Luba hissed scornfully.

"You knew that before," Karina replied evenly.

"True, but I didn't know what it meant. That's also why you dress that way, isn't it?"

"Yes."

"Natalya asked me about it yesterday. She didn't dream of the real reason."

"Thank G-d for that. At least there's no law here against dressing as you please."

Luba actually guffawed in response, and her anger immediately abated. "Natalya just assumed that it's yet another one of your eccentricities. Like being a vegetarian and everything else."

"What else?" Karina asked curiously.

"You know… everything. The way you act, your personality… I don't know… You're just… different, somehow. But for some weird reason, instead of being repelled, Natalya really likes you. She thinks you're special, and she's enjoying hosting you."

Karina wasn't sure if she should take that as a compliment or as a cause for concern, but at least for the meantime, she had managed to calm Luba.

"Why did you get up so early?" Luba repeated her original question.

"It's not early at all!" Karina chuckled. "Didn't you notice the time?"

"Ten-thirty is early for the summer. I didn't think we'd be up before noon!"

"So go back to sleep. I won't bother you."

"But why did you get up? You must be just as tired from yesterday as me."

"I told you already," Karina replied patiently. "I wanted to pray."

"Couldn't you have prayed later?"

"Yes, but I would have missed the morning prayer."

"You know that you'd better make sure that Natalya doesn't see you praying."

"Of course! But she doesn't get home before three, does she?"

"No, and some days not until four. You know what? I think I'll call my mother now."

"I thought you were going back to sleep," Karina teased.

"Guess not. I'm not tired anymore. I spoke to my mother last night, but I promised I'd call her again today when it was just us here."

"I hope she thought to call my mother and tell her that everything's okay."

"I'm sure she did, and your mother probably called her first anyway, to find out if she'd heard from us yet. Anyway, let's call now."

The conversation was short, sweet, and to the point.

"Hi, Mama," Luba began. "Karina wants to know how her mother is doing, and if everything is okay over there."

"That's exactly what her mother wants to know about her. What can I tell her?"

"That so far, everything is going according to plan."

"Good," Katerina exhaled a sigh of relief. "And remind Karina to call her mother when you go out, like we agreed."

"Sure. And, try not to worry. It doesn't look like we'll run into any trouble."

After ending the call, Luba turned to Karina. "Did you eat breakfast already?" When Karina shook her head in reply, she continued, "So, let's eat now, and then we'll go out to find a payphone and call your mother."

"Is that what your mother said?" Karina asked cautiously. "My mother told me not to go out specially to call, but to be discreet about it, you know, to go on an outing and call her from some random place along the way. Nowhere near Natalya's home."

Luba froze. "You're right. But we didn't make any plans for today."

"So we'll make plans over breakfast. We can go to a mall or something, and look for a payphone in between window shopping. That shouldn't attract undue attention."

"What about Natalya?" Luba asked doubtfully.

"What about her?"

"What if she gets upset that we went out without telling her?"

"How will she find out? We'll get back before she does."

Luba nodded. "You're right. And I can't wait to go out on my own exploring, without Natalya pointing out every statue in sight. There must be better things to do in Moscow than visit museums."

Karina grinned, packed her little book away in her suitcase, and then headed to the kitchen to prepare breakfast for the two of them. It was such a relief to eat a meal without Natalya around watching her every move and constantly questioning her "strange, extreme diet."

"I need to speak to your mother about this!" Natalya had complained over dinner the previous evening. "This diet is far too strict for someone of your age. Whoever heard of a teenage girl removing chicken, meat, and fish from her diet! It can't be healthy. What if you become anemic? I can't be expected to monitor your health while you're here."

"Natalya, really, you don't have to worry," Karina had hurried to appease her hostess. "I eat three hard-boiled eggs a day, and that provides me with all the protein I need."

"Maybe, but eggs aren't a substitute for meat!" Natalya had argued, and Karina had begun worrying that she really would ask for her mother's telephone number.

Just as she finished dicing the vegetables, Luba pranced back into the kitchen. "I've got a great idea!" she announced. "I just remembered about one of the big theaters here, in the city center, that my friends told me about, where there are performances all day long during the summer months. I'm going to call my mother back and ask her how to get there. It will be a great way to pass the time until Natalya gets back from work."

"Luba," Karina said quietly, "I don't go to the theater."

"You don't go to the theater?" Luba repeated in disbelief. "Why on earth not?"

"I have my reasons," Karina replied flatly.

A cloud crossed Luba's pretty face. "What reasons, may I ask?"

"Because the theater isn't a place for Jews. That's all."

"Oh, don't give me that! Some of the most famous actors in the world are Jewish, not to mention producers and directors."

"That may be so, but that's irrelevant for me. Not all Jews are religious, but I am, and religious Jews don't go to the theater."

"Why do you have to spoil everything?" Luba retorted, her eyes narrowed in anger. "You don't have a better suggestion, in any case, and I want to go to the theater! It's one of the things I planned on doing while I was here, and I didn't dream that anyone would tell me that they can't go for some stupid religious reason."

"I'm sorry, Luba," Karina said softly. "I understand you're disappointed. Maybe we could go back to the Kremlin, instead? One day spent there really wasn't enough to see everything, and we can probably find a public phone somewhere around there."

"Oh, *great*. So I get to wander around another ten dusty museums," Luba retorted. "I never dreamed it would be so boring spending the summer with you."

CHAPTER 10

It was their first argument, but it wasn't completely unexpected. After all, the girls had only known each other for four days, during which Luba had gone out of her way to make Karina comfortable. She was well aware of the sorry circumstances that had brought the girl across the ocean, and she sympathized with her plight. After hearing her story, she had assured her mother that she was willing to help Karina with whatever she needed – and, of course, she had been delighted at the prospect of a summer spent in Russia's capital city, too.

Now, however, things weren't turning out exactly as she had imagined they would. Karina was a nice enough girl, but she was just so… different. Her spoken Russian was fluent, but her mannerisms were so foreign, and her customs so strange. If she couldn't eat certain foods because of her silly religious reasons, then that was one thing, but what did religion have to do with going to the theater? And what right did she have to spoil her friend's vacation?

"I'm really sorry, Luba," Karina said apologetically. "I didn't realize you didn't like museums. Are you sure there isn't even one that interests you? Or maybe we could go to one of the parks, or something?"

Luba exhaled sharply in frustration. "Don't you get it, Karina? Today I just want to have a good time, and this theater is world-famous. I was really looking forward to going."

Karina nodded slowly, and her eyes were sad. "I hear you. I'm really sorry. Maybe we can figure out some other way for you to go, without me."

"I don't want to go by myself!" Luba protested. "Can't you make a compromise, for my sake? Think of all the things I'm doing for you!"

"I know, and I would compromise if I could, but just not on this issue," Karina replied firmly. "This isn't a personal issue – it's a matter of sticking to my principles."

Luba raised her eyebrows. "I never heard anything about religious people not going to the theater. My grandmother mumbles prayers all day long but she still knows how to enjoy herself. What – are you like a nun, or something?"

Karina stifled a smile. "No. And I also know how to enjoy myself. But…" she struggled to find the right words, "the theater is full of all kinds of immorality. I don't want to expose myself to that."

Luba frowned. "I have morals, too, and I don't need to be a vegetarian or wear weird clothes to be a moral person. And going to the theater isn't going to make me a bad person!"

Karina gave up. "Okay, okay. So we'll call my mother tomorrow."

Luba looked like she was about to scream. "That doesn't solve the problem at all! I want to go to the theater, whether or not we call your mother!"

"So go."

"I *am* going. And what about you? What will you do while I'm gone."

Karina shrugged. "Don't worry about me. I'll find something to do here."

Luba thought it over again. "Skip it," she sighed. "It's not a good idea. Let's go to the city center instead. You can call your mother at the first payphone we find, and then we'll figure out what to do."

Karina looked uncomfortable, unsure as to exactly what Luba had in mind. "If you think I'm going to give in and join you at the theater, it's going to be very awkward for both of us when I don't."

"I'm not thinking anything. I just hope we can find somewhere that both of us will enjoy."

It was a long journey to the center of town, and Karina trusted that Luba knew where she was going, even though the girl wasn't much more familiar with the capital than she was. After a long ride on the Metro, and crossing several streets on foot, they came face to face with a stunning edifice.

"Here we are!" Luba announced festively.

Karina narrowed her eyes. Luba had led them straight to the theater. "*This* is the place we're both going to enjoy?" she countered cynically.

"I couldn't think of anywhere else," Luba said nonchalantly. "And we're here now, so we might as well go in. I've been dying to see a live show in a place like this, and the next play starts in half an hour."

"You could have left me at home. Why did you drag me out here for nothing?" Karina complained.

Luba quickened her pace, walking purposefully toward the entrance to the theater. "This way, you can call your mother while you wait for me."

"My phone call isn't going to last for even a fraction of the time it'll take you to watch the show!"

"So why not join me? At least ask your mother if she lets! Your mother and my mother went to the theater together lots of times when they were girls. Why should you be any different?"

"Back then, my mother knew nothing about her faith," Karina replied. "We became observant only after we escaped to the United States, and it was a long, complicated process. Besides, my mother had no idea that you were planning on taking me to the theater, so there's no way she could have thought to forbid me go to."

"And she won't know if you come with me now. I won't tell her, that's for sure!" Luba laughed.

Karina paused mid-step. "You think that's the problem? That my mother doesn't let?"

"She's the one who made you go all religious, isn't she?"

"She's the one who introduced me to the beauty of Judaism, but today, I choose to be observant of my own accord, and I want to stick to my principles – however hard it is sometimes. It has nothing to do with my mother knowing or not knowing what I'm doing."

They reached the entrance to the theater. Luba's eyes were gleaming in excitement. "Look Karina, I'm going in. It's a bit early, but I want to get a good seat, plus I want to have a look around before the show starts. Are you coming or not?"

"Not."

"So will you wait for me?"

"Do I have a choice?"

"Where do you want to meet?"

"I'll wait for you outside in the square, near the grass over there. How long do you think you'll be?"

Luba's expression was at least somewhat guilty, but even so, she wasn't about to give up now. "I hope not more than an hour, an hour-and-a-half max. What are you going to do in the meantime?"

Karina made a face. "I'd go back to Natalya's if I knew the way. Can you give me directions?"

Luba looked doubtful. "It's pretty complicated, and I don't know if it's a good idea for you to wander around the city by yourself. You could get totally lost, and you'll be in real trouble if anyone finds out you're American. Don't forget that Natalya doesn't have a clue."

Karina gritted her teeth but said nothing. She was angry at Luba for misleading her, but given her dependency on the girl, she couldn't afford to pull the rope too tightly. Instead, she resolved to wait it out. She watched Luba disappear through the ornate entrance and then set about finding a payphone.

Not far away, she saw a row of three payphones. Karina wasn't thrilled to note that they were in such close proximity to each other, but there weren't many people around at that hour of the day, and she could always cut the conversation short if anyone got too close for comfort. Her heart beating fast, she dialed the number and spoke as quietly as possible.

"I can barely hear you!" her mother repeated anxiously, and Karina realized she would have to speak a little louder.

"It's Karina!" she repeated, raising her voice.

"Karina! How are you? It's so good to hear your voice! I've been so nervous since you left, and even before you left… I hope it wasn't a mistake to send you. This was my mission, and I shouldn't be endangering you like this…"

"Mama, everything's fine. Please don't worry. The only reason I didn't call until now was because you warned me so many times not to. But I really don't think anyone's bugging Natalya's phone. Why would they?"

"I don't know, but you still need to be careful. This isn't a game, Karina – this is serious. How are you getting along with Natalya and Luba?"

"Great. They're both really nice." She didn't mention Natalya's frustration with her diet, or her recent spat with Luba, but her mother insisted on hearing more details.

"Weren't the two of you planning a quiet day today?"

"We were, but Luba was in the mood to go out, so we did."

"Without telling Natalya?"

"We only decided to go after she'd already left to work. Natalya isn't our babysitter, after all. We can't go out without telling her?" Karina didn't remember this being one of the conditions of their trip, despite there being a very long list of do's and don'ts.

"You're not little girls," her mother agreed, "but I still don't think you should do anything that may upset or anger her. We need her. A little too much, in this case."

"I should have been more careful," Karina agreed regretfully. "But I didn't know how to stop Luba. She was dying to get out and have fun."

CHAPTER 11

Karina heard the heavy silence on the line and felt her heart sink.

"Mama?" she asked gently.

"Yes, Karina?"

"What's on your mind?" *How bizarre to be asking such a question during an international call when she was standing in the middle of a busy public square in central Moscow.*

"I'm thinking that despite everything that we took into account, we never really thought about Luba or what she might want to do while she's in Moscow. We planned, deliberated, weighed every option, sought advice, and warned both of you. But we completely forgot about this point."

"You're right – we did," Karina whispered her agreement.

"Where are the two of you now?"

"Luba went to the theater, but I told her I couldn't go. So I'm waiting for her outside."

"Waiting for her? What are you doing in the meanwhile?"

"Talking to you on the phone." *And missing you so much...* She didn't dare add that.

"I'd love to continue talking, darling, but we can't speak for an hour. It'll cost a fortune. What are you going to do until she comes out?"

"I don't know. I guess I'll walk around a bit, or sit on a bench in a park somewhere. I'll pass the time somehow or other." Karina could see her mother's eyebrows rise in displeasure.

"Of course the time will pass, but that's not the issue, Karina. What if somebody notices you hanging around? The last thing we need is for you to draw attention to yourself! You need to be more careful!"

"I know, Mama. But, really, why should anyone pay attention to a teenage girl sitting on a bench in a busy city?"

"You're in the Soviet Union, Karina, not the United States! When will you finally understand that things there are unlike anything you've ever known?"

Karina scanned the square again, wishing that Luba would appear suddenly and tell her that she'd had a change of heart. All around her, the sights and sounds were those of a busy, modern city, but her mother was right, she knew – behind the façade of normalcy, danger lurked on every corner.

"I'm sorry. I am being careful, but it is very different from anything I'm used to," she tried in vain to allay her mother's fears. "I'll try to blend in with the crowds, but I just hope I won't get lost," she concluded glumly, realizing suddenly that keeping herself occupied while Luba was in the theater wasn't going to be simple at all.

On the other end of the line, her mother paused a while before replying carefully, "So take it one street at a time. Walk up one block, cross the street, and then walk back to your starting point on the other side. Then do the same on a different street. Just be organized about it so you don't forget how to get back to the theater."

"Okay," Karina said, buttoning the top button of her jacket. It was an unusually cold day for the summer, and the Moscow chill penetrated even into the tiny phone booth. She wasn't accustomed to such weather in the middle of the summer.

"If anyone is following you, though, he'll catch on immediately to what you're doing. I just hope that nobody has spotted you yet."

"Oh, Mama!" Karina sighed. "Why would it occur to anyone that I came here for any reason other than a vacation? Who even knows that I'm here?"

Her mother gritted her teeth in frustration. "Karina, you just don't get it! The KGB makes it its business to know everything about everyone, literally! Especially foreigners, and even though your documents are flawless, they may still have caught on. Look around you, Karina. Do you see anyone just hanging around? No, right? Everyone is busy, running here or there. Anyone who stops to loiter automatically comes under suspicion, which is why people don't hang around or hold conversations in the street. Chances are, if you do see anyone hanging around, it's a KGB agent. So if Luba gets any more ideas into her head about having fun, then you make sure to stay put at Natalya's apartment, okay?"

"And how will I call you?"

"You'll have to manage to call me while you're out with Natalya," her mother replied. "You'll figure out how to tell me things without arousing her suspicion. There's just no other way."

"Can you girls be ready in a half hour?" Natalya asked brightly, shortly after returning from work. "There's a beautiful park not far away, within walking distance. I'll prepare sandwiches with fruit and drinks, and we can have a picnic supper under the trees."

"Why don't we prepare the sandwiches?" Karina offered. "You were out all day, and you're probably tired, so at least rest up for a few minutes before we go."

Natalya hesitated for a moment, unsure whether she really wanted to abandon her spotless kitchen to two teenage girls, but Karina's offer touched her, and moreover, she really was tired, and the thought of a short nap was tempting. Thanking the girls, she showed them where she had placed the fresh loaf of bread that she had just purchased on her way home, and she was about to head to her room when the shrill ring of the doorbell interrupted her.

Natalya went to answer while the girls washed and cut fruit and sliced the bread. Within a few minutes, they had finished their preparations, and Karina started to clean the counter and wash the few dishes in the sink.

"Do you think we should wake her up?" Luba asked.

Karina paused for a moment with the dishrag in her hand. "You know, I didn't hear her shut the door to her room. She went to open the front door, and then… Did she even go to take a nap, in the end?"

"Let's go and see," suggested Luba.

"Go and see what? We can't just walk into her room," Karina pointed out.

"Right, but maybe she didn't go to lie down after all?" Luba was already out of the kitchen and down the hallway before Karina could stop her, and then, suddenly, she called out frantically to her friend, "Karina, come quick! Something's happened to Natalya!"

Karina ran out of the kitchen, to find Luba standing in concern over their hostess, who was sitting on the couch in the living room, her face as white as a sheet, clutching an old, tattered book against her heart with trembling hands.

"Natalya?" Karina asked gently, her tone caressing. The woman lifted her gaze, and Karina saw that her eyes were red and damp with tears.

"Is everything okay?" Luba tried.

"Somebody just returned this book to me," Natalya mumbled in a strangled voice, almost as if she were talking to herself. "It's an old book. I'd forgotten all about it."

The girls glanced at each other, stricken in fear. Natalya's voice sounded hollow, almost lifeless. She spoke simply, but the pain in each word was evident.

"What's wrong with the book?" Karina whispered.

"Nothing's wrong with it," Natalya replied with closed eyes, her breathing shallow and her face still pale.

"So why do you look so upset?" Luba asked. Karina had to restrain herself from pinching the girl; did Luba really not realize how inappropriate her question was?

"This book belonged to my son," Natalya replied finally. "His name is written on the inside cover. This is his handwriting." She choked over the words, but her reply left the two girls no less baffled than before.

Meanwhile, Natalya was trembling, and she held the book close to her, as if it were a child.

"Can I get you a drink of water?" Karina asked softly. Natalya nodded, and Karina hurried to the kitchen to fetch it.

As Natalya sipped the cold water, her color gradually returned. "Thank you," she managed to say. The girls were relieved to see that her trembling had subsided.

"Did something happen to your son?" Luba couldn't restrain her curiosity.

Natalya waved her hand dismissively. "It's been a long time."

"What's been a long time?"

"Since anything has happened to him."

The girls stared at her in confusion.

"You look so broken," Karina said gently.

Natalya treated her to a hard stare. "Do I?"

"Um, less now than before," Karina tried to soften the blow.

"Well, it hurts to receive something that belonged to my son — six years after his death."

"Your son died?" Luba gasped, and Karina bit her lip sympathetically. They were both shocked at the sudden revelation, but even before Natalya could add any further details, Karina guessed that the conversation would lead them toward dangerous territory. She wanted to end the discussion as quickly as possible, and tried glaring at her friend in order to shut her up, but Luba was too curious and refused to take the hint.

"Yes, my son died," Natalya shared in a melancholy tone. "But it wasn't yesterday or even a year ago. It happened over six years ago."

"Can I ask what he died from?" For once, even Luba called upon her limited tact.

"Pneumonia."

"He died of *pneumonia*? But no one dies of pneumonia today! That's what antibiotics are for!" If Karina could have kicked Luba, she would have done so right then.

Natalya gave a curt chuckle. "Antibiotics aren't freely dispensed in jail. Medical intervention came too late. Way too late."

"You mean your son was in jail?" Luba wasn't sure how to digest this information. It was so unlike prim and proper Natalya to have a son who had ended up in jail that she didn't know how to react.

"Yes, my son was in jail," Natalya replied in a high-pitched tone. "He went out of his way to help my best friend in the whole world, and then she betrayed him and destroyed his life."

"Your friend betrayed him, even though he helped her?" Luba repeated in disbelief. How could it be that her mother had never breathed a word of such a scandal? Natalya and Katerina had been close friends for years – there was no way she didn't know about what had happened to Natalya's son. She opened her mouth again, about to ask another question, when she noticed Karina staring at her.

"Stop it, Luba," she said quietly, though there was steel in her tone. "Don't you see how much your questions are hurting Natalya? She doesn't deserve to suffer just to satisfy your curiosity."

Luba's jaw dropped, but she knew that Karina was right. "I'm sorry, Natalya," she mumbled hastily. "I didn't mean to cause you any pain. I was just asking because I care, because I feel so close to you, almost like your niece…"

"Even close relatives don't have the right to dig into other people's pain," Karina emphasized firmly, earning Luba's glare.

Natalya rose from her position on the couch and placed the book reverently in the breakfront. "It's all right, girls. You don't have to argue the point. Both of you are right. I'm feeling better now, and I appreciate your sensitivity and concern. Now, why don't we go back to the kitchen and finish preparing those sandwiches?"

CHAPTER 12

"Such a weird story with Natalya's son." It was the morning after the picnic, which, despite the painful incident that preceded it, ended up being pleasant enough. Natalya and the two girls had sat together in the park until late, watching the sun go down and making small talk about their high school, friends, and relatives in other cities.

The next morning, Natalya left for work before the girls woke up, and Karina, as usual, got up before Luba in order to pray undisturbed. By eleven o'clock, they had tidied their room and sat down for breakfast.

"Yes, it's weird. I mean, Natalya and her husband are both influential people – wasn't there anything they could do to help their son?"

Luba shook her head. "You have no idea how things work here. Nobody has influence. There are a few people – literally a handful – who control what happens to just about everyone else. Apart from them, everyone lives in fear. I don't even know if I should be speaking like this," she paled suddenly. "I mean… we all know this, even as little kids, but it's not the same as talking about it."

Suddenly, loud knocks sounded on the door, interrupting their conversation. Luba looked up in fright, and even Karina started, but she recovered quickly. "Just a nasty coincidence," she quipped, trying to calm Luba.

"Yeah, right," Luba mumbled. "But I'm not opening the door to anyone."

"Right – nobody needs to know we're here," Karina agreed. "Though I just want to see who it is."

"Don't—" Luba tried to stop her, but Karina had already tiptoed to the door, and was now peering through the peephole.

"It's three men in business suits," she whispered to Luba after joining her at the opposite end of the corridor. "And they don't look very friendly."

"Shh!" Luba put a finger to her lips. "Nobody's friendly in Russia! You're not opening that door, okay?"

"Okay, no problem! Calm down, will you? It's just someone looking for Dmitri, probably. Nothing to get worried about."

The girls retreated back to the kitchen, at the far end of the apartment from the front door. Meanwhile, the knocking continued for another few minutes before the men presumably gave up and left.

Karina felt a chill run up her spine, as she recalled the blood-curdling stories she had heard. They weren't just fictional tales, but real-life stories that her family had lived through and survived. Was she on the verge of getting caught? Would they dare arrest her – an American citizen? Was she about to be taken to that awful building where her mother had worked? Karina began to tremble violently. She had imagined the possibility more than once, but it had always been a vague warning, nothing that she had ever really envisioned taking place. Only now did the possibility seem real, and she wondered how on earth Luba could survive living in such a country, with fear as a constant companion.

Please, Hashem! Save me! she *davened* from the innermost depths of her heart. *Give me the strength I need to see the plan through to the end.*

"They stopped knocking," Luba interrupted her terrified thoughts. "Let's just check that they've really gone." She tiptoed back to the door and peered through the hole – Karina didn't dare follow her.

"They really are gone," Luba announced in relief. Karina nodded and exhaled slowly, suddenly realizing that she had been holding her breath. They were gone, but who knew if they wouldn't be back?

Less than five minutes later, the phone rang, and before Karina could stop her, Luba answered.

"Luba? Karina?" It was Natalya.

"It's Luba."

"You went out earlier?" The surprise in her voice sounded clearly through the line.

"No, we were home all the time." Luba was relieved that she had listened to Karina and stayed home.

"So why didn't you answer the door? Didn't you hear the knocking?"

"You want us to answer the door if you're not home?"

"Why not? I sent a courier from my office to fetch an important file that I forgot at home. They're coming back now, so please open the door this time. The file is lying on the bottom shelf in the cabinet right above my desk."

"I'm sorry," Luba apologized. "We didn't know that you'd want us to answer. I didn't realize people knew we were here."

"I guess I should have told you first," Natalya conceded. "In any case, they just called me from a payphone, and they should be back in a minute or two."

"Okay. Sorry again."

When the men returned, the girls opened the door immediately and handed them the file.

"Thank you," the taller one said. "And we're sorry if we alarmed you. Are you girls related to Natalya, or to Dmitri?"

"We're not relatives, but my mother is a close friend of Mrs. Kolchik, and we're spending the summer here with her," Luba replied politely.

"Is your mother also Natalya's friend?" the second one addressed Karina. Karina felt her heart skip a beat. Why did he want to know? What business was it of his? Something inside her screamed that these men were there more for the questions than for the forgotten file.

"I'm a good friend of Luba's," she replied, and was horrified to realize that her voice was trembling.

"A friend brings a friend," the man replied. "Where are you from?"

"Zagorsk," Luba replied. Karina was silent.

"You're also from Zagorsk?"

Karina nodded, delivering a silent prayer to Hashem that the man wouldn't question her any further.

"I have friends in Zagorsk," the man continued. "They probably know you, or at least your family. I'm sure they'll be happy to receive your regards." His gaze bored through them, as if trying to intuit their deepest secrets. In just a moment, Karina was sure, he would pull out the handcuffs and shove them both into a waiting KGB car.

"If we know them!" Luba exclaimed. "We know lots of people from Zagorsk, but not everyone, of course."

"Zagorsk isn't a very big town. If our friends don't know you, then they probably know your neighbors, or some of your friends. People don't live in a vacuum."

"Of course not," Luba agreed.

The men said goodbye and turned to leave. Luba closed the door, and the girls faced each other, stricken in terror.

"Was that what I thought it was?" Luba asked shakily.

"What did you think it was?" Karina's voice was unnaturally high.

"People checking up on us."

"But Natalya said that they were coming from her office!" Karina reminded her friend.

"So why were they asking us such crazy questions, and why that weird remark about not living in a vacuum?" Luba asked in a panic.

"I don't know," Karina whispered, trying to calm her own pounding heart.

"Do you think I should call my mother?" Luba asked, her terror gaining momentum.

"No! Why scare her when there's nothing she can do, in any case?" In fact, Karina was thinking of her own mother and how petrified she would be to receive such chilling news.

The girls returned to the living room, and Luba sank weakly onto the couch. "I wonder if your mother realized what kind of danger she was sending you into," she said with a shake of her head.

"She knows, and she's trembling the entire time I'm here. The last thing I want to do is frighten her even more."

"Why didn't she come herself?" Luba demanded.

"She wanted to, but that was way too dangerous."

"I don't get it!" Luba exploded. "It was too dangerous for her, so she sent her daughter instead?"

"It's not so dangerous for me."

"But you just said yourself that your mother knows that you're in danger and is trembling in fear!"

"I didn't mean real physical danger. But my mother was on the KGB's Wanted list eleven years ago. I'm nervous that they'll discover that I'm here from America, but even if they do, I won't be in any real danger. A lot of Americans visit here – I'm not the only one."

"Do you think those guys were KGB agents?"

"I doubt it," Karina tried to reassure her friend, although she didn't even believe her own words.

"They were too curious, with no good reason," Luba added.

"Well, if they know Natalya, then they were probably wondering who her houseguests are – you know, if we're family or friends," Karina suggested hopefully.

"Well, let's just hope that they don't decide to investigate in Zagorsk to find out who exactly you are," Luba said, frowning. "At least nobody would suspect you're American from your perfect Russian accent, but I still don't like it."

"Oh, Luba, stop worrying so much, will you? What's wrong with Natalya having guests? Do you really think the KGB doesn't have anything better to do than check up on random people?"

Luba rose furiously from her perch on the couch and began pacing the living room. "Stop trying to make everything sound like it's fine, will you!"

"What's the problem? Would you rather I tried to scare you?"

"I'm just wondering what could happen if my name gets connected with anything illegal," Luba said suddenly, turning a harsh gaze on Karina.

"What could happen?" The turn in the conversation took Karina by surprise.

"I'll lose any chance of getting a scholarship, for one. And maybe I won't even get accepted into university at all."

"Luba, can you take it easy for a minute? Natalya just called and explicitly stated that she was sending a courier from her office. You're blowing this completely out of proportion!"

"So maybe she's collaborating with them?" Luba suggested aloud. Reading Karina's expression of disbelief, she added, "In this country, anything's possible."

"Come on, Luba. You mean that Natalya would invite us to her home just so she could hand us over to the KGB? Would you really accuse her of doing something like that to your mother?"

The question was enough to make Luba stop and think. "I guess you're right. It's hard to believe that she would do something like that. My mom and Natalya have been friends forever… unless she guessed that your mother is mixed up in all this too…"

"There's no reason whatsoever to assume that," Karina said resolutely. "Besides, even if she did stumble on that fact, then she'd take care of me but leave you out of it."

CHAPTER 13

"It's been three days now, and nothing's happened yet," Luba announced as soon as she woke up after sleeping late once again. Natalya had been behaving completely naturally, and no other uninvited visitors had come knocking at the door. "I think we just let ourselves get nervous for nothing."

"I guess so," Karina inclined her head in agreement.

"Were you scared?" Luba asked. If anyone had been acting strangely of late, it was Karina herself, who had been even quieter than usual. Although Karina chose not to share her thoughts with her friend, Luba guessed that she was frightened.

"Yes," Karina admitted, "I was." She smoothed out the sheet and spread the comforter neatly on the bed.

"What, exactly, were you scared of?" Luba asked curiously. She suspected that Karina had turned around on purpose, so that Luba wouldn't be able to see her expression.

"You know, complications, interrogations… What everyone warned us about."

"Well, now we know that there was nothing to worry about. Those men must have really been from Natalya's office. In fact, she told us they were. Why did we think otherwise?"

"*Baruch Hashem*," Karina muttered, her face still turned to the wall. Stalling for time, she refolded her clothes neatly in the closet and then went to gaze out of the window.

"What did you say?"

"Nothing."

"You did say something! In fact, I've heard you say the same things lots of times. Is it English?" Luba persisted.

"No," Karina admitted, "it's actually Hebrew."

"Hebrew? Is it, like, a religious rite or something?"

"Something like that."

"I knew you'd answer that. And you know what? It's really annoying! Can't you give me a straight answer for once? Why all the secrecy? Don't you trust me?" For the first time, Karina detected a note of hurt in Luba's voice, and she turned around to face the girl.

"What would you like me to say?"

"I don't know, just more than you're saying. Talking to you is like getting a telegram – like every word costs you a fortune or something!" Luba exhaled in frustration.

Karina gave a wry smile. "This is the Soviet Union, isn't it? Everyone warned me that the less said here, the better."

"That's to the KGB! Not to me!" Luba practically exploded. "And if you keep on treating me like a KGB agent, then I'm leaving!"

Karina was shocked. "Why do you say that I'm treating you like the KGB? Don't we talk like friends?"

"No! Sure, we talk, but you're not open with me. You haven't told me a thing about yourself, about your mission here, whatever it is. You guard every word, and you share nothing with me! With all I'm doing for you, you don't even trust me. It's not right, and it's actually insulting."

"I do trust you, Luba," Karina said softly. "I trust you because of your goodwill and your heart of gold and because of everything you're doing for me. It's only because of you that I'm even able to be here now. I'm being extra cautious not because of you, but because of where I am and my mission—"

"That's exactly what I mean – your *mission*! I can't stand all the secrecy! Don't you think it's time you told me the truth? I mean, I'm here only because of you, as you freely admit. We've been together here for two weeks already. We're sharing a room, eating together, spending time together, getting scared when strangers knock on the door together, and dealing with Natalya. *Together*!" she emphasized the word strongly and then paused just long enough to take a deep breath. "Don't you think it's time you told me why you're here?"

Karina stared long and hard at Luba who met her gaze evenly.

"I'm sorry, Luba, but not yet. Soon, but not yet," she finally replied.

"And you still expect me to believe that you trust me?!" Luba exploded, the hurt in her eyes almost tangible. Karina cringed.

"This has nothing to do with you, Luba. I promise you! The whole situation is just so complex and delicate and dangerous, that if I'm not careful, I could mess everything up. Please believe me. *Please!*"

"You can't ask me to do everything I'm doing for you, and then to top it off, ask me to believe you, without telling me why! When my mother first told me about you and your planned visit here, I didn't think it would bother me not to know exactly why you're here and what you're doing. But now that we're both living here at Natalya's, I'm going nuts. I can't keep on playing this game without knowing why I'm playing it. It's not fair, and I can't do it! If you won't tell me, then I'll just have to call my mother and ask her to tell me the truth."

Karina took a deep breath, trying to steady her roiling emotions.

"Luba, let's keep both our mothers out of this for now, okay? They're going through enough with us so far from home, and they really can't do much to help."

"*Your* mother can't," Luba pointed out.

"No, she definitely can't, but your mother is also deeply involved in this, and she's a wonderful, caring person. She's committed to do everything she can to make this work."

Luba didn't budge. "Well, unlike me, she knows what's supposed to work. Come on, Karina! Just tell me what it's all about. It'll be so much easier to help you if I know what's really going on."

"I need a drink," Karina muttered, dragging her feet heavily to the door, trying desperately to figure out what to do. To her chagrin, Luba followed her right down the corridor to the kitchen, where Karina poured herself a drink of water, recited the blessing. and sipped from the cup. She wondered if Luba would comment on the *brachah*, but the girl was too absorbed in their argument to even notice.

"Would you like a drink?" she offered, trying to smooth the atmosphere.

"Water won't help you or me," Luba replied. "I want information. And something more than a 'telegram.'"

"Okay, you want to know the truth?" Karina's eyes narrowed as she turned to face Luba. "So, I'll tell you. I'm here for my father. He's here in Moscow, and I want to help him."

Luba's eyes widened in shock. "Your father is here in Moscow? You mean you managed to meet him without me knowing? When? But we've spent every minute of the day together! Have you been slipping out of the house in the middle of the night?" she demanded.

Karina couldn't hide her smile. "You're already way, way ahead of yourself, Luba. All I said is that my father is in Moscow. Everything else was just your own conjectures. But in case you're wondering, no, I haven't met up with him yet, and certainly not in the middle of the night when you were sleeping!"

"So you're saying that your father is in Moscow, but you haven't seen him yet?" Luba countered skeptically.

"Right. My father is in Moscow, and I haven't seen him yet," Karina confirmed.

"Why not? And what's the big secret about your father?"

"That *is* the secret, and I hope you'll be able to keep it that way."

"That's not the problem at all," Luba protested. "But… how come your father's here? Why didn't he move to America together with you and your mother? I mean… I knew there was a whole complicated business with you and your family reaching America, but I just assumed that your father was with you, or something. Is he in jail? And your mother really believes that you can get him out somehow? She must be out of her mind! She's being totally unrealistic, to send a kid here to achieve the impossible."

Karina frowned. "Luba, you're judging my mother for the second time without any knowledge of what's really going on in our lives. Why in the world do you assume that my father is in jail and that I need to rescue him? Come on, Luba, be realistic. Do you really think my mother's that crazy? Or your mother, who knows why I'm here?"

"Does my mother know what you're planning to do?"

It was a fair question, and Karina responded honestly to it. "I'll tell you one thing: It was your mother who concocted this entire plan. I'm here because of her, and not only that, but it was her idea to bring you along too!"

CHAPTER 14

The summer days passed with trips to the city center, many of the museums and parks, and then the countryside surrounding Moscow, where Natalya and the two girls went for long walks before returning to Natalya's apartment in the evening. Often, they chatted until late in the night, exchanging stories and discussing topical issues, and Natalya felt as if she had been catapulted back into her youth, back to her own teenage years when her life had still been full of light and vitality.

That evening, Luba was regaling them with stories of school and friends, with Karina interjecting occasional anecdotes, and their descriptions of high school life sent Natalya spiraling back decades into her own past.

"I was fourteen when I started high school in Moscow," she related, her eyes sparkling. "Before then, I attended the small regional school in my rural town, but my parents knew that in order for me to advance in life, I would need a better education than our small town could provide. They made arrangements for me to stay with my aunt in Moscow, and that's how I ended up in the city."

"It must have been a major transition for you," Karina remarked.

"It was. Everyone assured me that it would be an amazing experience, and it was, but it was also very draining, and painful at times too. In fact, I almost gave up and came home after two months," Natalya recalled, a distant look in her eyes.

"What was so hard about it?" Luba asked.

"The truth was, that although my parents sent me to Moscow for the superior level of education, the main reason I wanted to go was the social scene there – but I had no idea how hard it would be for a country girl in the big city," Natalya replied. "I desperately wanted to be accepted, but I was barely noticed."

"But you found your place eventually," Luba noted.

"How do you know?" Karina interjected.

"Because Natalya didn't go home, right Natalya? You persisted until the end of the year, and even then, you didn't go back to your home town. In fact, I think my mother said that you've been in Moscow ever since – isn't that so?"

"Yes, that's right," Natalya nodded. "And that was largely thanks to your mother, Luba. She did so much for me, even though it took her time to notice me. The truth is, that it took me time to notice her too and recognize the potential friendship there."

"How long did it take?" Karina asked, her tone of voice conveying the sympathy she felt with a young Natalya, alone and lonely in the big city. The soft tenor in her voice touched a chord deep within Natalya's heart, and, for a moment, she even felt that Karina had somehow tapped into the profound depths of pain and emptiness that she had known during her first months in Moscow.

"Long enough that I never forgot that painful period," Natalya replied. "I've been through a lot in life, girls. My son was arrested; we were pursued by the KGB; my son passed away while in jail. There's a void in my heart that can never be filled. But despite all that, I'll never forget the pain I endured in my teenage years, when I felt so rejected by my classmates."

"Although it is normal for people to find it hard to adjust to a new environment," Luba remarked thoughtfully.

"That's true, but in my case, it was much worse than the average," Natalya replied. "It wasn't just a normal adjustment period. I remember feeling literally invisible, like a spare chair in the classroom that nobody needed or would even notice if it was there or not." She took a deep breath before continuing. "The class dynamics were complex with everything centering around one clique of girls that the others worshipped. They were at the center, and everyone else just orbited around them. If one of them deigned to speak to anyone who wasn't part of the group, that girl would feel like she was walking on air for the rest of the day. There were eight of them, with two at the top, and the others like their ladies-in-waiting. The most powerful of all was Anya. She was the queen, and your mother, Luba, Katerina, was the second-in-command – the princess. The others weren't even friends – rather, they were in a constant power struggle to reach the top of the social ladder. I didn't even try speaking to them because I knew that they wouldn't deign to look at me. I was just one of those miserable wallflowers who sat in the far corner of the classroom, even during recess, waiting and hoping that someone would notice me."

"Anya was the most popular girl in the class?" Luba asked in surprise, casting a meaningful look at Karina.

"She sure was! She gave the impression of the classic snob, arrogant, condescending, disdainful of others. Only much later, when we became close, did I discover how much beauty and wisdom she had inside her. In fact, she wasn't snobby, but regal, kind, and refined."

"How can you call her kind if she treated others condescendingly?" Luba queried. Out of the corner of her eye, she saw Karina cringe, and immediately regretted her impulsive question.

"Today, I understand that it wasn't intentional," Natalya hurried to defend her one-time friend. "Anya was simply a cut above the rest, maybe even several cuts above. She was an exceptional person, and we couldn't relate to her or appreciate her. Despite her lofty attitude, she never intentionally hurt anyone. She acquired her queenly status without ever fighting for it; it was simply who she was, and we all automatically fell into our own roles around her."

"But you did suffer," Luba pointed out.

"Yes, I suffered terribly! I was so homesick, as well as lonely and rejected, and I didn't know how to deal with my feelings. At first I tried to push my way into being accepted, but of course it didn't work, and after that I was even more self-conscious. Things got worse and worse – until, finally, your mother noticed me."

"How did it happen?" Luba asked curiously; she had never heard this part of the story before.

"It wasn't in school. We actually met up in the doctor's office, while we were both waiting for appointments. Katerina came in a bit after me, and since there was an empty seat beside me in the waiting room, she sat down next to me. I was so nondescript that it took her a moment to recognize me, but when she did, she blurted out, 'Hey! Aren't you the new girl in our class?'

"I couldn't contain myself and replied that I had actually been part of the class for the last four months. Your mother, to her credit, blushed in embarrassment, and then apologized. She was even more embarrassed when it emerged that she didn't even know my full name, and she said that I had every right to feel hurt and upset, and that it was wrong of her to have never spoken to me until then. I kind of shrugged in response. To my surprise, she looked earnestly into my eyes, asked me to forgive her and also asked if I'd be willing to give her a chance and if we could maybe get to know each other? In my heart, I was so humiliated and hurt that I was tempted to rebuff her attempt, but I craved friendship and company so desperately that I actually agreed. Well, sort of.

"I told her, 'If you're planning on spending the waiting time here together but forgetting that I exist tomorrow morning in school, then I'll pass.' Katerina hesitated for a moment, but then she agreed that it was only fair. And, from then onward, I was never lonely in school again. We spent about an hour talking, and the next morning, I was invited to join her inner circle of friends. Anya began noticing me too, and we became close. Like I said, Anya was always special, and the more our friendship deepened, the more I grew to respect and love her."

"What was so special about her?" Luba asked, exerting enormous self-control not to wink at Karina.

"It's hard to describe. It was like she had a magic about her, unusual charisma and charm. She was extremely bright; brilliant, I would even say, and she was a go-getter who knew how to achieve exactly what she wanted without using force or manipulation. She was also a fascinating person to know and every conversation with her was memorable. There was never a dull moment with Anya around."

"And yet she still came off as a snob and didn't talk to you for four months?" Luba persisted, unable to connect the two seeming disparities.

Natalya rose to draw the curtains. "Actually, a lot of that changed after some of our early discussions. When I felt comfortable enough with her to share my feelings, I told her how much I'd suffered and how other girls in the class were suffering as well. I opened her eyes, and she began noticing the others girls in the class and treating them with warmth and consideration. Anya was always a learner and a grower."

"You sound like you admire her until today," Luba commented with a smile.

"Not anymore. Honestly, today, I'm furious at her, and I don't think that I'll ever be able to forgive her."

A heavy silence settled upon the three, and Luba suddenly recalled what Natalya had said several days earlier about the son she had lost. She understood that Natalya's tragedy was somehow connected to Anya, although she didn't yet know how. The questions were at the tip of her tongue, but a warning look from Karina made her swallow them. Recalling Karina's previous sharp rebuke, she wisely decided to stay silent, even though her curiosity was burning a hole in her heart.

"You know, Karina," Natalya said softly, "there's something about you that reminds me very much of Anya. The Anya of my youth, of course, not the one who betrayed me," she hastened to add. "I think I told you that right in the beginning, when you first arrived here. Your posture, your expression, your finesse, even the look in your eyes – they remind me so much of Anya that it's almost uncanny." Seeing Karina's deep blush, Natalya chuckled uncomfortably. "I don't know why I'm dwelling on this. It's not like the two of you are related or anything. Sometimes you just meet a person who has a striking resemblance to someone else you know, and you really do remind me of all that was good and beautiful in Anya. When I see you, I miss the friend that I once had and, suddenly, I forget the anger and resentment that I normally harbor against her. Funny, isn't it?"

Late that night, when the girls were in the privacy of their room and the door was shut, Luba turned to Karina. "Did your mother ever tell you about her childhood? Did you know how special she was?"

"I know how special she is because of all that we've shared together." Karina choked up as she spoke.

"What's the story with Natalya's son? Your mother really handed him over to the KGB in order to save herself?"

Karina jumped out of bed as if bitten by a snake. "Don't you ever, *ever* say or even *think* such a thing about my mother, as long as you live! My mother would never do something like that!"

Luba lifted her hands in a show of surrender and then placed a warning finger on her lips. "Take it easy, Karina. If you don't tone it down, you'll wake up Natalya and Dmitri!"

CHAPTER 15

Moscow, 1976 (eleven years earlier…)

Anya cast tired eyes upon the large wall clock. Nine o'clock! Was it really nine o'clock already? Had she really spent the last thirteen hours at her desk? She hadn't even lifted the phone to call Jenya or Lev to ask about Karina, and she could already picture her husband's disapproving gaze when she returned. On the other hand, her efforts had yielded results; another two learning groups had been exposed that very night, an achievement she couldn't recall in all her years of working for the KGB. Anya had just received a communiqué from Fyodorev, congratulating her on her success and hinting at a potential promotion as remuneration for her contribution to cleansing Moscow of undesirable elements.

Noontime the next day, the Agency was celebrating the capture of a third learning group at the university when Svetlana entered with a steaming mug of coffee which she set down in front of Anya.

"Thanks, Svetlana," Anya smiled her gratitude. "It's just what I needed – but how did you know?"

"It was written all over your face!" Svetlana chuckled. "Would you like to see the list of detainees? In the meantime, that's the only prize I can offer you in exchange for your hard work the last few days."

Anya hesitated. Despite the immense amount of thought and planning she invested into tracking down the enemies of the Soviet state, she had never felt the inclination to learn of the identities of those swept up by her deputies. She preferred that the victims – her victims – remained anonymous, at least partly out of fear that one day, one of the names on the many lists would be that of an acquaintance, or worse. As long as she never knew who had suffered at her hands, she could continue working and achieving results. But when the day arrived when she recognized the name of someone on the list, Anya knew that all her strength – and worse yet, her peace of mind – would falter.

As if reading her mind, Svetlana continued, "I know you don't usually like to, but if you do want to take a look, I'm placing the list on Tina's desk. She'll be in soon to add anyone whose name comes up during the initial interrogation."

Svetlana returned to her office, leaving Anya alone with her thoughts. It suddenly occurred to her that the detainees were all students in the university where Lev taught, and she wondered if he'd be interested in hearing their names. The thought drew her like a magnet to the adjoining office where Tina worked, but at the threshold, she stopped and made an about-face, returning to her own office. No, she wouldn't look. She didn't need to know.

A minute later, Svetlana poked her head back in Anya's office. "Did you look at the list, Anya?" she asked.

"No. Why?"

"Because there's someone on the list with the same last name as yours."

"Really? That's surprising. I don't have any relatives here in Moscow," Anya replied, astonished.

Svetlana gazed at Anya for a moment, and Anya couldn't quite figure out what she saw in her expression. "Oh? So... maybe he's a relative you didn't know about," she suggested. "Or... well, whatever." Nodding curtly to her colleague, Svetlana disappeared again, and this time, Anya, her curiosity piqued, followed her out of the room and headed straight for Tina's desk.

Scanning the list of detainees, it didn't take long for her to single out the name:

Lev Ilyevich Krasnikov.

Lev Ilyevich Krasnikov! What a coincidence, that there were two men with the identical name in the university, although her husband was a professor and the other was presumably a student...

Unable to restrain herself, she turned and hurried out of the office and down the steps, headed to an area of the building where she had never previously dared to venture – the interrogation rooms. She needed to see this Lev Krasnikov for herself. Too unsettled to wait for the elevator, she hurried down the stairs as fast as she could, catching herself at the last second before she missed a step and fell hard. She was still tired after yesterday's brutal workday, but she ran down four flights of stairs at top speed, stopping only when her entrance to the interrogation wing was barred by an armed security guard.

"Anya Krasnikov!" she announced imperiously, flashing her badge. "I'm commanding this operation, and for the purposes of the investigation, I must see the detainees at once."

A quick glance at the title beneath her name was enough to cause the low-ranking officer to open the door for her, and Anya entered. The arrestees were clustered together in an anteroom, their hands cuffed and terror written all over their faces. She scanned the room quickly, but didn't recognize any of the faces.

"Lev Krasnikov!" she called out in a loud voice, and then noticed a small stir coming from the far left corner of the room. A tall man approached, but Anya didn't have to look twice to identify him. All color drained from her face, and she felt her knees buckling beneath her. She reached frantically for the wall to steady herself, knowing how critical it was that the guard should not see her fall.

Her husband approached slowly, his face an inscrutable mask. Anya took a deep breath and commanded herself to maintain her equilibrium. "You will join me in the next room," she instructed in a low voice, hoping that no one heard the tremor. She indicated to a door that led to an adjacent room, and then followed her husband inside before shutting and locking the door behind them.

When it was just the two of them, she rasped, "What are you doing here?" Lev didn't reply, studiously avoiding her gaze.

"What are you doing here?" an unfamiliar tearful note wriggled its way into her words. "You happened to be passing by when the KGB stormed the Talmud class someone organized on campus? Are they claiming that you're part of the group?"

Lev still didn't reply, and Anya sank onto the solitary chair in the room feeling as if all the wind had been knocked out of her. She hardly noticed that her husband remained standing.

"Lev…" she finally said, "I understand that you must be in shock to find yourself here, but if you don't conjure up a mighty good excuse, it's going to be really tough for me to get you out of here."

"It really is going to be tough to get me out of here," he finally spoke his first words, but in a tone that terrified her.

"Lev! What are you saying? What's going on?" she pleaded, wishing desperately that he would snap out of his stupor. "Don't you realize that you're under suspicion?"

"Anya, I know that you'd like me to say that it's all a mistake, but I don't think they'll believe that."

"Who won't believe it?"

"The interrogation committee. It's not easy to get anything past them. They'll squeeze the truth out of one of the others. It won't work."

"What won't work?" Anya practically shouted.

"To claim that I was just passing by and was there by chance."

She studied her husband in anguish. "You mean they'll lie to save themselves?"

"They won't lie, but it's hard to stay strong under torture."

"Lev…" Anya's eyes were wide, and her heart palpitated wildly in her chest at a rate she'd never known was possible. "Why won't they lie? What were you doing there?"

Lev lowered his head, and Anya suddenly noticed that all the color had drained from his face. *No, it can't be! It's impossible!* a voice screamed inside of her.

"I think it's best that you don't know," Lev said finally. "Better that you shouldn't know the truth."

"Stop it, Lev, and talk sense for once!" she spat angrily. "If I'm going to get you out of here, I need to know exactly what you were doing and how you ended up there. And you'd better hurry up if you don't want the guard barging in on us!"

"Anya, it's going to be very difficult for you to absorb this." Lev's voice was barely above a whisper, and Anya felt her heart clench in terror.

"What, Lev? For heaven's sake, just tell me what! I can't take this anymore!" she cried.

"I'm telling you, Anya, but you need to be strong. I was doing exactly what all the other students there were doing. I was learning about Judaism, about the truth."

She jerked back as if bitten by a snake, dragging the chair along with her, as if the physical distance between her and her husband would save her from his impossible confession.

"No," she said, shaking her head. Lev gazed at her, heartbroken.

"No! It can't be true!" she repeated in a whisper, on the verge of hysteria. "You... You? You were learning about... *You?*"

This time, Lev met her gaze evenly. Something sparked in his eyes, and he suddenly appeared strengthened. "Yes, Anya," he replied confidently. "I was learning about Judaism. I've been learning Torah for two years now. I've wanted to tell you for so long, but I knew that it would be too dangerous for you to know about it. I'm so, so sorry that you had to find out about it like this. But it is the truth, and I can't deny it. I won't deny it."

"You... You're studying... Judaism?" she repeated the words, choking over them, unable to believe that they were true, refusing to absorb them. Suddenly, in place of shock and terror, she was besieged by an uncontrollable rage. *How dare he! How dare he risk himself and his family by learning the forbidden in Soviet Russia? Studying Judaism was a crime! He was a husband and a father! Where was his sense of responsibility? How dare he!*

"How dare you!" she voiced her fury.

"Anya," Lev's soft voice rose above the shouted echoes in her mind. "I beg your forgiveness. Please, please forgive me. I never wanted to harm you, and I don't want to hurt you now. Leave me here. Tell them the truth; tell them that you knew nothing of any of it. Let me accept the punishment for my own crimes. This has nothing to do with you – or Karina."

"How can you ask me to do that?" she wept. "Do you think I can just go about life knowing that you've been sentenced to years of hard labor in a camp in Siberia? Don't you realize that whatever they do to you will destroy me?"

"I'm so sorry, Anya! There's nothing I can say or do to make it up to you. But, please, just stay strong. If not for me and not for you, then at least for Karina! For our beautiful, precious child!" Lev's voice cracked, and Anya felt her heart shatter.

"How could you, Lev? How? *Why?*" she begged. "Didn't you know what could happen?"

"Anya." The intensity with which he spoke her name made her lift her tear-filled eyes to meet his, and in them she saw a fire that she had never seen before. A sudden radiance illuminated his pale features as he expressed his deepest feelings. "Anya, I promise you that I thought many, many times about what could happen. I knew exactly what I was doing. Not a day passed when I didn't consider the potential ramifications and what the future could hold. Many times, I was about to leave it all behind, to close the door to those lessons, to leave the danger and never return. But I couldn't."

Anya stared at him in confusion. "You mean they forced you to attend?"

"No, Anya. Nobody was forcing me to be there. Only the soul within me. I couldn't escape the yearning in my soul. Once I discovered Truth, I couldn't just walk away. I couldn't deny it any longer. I need it like I need water to live."

Anya didn't comprehend a word of what he was saying, but she didn't have time to wonder. She needed to get her husband out of that place, and fast.

CHAPTER 16

The door to the tiny interrogation room was still shut, and Anya looked around in desperation. She was one of the senior employees in her department, and there was no way she could allow her husband to fall into the cruel clutches of the KGB. On the other hand, as a senior officer, she was well aware just how impossible it was to escape this fortress of evil. Neither her rank nor her exceptional record would be of any help in such circumstances.

"What do we do now?" she whispered pitifully, unable to believe this was really happening to them.

"There's nothing that can be done," Lev replied calmly. "You go back to your office quietly, and I'll return to the next room. And then," he exhaled slowly before continuing, "whatever happens, happens. You'll just keep insisting that you knew nothing, and I'm sure that your record here will at least achieve that much, that they'll believe you."

But Anya shook her head, trying to fight back the tears that threatened to cascade down her cheeks. "I won't leave you here to be tortured!" she cried fervently, clenching her fists tightly together. "I won't abandon you, Lev!"

"But think of Karina. Think of our little girl! What will happen to her if we both land up in jail?" Lev was struggling to be rational and to direct her to use her common sense, but right then, it seemed like an impossible task.

"How will I face Karina one day when she gets older and asks me what I did to save her father? How can I continue just living and working here when I know what's happening to you?"

He exhaled a bitter sigh. "Oh, Anya, I'm so sorry! I wish it didn't have to be like this. I wish I hadn't hurt you like this. I don't even have the time to explain now why I had to do this, how important – how vital it was. Please, I beg of you, stay strong. I know you can do it. You'll pull through this – if not for yourself, then for Karina. When she gets older, you'll tell her that—"

"Stop it! I'm getting you out of here! That stupid guard outside has no idea what my position here is, and he won't dare stop me."

"Anya, you know as well as I do that it's impossible. My name is already on their list, and the moment I disappear, they'll go after you. Why is my blood worth more than yours?"

Anya swiped away her tears; she couldn't afford any display of how weak she truly felt, in case the guard discerned that something was awry. It was even dangerous for Lev to realize how terribly shaken she was – if he knew, he would never let her go ahead with the plan that was beginning to crystallize in her mind.

"It will be okay," she announced finally. "I know how to deal with this. I can figure it out – trust me. I didn't start working here just yesterday."

Lev shook his head. "You're blinding yourself to the truth, Anya. They'll come after you. If not in a half-hour, then in an hour, or a day. Maybe even within minutes."

"I'll have help. There are people here who are loyal to me and will be willing to help us out, even if it means circumventing the rules." She rose from her chair and walked to the door, maintaining a stiff posture.

"Comrade!" she called to the security guard as she opened the door, "there's a prisoner here who refuses to be interrogated."

Lev gave her a shocked glance, but then immediately scurried into the next room, crouching low between two other prisoners. He managed to whisper several sentences to one of them before the guard's strong hand grabbed him by the wrist and dragged him out of the room into the corridor.

"Where should I put him?" he asked Anya gruffly.

"I'm taking him upstairs now. If there's any trouble, I'll call you."

The guard treated Lev to a withering stare. "I advise you to do as you're told. The alternative isn't very pleasant, even though you'll probably experience it in any case."

Lev nodded and followed Anya silently down the long corridor until they reached a staircase. They walked up a flight of stairs and then immediately descended another one that led to the far side of the building, not exchanging a word throughout until they reached an abandoned, unused wing of the upper basement floor. Anya passed her eyes quickly over the unpainted cement walls until she located an old metal chest which she tried to drag.

"Leave it. It's too heavy for you," Lev said softly. "Do you want me to move it?"

"Just a drop forward. Just enough so you can stand behind it."

"You want me to hide here?"

"Just for a few minutes until I get a key."

Lev took a deep breath and closed his eyes, speaking with difficulty. "Anya, I'm asking you again. For the sake of logic and safety, please take me back to the other prisoners. We're still before the point of no return."

"We reached that point the moment I laid eyes on you," she

whispered back, her expression taut. "Just promise me that you'll wait here quietly and won't budge an inch. No one's likely to come this way, and I should be back in ten minutes, tops." Without awaiting his reply, she ran back up the steps, forcing herself to resume a normal pace when she reached the main entrance level, which was, as usual, bustling with people. From there, she continued at a regular pace until her color returned to normal by the time she reached her office.

There was no time to plan the most innocent-sounding phrase to use – Anya simply uttered the first words that came to her: "Svetlana?" she called out, as she passed the woman's office, "can I borrow your keys for a minute?"

"What for?" Svetlana returned in surprise.

"I lost something, and I think it might be downstairs in one of the rooms."

Svetlana studied her curiously. "What did you lose?"

"Um… a bracelet," she said quickly.

"I'll help you look for it. Two pairs of eyes are always better than one," Svetlana replied with a smile.

Anya took the keys out of her hands. "No, it's fine. I wouldn't want to waste your time. It's enough that my time is going to waste with this."

Svetlana looked surprised. The answer was so out of character for the Anya she knew, that she wasn't sure how to respond. Eventually, all she could think to say was, "You sure?"

"Positive." Anya forced a smile, hoping that she was at least succeeding in masking her terror.

The way back to the old, decrepit wing seemed shorter than before, although it took enormous self-control to smile and nod politely at the colleagues she passed on the way. She hoped that Lev was still waiting for her. His initial reaction had shocked her, and she couldn't comprehend his reluctance to let her help him. She had to try! How could he even imagine that she would give up on him so easily? How could he give up on himself?

She returned to the basement level within several minutes and immediately noticed that Lev's shoulder was protruding from behind the chest. But the main thing was that he hadn't been noticed – yet.

"I'm back," she whispered, "and I'm getting you out of here. There's a door here that leads outside."

"Where should I go?"

"As far as you can. Far from Moscow. Don't go home or to anyone we know. Don't let anything delay you. Stop the first taxi you see and get in, even if it's only a local driver. You can get out later and take an intercity cab. Whatever you do, just get as far away from here as you can."

"I don't have any money," he whispered. "They took everything I had."

"I already thought of that. Take my wallet. I don't have much cash, but it should be enough for the beginning. We'll have to figure out a way to get you more money later."

"Anya, if anything goes wrong, I'm coming back. I won't let you suffer for me."

"If anything goes wrong, it won't help for you to come back! You'll just be arrested, and I'll already be in jail. You know that."

"Anya, please. Take me back to the others. It's not too late! I won't endanger you."

"No!" With that, she approached the old iron door and began sorting through the keys on the key ring until she found the right one. "Besides, nothing will go wrong. I know what I'm doing." As she spoke, the door swung open.

"Anya!" Lev cried in a choked voice. "Come with me. We'll run away together!"

"What about Karina?"

"We'll send someone to bring her to us. Maybe we should just go home first. It will take them time to figure out what happened."

"You think? The KGB is much quicker than that. As soon as they discover that we're both gone, which will happen in about five minutes if I don't hurry back to my office, the first place they'll check is our apartment, and they won't hesitate to take Karina prisoner."

CHAPTER 17

Anya tried desperately to calm herself, knowing that maintaining a cool façade was crucial during those moments, but it still took her almost half an hour before her breathing returned to normal. All the while, she was haunted – both by the image of her husband escaping through the ancient iron door, and by his last words to her. Had Lev been right? Should she really have tried to escape together with him?

Worse still, she had no idea whether his escape attempt had succeeded. He could easily have been picked up by any one of the security guards in the vicinity, and in that case, it wouldn't take long before fingers were pointed at her, implicating her in his escape. And if both of them were jailed, then what would become of Karina? She would probably be taken into custody as a ward of the state, most likely never to see either of her parents again.

How impulsive – how foolish she had been! And yet, Anya knew that she could never have sat idly by while her husband was in a KGB dungeon. There had been no choice, regardless of the consequences. That was the bitter fate of living in Soviet Russia.

A chill passed through her, and she began to tremble. No choice? She had blindly followed her instincts with no thought as to the consequences, which, she now realized, were likely dire. It was a matter of hours, maybe even mere minutes, until her husband's disappearance was noticed and the guard recalled her visit to the interrogation rooms. What had she been thinking? Her rank, her reputation – neither of them would stand her in any stead when the truth came out – on the contrary; they would only add to her perfidy, in the eyes of her superiors. Fyodorev would not hesitate to throw her to the Siberian wolves, and he would probably even manage to manipulate the whole terrible story to his own personal advantage.

Anya felt her heart sink as she came to the realization that her fate was sealed. Sitting in her office, she watched the hands of the clock drag themselves around the dial. Ten minutes passed in quiet. How much longer would it be before they came for her? How long could it take for them to realize that they were short one prisoner? A quick scan of the names would be enough for them to identify the missing person, which would spare them a superfluous investigation. They would storm into her office and demand to know how she had achieved what was thought to be impossible, and then she would be thrown into the dungeons herself, probably in an isolated cell, to be tortured before her bogus trial and further tormented afterward. How many years of her life would they steal? Would it be years, or decades? Or… would she end her life in Lubyanka, under the earth, or under the frozen steppes of the Siberian tundra?

Anya shuddered. Her deepest pain was not for herself, but for Karina. Where would they take her little girl? Would she ever see either of her parents again? How had she dared to risk Karina's safety and future? What kind of mother abandoned a four-year-old to her fate?

Anya tried sipping from a cup of water, but she couldn't even swallow. She only hoped that the day would come that Karina would learn the truth and appreciate that her mother hadn't abandoned her for nothing – that she had sacrificed herself rather than leave her father to a miserable fate.

"Anya!" Svetlana's voice interrupted her reverie as she burst into her office. "Didn't you hear? One of the prisoners just escaped!"

Anya sat up bolt upright and stared in horror. "Escaped?" she stammered, trying to control the tremor in her voice. "How?"

"Nobody knows yet. They're searching the surrounding area. The guard claims that a senior official summoned the prisoner and took him out, and he swears it was a female interrogator, but nobody believes him, of course – there aren't any female interrogators on staff right now."

Anya opened a window and inhaled the fresh air; her office suddenly felt stifling. "The guard will pay dearly for his stupidity," she noted, breathing out slowly before she turned back around to face Svetlana.

"Oh yes!" Svetlana confirmed. "He's being interrogated even as we speak."

Svetlana continued to regale Anya with all the other details she was privy to, and then to offer her own conjectures as to the most likely methods used by the prisoner and his accomplice, and Anya nodded along, still trying to stop her whole body from shaking in fright. How long would it take for Svetlana to make the connection between the keys she had requested and the prisoner's escape? Was Svetlana really so dense – or was something else going on?

When Svetlana finally left her alone, Anya forced herself to return to work, this time working at top speed. Sitting in the office and doing nothing while waiting for them to come for her was the worst of all her options; best that at least she should try to accomplish something in the meantime.

Another two hours passed. Anya wanted to savor every last moment of freedom, but it was impossible; the fear was paralyzing. Each time she heard footsteps in the corridor or somebody knocked on the door, she was sure that the dreaded moment had arrived, and as time passed, she began to wish that they would just come already, and end the nightmare of suspense. Fear of what lay ahead in the future could sometimes be worse than the future itself, although in this case, Anya had no doubt that reality would be much, much worse than she could possibly imagine.

At four o'clock, she received a message from Fyodorev regarding an emergency meeting of the senior members of the department. Anya's heart clenched in terror; was he planning to confront her there in front of everyone?

With her remaining strength, she marched to the conference room like a condemned man on his way to the executioner. Never had she known how terribly anxiety could sap a person of his energies. Yet, to Anya's shock, Fyodorev acknowledged her arrival in his typical, perfunctory manner, and opened the meeting with a regular briefing, as if nothing out of the ordinary had occurred that day. Only after forty minutes of dry discussion did he turn to the hot topic of the moment, summarizing the findings resulting from the interrogation of the guard, Ivan Daminsky.

Apparently, Fyodorev related, the guard had confessed to having received a hefty bribe, in dollars, for releasing the prisoner. He had also given an outline description of the two people, a man and a woman, who had bribed him, and they, along with the escapee, were now being sought in the environs.

"So where's the money?" Sergei Rashiknikov of Planning and Development asked.

"What's the difference? He says he spent it already," Fyodorev replied curtly.

Anya listened quietly, baffled as to how her superiors failed to recognize that the guard had said everything the interrogators wished to hear in order to spare himself further torture. Not that it made any difference to her – the main thing was that meanwhile, nobody was pointing a finger in her direction, although Fyodorev did ask her opinion.

"Who do you think would invest money and endanger himself in order to rescue a prisoner?" he asked.

Her natural response would have been to ask the identity of the prisoner, a pertinent fact that had seemingly escaped everyone's attention, but Anya would not be the one to draw attention to herself. "Someone who has more to lose by the prisoner sitting in jail than by risking himself to set him free," she answered simply.

"What's the prisoner's name?" someone finally thought to ask.

"Boris Smirnov," Fyodorev read off the document. Anya struggled to maintain her equilibrium, wondering if she had somehow heard wrong.

"Any information about him?"

"What we know so far is that he lives in one of the suburbs of the city, and that he's in his second year at the university, studying Geological Science. He's considered a brilliant student and was seen as a loyal citizen – no black marks against his name until this 'little episode.' His family lives in Leningrad, but he hasn't seen them for the last six months, and it seems unlikely that they know of his illicit activities, although we will certainly investigate that."

Anya pinched herself to make sure she was hearing right. Was she dreaming? Had her terror confused her senses or perception? Was she hearing things?

"What do the other prisoners say?" Sergei asked.

"That he was taken by one of our interrogators and murdered during questioning. Some suggested that the interrogator must have hidden the body."

"What are the chances of that being true?" Viktor Grinin from Forensics asked.

"Anything is possible," Fyodorev conceded, "and we aren't ruling anything out for the time being. Of course, once all the prisoners have gone through a preliminary interrogation, matters will likely become clearer."

The meeting adjourned, and the attendees began to file out. "Comrade Krasnikov?" Fyodorev called out, just as Anya was about to step over the threshold. Anya froze, and then forced herself to turn around calmly.

"I hear that a certain relative of yours is among the prisoners," her boss said, so softly that she might have mistaken his tone of voice as compassionate, had she not been otherwise informed by the coldness in his eyes. "This will doubtless impact upon the way in which we regard your work here in the department. In the meantime, it is 'business as usual' – but naturally," he paused, eyeing her like a wolf about to consume his prey, "this could change, depending on what emerges when your 'relative' begins to talk. Comrade Krasnikov, watch your step."

Anya nodded mutely, balling her fists in her pockets as she turned and walked out of the room.

CHAPTER 18

Back in her office, Anya collapsed into her chair and stared at the pile of documents on her desk. She had clearly underestimated her husband's ingenuity; the idea to switch identities with a fellow prisoner had obviously been his, concocted in the split second he had to implement the plan. Would it work? Only time would tell.

Or rather, she reflected, the plan gave her some time, but probably still not much. It might be enough to get home, pick up Karina, and escape somewhere with her. How she would manage to locate her husband once she left home and he had no way of finding her, she had no idea, but nonetheless, her immediate priority was to flee. She would have to travel as far as possible in the first few hours of her escape, as she would come under suspicion right away the next morning when she didn't appear in her office as usual.

But where could she go? Seeking refuge in the home of a relative was clearly out of the question – it would be the first place they would look . And yet, who, other than a loved one, would risk life and liberty to offer her shelter? Anya nodded grimly to herself as she admitted the answer: No one. She didn't even dare to ask anyone to endanger himself on her behalf. So how could she flee? It would be hard enough for Lev to make his escape, a man on his own who could sleep in barns in the countryside if necessary and somehow procure food and water for himself. But there was no way she could attempt a similar escape with a four-year-old child.

The more Anya thought about it, the more she realized that her escape would have to be carefully planned. Meanwhile, she had to hope that the interrogation of the man now posing as her husband would be one of the last ones on the list, buying her some more precious time to make all necessary arrangements. Maybe Lev would even manage to contact her in the meantime, and help her think up a way to join him.

So, she would have to remain at work, for now. At least now that it was in the open, that a 'relative' of hers was a prisoner, she wouldn't have to feign a tranquil state of mind. She would be under close observation, to be sure, but nobody would think it strange for her to be distracted, tense, and anxious.

The relief that had flooded her only an hour earlier dissipated quickly. She was living a dangerous, temporary existence, and it was impossible to know how temporary it really was. She was safe only for the time being, but that security could vanish in a day, a week, or even before she exited the building that afternoon. Yet, she could not allow herself to succumb to the terror. She needed to be strong, and, as Lev had pleaded, if not for herself, then for Karina's sake.

She forced herself to sit up straight, arrange the papers on her desk, and focus on the tasks at hand. When the clock struck six, she rose slowly, collected her belongings and made her way leisurely out of the building, as always. *Don't run,* she ordered herself. *Act natural. Stay calm,* although she knew that the word "calm" would never again be a part of her lexicon. She couldn't wait to be home, even though she knew that the four walls of her apartment no longer offered her shelter or haven.

It was midnight, and only a dim bulb burning in the hallway illuminated her room with a faint yellow glow. Fear for her daughter consumed her, and she had brought Karina into her bedroom for the night. The little girl, naturally, was thrilled by the special treat. The apartment was silent except for Karina's steady breathing. Too silent. The silence only underscored the loneliness and terror that gnawed at her heart. For an hour she had held the telephone in her hand, debating whether or not to call Lev's mother to tell her what had happened. She craved someone's support and reassurance so badly that she almost dialed – until logic prevailed. It would be insanity to involve her mother-in-law. It would endanger not only her, but Lev, as well.

Nonetheless, the impossible fear of what would become of Karina if she were discovered was making her lose her mind. Anya resolved that the first task at hand was to find someone who would agree to look after Karina in the event that she was caught. But who? The authorities would doubtless seek to make Karina a ward of the state, meaning that she would be entrusted to a government-run orphanage, to be indoctrinated in blind loyalty and obedience to the Communist ideal. Who would risk himself to hide Karina? The only person who came to mind was her neighbor, Jenya Idelevitz, who loved Karina dearly, but although the woman was good-hearted, she doubted that she would be so devoted as to place herself in danger for her neighbor's child.

It was a moonless, starless night, and the darkness outside seemed to be almost thick, practically choking Anya. Karina, sound asleep, looked so vulnerable that Anya just wanted to hold her tight and never let go. What kind of future would her daughter know? She tried to escape her fearsome thoughts, but they swirled steadily in her mind, refusing to leave her.

In the haze of her terror, she recalled Lev's parting words to her, spoken just before he had escaped through the iron door. She had been so frantic at the time that she had hardly paid attention to them, but now the dark quiet caused them to echo in her mind.

"I don't know if we'll ever see each other again. I don't know if I'll ever see Karina again," her husband said, his voice cracking in pain. "But tell her that her father discovered the truth of life, and that it's to be found in a place where few believe it to be. Tell her that my final request to her is that when she gets older and understands, she'll search for it too and never give up until she finds it." Anya hadn't asked him to explain; her thoughts and heart were elsewhere, waiting for him to flee before they were discovered.

"Go, Lev! Run!" she had pleaded. "And take care of yourself. One day, we'll be back together, a family again!" These had been her final words to her husband before he had disappeared. Hers were words of parting, of hope and faith, although neither could know what the chances of them being realized were.

Now, as she replayed the scene in her mind, she was surprised to notice that she wasn't even angry at him. Lev and Anya shared a wonderful marriage and close relationship. Their lives had been comfortable and secure, with both working and earning respectable salaries. Moreover, they were blessed with Karina, the light of their lives. What had Lev done? Why had he risked all of that – what for? What had he felt he was missing?

The question weighed heavily on her mind and she knew she had to discover the meaning behind his words, the explanation for the extraordinary radiance that had illuminated his countenance when speaking of the truth he had found, despite the hunted look in his eyes. She wanted to be angry at him, to feel the pleasure of revenge; he deserved it. But she couldn't. The innocence in his expression and the hypnotic glow that radiated from within vanquished all fury in her heart even as she couldn't fathom why, *why*, he had done this.

Dawn was beginning to break over the horizon by the time Anya finally succumbed to a restless sleep, and she was barely able to rise to her ringing alarm clock. The only consolation for the impossible fatigue was that it dulled her fears and anxiety. She needed to exert physical and mental effort to dress Karina, prepare breakfast, and make sandwiches for the two of them. Usually, it was Lev who gave Karina breakfast. The little girl looked curiously at her mother as she poured hot water from the kettle into her red mug and asked, "Where's Papochka?"

Anya fought the trembling inside her. "He had to go somewhere."

"But he'll be back to pick me up in the afternoon?"

"No, my dear. He can't. He had to go away."

"When is he coming back?" Karina asked, clearly displeased.

"In a few days."

Karina banged her mug down angrily, sloshing hot tea on the table. "He didn't tell me he was going! Why didn't he tell me?"

Anya felt something warm and wet in her eyes, but she blinked back the tears. "He wanted to tell you, Karina sweetie, but he wasn't able to. He had to go on very short notice, and even I barely saw him before he left."

"Where did he go? To Babushka?"

Anya seized upon the idea. "Exactly. He had to go to Babushka, and he promised to bring back a gift with him, when he gets back."

Karina pouted. "I want to visit Babushka too! He promised he'd take me in the summer."

"It's not summer now, Karina. Remember? You have kindergarten this morning, and we can't be late."

"It's not summer for Papochka either! He teaches in the university!" the little girl stumbled over the word. "He could have taken me too!"

Anya didn't reply, hoping that the day's activities in kindergarten and then later at Jenya's house would distract the girl, if only temporarily. Maybe Lev would even manage to telephone them, and then Karina would speak to him, and calm down enough to wait patiently until he returned. But of course he could not return – and would they ever see him again?

CHAPTER 19

Just stay calm, Anya repeated to herself every few minutes that morning. *Calm down. Nobody suspects you yet. It's a regular workday, and there's nothing unusual on the agenda.* Her constant dialogue with herself eventually made an impact and her inner trembling quieted, which allowed her to set about her daily tasks.

At eleven o'clock that morning, a summons from Fyodorev caused Anya to break out in a cold sweat. Was this it? Had they discovered the switch? Or, did they 'simply' want to torture her with the latest developments with her supposedly imprisoned husband? Sooner or later, Lev's friend was bound to slip, and even if he didn't, it was inconceivable that it would take the KGB long to discover that he wasn't Anya's husband after all. The KGB knew *everything*. Even things that people didn't know about themselves, the Russians would say.

But how nervous should she appear, supposing that they still thought that it was Lev downstairs in the dungeons? What should she say? It was impossible to plan ahead for an interrogation – one could never anticipate the direction the questions would take. So, she would simply take each moment as it came, Anya resolved, as she headed down the corridor slowly, nodding to Svetlana as she passed by her open office door.

Placing a pile of documents on the chairman's desk, she relayed a fluid report about the files in her folder. Fyodorev nodded as he listened, asking the occasional pertinent question and keeping his steely eyes on her as he spoke. Anya's voice was unusually subdued, but surely he must have expected that.

"Thank you, Comrade Krasnikov," he said finally, indicating that the briefing was over. "Oh, and just one minute," he added casually, as she prepared to leave. "Your husband claims that he told you nothing about his learning. Which I find rather difficult to believe," he added, narrowing his eyes as he spoke.

"It's true," whispered Anya. "He didn't tell me, because… because he was scared." Tears pricked at her eyes but she didn't dare to wipe them away.

"He was right to be afraid," noted Fyodorev coldly. "A man with a wife and daughter is very foolish to take such risks, especially if he hopes to see them again in his lifetime. That's all for now, Comrade Krasnikov," he concluded, nodding at Anya. "You may leave."

Anya heard the telephone ringing when she was still in the stairwell, and she rushed to open the door and answer it before whoever it was hung up.

"Hello?" she replied hurriedly while trying to catch her breath.

"Anya?" the voice was unmistakably Lev's, and it was filled with a fear that terrified her.

"Yes! Are you okay?" she gasped, still short of breath.

"I'm all right. But what about you? They didn't catch on yet?"

"No. They didn't." *Not yet,* she added mentally.

"Thank G-d." *What had he said?* But Anya was too frantic to pay attention to such minor details. "I've been imagining the worst, and I almost returned home for fear."

"Don't you dare!" she cautioned. "Not even if I'm caught!"

"You don't know what you're saying. I've regretted this escape a million times already, and I can't forgive myself for endangering you and Karina to save my own skin. What will it help if they put you behind bars?" he lamented.

"Maybe it won't happen," she said weakly. She lacked the strength to deal with the future right now. Fear had pursued her all day long, and she had no answers, only questions.

"They didn't even interrogate you?" This was even more difficult for him to believe.

"No. Your idea to switch names was brilliant. At least in the meanwhile."

"In the meanwhile?" Lev didn't miss the hesitation in her voice.

"Not just in the meanwhile. I mean, it's working. Where are you? No, actually, don't tell me. It's better for both of us if I don't know."

"Why better?"

Her voice dropped to a whisper. "You know why. Do you have any money left?"

"A bit. Not much, but I hope that I'll be able to meet with one of my friends in a village somewhere and ask for help. I'd much rather not endanger anyone, but I don't see any other option."

"Don't tell them the truth. Just say that you're traveling to a conference and got mugged on the way. Ask for a loan, and as soon as you're far away, let me know who to repay."

"Okay…" Lev hesitated for a moment. "Anya, can I speak to Karina, just for a moment?"

Anya nodded wordlessly and passed the receiver to her daughter.

"Papochka! Why didn't you take me with to Babushka?"

"To Babushka?" Lev countered in astonishment, but then realized that this had been Anya's excuse for his absence. "I'm sorry, Karina, but Babushka is very busy now and so am I. She doesn't have time for guests right now – it's best for you to come another time, when she has time for you. So, I'll take you along with me next time, Karina, okay?"

"If Babochka doesn't have time, then how come you can stay with her?" Karina complained, clearly insulted.

"It's hard for her, but I'm out most of the day working. Are you helping Mamochka? Is it hard for her?"

"It's very hard," Karina replied with a maturity that surpassed her four years. "She cried last night, and this morning, her eyes were red, and she was sad. Maybe she's not feeling well."

"Karina!" Anya yanked the phone out of her daughter's grasp. "Don't mind her, Lev. It's not as bad as she's making it out to be. I'm all right mostly, just a bit tense."

"I understand." He choked over his next words. "And you must be very angry at me."

"I wish I could be," she confessed, "but I'm not. In my present situation, I can't waste my emotional energies on anger. At this point, I just want you to take care of yourself. For me and for Karina. Let's just get through this nightmare, and then we'll deal with everything else."

"Pray, Anya," Lev whispered earnestly. "I know you don't believe in the power of prayer or in a Higher Being at all, but there is a G-d above us, and He hears our every word. There is so much that I've learned that I'm aching to share with you – and I hope I will be able to, some day. But until then, I am asking you to pray. Pray, dear Anya! Try to speak to G-d as if He were standing right beside you – because He is! Believe me, it will do you good. Try it, for my sake if for nothing else."

Anya mumbled her agreement, even though she had no concept of what Lev meant. But now was hardly the time to differ with him – only if they held strong together did they stand a chance of surviving this ordeal.

Before tucking Karina into bed later that night, she tried to explain several important points to Karina. "Sweetie, it would be better if you didn't tell your friends or your teacher that Papochka is away."

"No?" Karina's face fell. "But when Tatiana's mother went to Ukraine, she told everyone, and Svetlana's father brought her presents when he traveled abroad. She even brought pictures to show!"

"I understand, my dear, but we're going to keep it secret, okay?" she coaxed, hoping that the excitement of a secret would have its effect. She was chagrined when Karina would hear nothing of it.

"Why do we have to keep it secret?" Anger crept into Karina's voice. "How come my friends can say when their parents go away, and I can't?"

"Every little girl does what her parents tell her to do. Tatiana's mother let her tell, but I want you to keep it a secret. It's really much more fun like that! Besides, why should you do what Tatiana does? Maybe she should do what you do?"

Her words confused Karina, enough to cause her to fall silent, but Anya knew that she would have to reinforce the necessity of silence each and every day. She was reluctant to scare her daughter and tell her that it was dangerous to talk about her father, but maybe the time would come when there would be no other option. Communist doctrine taught children to inform on their parents to their teachers, and Anya had never forgotten the time when she had been a small child and watched her neighbors being led away in handcuffs, never to be seen again. Rumors had spread quickly that it had been their eight-year-old child who had been the cause of their arrest. Would the same happen to them? Could Karina innocently and unknowingly bring about her family's destruction? The very thought of it caused Anya's blood to freeze in her veins, and she instinctively lifted Karina in her arms and hugged her tightly against her chest. *If only things would somehow work out*, she whispered to herself.

Suddenly, Anya realized that she had just uttered what must have been her first prayer, ever.

CHAPTER 20

At ten o'clock that night, knocks on the door were the last thing Anya wanted to hear, and at first, she was sure that the game was up – she was about to be imprisoned. As her heart raced, another idea struggled to gain traction in her mind, and gradually, she realized that the knocking was far too gentle to be heralding the arrival of the KGB.

With a sigh of relief, she opened the door and found herself facing Oleg Savitsky, one of her upstairs neighbors.

"Can I speak to Lev for a moment?" he asked. "I apologize for the late hour, but it's important, and I'll be brief."

"Lev isn't home," she replied apologetically.

"He's not home yet?" Savitsky countered in astonishment. "But he's always home at this hour. What time do you expect him?"

"He's away for the week, possibly a bit longer," she admitted. "I'm sorry that he can't help you."

Savitsky's eyebrows rose and he stared at his neighbor in disbelief. "Lev went away for a whole week, right in the middle of a semester?"

"He didn't have a choice. It was an emergency," Anya stammered, trying to still the tremor in her voice and hoping that her neighbor wouldn't notice it.

"The University granted him a leave of absence in the middle of a semester? How on earth did he manage to get it authorized?" Savitsky was also employed by the State University, and he was familiar with their rigid policies.

Anya grit her teeth in frustration at the nosiness of her neighbor, but she managed to control her emotions and maintain a calm façade. "Exactly how, I don't know. But, as you can see, exceptions are occasionally made, and this was one of them."

"Oh, so he must be traveling on behalf of the University," Savitsky suggested, shaking his head in wonder. "I can't think of any other reason why they would allow it."

Anya wished she could simply confirm her neighbor's words and end the dialogue there, but Savitsky was a close colleague of her husband's, and he would discover the following day that she had lied to him. "Actually, he went for personal reasons, but I can't really say anything more at this point."

Savitsky looked contrite. "I'm sorry, Anya. I really didn't mean to pry. When you speak to him, send him my regards, and I hope that everything is okay with the family. If you need help, you know I'm here for you."

The man bid her goodnight and returned to his apartment, leaving Anya with even more worries on her head. How much had Savitsky gleaned from their brief exchange? Was he hinting that he knew more than he was saying? And would he draw his own conclusions upon discovering that three religious groups had been unmasked right in the University?

After three nights with barely any sleep, Anya finally collapsed. She finished eating a late lunch with Karina and then sat down to relax on the rocking chair on the back porch where she fell into a deep sleep that stretched for over three hours. She was so exhausted that she slept, blissfully unaware of everything going on around her. Nothing succeeded in awakening her – not the ringing phone, not even Karina's incessant whining. When she finally opened her eyes, she was shocked to see that the sky was pitch black.

"What time is it?" she cried. A quick glance at her watch showed that it was half past seven, and she raced through the apartment in search of her daughter, whom she found crying in her room.

"Karina! What happened? What's wrong? Why are you crying?"

"Because you didn't answer me! I was talking to you and talking to you, and you didn't answer. I even shouted, but you didn't wake up!"

"I'm so, so sorry, Karina!" Anya gathered the child in her arms and hugged her tight. "I was just so tired that I fell asleep. What were you doing while I was asleep?"

"I ate cookies and I looked at books, and now I'm playing with my dolls. And crying." Karina's reply was refreshingly honest.

"What else?"

"I talked to Babushka."

Anya's first thought was that Karina was making up stories, but the sparkle in her daughter's eye stoked her anxiety. "You did?" she asked skeptically.

"Yes. She called, and she said she's coming to visit."

"She *what?*" Anya's heart began palpitating again.

"Yes!" Karina exclaimed, clearly overjoyed. "She called when you were sleeping, because she wanted to talk to you. I told her you were sleeping, so she said she's happy to talk to me instead! I asked her why Papochka can stay with her, and I can't, and she laughed and told me that he's not staying with her at all."

Anya inhaled sharply, wondering what was coming next. The onslaught was quick.

Karina narrowed her eyes imperiously. "Why did you tell me that Papochka went to Babushka? Papochka also told me he's there, but he's not! Now Babushka thinks I'm a silly girl who doesn't know what I'm talking about…"

"Of course she doesn't think like that!" Anya immediately protested.

"Yes, she does! And she also laughed and said that she has to speak to you and ask why I would think that Papochka would visit her in the middle of a semester, and what he would do there. So I called you, and I tried to wake you up. I screamed and I shouted, and I tugged at you, but you wouldn't wake up! Babushka got all scared and told me to call a neighbor, but I didn't want to, because I don't like when the neighbors come in when you're sleeping. So Babushka told me that she's coming right away and that she'll be here tomorrow. She also said that if you don't wake up in another hour, I must call a neighbor, because maybe you're sick…"

"Did you call somebody?" was all Anya could think to ask after her daughter's tirade.

"I… I didn't know how long an hour was," Karina replied in a small voice. Hearing this, Anya drew the little girl close to her.

"You're a wonderful girl, Karina, and it's good that you didn't call anyone. I was just tired. But now I'm wide awake and feeling very refreshed. See?"

Karina nodded.

"Are you hungry?"

Karina nodded again, this time more enthusiastically. A delicious supper was enough to distract the little girl from her worries and give Anya the opportunity to collect her thoughts, but not for long. As she cut Karina's food into small bites, Karina turned to her mother with huge eyes that looked so vulnerable that Anya felt her heart crack in two.

"Mamochka, why did you tell me that Papochka is at Babushka's house?"

Anya briefly considered telling Karina that her husband had indeed been there, but had already moved on – but she couldn't bring herself to lie yet again. Instead, her frank admission shocked even herself. "Because I wanted you to think that he was there."

"But he's not!" Karina retorted.

"That's right. He's not."

"So why did you want me to think something that's not true?" Karina's four-year-old innocence was too much for Anya to bear; if only Karina could remain unaware of how cruel and deceiving the world could be.

"I didn't have a choice, my dear."

"Why not?"

"Because… sometimes… different things happen, and… they're things that we're not allowed to talk about. Are you old enough to understand what I'm saying?"

"I'm very big!" Karina announced importantly, but incongruously, tears filled her eyes. "I'm big, and I won't tell anyone what you told me. *No one!*"

"Thank you, Karina. I see that you really are very mature and do understand what I'm saying." Anya allowed herself a small smile, but it was a smile laced with anguish.

"Where is Papochka really?" The girl refused to let up.

"I don't know." Anya spoke so quietly that her daughter had to strain to hear her.

"You don't know? But how can that be? Didn't Papochka tell you?"

"No, Karina sweetie. He didn't. Just like I'm not able to tell you, he's not able to tell me. I know that it's hard for you to understand, because it's hard even for me to understand it. Very, very hard." Anya's features contorted, but she forced herself to hold back the tide of tears that threatened to flow from her eyes. She wouldn't cry in front of her baby! If she had the strength to play the game of indifference at work, then she should be able to continue playing the game at home. And yet, she couldn't any more.

Karina gazed at her mother in shock. "Mamochka, are you really crying?"

Anya grabbed at a tissue and escaped to the bathroom, closing the door behind her just as the tide was unleashed. Karina followed her and began pounding on the closed door. "Mamochka! Let me in! Mamochka, don't cry! Please don't cry!" she screamed hysterically.

Unexpectedly, Anya opened the door and hugged her daughter again tightly. "It's all right, Karina. It's okay. Don't mind me. I'm just crying without a good reason. Sometimes, it happens to Mamochkas."

Karina began crying along with her mother. Now faced with the task of stopping her daughter's tears, Anya's own tears dried on her cheeks. Eventually, both returned to the porch, and Karina climbed into her mother's lap. Anya hardly noticed as the little girl stroked her face with her soft hands and wiped away the remaining moisture.

"Don't cry, Mamochka," Karina pleaded. "If you stop, then I promise that I won't ask you any more questions about Papochka." She was completely shocked that her vow was met with another bitter wave of tears.

The following afternoon, when she returned from work, the delicious aromas wafting out of her apartment into the stairwell informed Anya that she had a visitor even before she saw her. When she entered, as she had expected, she found Valeria, her mother-in-law, bustling around her kitchen stirring two large pots.

"You needn't have gone out of your way!" Anya reproached the older woman good-naturedly. "You just got here! Why are you already working in the kitchen? You probably didn't even sit down or have a drink."

"You just came home after a long day of work, and I'm pretty sure that you didn't have anything to eat or drink either!" her mother-in-law pointed out. "I did do some stuff around the house, but I'm glad I did because it was a good distraction."

Anya sank onto the couch before burying her head in her hands. Her mother-in-law took the seat beside her and placed a warm, comforting arm on her shoulder.

"What's happened, Anya? I was so worried after speaking to Karina. Is Lev okay? Are you okay?"

"You shouldn't have come!" Anya wept. "It's too dangerous!"

"Dangerous? Where is Lev? When does he get home?"

Karina's voice rose loudly and clearly above the others. "Babushka, Papochka traveled very, very far away, but he's not allowed to tell anyone exactly where he is. If you ask Mamochka, you'll make her cry. Please Babushka, don't ask Mamochka about Papochka. Asking her will only make her cry harder, and she already cried so much yesterday."

CHAPTER 21

Valeria Krasnikov's features were creased with worry as she stared in trepidation at her daughter-in-law. The dread that was never far from life in Soviet Russia had descended on the apartment, engulfing the family in despair. The noose was tightening around their necks, and Valeria felt herself grow short of breath even as she tried to remain calm.

"Right now, Lev is in a safe place. Nobody knows where he is, including me, which is the best for all of us," Anya tried to reassure her mother-in-law, after briefly outlining the events that had led to this terrifying situation.

For now, Lev was safe, but no one could possibly know how long that would last. The odds were not in his favor; in all likelihood, the KGB would, eventually, track him down, pluck him from his hiding place, and crush him beneath their boots just as they did to every other law-breaking citizen. Yet, Valeria also knew that now was not the time to surrender to her emotions and fears; her daughter-in-law and precious granddaughter were facing her, studying her every feature and relying on her emotional support and wisdom. Later, when she was alone, she would be free to give vent to her emotions, but now, she couldn't afford to show weakness.

"Well, at the very least, I can help out with the financial aspect of all this," she said finally, after a long pause. "I can try to locate Lev, and bring him whatever he needs. Maybe I can even stay with him and help him out – you know, like with cooking and laundry and basic things – until he manages to finalize an escape plan."

"Thank you. That's very generous of you," Anya forced a smile. "It'll make things so much easier for him, which will also make it easier on me knowing that he's being taken care of."

Valeria nodded and then glanced at her valise, still standing unopened in the corner. "In that case, I won't bother to unpack for the time being." Suddenly, a thought crossed her mind. "Anya, who will care for Karina… if you… if they… I mean, you know what I'm asking."

Anya exhaled a miserable sigh. "That's the issue that's given me no rest. I would even consider sending Karina with you, but…"

Her mother-in-law inclined her head questioningly. "But what?" she murmured, softly, so that Karina wouldn't hear.

"I'm worried that it will draw unnecessary attention to us. What will I tell her preschool teacher, especially if I'm still here? People are already starting to notice that Lev is gone. I left a message with the University that he's ill and unable to teach, but if Karina disappears too, it'll look even more suspicious."

Valeria looked back and forth from Anya to Karina. With her mother's heart, she knew what Lev would have wanted most, and she resolved to do it. "Anya, I'm staying here with you and helping you."

"Lev needs you more than I do," Anya argued.

"He needs me to be here with you."

"We're managing fine!" Anya insisted. She couldn't bear the

thought of endangering her mother-in-law too. It was impossible to know how the KGB would treat an older woman if they arrested her.

"Anya, I know Lev, and if we could speak right now, I know that he'd ask me to stay here and help you with Karina… and to take her home with me if… if anything should happen."

Anya looked straight into her mother-in-law's eyes. "Mamochka, I can't tell you how much your offer to means to me. If I am arrested, at least I'll know that Karina is in good, loving hands. But I can't lie to you and tell you that your offer doesn't come with risks attached. You might also be arrested as soon as they discover that Karina is with you."

"We're all in danger, and we all put ourselves there," Valeria agreed, sipping from a cup of cold water and moistening her dry lips. "You endangered yourself when you forced Lev to escape. Lev endangered himself when he decided to learn… that."

Anya nodded. Barely a week had passed since her life had been turned upside down, and she still hadn't quite grasped how much had changed, how there was literally no going back to the way things had once been. She was no longer the same woman who had gone to work each morning and looked forward to the end of a day, no longer the mother who browsed through exclusive shops in search of the perfect doll for her daughter. Today, every ring of the phone made her heart race in anxiety, and every footfall outside her apartment caused her face to pale. Her sleep was punctuated with nightmares from which waking provided no solace. Her old life was as remote a distant planet.

"Anya?" The voice startled her back to reality, and only when Anya realized that her mother-in-law was staring at her expectantly did she realize that she had asked her a question and was awaiting her reply.

Uncomfortably, she stammered, "I'm sorry, Mamochka, I was just thinking about something else. What did you ask?"

"I asked if you're angry at him."

A wave of fury rose from the pit of her stomach, and she bit her lip to control herself. "Lev asked me the exact same thing."

"And what did you answer him?"

"What did I answer?" Anya's eyes flashed. "What do you want me to say? That I'm angry at him even though his life is in danger?"

Valeria fought the tears that rose to her eyes. "Yes, Anya dear. Even though he's in danger, you are allowed to be angry. He risked the wellbeing – the safety of your family, and he… he destroyed your lives. You don't have to deny your feelings."

"I'm not denying anything," Anya whispered, wiping the tears from her own eyes.

"I'm angry at him," Valeria admitted, "and I'm also petrified. And yet, at the same time, part of me admires him."

"You admire him?" Even as she questioned the older woman, Anya recognized her feelings mirrored in her own. She, too, admired her husband, even though she was at a loss to explain why. She had no concept of what had caused him to act as he had, but she knew Lev well enough to know that he would never sacrifice his wife and child for a trivial matter. Something ideologically deep had been ignited within him – she had seen it in his eyes – and he had felt compelled to act according to it, regardless of the peril. How could she not admire him – even as the anger burned within her?

"He reminds me so much of my father!" Valeria burst out. "I was the only one of my siblings who knew that my father continued observing Judaism in secret. On the outside, there was no hint of his activities, and he played the part of a committed communist, completely loyal to the regime. But his heart was broken, and he never ceased mourning the Judaism that had been lost to our nation. He was actually jealous of those Jews who were fired from their jobs or stripped of their privileges because they remained true to their faith. He often whispered to me that their lives – miserable and wretched as they appeared to be – were actually real and authentic, whereas his own life was a sham. To the outside world, he was a stunning success, but inside, he was so deeply ashamed of himself, of what he had become. Our academic achievements never brought him pleasure or pride. As a young adult, I despised his attitude and beliefs, and I was convinced that it was impossible to advance in life without breaking what I saw as his addiction to religion. I really thought that religion just held people back and stifled their creativity and potential…" Valeria sighed. "Today, I'm older and wiser. Today I understand my father a little, and maybe I can understand my son, too. I even wonder…" her voice trailed off.

"You wonder what?"

"I wonder if Lev is somehow the answer to my father's prayers? After all, none of his own children inherited his attachment to our faith, but Lev somehow found his way back…" she mused thoughtfully.

Anya remained silent. What was there to say? A mystery called Judaism had suddenly appeared in her life, and although she hadn't ever wanted to have anything to do with it, now it was being forced upon her. Her own parents had told her nothing of her heritage, save that it existed in the past only, and was best buried in the present. She had shared their views, but now? Now what should she do?

And so, Valeria settled into her daughter-in-law's apartment, doing her best to remain unobtrusive and avoid attracting unnecessary attention. She left it to Anya to take Karina to kindergarten and to pick her up at the end of the day – it was well known that teachers were usually the most enthusiastic government informers, and there was no sense in giving Karina's teacher cause for suspicion. Therefore, it was also vital to ensure that Karina herself didn't let anything slip, and daily candies were the bribe that persuaded the little girl not to talk about her father's whereabouts or to mention that her grandmother had come to visit for an extended stay.

Gradually, the days fell into a semblance of a routine, and somehow they learned to live with the fear, even though it never abated.

"I wonder if the KGB forgot about the 'mysterious case of the disappearing prisoner'?" Lev dared to suggest one day to Anya, during one of their infrequent phone calls.

"The KGB doesn't forgive or forget," his wife replied warningly. "Even though things seem quiet on the surface, appearances are deceptive. They're still interrogating the prisoners, as far as I can tell, and sooner or later… well, never mind." Anya sighed.

Lev felt his heart lurch. "I'm trying to make arrangements – really I am, but it's not easy. Leaving the country means obtaining so many types of documents, and I haven't made the necessary connections yet. And you'll need your own set of documents, too. I just wish I knew when this was going to end…"

Anya cringed. She had never been optimistic by nature, and she felt a dread in her bones that already told her that she knew how this would end. But maybe Lev could still escape before the inevitable befell her, and maybe she could even manage to squeeze out a few drops of tranquility from the days remaining to her…

CHAPTER 22

Tina closed the door behind her and pierced Anya with a sharp gaze. "Anya, I hung the 'Do Not Disturb' sign on the door. You'll never believe what I just saw!"

A violent tremor passed through Anya's body, but she had become a master at hiding her feelings. "Oh, what did you see?" she inquired with just the precise note of curiosity.

"I was shopping in the Orbit Plaza, and who did I see hanging out with a group of American tourists?" Tina paused dramatically.

"Who?"

"Yvgenya! She was walking right alongside them, almost as if she were part of the group!"

Anya shrugged. "Walking alongside them? So?"

"To me, it looked like she was meeting up with them. I mean, not exactly a meeting because it was in the middle of a crowded square, but I think I even saw her exchange a few words with one of them."

They were both quiet, studying each other's features and waiting for the other to speak first. Finally, Anya broke the silence. "What are you trying to tell me, Tina?"

"That we could easily get Yvgenya arrested for consorting with enemies of the state. Come on, Anya, don't tell me you didn't think of that?"

"But why? You're not even sure that you saw her speak to them!" Anya protested.

Tina winked. "She spoke to them. I'm telling you she did."

Anya's eyes flashed. "Who are you out to get, Tina? You're playing with fire! We both know very well what could happen to Yvgenya if she's arrested!"

"Exactly, which is why I want your help, Anya. I want the hit to be sharp and direct."

It required enormous self-control for Anya to respond calmly. "What hit? Tina, please talk clearly."

"I didn't think that was necessary," Tina said disdainfully. "What happened to your famous intuition, Anya?"

"Maybe I never quite had it," she replied dryly. "I don't understand you, Tina. Are you attempting to frame Yvgenya, or do you have hard facts?"

Tina leaned over until her head was close to Anya's, and her voice was barely above a whisper as she spoke. "Look, Anya. I'm trying to take advantage of an opportunity that's come my way. That's all. Nothing more, nothing less. And I want your help, because if I don't have it, then she'll probably get away scot free."

"What kind of opportunity?"

"To get her out of the way. Do you really not understand?"

Anya made a show of arranging a pile of paperwork on her desk, knowing that it would be dangerous to say what was at the tip of her tongue.

"What's the problem?" Tina's eyes flashed challengingly.

"You're jealous of her promotion, aren't you?" The promotion that Yvgenya worked so hard for, the one she so richly deserved… Yvgenya worked in the parallel department to hers and Tina's. Parallel – and competing.

"That took you long enough," Tina replied mockingly. "And this is my way of reclaiming what should have been mine."

"And if I had been the one to earn the promotion, would I be on your hit list too?"

Tina's expression changed to something Anya couldn't quite decipher. "Why ask such a question? We work together, and it's best that we get along. Sometimes, I help you out, and sometimes, it's the other way around. It's best for both of us that way. And this time, you'll help me. Yvgenya didn't earn her promotion – she got it unfairly, and she'll pay for it now."

The chill inside Anya was slowly freezing the blood in her veins. "She didn't buy her way up to the top, Tina. She worked hard and was selected by the chief directorate."

Tina narrowed her eyes. "That's what you think, Anya. Obviously, I have some important information that you don't have access to. She did a lot of maneuvering to get where she is today, with help from people that common folk like you or I could never dream of recruiting. She advanced by stepping on us, and she knew that very well."

"I don't think she stepped on us as much as skipped over us," Anya forced a grin, trying to lighten the tone of the discussion. "But, by the nature of things, all promotions are 'at the expense of' others. That's just the way things work."

"That may be so, but it doesn't change the facts," Tina retorted. "I can't understand why you're taking her side in this! What's in it for you?"

Anya stared. "What's in it for me? Nothing! I'm not taking anyone's side, not yours, and not hers either. I'm just presenting the facts, the situation, as it seems to me." Anya picked up her pen and started to doodle on her memo pad, using the physical activity to avoid having to meet Tina's cold, accusing gaze.

The fury on Tina's coarse features grew even more pronounced. "Don't go all noble on me, Anya Krasnikov! Both of us stand only to gain from getting Yvgenya out of the way, and that's exactly what we're going to do. All you have to do is submit a report of the sighting when you present your next set of reports to Fyodorev. I'll take care of everything else – I just need you to document the date and time that I saw Yvgenya in the plaza with those Americans and note that I was the source. That should be enough to accomplish things."

Anya clenched her teeth in frustration. She wanted so badly to tell Tina exactly what she thought of her, but what would that achieve? Instead, she resolved to appeal to the woman's humane side – if it existed.

"Tina, you know that this little report – baseless though it probably is – could destroy Yvgenya and her entire family. This isn't just about her position here, but her life itself! She could be sent to the gulag, and who knows if she'll ever make it back? Think about her husband, her poor children! They'll be orphaned of their mother! Don't you think it's too harsh a punishment?" Somehow, Anya managed to keep her voice low and her tone steady, despite the roiling emotions within her. "Tina, have mercy!"

But a glance at Tina's face told Anya that her words had been spent in vain. "I came here for help, not a lecture on ethics," Tina hissed. "Time is limited. Do what I say."

Anya was silent.

"I'm waiting for your answer, Anya."

"I heard what you want."

With that, Tina rose from her seat. "Good. I'll wait for Fyodorev's summons. There's no purpose in me approaching him before you've given him the background."

Anya shrugged, unsure why she didn't feel strong enough to state her refusal aloud. Perhaps it was the vicious spark in Tina's eyes? Tina was tough, ruthless, heartless, and Anya didn't have the courage to rebuff her openly. When Fyodorev's summons never arrived, Tina would get the message on her own, loud and clear.

Anya scanned the schoolyard outside Karina's nursery, looking for her daughter. A quick glance was enough to tell her that Karina wasn't there. In fact, the yard was empty, which meant that the other children had already gone home. She had rushed back from work that day, hoping to make it in time to pick Karina up before her friends left, but now her heart sank as she realized she had arrived late, yet again.

Recently, Anya had been coming late almost every day to pick up Karina, however much she hated to do so. Fyodorev was keeping an eagle eye on her movements, and almost every day he presented her with an additional assignment that supposedly needed to be completed before she left that afternoon. Anya knew that his motivation was simply to test her loyalty and let her know how tenuous her position was, and her loathing of the man grew from day to day.

But what could she tell Karina's teacher? Nothing – simply nothing – and therefore, she had even offered to compensate her for the extra time she spent waiting in the building for Anya to arrive to pick up the last child of the class. The last thing she needed was to acquire an enemy, and so Anya made sure to apologize profusely each time she arrived late, but she couldn't fail to notice the spark of resentment in the teacher's eyes every time it happened. The woman had refused to take any compensation for the extra time, probably fearing that she could later be accused of taking a bribe, and Anya could only hope that the teacher wouldn't take out her frustration on Karina herself.

Now, as she approached the building, her heart pounded, and she found herself wondering if something as simple as picking up her daughter from preschool would ever become simple again. As she raised her hand to knock at the door, it suddenly opened before her, to reveal the teacher herself.

"Hello, Mrs. Krasnikov," she greeted her with a wisp of a smile. "Karina is waiting for you inside. And, today I'm actually glad you arrived late, as there's something that I would like to discuss with you."

Anya's bland expression masked the pounding of her heart. "Of course, Anastasia."

"I don't wish to pry," the woman said, clearly somewhat uncomfortably, "but is something wrong with Karina's father?"

The moment of truth had come… but what now? Should she continue with the charade, or lay all her cards on the table and hope that the teacher's compassion outweighed her loyalty to her masters?

After the briefest of pauses, Anya chose the easiest way out. "Why do you ask?" she inquired, feigning nonchalance with the ease of a pro.

"Something rather strange happened today in class," the teacher replied, her eyes darting between Anya's face and the wall behind her. "Karina has a friend called Nina, Nina Dorosh. A petite blond girl – perhaps you know her. In any case, Nina's father left on a trip overseas about six months ago, and Nina told everyone all about it, and how when he returned, he would bring her expensive gifts…" Anya felt her heart sink; she already thought she knew how this story would end. "As time passed, Nina spoke less about her father, but today she told everyone that he's not coming back, because he unfortunately passed away."

"How terrible!" Anya exclaimed, genuinely horrified to have her fears confirmed. "The poor child! Did she manage to see him before he died?"

"No," Anastasia's face twisted into a contorted smile. "It seems that the story of his journey abroad was fabricated in order to hide his real condition from Nina. Obviously, the child has taken the news very hard, but that's understandable. What really surprised me was your daughter's reaction to the story."

Anya stared at the teacher, hoping desperately that her face had not noticeably paled. "Oh? How did she react? She is a sensitive child, after all."

"Sensitive is one thing, but her reaction could only be called extreme. Karina burst into tears and started screaming that she didn't want her father to die too."

Anya's jaw dropped in horror, and she didn't even attempt to conceal it. "That's what she said?"

"Yes," the teacher nodded. "She was inconsolable, and I wanted you ask you, Mrs. Krasnikov, why your daughter would be afraid that anything would happen to her father?"

Anya made her decision on the spur of the moment. "Very simple. My husband is away right now, on business, not abroad, but across the country. Karina must have grasped the superficial resemblance between the two stories, but I'll find a way to calm her down. Thank you for calling this to my attention."

"Mrs. Krasnikov, may I ask if your husband said goodbye to Karina before he left?"

"Of course! Why wouldn't he?"

The teacher narrowed her eyes suspiciously. "I understood differently from Karina. From what she said, it sounded very much like he ran away without saying goodbye. If that is indeed true, it was neither wise nor fair to the child."

Anya stiffened. How dare the simple kindergarten teacher criticize her parenting! And, more critically, where were all her questions leading? Taking a deep breath, she forcibly silenced the angry voices that threatened to protest the injustice of it all.

"Of course that would not be a wise thing to do, but you can't believe everything you hear from a four-year-old! The truth is that my husband did leave late at night, and she was very tired. It could be that Karina didn't entirely absorb that he wouldn't be back for an extended period, but that is as far as it goes."

The teacher nodded, her expression grim. "Mrs. Krasnikov, I am experienced enough to distinguish between fact and fiction quite well, even in four-year-olds. What I am really asking you is, whether your husband is truly away on business, as you claim, or if he is ill, or something else entirely…?"

Anya shook her head. "Anastasia, please! Why on earth would you think to doubt my word?" Anya stared at the teacher, daring her to persist in her suspicions.

The teacher, however, refused to back down. "Well, that is exactly why I wasn't too concerned, to be honest. I was just thinking that you might be interested to know that the story with poor Nina's father is not quite as the family is claiming. The father never traveled abroad; his 'journey' was to your place of work, although in less than comfortable accommodations. It was there that he met his untimely demise. I very much hope that Nina doesn't discover the truth at her tender age, and… and that Karina has nothing unpleasant to discover on her own horizon."

Anya forced herself to chuckle. "What a suggestion! How bizarre that such a thing should even occur to you, my dear Anastasia. And now, let's leave all this fairy-tale imagining behind, shall we? Where is Karina?"

"She's playing inside," the kindergarten teacher replied, her eyes still mocking. "Let's call her now."

CHAPTER 23

It rained incessantly that afternoon, and as the temperature fell, the droplets turned into icy needles. It wouldn't be long before it started to snow.

Where is Lev now? Anya found herself wondering for the thousandth time. *Where is he hiding? Is he protected from the cold? He doesn't even have his fur coat with him!* Three weeks ago, when her husband had fled the KGB fortress, the weather had been significantly warmer, but winter had shown its face earlier than usual this year, too quickly for Anya to send him his coat or money to buy another one. Her office in the KGB complex was well-heated, but that only compounded her anguish. How could she sit in comfort when Lev was wandering, a lost and broken soul, from city to village to town without even a decent coat to keep him warm?

She reminded herself that Lev wasn't a child, but a grown man who was perfectly capable of looking after himself. He was intelligent and highly resourceful, and she could rest assured that he would manage to get hold of a coat somehow. Yet the snow would make it more difficult for him to travel… What if he fell ill? How would he obtain medicine?

Stop it! she commanded herself, trying hard to rein in her imagination. Why should she worry about Lev falling ill? He was as strong as an ox! But maybe his emotional state had weakened him, and he needed her help? Anya shook her head hard from side to side, as if to banish the anxiety. Worrying wouldn't help anyone, least of all Lev… and yet, how could she not worry?

Sighing, she picked up her pen again, and tried to get back to work. Suddenly, the door to her office opened, startling her. It was Tina, and the woman walked slowly toward Anya's desk, traversing the distance in three brisk steps and then glaring at her for a long moment in silence.

"I'm waiting," Tina said finally.

"For what?" Anya raised her eyebrows, meeting the woman's gaze.

"For you to pass the message on to Fyodorev."

Anya measured her words. "This has nothing to do with me, Tina."

"What doesn't have to do with you? We spoke about this!" Anger flooded Tina's white face, and two bright spots appeared on her cheeks.

"Yes, we did. I shared my position with you then, and I'll repeat it now: To tell Fyodorev would be cruel and heartless, and I won't be part of it. I'm still shocked that you would consider such a thing, if you really want to know."

"Why shocked? This is how everyone operates here! You think Yvgenya wouldn't do it to me, if she got the chance? She deserves this, one hundred percent, and I intend to make sure that she is 'removed' from her position, shall we say. The only question is, how it comes about." The wild fire in Tina's eyes frightened Anya, but what option did she have?

"Tina, I'm trying to get an important assignment finished, and you're disturbing me," she said firmly. "There's nothing more to discuss."

Tina's expression turned mocking and sinister. "As you wish, Anya. I won't force anyone to continue a conversation with me, but I will add one last point: Either you submit that report to Fyodorev, or you'll pay the price of your refusal. It's up to you." Without awaiting a reply, she spun around and exited as abruptly as she had entered.

What is Tina plotting? Anya wondered fearfully. Though she tried to stay calm, the room spun dizzyingly around her. Had she only imagined it, or had Tina really just threatened her? The woman's tone had been just a touch more than scornful, but that was only natural; it was dangerous for her to leave behind clear evidence of evil intent. What really lay beneath her words? What kind of price would she demand from Anya for her refusal to comply with her request? Even though the room was warm, Anya shivered. Was Tina hinting at something terrible? Did she know something about Lev?

No, that can't be, Anya reassured herself. *Surely, if she knew, she would have openly hinted at it, in order to better manipulate me. But what if she finds out? Then what?*

Once again, Anya felt the familiar tug of the noose around her neck and her lungs being drained of oxygen. Should she just submit the report that Tina wanted? Was Yvgenya's blood any redder than her own that it was worth flouting Tina and risking her vengeance? Was Karina any less deserving than her colleague's children?

Stop driving yourself into a panic! Just stay calm and think clearly, Anya told herself sternly. *Tina knows nothing about Lev or about me; if she knew, she would have used that knowledge already, and not just to get me to talk to Fyodorev – she would use the knowledge against me directly, and try to acquire my position for herself. That woman would stoop to anything...* And then, with a shock, Anya realized that Tina was hardly the only one of whom that could be said. Most likely, any one of her colleagues would feed her to the wolves if they thought it would save their own skin, if necessary. That was what Communism did to people.

Svetlana, Fyodorev's secretary, found Anya gazing outside at the falling flakes of snow. "I'm glad you're taking a few minutes to relax now," she noted, "because Fyodorev's got a new operation in store for you. He wants to speak to you first, though, and he's waiting for you in his office now."

"Now?" Anya hoped that her voice wasn't trembling.

"Now." Svetlana treated her to a strange look and motioned for her to follow.

Anya rose heavily from her seat and dragged her feet toward the chairman's private office. Had Tina worked so quickly that she had already arranged Anya's undoing? Logically, that was impossible, and yet… Nonetheless, the last thing she wanted now was a new operation to head. Surely Fyodorev must realize for himself that she was hardly in an appropriate state of mind to take on such a project. What could he be planning?

Taking a deep breath, she knocked on the door and heard the steely voice invite her to enter.

"We've been discussing the possibility of transferring you to our branch in Leningrad," Fyodorev announced without preamble, the moment Anya stepped over the threshold.

"To Leningrad?" Anya repeated in disbelief.

"Precisely," he nodded in satisfaction. "Several months ago, a position opened up in one of the senior offices there, and they keep complaining that the management has been limping along ever since because they haven't found a suitable replacement. You remember Genya Blasky? She worked here several years ago, and she recommended you highly for the position. At first, I refused to authorize the transfer, because I wanted you here, but I am no longer so sure that here is the best place for you to be." Fyodorev's eyes narrowed and he exhaled slowly, reminding Anya somewhat of a snake, readying itself to attack its prey. "We no longer need your services here, Comrade Krasnikov. Your name is already too strongly associated with illegal activities and news is starting to spread around the departments. You will make immediate arrangements to leave. In two days' time." As Anya stared at him, her expression bewildered, he rapped his pen impatiently on the leather surface of his desk. "The day after tomorrow, you will be on the midday train to Leningrad. You may pack up your personal effects now."

Anya remained rooted to the spot, too shocked to respond, but then, slowly, she unfroze her limbs and managed to nod her acquiescence. Fyodorev swung his swivel chair toward the window, turning his back to her. "That is all, Comrade. You may leave."

CHAPTER 24

Three weeks earlier…

Lev still couldn't quite believe what had happened. Even though he knew that the first few moments of the escape were the most critical, he still marveled at each additional kilometer that he managed to travel away from Moscow, putting more and more distance between himself and his pursuers.

The train sped through the countryside, passing stunning scenery, but Lev kept his face buried in his newspaper, trying to appear unobtrusive. He knew only too well that all intercity trains were patrolled by undercover agents, and that his only chance of evading capture lay in his ruse of having switched identities with Boris Smirnov. If his friend managed to sound convincing and the interrogators' suspicions were not aroused, then the KGB was out looking for Boris Smirnov, not Lev Krasnikov. Lev Krasnikov, on the other hand, was supposedly languishing in the dungeons of Lubyanka, not traveling through the Russian countryside in an attempt to break free of the Soviet bear hug. If his papers were inspected, and if some eagle-eyed secret service agent noticed how nervous he was, though he tried to conceal it, there was no guarantee that the whole ruse wouldn't be exposed.

Lev breathed in deeply and slowly, and then exhaled as he tried to calm himself and slow his racing pulse. Nine hours had passed since his train had pulled out of the Moscow terminus, and he still didn't feel in the slightest bit secure. He had hardly slept during his time in incarceration, and he was exhausted, both physically and emotionally, but he was too frightened to shut his eyes, even for a moment. And yet, as the rhythmic motion of the train lulled him, he found his eyelids fluttering closed from time to time, and he would have to jerk himself awake and once more scan his surroundings for any sign of danger.

And yet, it wasn't the danger to his own life that he feared as much as the danger his wife had put herself in. *No, Lev, the danger you put her in*, a little voice mocked inside his head, and Lev cringed. It was true – it was his fault. He had wittingly endangered not only his wife, but his young daughter too, in order to drink from the wellspring of life, to learn the holy Torah. He had no doubt that he was personally willing to pay the price, but what of his family? Did he have the right to make such a choice on their behalf, especially when they were not even aware what they could be sacrificing themselves for?

As the train crossed a wide river, swaying slightly on the bridge as it passed, Lev realized suddenly how tenuous his life – indeed, all life – was. The slightest engineering fault in the bridge would send the train hurtling into the depths of the waters below; the slightest slip in his mask of normalcy could condemn him, along with his wife and child, to the nightmare of a Soviet 'mock trial' most probably followed by an icy exile in Siberia.

And if that happened, his world would come to an end. He would never find solace nor forgive himself for what he had done to Anya and Karina.

The train whizzed past endless miles of ploughed fields, and his red eyes gazed sightlessly upon the horizon where the green-brown kissed a cloudy gray sky. *I should never have run away,* he thought again for the millionth time. *All I did was endanger Anya. Oh, Anya…* It was Anya who had forced him to flee, Anya who hadn't given him a choice. She had ordered him to follow her down that dim hallway and forced him out the door. But perhaps he could have surrendered to the authorities, regardless? They didn't have to know how he had somehow found his way out of the building. He could have concocted some excuse – anything, to avoid implicating his wife. Anya would have been furious, broken, and her career would have been ruined simply by association with him, but at least she wouldn't actually be in danger.

Should I just alight at the next station and take the first train back to Moscow? It's so simple…

But it wasn't. By now, it was too late for that. He had been missing for too long, and it would be obvious that only someone with real authority in the building could have enabled him to evade capture for so long. He had no choice but to go through with it, and try to escape, along with his wife and daughter, as soon as humanly possible.

Tiny pellets of hail tapping against the windowpane stirred Lev from his thoughts. *Why am I losing hope so quickly? Where is all that faith and trust in Hashem that I learned about over the past two years? It is forbidden to despair!*

Again Lev dozed off, this time only to awaken over an hour later to the sound of the next train stop being announced. They were approaching Kirov, a large city north-east of Moscow, and Lev considered getting off there. He had a few acquaintances in Kirov – maybe they would be able to help him out – if he dared to approach them.

Slowly, Lev got to his feet, folding his newspaper and trying to look nonchalant, even though he realized that his lack of suitcase or even small valise must look strange. Once off the train, however, he hoped he would be able to blend in with the crowds. It was late already, and he would have to quickly find somewhere to spend the night if he didn't want to be picked up by the local police and accused of loitering.

Lev's exit through the huge Kirov train terminus passed without event, and he forced himself to walk slowly down the street without looking over his shoulder. Now, to find a hotel, preferably a smaller establishment where they were too lazy to submit his personal information to the authorities to check that he wasn't on any Wanted list. Lev ducked into a narrow alleyway, turning randomly left and then right as the fancy took him, until, to his relief, he spotted a faded sign advertising a small guesthouse. Perfect. He entered, casually placed his ID card on the reception desk, and asked for a room.

The clerk behind the desk glanced at the photograph on his ID card for just a split second, and then nodded before returning it to him. "Room twelve," he muttered, slipping Lev a key and turning back to his paperback novel.

Lev strode down the narrow, dimly-lit corridor until he found his room. It was dingy, and furnished with nothing more than a narrow bed and a small closet, but it was privacy and certainly comfort when compared to accommodations courtesy of the KGB. Luxuriously, he stretched out, fully clothed, on the bed, and fell asleep instantly, dreaming of train journeys, the screech of iron doors, gloomy corridors, and Anya's face as she said goodbye – forever?

CHAPTER 25

Pale sunlight streamed through the window of Lev's hotel room, rousing him mercifully from his nightmares. A new day was upon him, and miraculously, he was still free. But what of Anya? Was she under suspicion – or worse? He had to find out, but the last place to phone her from was the hotel; everyone knew that hotel phones were bugged. He would have to find a public telephone – but what if his home line had been bugged? Somehow, he would have to find out if it was safe to call home – he didn't dare to try before knowing.

It was still early, but sleep was out of the question now that his mind had started whirring with worries and questions. Lev swung himself out of bed and headed straight for the sink, to wash his hands with a plastic cup that he was pleased to find there. He had already been careful with *netilas yadayim* for months, but today would be the first day of his life when he could pray immediately afterward, instead of waiting for Anya to leave for work.

Is she leaving for work this morning? Or... Lev's eyes filled with tears and he could barely pronounce the words of prayer that now came straight from his heart. Precious few of them had he managed to commit to memory, but they were his solace now, and when he completed what he knew, he begged Hashem in his own words to protect his family, and even, ultimately, to reunite them in freedom.

Afterward, Lev gulped down a glass of water and exited his room, walking down to the lobby on his way out of the guesthouse. As he crossed the threshold, someone brushed past him on his way in, but a moment later, the person turned around and started to follow Lev down the street.

Lev felt his heart sink. *That's it – the game's up. It's all over.* He continued walking, almost blindly, barely aware of his surroundings, until he spotted a small café which he entered. *So they'll arrest me here*, he thought to himself morosely. *I wonder why they let me sleep so comfortably last night, if they already knew where I was?*

Lev sat down at a table and ordered a glass of tea. A moment later, the man who had been following him entered and took a seat at the next table. The waiter hurried over, and he, too, ordered a glass of tea, before settling back in his seat and fixing Lev with a stare.

Lev met the other man's gaze coolly, without flinching, and then pulled his trusty newspaper out of his pocket. The tension was almost unbearable as the minutes passed. Lev's tea arrived and he sipped at it slowly, every so often glancing up to see what his companion was doing.

Five minutes passed, and then ten. Finally, the man at the next table got up, looked around for a moment at the empty tables surrounding them, and sauntered over to where Lev was sitting.

Lev looked up sharply. "Is there a problem, comrade?" he asked politely.

"Aren't you Anya's husband?" the man replied with a smile.

Lev coughed, trying to buy himself time while he tried to decide how to answer. Surely, if this man was planning to arrest him, he would have done so by then? What was going on?

"Anya?" he replied eventually. "How do you know her?"

"We met at a wedding a few years ago, and I'm sorry I don't remember your first name. But you're Krasnikov, isn't that right?"

Lev nodded cautiously and waited for the other man to continue.

"Have you finished your tea? Why don't you have something to eat?" the man questioned him. "You probably haven't had anything to eat since you left… wherever you came from."

Lev stiffened. What did this man know? More critically, *how* did he know?

"Oh, I prefer not to eat in restaurants," he replied casually.

"Really? Same here. How about taking a walk to the open-air market and we'll pick up some fruit and eat in the park while we catch up on things?" the man suggested.

Lev's eyes widened. "Okay," he replied cautiously. This was no KGB agent, that was for sure. If it had been, he would have been in an armored car by now, speeding back to Moscow. So who was this man?

"Please remind me of your name," Lev said, as the two of them left the café and started to walk down the street.

"Andrayev," the man replied with a broad smile. "You can call me Anatoly. But, seriously, Mr. Krasnikov, aren't you wondering why I'm here?"

"I don't like to pry," Lev said resolutely, hoping that his reply would be enough to hint to the man that he shouldn't be meddling in his business either. To his dismay, the man continued to talk, as if they were old friends.

"I'm surprised that Anya never told you about me. There were three of us high-ranking officers who were transferred suddenly from Moscow to Kirov in one week. It was the talk of the department at the time."

Lev wracked his brain, trying to recall if Anya had mentioned anything about such an episode, but nothing came to mind. The trauma he had endured during the past few days of his life had caused every piece of trivial information to converge into one unimportant mass in his mind.

He chose his words carefully to protect both himself and his wife. "Anya is pretty selective about what she tells me when it comes to her job. Much of what she deals with is classified, and therefore it's just easier to avoid the entire topic instead of accidentally spilling the wrong information."

"So you're here, while your wife is still in Moscow? You have a little girl too, if I'm not mistaken?"

Lev nodded.

"And what brings you so far?"

"I'm traveling on behalf of the university where I teach." As he spoke, he knew that it would take Andrayev but an instant to verify whether his claim was true, and that every extraneous word could further compromise his already-perilous position. On the other hand, as long as the curtain was still up and the spotlight was turned on him, he would continue acting the part to prolong his freedom and life.

"How much longer do you expect to be here?" Anatoly asked.

"Well, I just got here, so several days, I believe, but not long," Lev replied. They reached the market, and Anatoly bought a bag of apples, offering one to Lev, who accepted it gratefully.

"I've been thinking," Anatoly mused thoughtfully as they continued to walk. "It's been nearly a month since I've been in Moscow, but I do try to keep up to date on what's going on there. I've heard excellent things about Anya's work at the Agency and the way she exposed those religionists in a university. It was Moscow State, wasn't it?"

Lev nodded again. He tried forcing a smile, but wasn't particularly successful.

"Did you know any of those arrested? Did you give your wife any inside information?"

"Really, Anatoly!" Lev allowed himself a burst of righteous anger in a pathetic attempt to cover the wild fear that was wrapping itself around his heart. "First of all, I'm sure you're aware that she's not allowed to involve me in any of her operations. Second, if you know Anya, you also know that she prefers to avoid looking at the list of those arrested."

"Yes, but every rule has its exception, especially when the going gets tough." Andrayev pierced Lev with a serious gaze, as if trying to decipher a riddle on his face.

CHAPTER 26

I should have been a KGB agent too, Lev found himself musing. *I never knew that I had the ability to remain so calm and level-headed even when under such pressure.* They had just reached the entrance to the park, and Lev suggested they sit on a bench near the ornamental fountain.

Anatoly agreed absently; his mind was clearly elsewhere – on his cross-examination of his newfound quarry.

"So you didn't see the list," Andrayev was now saying. "But, nonetheless, Anya surely told you the sensational news that one of the detainees somehow managed to escape detention prior to the preliminary interrogation. Now *that* was news indeed!"

Lev nodded vaguely. "Yes, I believe she did mention it. She was a bit worried that it would be counted against her." Even as he uttered the words, Lev realized that he had slipped, and Andrayev wasn't one to let the slip go unnoticed.

"Why on earth would it be counted against her?" Anatoly raised his eyebrows.

"Well, it was her operation," Lev replied weakly. "Though you're right – she wasn't responsible for the detainees at that point. Her role in the operation was already over."

"And you know what her exact role was?"

"No. I already told you – we didn't... we don't talk about her job."

"And yet, even if that is really so, it surprises me that Anya didn't mention that one of the prisoners just so happens to have the exact same name as yours."

Lev exhaled slowly and, he hoped, unobtrusively. "Really? That's interesting."

"It's very interesting indeed. Krasnikov... ah, yes, now I recall. Your first name is Lev, is it not?" Andrayev didn't wait to have his observation confirmed, but continued speaking, his eyes still fixed on Lev. "Lev Ilyevich Krasnikov. That was the name I saw on the list. A professor at Moscow State University, who just so happens to be sitting at my side in the Byelski Park in Kirov. Well, Lev, I'm glad you're here, and not there. Would you like me to send regards to Anya, perhaps?"

Lev was trembling, visibly, by this point, his teeth clenched together to disguise their chattering from fear. "Andrayev... you... please... I just..." He tried to get to his feet, but stumbled and fell back onto the bench. "Who are you, and what do you want?"

"I already told you. I can send regards to Anya, if you like."

Lev's face was unnaturally pale and his breathing was shallow, but he was trying desperately to pull himself together. "You're going to Moscow?"

"No. Why should I be going to Moscow? But Anya is only a phone call away. And you're scared that her phone is bugged, so you won't call her. But I can."

"Bugged? I mean... why?" Lev gave up. Why pretend, when this Andrayev clearly knew everything already? But what was he trying to achieve?

"Lev, calm down. I can help you," Andrayev suddenly told Lev seriously, his voice low but his tone warm and full of compassion. "I want to help you. Just tell me what I can do for you."

Lev shook his head. "I'm fine. Thank you, but I don't need your help." He had never heard of KGB agents engaging in such a long-winded procedure when trying to ensnare a target, but that didn't mean that they hadn't broadened their repertoire. Maybe it was all a ploy, to get him to trust Andrayev, and then, they hoped, he would give them yet more names, yet more innocents to be drawn into their trap and condemned to a bitter future. He resolved to maintain a stern façade.

Anatoly didn't seem put off by his abrupt manner, however. "Lev, you're going to be needing *a lot* of help in the coming days, so please don't dismiss my offer so quickly. Another thing I can tell you is that your ruse worked. They still think Smirnov is you, and you owe the man big time. I'm sure he had no idea what he was getting himself into when he agreed to the switch, and I hope I'll be able to save him from the consequences. As for you," Andrayev paused carefully, "I also hope I'll be able to save you from the consequences: you, your wife, and your little daughter. But it isn't going to be easy. I imagine you know that already."

Lev got to his feet, and this time, his legs held steady. "Anatoly, enough. I have no idea what any of this is about, and quite frankly, I have no wish to be enlightened. It was pleasant meeting you." He turned and began to walk away, quickly, without looking back, almost certain that the man would follow him, perhaps clapping handcuffs over his wrists, maybe even wrestling him to the ground – but instead, nothing happened at all, and when Lev did finally turn around to see what had become of Andrayev, he saw that he had disappeared.

Lev didn't waste another moment wondering if he could really hope to shake the man off his trail. He was tempted to hurry straight to the train station and board the next train out of Kirov, but he knew that if he failed to pay his hotel bill, the manager of the guesthouse would contact the police immediately, probably as early as that evening. The detour to the hotel wasted almost an hour of his time, but finally, he was on his way to the station, trying to plan his next step.

At the ticket office, he purchased tickets to three different destinations, in order to confuse anyone who might be trailing him, and he determined to board the first train to depart. To his shock, when he reached Platform 5, Mikhail Gadorovitch was there waving at him.

Gadorovitch, a former colleague and friend from the faculty at Moscow State University, had been the one to invite him to join the Torah classes that were held secretly in the basement of the science faculty. Approximately a year ago, however, Mikhail had begun to suspect that he was being followed, and he managed to escape Moscow before the KGB could lay their hands on enough evidence to frame him. Since then, the two friends hadn't met, and Lev had often wondered what had happened to him.

"Lev! I'm so glad I didn't miss you!" Gadorovitch opened his arms expansively to greet him. "What are you doing here? Did you know that I live here?"

Lev knew that he should have been surprised and delighted at this unexpected reunion, but something about Gadorovitch's greeting didn't make sense.

"You mean you came here looking for me?" he asked, baffled. "How did you know that I was here, and what made you think you'd miss me?"

"It was Anatoly Andrayev. Don't worry, Lev. He's one of ours. He wants to help you, and he *can* help you."

Lev paled. Of all people, had *Mikhail* been sent by the KGB to trap him? Lev would never forget the long conversations they had once shared, the discussions that had turned his world and beliefs upside down and replaced them all with truth. Mikhail had taught him privately for six months before introducing him to the group, and even then continued teaching Lev one-on-one until he fled the capital. If he couldn't trust Mikhail, who then could he trust?

"Anatoly Andrayev is a senior operative in the KGB," he informed Gadorovitch flatly. "He's clearly onto me. Why would he want to help?"

"Well, maybe because he's been participating in Torah classes for several years and observes Shabbos faithfully. Your meeting this morning was carefully planned so that he could ensure that what he assumed was true, and it clearly is. He wants to help you, and he, more than anyone else, is actually in a position to do so."

Lev gazed at his friend in disbelief, trying to digest this startling piece of information. "How can he help?" he finally stammered.

"First of all, he can obtain and relay information. He's our most senior operative, one of the top brass, and he has full security clearance. If anything happens to Anya, he's the only one who'll be able to help her. Remember that, Lev. You know that you can trust me, and I guarantee that you can trust Anatoly too."

Lev decided that he had no other choice than to heed his friend's advice. He would have to trust Anatoly. The first piece of information solicited by Anatoly made it possible for him to finally contact Anya.

"Your home phone isn't bugged," he informed Lev several hours later. "As I told you earlier, Smirnov is doing a great job, though I can't predict how much longer he'll be able to hold out. In the meantime, Anya is tainted by association with a criminal, but that's as far as it goes. But I must warn you not to breathe a word about me. My identity is one of the most closely-guarded secrets in all of the Soviet Union, if you know what I mean."

Lev knew exactly what he meant.

CHAPTER 27

The conversation with his daughter drained Lev of his final reserves of emotional strength. In her innocent way, Karina gave away exactly what her mother had tried so hard to conceal. Anya was anxious and weepy, two traits that were completely out of character for her. Though she often tried to project otherwise, especially at work, Lev knew that his wife's heart was not fashioned of stone, but she was certainly not given to open expressions of emotion, and if Karina had actually seen her crying, then things must be very bad.

What did a Jew do when things were bad, especially when things were this bad, and there was virtually nothing he could do at all? Lev's *Sefer Tehillim* had been left behind in Moscow and he only knew a few chapters by heart. What he did know to do was to speak to Hashem in his own words, from the depths of his heart, and this he did, almost all day long, pleading for Divine assistance and for mercy. Yet, Lev was close to despair, so far away from his beloved family, tortured by images of their suffering and by his fears of what they risked suffering in the future. Somehow, he had to save them!

Lev reviewed his brief conversation with his wife, trying to analyze exactly what she had said and what she had withheld. Once again he felt incredible admiration for her, for her self-sacrifice, her willingness to risk everything to set him free. Even after all the years of working for an organization that was the epitome of cruelty and inhumanity, she had remained human – and not just human, but so Jewish in essence, despite barely knowing what Judaism was and how it related to her. Generations of Communist indoctrination had not succeeded in erasing the Jewish spark in his wife's soul, and Lev could only hope that his wife was the rule, and not the exception; that his Russian Jewish brothers and sisters would yet rise again as proud Jews and reclaim their heritage.

Of all people, why had Anya been the one appointed to devise the operation that would lead to the arrest of their learning group…

Ever since the start of his religious journey, Lev had mentally prepared himself for the day when he would be discovered and arrested, and all that would follow. Never had he imagined, though, that it would be none other than his wife who would lead the operation. It was so unreal that it was almost as if someone had planned it – or, rather, "Someone." But why? And, more importantly, what for?

Anya's job with the KGB had never been a simple issue in their marriage. On one hand, they enjoyed frequent benefits as well as a standard of living that few others had, but never for a minute did they forget that they were walking at the edge of a steep precipice where one wrong move could send them both hurtling to devastation. Anya had full security clearance, and although she shared almost nothing of her job with him, one thing he did know well was that all positions, without exception, in the KGB were precarious in the extreme. Even Fyodorev himself was not immune to the terrible stresses of the job, hence the pressure to advance at the expense of others, to scheme and backstab, fawn and flatter. Somehow, Anya had managed to stay out of most of that – or, at least, Lev hoped that she had.

Other Jews, however, had not succeeded in preserving their integrity, and suddenly Lev's thoughts turned to the one example he could recall when Anya had shared something of her work life with him. The episode involved a senior-ranking KGB officer, whose name she had refused to share, instead referring to him as Agent X, who, apparently, was someone whom even Fyodorev treated with utmost respect. Agent X was charged with some of the Agency's most sensitive missions and operations, including many with a political slant, and his level of success was unparalleled. Over time, he gained a formidable reputation, and it was rumored that his missions were ordered directly from the Kremlin.

One day, Svetlana had chanced to ask Anya if she had known that Agent X was Jewish. Anya had shrugged, annoyed by the question.

"Since when does faith concern anyone in the Soviet Union?" Anya had retorted shortly.

"As soon as the person begins to act upon it," Svetlana had replied in a low voice. "I have substantial information indicating that Agent X is observing Judaism, at least partially."

"That's ridiculous!" Anya had scoffed. "He never could have reached his position if anyone suspected him of observing any faith, let alone Judaism!"

Svetlana had not been swayed by Anya's argument, and a small smile had played at the corners of her lips. "From what we know about Agent X and his exploits, you can believe me that his religion plays a significant, multi-faceted part in his mission."

"Since when does faith correspond to any mission here?" Anya had replied, completely baffled.

"That depends on the angle from which you view your faith and your mission. Really, Anya, I didn't think you could be so dense."

Anya had been appalled to discover that Agent X was playing the role of a secretly-observant Jew in order to expose those who were genuinely religious. It was no secret that the man was personally responsible for the arrests of tens, if not hundreds, of his co-religionists, but the means by which he had chosen to frame them disgusted her, and when Agent X left the Moscow branch of the Agency, she had been relieved that she would no longer encounter him at department meetings.

Now Lev wondered why he had suddenly recalled this episode. Agent X had been transferred out of Moscow almost two years earlier, and Anya hadn't mentioned him since. What had suddenly caused Lev to recall him? He had enough worries on his head, but he couldn't avoid the thought that the episode hadn't surfaced without reason.

It hit him with a sudden force. The details of the story corresponded far too closely to… *No, it couldn't be.* Lev began trembling violently, certain that he had inadvertently stumbled upon the truth. Agent X could only be Anatoly Andrayev; he was sure of it. And Mikhail trusted him…

Lev felt sick to the stomach, yet he knew what he had to do. He was obligated to warn Mikhail of the danger, and he only hoped it wasn't too late. How many others still trusted Andrayev? Had he already begun to expose the Jews of Kirov, and where would he move to next? Maybe, if he told Mikhail now, at least some Jews would manage to escape in time, and others would be spared.

Lev met with Mikhail that evening, and Mikhail listened silently as Lev shared all that he knew. A long silence passed between them until Lev spoke again. "Mikhail," he said gently, "I understand that this is hard for you to hear. You've known Andrayev for a long time, and you trust him. It really is heartbreaking to learn the truth at this point. Especially if… well, whatever. Let's just hope that too much damage hasn't been done yet."

"No, Lev, it's not what you think," Mikhail waved away his words. "There's a lot more that you don't know, but I'm just not sure if I'm permitted to share it with you."

"You mean you already knew all this?" Lev gaped.

"Yes and no, but as far as you're concerned, I can assure you that it's definitely safe for you here in Kirov. At least for the meantime. Trust me – you're not in any danger here."

Lev stared quizzically at his friend.

"People change, Lev. Who knows that better than us? People arrive at new conclusions, new understandings. What happened two years ago doesn't necessarily reflect on today's reality." Mikhail opened his mouth again, as if to add something, but then promptly fell silent.

"I don't understand," Lev said bluntly, leaving no room for his friend to evade the question. "What are you trying to tell me, Mikhail?"

"I'm trying *not* to tell you, Lev."

Lev's face darkened in anger; what was Mikhail hiding from him? They were all in danger here, all in the same boat – each and every Torah-observant Jew in Kirov and in all of the Soviet Union. And yet, instead of taking immediate action to save his fellow Jews, Gadorovitch was speaking in riddles!

His friend tried to console him. "I'm sorry, Lev, but I can't really say much more. That doesn't mean that you can't try to figure things out for yourself. But Lev, I assure you again, you don't have to worry. Trust me, my friend. You're safe."

Lev shook his head sadly. He, like everyone else in Soviet Russia, knew that to trust anyone was foolhardy and that safety was always an illusion. Traitors lingered behind the most open, smiling faces.

Still, Mikhail was one man whom Lev couldn't afford not to trust.

CHAPTER 28

Gadorovitch's one-room apartment overlooked a tiny park, located in a quiet suburb of Kirov where only the occasional car passed through – but the pastoral beauty couldn't fool Lev. In Soviet Russia, there was no such thing as peaceful tranquility. The long arm of the KGB reached everywhere.

"I trust you, Mikhail," he said hesitantly, "but only you, yourself, because of what we've been through together. That's not the issue; the issue is that you've been deceived. I'm convinced that this man, Anatoly Andrayev, is the officer whom my wife always called Agent X, which means that you're in terrible danger! I just hope that he hasn't infiltrated the groups here – if they exist, that is – but if he's been here for two years already, then he's probably already done terrible damage. You have to protect yourself somehow! Otherwise, we'll all end up behind bars, and *that* I know from a very reliable source."

"Then your reliable source isn't up to date."

Lev stared quizzically at his friend. What was Mikhail hinting at?

It took a moment for the realization to dawn on him. "Mikhail, are you trying to say that Agent X now observes the *mitzvos*? Mikhail, people like that don't return and don't repent; there are some people in the world – even Jews – who don't deserve to do *teshuvah* because of what they've done, and so they aren't even granted the opportunity. And a traitor certainly falls into that category!"

"Who says you're right? Who told you such a thing?" The anger in Mikhail's voice startled Lev. "The gates of *teshuvah* aren't locked for anyone!"

Lev shrugged. "Theoretically, you may be right, but I'm talking about in practice. Jews who go undercover in order to betray their own brothers are very far from *teshuvah* – just about as far as anyone can get. I don't believe that someone so evil, so corrupt, would ever turn his life around. A person has to be open to absorbing truth, but if he's too busy fighting it, he won't see what's right before his eyes."

The anger in Mikhail's eyes softened. "You may be surprised to hear this, Lev, but *teshuvah* is a gift that Hashem offers to every Jew, no matter who he is or where he's holding. Even those who have sinned and fought tooth and nail against *emes* can grasp hold of it and come back. I think that *teshuvah* is one of the few things that completely overrides logic and common sense. Even when it seems, like you say, that the person doesn't even deserve to see the truth, the merit of the *Avos* and *Imahos* still stands in his stead, as well as all kinds of merits of his own personal ancestors which he knows nothing about; and then, Hashem just pulls him close, regardless of everything."

"So you're saying that after betraying dozens of Jews to the authorities, Andrayev turned around and found the truth himself?" Lev was still skeptical.

"Do you deny the possibility?"

Lev visibly hesitated. "I don't know," he said finally. "But even if it's possible… the real question is, after all he's done, can Andrayev be trusted? He played the same game so many times, joining groups of learners only to expose them, without mercy. What makes you think this isn't just another ploy of his? It's just as possible as what you're suggesting," he challenged.

Gadorovitch couldn't hide the fear that flashed across his countenance, and Lev could see that he was torn between two conflicting desires. "Let me tell you a story," he said, after a long moment of silence. "A story which I hope will strengthen your faith in… the man you call Agent X. It seems to me that you're going to need that faith, because he's the one man who can make the difference between you managing to escape and… well, you know what."

"So you admit that Andrayev is Agent X."

"I don't admit anything. I'm just telling you a story." Another pause as the two friends studied each other before Mikhail picked up where he had left off. "This person, Agent X we'll call him, lost his father at a very young age. His mother raised him with his two younger siblings in abject poverty, and his childhood was miserable. The children often went hungry, and the mother was almost always out of the house working at one job or another, trying to make ends meet. Somehow, this boy managed to succeed in school, and when he grew older, he joined the KGB, hoping that it would provide him with a measure of security and financial stability. Yes, he was wrong about the security," Gadorovitch admitted, noting the incredulous expression on Lev's face, "but you'll surely agree that high-ranking employees are relatively well paid, no?" Lev nodded reluctantly.

"Anyway, about a year ago, something strange occurred. In the course of his duties, this man, Agent X, needed to locate a certain file in the KGB archives, and while he was searching for it, he happened to stumble across another file, bearing his father's name on its cover. Curious, he opened it, and began to read the life history of none other than his very own father. He discovered that his father had been arrested, years ago, and incarcerated on charges of disseminating religion. After a show trial, he was sentenced to ten years in a labor camp in Siberia, and he met his death there, just three years into his sentence. The report actually included a description of his father's continued *mitzvah* observance, even in the labor camp, and though I imagine it was written in very official language, he was still awed by the greatness of his father's spirit."

Lev shut his eyes, trying to imagine what could have gone through Agent X's head. At the time, he had been a seasoned, heartless officer, under the influence of years of Communist brainwashing, one who had used all his cunning to battle and defeat the enemies of the state, amassing awards and commendations following each additional success in exposing traitors. Then suddenly, with no forewarning whatsoever, he discovers that his own father, whom he had loved and lost so tragically as a young boy, was actually one of those very same traitors that he was working so hard to root out. And, not only was he one of the traitors, but he was a leader among them, a man whose spirit refused to be quashed even under the harshest of circumstances.

In place of the scorn and hatred he was accustomed to feeling toward those who stubbornly opposed Communist doctrine, a strange, unfamiliar feeling – most probably something verging on respect and awe – begins to penetrate his heart. Stunned, he finds himself wondering: Why? Why did his father risk his life, the well-being of his family – everything – to adhere to the laws of an ancient, and, to his mind, discredited, religion? Where did he find the inner strength to do so? What power on earth – or above it – could motivate a person with such a fiery spirit to battle against forces so overwhelmingly slanted in his enemies' favor?

The next step, the logical conclusion, is, of course, to learn more, to trace his father's mental steps and then, to consider actually following in his path.

Lev was startled to realize that Mikhail had continued speaking, leaving him lost in his reverie, and he shook himself free of his thoughts. "The revelation must have been shocking."

"Shocking doesn't begin to describe it," Mikhail agreed. "He dove headfirst into his religious studies, and only his solid reputation in the KGB saved him from being arrested. His superiors were aware that he was studying, but they were certain that he was doing it in order to improve his cover and enable him to betray yet more Jews. For his part, at one point, he was so tormented by the memories of what he had done that he considered turning himself into the KGB in an attempt to end his life in Siberia, like his father, hoping that it would serve as at least partial atonement."

"And despite all this, he's still serving in the same position as before."

"The Torah forbids a person to turn himself into the authorities and place his own life in danger. His rabbi told him to continue learning while maintaining his position and actually utilizing it to rescue Jewish captives, and that's what he's been doing ever since."

"So that's the end of Antoly's story?"

"That's Agent X's story."

Two-and-a-half weeks later…

The phone rang for several minutes, but Anya still didn't answer, and Lev was fuming. Anya knew how anxious he was and that every delay drove him crazy with worry. Why was she making him wait and compounding his agony? He dialed a fifth time and listened to the infuriating ring of the telephone while silently whispering familiar words of *Tehillim* by heart.

At long last, she answered.

"What took so long?" he demanded breathlessly, without even saying hello.

"Oleg Savitsky came by again, asking if everything's okay. I didn't dare to answer the phone while he was here."

"Do you think he suspects something?"

Anya took a deep breath. "I think he's concerned, and he doesn't really understand why your mother is here with me while you're undergoing surgery far away. And it's true – it does look strange."

Lev sighed. "You're right. We should have thought of that before concocting such a story."

"You mean, *I* should have thought of it," Anya corrected him. "But it's simply impossible to anticipate everything when I'm improvising under pressure. And another thing: I got a call from the university the day after you disappeared. They made it sound like you were the first professor in history not to show up without informing them ahead of time."

Lev listened to his wife's account of the excuse she had offered, and reflected that she had done an admirable job of covering for him. Her excuse, that he had been examined by a doctor and sent to distant Kiev for an emergency surgery, had been accepted, and then, a week later, she had called the university to inform them that there had been a complication, and that Lev wouldn't be returning as soon as he had hoped. *So far, so good*, Lev reflected, trying not to wonder what would happen when the university finally got tired of Anya's phone calls and demanded to see at the very least a doctor's note of referral. *Why worry about tomorrow, when there's more than enough to worry about today?* he thought to himself. His neighbor and colleague, Oleg Savitsky, was already beginning to spot the holes in the story – what would happen if he became truly suspicious, and then, loyal citizen that he was, decided to inform the authorities?

"What did you tell Oleg?" Lev returned to the original topic of conversation.

"I said that I need help with Karina, and there just isn't any other option, since my work day is impossibly long, and I need someone to look after Karina until I get home."

"Sounds plausible enough."

"Maybe, but he still wanted to know who's taking care of you in Kiev. I think I made a pretty awful impression on him as a wife who isn't even concerned about her husband's well-being. He even suggested that I might be eligible to a few days of leave in order to be at your side before and during the surgery and then for the initial recovery period too."

"I wonder if he would do for his wife what you did for me," Lev commented, his voice full of admiration for Anya's sacrifice.

"Most people don't face such challenges," she replied softly, wondering not for the first time what she had done to deserve such a challenge.

"How's Karina?" Lev changed the subject to something more pleasant.

"Okay."

"Is her teacher still giving you the third degree?"

"Since our discussion, she hasn't said anything, but she looks at me with these penetrating eyes, as if she suspects that something's not quite right."

Lev felt it was his duty to calm her. "You probably only feel that because you're so worried yourself. You're afraid that she suspects something, so you see suspicion in her eyes."

"Probably," Anya agreed tiredly, and then dropped the bombshell. "Lev, I don't know how to tell you this, but Fyodorev just summoned me today to tell me that I'm being transferred to Leningrad."

"*To Leningrad?*" Lev repeated dumbly and then listened quietly as his wife filled him in on the details.

"Well, it's understandable," he said finally, after a long silence. "In a way, it's amazing that they let you continue until now. Unless they had some reason for it," he mused. "I wish I could fathom the mind of the KGB, and yet I'm glad that I can't – glad that I don't think like they do. The question is what to do now."

"There isn't any choice in the matter," Anya replied sadly. "Fyodorev told me to be on the midday train the day after tomorrow. Your mother will probably leave a few hours before me and we'll arrange in advance a place to meet up there. It's not going to be easy – I don't know a soul in Leningrad."

Lev paused a moment before replying. "Well, I know someone here, in… well, where I am, who can possibly help you out there. I'll speak to him, and get back to you."

"You know someone? Are you sure you can trust him?"

"Yes." Lev's tone was certain. He could trust him, and, in any case, as Gadorovitch had stressed, there was no other choice. Nobody else was in a position to help him, and certainly not Anya, whose position was precarious in the extreme. Hopefully, Andrayev would have some ideas, some suggestion as to how Anya would manage to escape Leningrad and meet up with Lev before they slipped over the border with Karina. Even as Lev let his thoughts wander as far as crossing the Iron Curtain, he realized how fanciful it all seemed – how many escape attempts had succeeded in the past, after all? Yet, with faith and *siyata diShmaya*, anything could happen, he reminded himself.

"I'll call you back tomorrow, in the afternoon when you get home from work, to let you know what this person says," he told Anya, before ending the call on an optimistic note. Maybe, just maybe the end of their ordeal was in sight.

But the following day, all of Lev's excitement and hopes vanished instantly, only to be replaced by a terrible, gnawing fear. Anya didn't answer his call at five in the afternoon, nor a half hour later, nor at any of the other times he called, becoming increasingly desperate as time passed.

Something had gone wrong, and Lev was left groping in the dark.

CHAPTER 29

Lev sat at the kitchen table in Gadorovitch's apartment, his fingers aching from the constant dialing and redialing. Why wasn't Anya picking up the phone? Even on the days when she had to work late, she was usually home by six. What could have happened?

What had happened? Exactly what he had been dreading all along. Lev started to tremble as he let his thoughts run wild. *They've arrested her. They finally caught on to the switch, and realized what happened. They're probably interrogating her right now!* Lev buried his face in his hands, but it was impossible to escape the emotional torment at the thought of his wife in captivity. If only it could be him instead of her! Why had she insisted on things being this way? Why?

Gadorovitch entered the kitchen and frowned as he caught sight of his friend – his ashen pallor, his sunken shoulders. "She still didn't answer the phone?"

Lev opened his mouth to answer, but sufficed with shaking his head when he realized that he was beyond speech. Just then, he was assailed by a second fear, no less paralyzing than the first: Where was Karina? Where was his mother? Had the KGB placed their vile hands upon those innocent ones as well? Were they using them to break Anya?

Stop it! he shouted mentally at himself. *Stop letting yourself get carried away. There's a limit to what a person can handle. Daven. Focus on tefillah, on emunah.* He willed himself to rein in his emotions and as he exhaled slowly, he raised his eyes to meet those of his friend. "We have to do something, find something out," he managed to utter.

Gadorovitch's expression was grave. "I'll speak to Anatoly right away, but I'll go to him in person. I don't think it's wise to discuss this over the phone. Wait for me here, Lev." Lev reluctantly agreed, knowing that he had no other choice. His friend disappeared, leaving him alone with his thoughts which he struggled to divert to *tefillah*. Waves of despair threatened to engulf him, but he battled against them valiantly.

Ribbono shel Olam, please let me be wrong! Please let me find out that Anya is safe, that Karina and Mother are safe, that they didn't take them. Please let it all be nothing but my wild, faithless imagination. Let Mikhail and Anatoly laugh at my fears. Only You can decide what is imagination and what is reality.

During those minutes when Lev pleaded with his Creator, he knew he genuinely believed that his life, as well as the lives of his family, were only in the Hands of Hashem. But even as he wept and prayed, the image of his wife in the custody of the KGB kept stealing into his mind. If she was really a prisoner, what then? On one hand, he longed to deny the possibility and erase it from his mind, but he also knew that regardless of all his prayers, there were no guarantees that Anya was safe. *And if she isn't, if she was arrested and imprisoned, then my faith must remain as strong as ever,* he told himself. *I cannot fathom the will of G-d. His plan for His People is something way, way beyond human comprehension.*

If the worst was true, Anya would not be the first Jew to pay the price of cleaving to Torah and *mitzvos*. And yet, she didn't have even the slightest awareness of the greatness of her sacrifice. Did that make it less valuable, less real? If only it were he, and not his wife, paying that ultimate price. He, at least, was fortified with his newfound belief and the knowledge that his suffering was achieving something of eternal value. But how would Anya fortify herself? Why had he let her go through with her crazy plan? Why? Surely there was something he could do? Anything!

An excruciating two hours passed before Mikhail returned. Lev had only to steal a single glance at his friend's ashen features to know that his worst nightmares had become reality. "I'm so sorry, Lev," Mikhail choked out.

Although he had suspected it was coming, the blow was still brutal.

"What about my daughter? My mother?" he finally managed to ask.

"Your mother escaped with the child. They're searching for them, but in the meantime, nobody seems to have any idea where they are."

"*Baruch Hashem*," Lev whispered. Mikhail handed him a glass of water and ordered him to drink it.

"It's my fault, Mikhail!" Lev groaned. "It's all my fault. I should have taken responsibility for my actions. I never should have let her sacrifice herself for something she doesn't even understand."

Mikhail disagreed. "You're wrong, Lev. Your wife risked herself for the husband she loves. Many women have done the same throughout history."

"But she doesn't even understand why I was willing to endanger her! She has no idea about anything – I never breathed a word to her. They're torturing her, Mikhail, *torturing her!* She must hate me now. What can she be thinking?"

"She went into this with her eyes wide open, Lev. She knows how the KGB works, after all. She had no illusions."

It was poor comfort for Lev. "You're right, but I can't bear it. Mikhail, I'm going back to Moscow. I'll surrender on condition that they let her go. I won't let her suffer in my place."

Mikhail automatically blocked the doorway. "You can't, Lev. It will never work. The KGB won't be cowed into anything; they won't release her even if you give yourself up. You'll lose everything and gain nothing in return."

Lev shook his head. "But there has to be something I can do to help her! I won't let her suffer because of me!"

"I understand your feelings, but it won't help anyone, least of all Anya, if you give yourself up! They'll just play you against each other. Anatoly says to sit tight until he can come up with something. There's nothing we can do right now. We have to wait and see what develops."

Lev cringed as knives and daggers twisted painfully in his heart. "I can't just wait, Mikhail. I can't."

"You have to. There's no other choice. Anatoly is working hard to find a safe house for your daughter and mother. The trouble is that nobody knows where they are, but that can be worked out. Even if the KGB finds them first, Anatoly should be able to use his connections to save them."

"Why can't he do the same for Anya?"

"Anya is a different story. She's under heavy guard, and it's too risky to try anything at this point."

Lev shook his head, wishing there was some magic potion he could ingest that would dull the terrible pain. If he had once imagined how terrible life could be under KGB imprisonment, he now discovered that knowing that his wife was there was much, much worse…

Anya's eyes closed of their own accord. It wasn't the dank, tiny cell that was closing in on her as much as the cruel thoughts that preyed upon her like vicious hawks. She had been confined in a dark cell for two days already, and the door had yet to be opened even once. It had been over fifty hours since food or water had passed her lips, and she wasn't sure how much longer she could survive like this. Her thoughts were beginning to become distorted, although her thinking was still clear enough for her to wonder why she hadn't yet been summoned for an interrogation. What was Fyodorev planning?

The very thought of her former boss caused her to tremble. Fyodorev would never forgive her treachery. If he was merciless with even the smallest infraction, she could not even fathom his reaction to what she had done. No doubt he was plotting a cruel, miserable end to her life. She wondered if he would simply dispense with the interrogation and show trial in favor of punishing her immediately, behind closed doors. Nobody would ever find out what had happened to her; she would become just another miserable statistic, yet another faceless victim of the regime that crushed all those who opposed it.

Even if she confessed, she doubted that it would help her. They already suspected that she had been somewhat complicit in her husband's illicit activities, but without proof, they had waited to act. Waited for what? What, exactly, had they discovered? Had Fyodorev been lying about a plan to transfer her to Leningrad, or had something happened in the interim? Probably, she would never find out.

And what of her husband? Would they ever meet again? Anya swallowed hard. There was no sense in letting her thoughts wander to the future. It was hard enough to deal with the present. Where was he now? Was he truly living the life of a religious Jew? What had he discovered that had so inspired him? As she brought to mind her last memory of him – his face a moment before he had stolen out of the building on Lubyanka – she realized that in all their years of marriage, she had never seen him so passionate about anything. A fire had blazed in his eyes, and Anya realized that even if she had known about his covert activities, she would have been powerless to stop him.

The question was now, did she, too, have the spirit inside her to survive the terrible conditions of her captivity? If the hunger had not been eating away at her insides, she could have thought it was all a nightmare. How much longer could she exist like this, trying to find a measure of comfort on the cold concrete? She stood up and stretched her aching limbs, but then sank down again, too weak to maintain an upright posture. How much longer could she survive this?

Despite herself, a hoarse, mirthless chuckle escaped her dry lips. *Just wait, Anya. This is just the beginning. Before long, you'll be pining for those comfortable days when your only tormentors were the hunger, the thirst, and the cold cement floor.*

CHAPTER 30

"When did your husband join the religionists in the University?"

"I don't know. He never told me about it."

"When did you start learning religion?"

"Me? Never. I knew nothing about my husband's religious activities."

The interrogator sneered. "For the moment, we'll let that statement pass. However, I do believe that you have quite a good idea about how your husband managed to escape this building."

Anya fell silent, the impossible thirst causing her tongue to stick to her palate. Really, it was a miracle that she was able to speak at all, and if her captors had intended to dull her instincts before the interrogation, then they had succeeded. She couldn't even recall what she had resolved to do before succumbing to her present state of apathy. Had she intended to confess to her crime? To deny it? Was there any purpose in pleading innocence? The KGB had condemned many for crimes far less severe than hers.

"No response," the interrogator snapped toward the stenographer who was dutifully recording every word of the interview. "I'll repeat my question. Who abetted Lev Krasnikov in his escape from this building?"

"I didn't help him to escape. I forced him to leave. He didn't want to cooperate, but I gave him no choice."

"Who notified you of his arrest?"

"I saw his name on the list of arrestees."

"As I understand it, you never so much as glanced at the list before. Who clued you in this time?"

Despite her lethargy, Anya recalled her oath not to incriminate anyone and subject them to this hell. "Then you understand it wrong. I don't usually glance at the lists, but from time to time, I do."

"For what reason?"

"Curiosity."

"And it was simple curiosity that led you to discover your husband's name on the list of arrestees?"

"Yes."

"And you expect us to believe that you knew nothing, *nothing at all*, about his forbidden studies."

Anya exhaled in frustration. Of course she didn't expect them to believe her, but nonetheless, it was the truth, and there was at least some evidence in her favor – or so she thought. "Had I known, is it logical that I would have devised an operation that could lead to his arrest?"

"Of course it's logical. Logic extends above emotional ties, and, as you must know, in the Soviet Union, every patriotic citizen is bound to our country above everything else."

Once again, Anya fell silent. The interrogator was telling her nothing she didn't know already. Would he willingly hand even his wife over to the authorities, if he discovered that she had transgressed? Anya had no doubt that the answer was positive.

"Anya, we'd like to offer you an opportunity to make amends."

Anya didn't even deign to reply. She had suspected from the outset that the KGB intended to force her to incriminate others in return for some form of a plea bargain, but she would have none of it.

The interrogator continued, ignoring her stony silence. "We have reason to believe that you are in contact with your husband. Which is why you'll do exactly as we instruct you. Today."

Anya stiffened, but then immediately regretted it, knowing that the worst thing she could possibly do was anger them. "I don't have any way of contacting my husband, and I swear that I have no idea where he is."

"You've been in telephone contact throughout the past two weeks."

"Yes, but I don't call him – he always calls me. My guess is that he's left the country."

"He hasn't, and stop playing games," the interrogator snapped. His expression hardened, and Anya quaked inwardly, knowing that worse was in store. The interrogator leaned closer to her and added, "If you want to, you can reach him. We know that."

She was tempted to shout that she didn't want to, but she held her tongue.

"Anya Krasnikov, you've committed an unforgiveable crime. Senior command is furious, and I imagine you know even better than I how this will all end. You have one – and only one – way to demonstrate your remorse, and that's by cooperating with us. If you help us capture your husband, we'll consider reassigning you to another unit and restoring your freedom – within certain limits. Of course, it goes without saying that you'll never be reinstated to your former position. Nonetheless, you can rejoin your daughter and live a relatively normal life. *If* you choose that option.

"Don't give us your answer just yet," the man continued as he got to his feet. "We'll give you another twenty-four hours to weigh your options. Tomorrow evening, when you've come to the right conclusion, you'll receive food and drink."

It was then that Anya passed out.

The interrogator and stenographer exchanged a baffled look, unsure whether it was the knowledge that she wouldn't be receiving food or drink for another day or the possibility of saving herself that had caused her to faint. Two cold buckets of water sufficed to revive her, and when Anya opened her eyes a few minutes later, she discovered that the interrogator's chair was empty. An unfamiliar young female officer helped her to sit up.

"Would you like to relax for a moment before I lead you back to your cell?" the officer asked with an unexpected touch of kindness.

Anya struggled to identify the face that peered at her from behind gray clouds of haze. She leaned back in her seat and tried to breathe deeply and slowly until she felt slightly better. She was tempted to ask this sympathetic officer for a glass of water, but held back, knowing that both of them would be severely punished for any infraction of the rules.

"What did you do to Tina?" the young woman gazed compassionately at her. "She turned the world upside down in order to destroy you, but even she didn't dream that she'd stumble across such juicy information."

Anya froze, but her wide eyes revealed the shock.

"What – you didn't realize it was her?" the officer stared.

Anya was barely able to speak. "You mean Tina Yeltsin?"

"Who else? How many other Tinas do you know around here?"

Anya tried to absorb the information, but her starved mind led her thoughts around in circles. After several moments, she finally choked out, "You mean, she did this? For revenge? Because I refused to help her destroy Yvgenya?"

"I have no idea what went on between the two of you," the young officer replied, "but you can be sure that Tina is responsible for this. She was obsessed with uncovering something that would destroy you, almost as if Fyodorev had appointed her to do it."

"Maybe he did…"

"No," the officer insisted, waving her hand dismissively. "He was the last one willing to believe her accusations. He really trusted you. Until all the evidence was sitting on his desk, he refused to even listen to her, but once it was proven beyond doubt that it was your husband who escaped the building, and not the other guy, he hit the roof."

For a moment, Anya let her memories take her back to that day in her office, to the day when Tina had confronted her and demanded her cooperation in reporting Yvgenya to the authorities. The viciousness on her colleague's face had shocked her, but the knowledge that she had acted on her threats was still devastating to hear.

"Are you ready to go back to your cell?" the young guard changed the subject.

Still too stunned to reply, Anya simply nodded and rose automatically from her chair, but just as she was getting to her feet, the room performed a maddening swirl around her, and she nearly fell again. At that moment, a tall, broad-shouldered warden entered the room.

"Is she making trouble, Sonya?" she asked curtly.

"No. It just took her time to come to," the guard replied quickly. Anya felt the two women grab her by the arms and lead her roughly out of the room and down a long corridor. Before she knew it, she was back in her cell, sitting on the freezing cement. Her feet were swiftly becoming numb, and she debated whether to remove her sweater and wrap it around her toes to warm them. Ideally, she would have paced back and forth to keep warm, but she was too weak to stand unsupported for more than a few minutes. Vaguely, she reflected that her bemused state of mind was probably a blessing, as it dulled her senses and prevented her from appreciating the full horror of her situation.

In the misery of her cell, Anya found herself wondering if she had been wrong to refuse Tina. She had known Tina was ruthlessly ambitious – why hadn't she taken her overt threats more seriously? For her own sake, Anya might have been willing to suffer rather than betray another colleague and friend. But what of Karina? Should her daughter be forced to suffer as well? *Poor, poor Karina…*

Maybe I should have just bowed to Tina's wishes and written that report, she sighed. *But that would have meant sacrificing not just Yvgenya but also her entire family to save my own skin.*

"No!" she screamed suddenly, her cry echoing against the cold cement walls. *This world isn't meant to be a jungle with the only rules being the survival of the fittest. A woman shouldn't be forced to destroy her friend's life in order to spare herself. It's wrong. It's illogical. It's inhuman! I never could have lived with myself knowing that I had ruined Yvgenya.*

It was at that moment, in the freezing cold cell of the KGB dungeon, that Anya Krasnikov discovered exactly how depraved the Soviet regime really was. It caused its own citizens to turn their backs on each other and descend to unprecedented levels of cruelty.

Her only solace was knowing that, somehow, at least this once, she had remained above it all.

CHAPTER 31

Two days earlier…

Valeria Krasnikov hurried down the street. From afar, she could already see the green painted gate of the kindergarten, which was still closed. Glancing at her watch, she noted that she was early again; there was still another ten minutes until the end of Karina's day at kindergarten. The preschool teacher had already hinted to her that she was disturbing when she picked up Karina before dismissal, and so Valeria decided to wait on the bench across the street until a minute before four, which would still give her just enough time to be on her way with Karina before the other mothers arrived to pick up their children.

Although Anya had wanted to maintain her regular routine as far as possible and pick up Karina herself, of late it had become harder and harder. Her boss seemed to be delighting in giving her last-minute tasks to complete at the very end of the day, and when one day she arrived half an hour later to pick up her daughter, both she and Anastasia, the preschool teacher, realized that things couldn't carry on that way. From then on, Valeria had been coming to pick up her granddaughter, but the fewer people who knew about that, the better.

At a minute to four, the gate was still locked, but Valeria, impatient, crossed the street and rang the bell, just as the teacher exited the building, a long line of children following closely behind. She caught sight of Valeria and smiled. "I'm glad you came on time today," she called out. "Karina isn't feeling well, and I think she might be coming down with something."

The gate opened, and Valeria felt a thud in her heart. "Where is she? What's wrong with her?" She scanned the group of children, but didn't find her granddaughter among them.

"Karina's still inside. Ina made her a cup of tea."

Karina immediately abandoned the mug in favor of her grandmother who approached her with outstretched arms.

"My head hurts," she whimpered, burying her face in her grandmother's skirt, "and I'm coughing."

"You poor thing," Valeria crooned. "You must be coming down with a cold." She took Karina's lunchbox from the teacher, thanked her, and then retrieved Karina's coat and hat from the peg on the wall. She tightened the fur cap on the little girl's head, making sure to cover her ears well, before exiting into the bristling cold. They walked home together hand-in-hand, with Valeria promising her hot tea with lemon as soon as they got home, before tucking her up in bed for the rest of the afternoon.

Ten minutes later, they turned the corner into the street where Lev and Anya lived. As they walked down the street, a broad figure suddenly emerged from the shadows between two buildings and blocked their path. Valeria looked up in shock. She didn't recognize the man standing there, but she could only guess who he might be, and she started to tremble. Should she run – but where to?

Noting the fear on her face, the man began speaking, in a quiet, but urgent tone.

"Mrs. Krasnikov, you don't know me, I see, but I know you. I am Lev and Anya's neighbor – my name is Oleg Savitsky. I've been waiting here for you to get back, to tell you not to go home." Savitsky cast a panicked look behind him before continuing: "A few hours ago, three men entered the building and then Lev's apartment. They must have had a key, because there was no sign of damage to the front door. I don't think they realized that I saw them – at least, I hope they didn't. They left not long ago and I waited a bit before going downstairs to warn you."

Valeria turned white and stared back at the stranger in terror.

"I advise you to get as far away from here as possible. If… I mean… when Anya comes home, I'll tell her that I sent you away. I just hope she does come home," he added, under his breath.

Valeria scooped up Karina and held the little girl tightly to her chest. "But where can I go?" she whispered despondently.

Savitsky pressed a small, crumpled square of paper into her hand. "Go to this address. You should be safe there. It's my mother's house, and she's a widow and lives alone. Tell her that I sent you. I'll do my best to stop by there tonight and let you know what's happening."

She thanked him weakly and turned, confused, toward the bus station.

"Wait, Mrs. Krasnikov!" he followed her with quick strides. "I don't mean to pry," he added uncomfortably, "but do you have money for the ride?"

In her confusion, Valeria had forgotten all about the fare. "Um… no, actually I don't. I just went to pick up Karina, and I didn't take my wallet with me."

Savitsky wordlessly handed her several bills and coins. "This is what I have on me, and it's enough for the ride plus a little extra. You should hurry, though. And, don't go to the bus station," he added. "Go to a stop further away and take the bus from there."

Valeria stuffed the money into her coat pocket. "Thank you," she whispered again, before turning back around to hurry down the street. Karina's added weight in her arms slowed her pace, but she pushed herself forward, knowing that it was vital to get away before they came after her too.

Weak and feverish, Karina let her head rest on her grandmother's shoulder, and she soon dozed off into a fitful sleep. Valeria hoisted her up to a more comfortable position and kept on walking determinedly, turning randomly left and right as she tried to collect her thoughts. Her arms were aching, and when Karina woke up and began to whimper, she took the opportunity to enter a small park and sink down on to a bench to catch her breath for a few minutes.

"I want to go home," the child begged her. "I'm so cold, and my head hurts. Why aren't we going home?"

Valeria swallowed her tears, tears of exhaustion, terror, and despair. "We can't go home right now, Karina. Bad people came into our house, and we have to go somewhere else."

"Where's Mamochka? What if she comes home and finds the bad people?" Karina began to cry and Valeria felt like crying along with her.

"We'll meet up with Mamochka later," Valeria tried to keep her voice calm. "As soon as we get where we have to go, we'll see what we can do." As she spoke, she shivered. Where were they headed? Were they walking into a trap? She remembered Anya mentioning Savitsky as a too-curious neighbor who had stopped by on several occasions to inquire after Lev, and she wondered now if she had been overly hasty to heed his warning. Anya had suspected him too and hadn't dared to breathe a word about her husband's situation to him. Did her daughter-in-law fear that Savitsky would report them to the authorities? Why had she been so afraid?

On the other hand, if Savitsky really wanted to see her arrested, he had no need to wait outside the building to warn her. He could have simply let her arrive home and then called the authorities to inform them of her presence. If so, she could most probably trust him – and, in any case, she didn't have much choice in the matter.

Valeria retrieved the scrap of paper he had given her from her pocket and smoothed it out, squinting to read the street address written there. She had never heard of the street name, but she saw that the neighborhood was located in a remote suburb of the city. Karina's loud sobs interrupted her thoughts, and Valeria realized that she couldn't delay any longer. Rain had begun to fall in a soft patter, and the temperature was dropping together with the advancing hour; it wouldn't be long before the rain turned to soft snowflakes. She needed to get both of them to shelter before Karina's cold deteriorated into pneumonia.

She boarded a bus at the nearest stop, and an hour-and-a-half later alighted at her destination well past sundown. The dim streetlights barely illuminated the faded wood of the door with the ramshackle sign that read *Savitsky*. Valeria knocked on the door with numb fingers, cradling a burning Karina against her chest.

The door opened to reveal a babushka wrapped in a thick woolen scarf who stared curiously at Valeria.

"Your son sent me," she somehow stammered, her teeth chattering from the cold. "I need a place to stay, and he said he'd come tonight to explain."

The old woman gazed at her with ill-concealed suspicion. "My son?"

"His name is Oleg."

"You know him?"

"He's our neighbor. He told me to come here."

The old woman continued peering at her suspiciously but finally relented and stepped aside, allowing Valeria to enter. "What's the matter with the child?" she asked. "Why is her face so flushed?"

"She's not feeling well, and I'm afraid she has high fever."

Nodding, the older woman led her to an inner room in the small house. "You can lay her down here on the bed. I'll make you both hot tea."

After forcing Karina to drink something, Valeria dared to ask her hostess if she had any fever-reducing medication."

"Damp rags always work best," the old woman replied.

Valeria nodded, knowing that most likely she had nothing better to offer. She followed the woman to the kitchen where she was given a small bowl of water and a bundle of rags, and then Valeria headed back to the inner room, hoping that Karina's condition wasn't bad enough to demand a more aggressive treatment.

Karina lay in a restless sleep, moaning sometimes, her face flushed and her forehead hot to the touch. "The fever is getting worse," Valeria muttered. "I just hope this helps."

"Would you like to sponge her body with cool water?" old Mrs. Savitsky offered.

"I don't think that's a good idea," Valeria replied. "If she hasn't caught pneumonia yet then she definitely will after a cold bath."

The old woman stared at her lengthily, as if trying to solve a riddle. "Who are you running away from?"

"I don't know," Valeria stammered. "All I know is that your son told me to leave immediately."

"And you took his advice." It was a statement more than a question.

"I was scared," Valeria replied frankly.

"Why?"

"Why? For good reason, unfortunately." Valeria sighed as she met the older woman's eyes, which were tinged with sympathy.

Old Mrs. Savitsky nodded. There was nothing else that needed to be said. In Soviet Russia, there are some things that are better left unsaid.

CHAPTER 32

It was getting late, and the rain outside had long since turned to swirling flakes of snow. The small gas heater in old Mrs. Savitsky's home barely took the edge off the frost, and Valeria shivered as she sat at her granddaughter's side. Karina lay beneath a layer of damp rags covered with two rough, heavy blankets, her face flushed and her breathing labored, sleeping fitfully and occasionally murmuring through her dreams.

Valeria grew more concerned as the evening progressed, and when Karina's fever didn't break but instead seemed be rising, she realized that she would have to find something to lower her temperature. She knew that knocking at doors at this hour of the night would rouse the neighbors' suspicions – but what choice did she have? In any case, if the KGB was really searching for them, she had no doubt that they would find them eventually, either sooner or later.

As she sat at Karina's bedside clutching her burning hand, her thoughts drifted to her son, his dangerous activities, and the faith that had motivated him to throw caution to the wind. Valeria was already in her sixties, and although Communism had successfully eradicated virtually all memories of living a life grounded in religion, she could still recall snatches of prayer and even a few ritual observances that she had seen in her grandparents' home. How they had hoped that something – anything – would remain of their faith in the coming generations, despite the perils it entailed. And what remained, now that both Lev and Anya were gone? Only Karina.

Only Karina, who now desperately needed medication, and she would bring it to her, somehow. Valeria stood up, buttoned her coat, wrapped her scarf around her face, and headed out into the dark, snowy night.

Mindful of the puddles of icy water lining the street she made her way carefully to the next building, knocking on one door after another in the hope that somebody would take pity on her. It took four attempts before the door opened to her insistent knocking, albeit only a crack, and a young man peered out at her. "Yes?" he growled, ready to slam the door in her face given the slightest excuse.

Nervously Valeria began to explain that her granddaughter was burning with fever and that she would like to purchase syrup to lower it.

The stranger stared at her through narrow, suspicious eyes. "Who are you?" he asked, the doubt and fear manifest in his voice. "How did you get here?"

"We're staying with a neighbor, and my granddaughter is sick. Please help me."

"No. I can't help you." The door was slammed in her face, and Valeria was left standing despairingly on the doorstep, on the verge of tears. Would anyone be willing to help a stranger? But she had to continue trying, and, finally, on her ninth attempt, she met her salvation. A young mother took pity on her and extended a single pill.

"I'm sorry. I can't spare more than this, but I hope it will help you." Valeria couldn't believe her ears. Was the mother actually apologizing?

"Thank you! Thank you so much!" she said quickly. "May you be blessed!"

The woman returned a sad smile and closed the door gently. Valeria hurried home with her precious find and despite Karina's weak protestations, force-fed her the pill. An hour later, to her relief, Karina began to perspire, and she called out hoarsely asking for a drink. Later that night, past midnight, Oleg arrived as promised. He greeted his mother warmly and accepted her invitation to join the women at the kitchen table for tea.

"Mrs. Krasnikov," he began hesitantly, "you are Lev's mother, correct? And you have some idea of his whereabouts?"

Valeria's face fell. If Savitsky had any good news, he would surely have begun with that. "I have no idea at all where Lev is," she replied quietly.

"I see." He bit his lip, wondering how he was going to break the news. "My wife and I have been taking turns watching from the window, and it's clear that Anya hasn't returned home. Based on what happened earlier today, it seems likely that she was arrested."

Valeria nodded slowly. It was no surprise to have her worst fears confirmed.

"I don't have any inside information, but logically speaking, they must be looking for Karina already. I have no idea if they know you were staying with Anya, but…well, as you must know, they tend to know most things." Savitsky sighed, not enjoying being the bearer of such bad tidings.

Valeria swallowed hard. At her age, to become a hunted person was no simple matter. It must be hard enough for Lev, a young, healthy man, to evade his pursuers, but how could she, an elderly woman, hope to remain out of the clutches of the KGB? Who would help her? Anyone who conspired to abet the escape of a wanted person was liable to be arrested himself, and suddenly Valeria realized that Savitsky had placed himself in grave danger by coming to tell her what he knew.

"Why are you helping me?" she asked him, full of admiration for a man who was almost a total stranger.

"Because I care about Lev and Anya. Lev is my colleague at the university, and a friend of mine. But even if he wasn't, I would still help you. What's a man worth if he isn't willing to help another person in need?"

His words brought tears to her eyes, and Valeria wondered how many other people in Soviet Russia would act in the same manner.

"You can stay here for the meanwhile," Savitsky's mother told her. "Whatever I have, I will gladly share with you. Nonetheless, you should be making plans to move on. This is not a long-term solution."

"No, you're right," Valeria agreed. "I just hope the neighbors don't start asking questions. Probably I should just stay indoors and they won't realize I'm still here. I had to knock on a few doors down the street," she explained, noting Savitsky's puzzled look. "Karina is sick, and I needed something to lower her fever."

Oleg furrowed his brow in concern. "She's sick? Is it something serious?"

"I hope not. Her fever went down, but I don't have another pill to give her if it rises again. She's still coughing, and I'm worried that she has pneumonia."

Oleg strode quickly to the bedroom where Karina lay sleeping. Her breathing was raspy, and her cheeks were still bright from fever.

"She needs to be seen by a doctor," he pronounced. "We'll have to find one who's willing to come here and write a prescription in my daughter's name."

Valeria gazed anxiously at the man who had unexpectedly become her savior. "Yes, but I hardly know a soul here in Moscow. I wouldn't know whom to approach."

For a moment, Oleg deliberated. "Let me see what I can arrange tomorrow morning," he said finally.

"Thank you, thank you so much," Valeria expressed emotionally. "You're a good man, Mr. Savitsky."

Anatoly Andrayev studied Lev, his gaze penetrating. "Lev, you know how dangerous this is. Dangerous isn't even the word. It's downright crazy, insane. There is simply no way you'll ever be able to pull it off. Even if you make it into Moscow without being spotted; even if you make it to Lubyanka without anyone noticing you… You really think that you'll manage to get into the building and get Anya out? You're out of your mind!"

"It's not as crazy as it sounds," Lev insisted. "I have some ideas that I'm working on, and I won't be doing this alone."

Anatoly rubbed his eyes, eyes that were red from exhaustion. "Give it up, Lev. I tell you, it's impossible. It's forbidden to place your life in such danger when there's so little chance of success."

"There's more than a small chance of success. I've spent hours thinking this through, and I won't go ahead until I have a solid plan. What's more, I've managed to enlist the help of three people who work right there, in the building. And, you gave me the building's blueprints, which will help tremendously – now I know where all the entrances and exits are. I'm not walking into this blindly, Anatoly. I know what I'm up against, and I'm not stupid."

"How do you know that you're not walking right into a trap? Who are these three people you're so sure will help? Even close colleagues can turn their backs on their friends. If that happens, they'll have both you and Anya."

"That's exactly what I want you to find out. For you to try to gauge the integrity of these three people. All three of them owe their positions, promotions and all, to Anya, not to mention other favors along the way."

"Lev, you know that every Soviet citizen is loyal to the state above all, and especially when the citizens happen to be KGB agents... although I can try to find out. But even if these people really are trustworthy, there's still no guarantee that your plan will work. At best, you have minimal chances of success."

Lev rose and began to pace the small room. "Anya also endangered herself when forcing me to leave the building after my arrest. Ever since, I've been trying to justify my actions by claiming that she forced me to follow her orders, but I never should have let her endanger herself like that. I should have refused. There was no question that it wouldn't be long before all fingers would point to her. We both know what kind of fate is in store for her, both before and after the trial. If you were in my position, Anatoly, would you act any differently?"

Anatoly preferred not to answer.

Andrayev returned with his answer by evening. "You can trust them, all three of them," he told Lev. "They're with you all the way, and they are actually in a position to help you, but I still don't agree with your plan. They told me what you're asking of them, and I just don't believe it will work." Andrayev sighed. "But you're not going to listen to me, are you, Lev? You're going ahead with this, regardless. So I have no choice but to help you as much as I can. So, what I will recommend is that you only use force in the case of a real emergency – it's far better to pull this off without any direct confrontations."

"Meaning?"

"Meaning, that what you were thinking of doing isn't the best way. I discussed it with them all, and we came up with some alternative ideas. Boris said he can arrange to be posted on guard at the main entrance to the building on that day, and you'll enter in uniform. Sergei says he'll try to get assigned to the cells, and Sasha will help you smuggle Anya out through one of the basement exits."

Lev considered the revised plan. "If that works, then we won't have to fire a single shot."

"That's the best we can hope for. But there's one thing you haven't thought of, and that's Anya herself. I have no idea what condition she's in, and it's possible that she doesn't even have the strength to walk." Andrayev cast a sympathetic glance at Lev, whose face had paled. "I wish I knew more, but Fyodorev has been keeping her file under wraps, and I have no idea what's going on there. I haven't managed to squeeze so much as a crumb of information about her."

Lev nodded slowly, his expression grave. "So we'll have to prepare a stretcher, but we can't just march it into the building. We'll have to set it up near the basement exit."

"And take a First Aid kit with you," Anatoly added.

"She'll probably need a doctor too. We'll have to locate someone nearby who can be trusted. After all, if someone's wounded during the operation, we can't just take him to the hospital."

"Good point," Anatoly nodded. "And don't worry – I know of someone who'll be willing to help out with that part of things."

Lev rubbed his eyes. "What about my mother and daughter? Don't any of your contacts have any idea where they are? The longer it takes to find them, the longer we'll have to wait to leave the country. I won't leave without them."

"Nobody found them yet. But that includes the KGB. They must have found somewhere really good to hide – I imagine someone's helping them. But I advise you to flee the country at your first opportunity. As soon as we find your mother and daughter, we'll find a way to send them after you."

Lev frowned and shook his head. "I'll send Anya, but I'm not going anywhere without them."

CHAPTER 33

It was a long journey back from Kirov to Moscow, and Lev used the time to rest and review his plan, making sure that it was as watertight as possible. He had spent most of the previous night with Anatoly Andrayev, analyzing each step and trying to account for all possible scenarios that could potentially arise. Nonetheless, Lev knew that all the planning in the world wasn't sufficient to guarantee success. At the moment of truth, it would be the *Ribbono shel Olam* alone who would guide his footsteps and determine his fate.

He tried to *daven*, but his thoughts and anxieties kept disturbing his concentration, frustrating him almost to the point of tears. How he wished that he could just leave all speculation aside and focus on his *tefillah*, which was, he knew, the only thing that would really help him now – but the fear refused to abate. Was this a bad omen? he wondered fearfully, a sign that he wouldn't merit the Divine assistance that he needed so desperately? *Stop worrying!* he ordered himself. *It's forbidden to think like that. It's these kinds of thoughts that really weaken a man.* Biting his lip, he forced himself to continue repeating the words of prayer that he knew by heart until the Moscow skyline became visible in the distance.

Lev alighted at the Metro station and made his way on foot toward his destination. He had donned his uniform back in Kirov, and he held a smart leather briefcase that concealed a loaded pistol. He approached the main entrance precisely at twelve, and during those final seconds before addressing the guard, he begged Hashem to help him remain calm and for everything to go to plan, even as he knew how steeply the odds were stacked against him.

Boris was supposed to be waiting for him at the entrance, but when Lev reached the double doors, he saw that someone else was stationed there instead. The guard studied him carefully. "Your ID. What is your destination and purpose?"

Keeping his wits about him, Lev proffered a forged ID that Andrayev had procured for him and brusquely stated, "I have an interview with Pavel Bantov."

The guard wrinkled his brow. "Bantov? That's impossible. He left for Leningrad today."

Lev nodded, unruffled; Anatoly had already given him this piece of information, which was why he had specifically used his name. "That's right. He told me that he might be out of town, and that if he was, I should speak to Boris Tolstoy."

"Tolstoy?" the guard's suspicions skyrocketed. "Since when does Tolstoy conduct interviews?"

Lev shrugged. "I really have no idea, but that's what I was told. Would you like to call Boris and ask him?"

The guard hesitated visibly but agreed to try. He scanned his list of names and extensions, searching for the right one. Meanwhile, Lev leaned casually against a wide stone pillar. His posture conveyed nonchalance, but his heart was thudding wildly in his chest. This was only the first obstacle in his path, but the next minutes would prove whether Andrayev had been accurate in his assessment of Tolstoy's character and integrity. And it was an assessment upon which his life and Anya's depended.

No! a voice within him protested. *The success of this mission is not dependent upon any man or his assessment, but rather upon the will of G-d! Not only the next minutes of your life, but also the course of your entire life, have been predetermined in a place on high.* The minutes passed by interminably as the guard argued vociferously on the telephone, but each minute filled Lev with greater calm and serenity as he repeated the message in his mind. His only fear was that he was drawing too much attention to himself while the guard struggled to locate Boris. Lev was aware of the curious gazes being sent in his direction, and he prayed that these would not be the final moments of his freedom. He tightened his clutch on the handle of his leather briefcase, wondering how long it would take before he would be forced to make use of the weapon.

At long last, Boris appeared at the entrance to the building.

"Do you know this man?" the guard pointed in annoyance at Lev.

"Not personally, but I'm aware that I'm supposed to be interviewing somebody. Is that you?" Tolstoy asked with feigned indifference.

"I'm scheduled for an interview with Pavel Bantov, or alternatively, a Boris Tolstoy," Lev replied with just the perfect measure of deference.

"Follow me," Boris spun around without another word, motioning for Lev to follow him. The guard, however, blocked Lev's entrance.

"Boris, since when do you interview new agents? Are you sure someone isn't out to get you into trouble?" the guard asked.

"Trouble?" Boris raised his eyebrows. "Here? At headquarters? What's gotten into you, Vasily? Yesterday, I received notice from Comrade Bantov that I'd be interviewing a new agent. I'd appreciate it if you'd let me do my job," he added coldly.

The guard didn't appreciate the jibe. "You may appreciate it, but I won't allow a stranger to enter without written authorization from your superior."

"Look, Vasily," Boris immediately changed his approach. "Theoretically, you're right, but do you realize that you'll mess up the entire schedule for the day? If I have to approach Kodorov for authorization, then it's likely to take another half hour, and then it will already be my shift on guard duty, and how do you expect me to interview someone while I'm standing here?" Boris spoke quickly, trying to confuse the man, who was clearly torn between his obligation to follow orders and the fear of what would occur if he disrupted the rigid schedule.

"Look, Boris, if you're willing to sign that he entered during your shift, then we'll leave it at that," Vasily finally relented.

Boris hesitated himself, but then agreed. He signed his name in the register book, and then Lev followed him down a steep flight of steps into a storage room. As soon as the door closed behind them, Lev turned to the younger man with a penetrating gaze. "What went wrong?"

"They changed the guard schedule," Boris said tautly.

Lev stared at the man as if he was out of his mind. "Why didn't you tell me? The whole operation could have failed because of this!"

Boris wiped the perspiration from his brow. "I didn't have a chance to tell anyone. They made the change only a few hours ago, and it wasn't just my shift that was affected. Sasha's shift downstairs won't begin for another hour."

Lev winced. "Which means that I'm stuck here until then, and someone could find me here during that time."

"If you prefer, you can leave in half an hour, when my shift starts, and I'll let you back in later just before my shift ends," Tolstoy suggested.

Lev pressed his lips into a thin line. "No. I'm not leaving this place without my wife. Anything could happen within the next few hours and there's no guarantee that I'll be able to get back in. It's not worth the risk of leaving."

Boris nodded in agreement. "So stay, but not here. Too many workers go in and out of here."

"So where should I wait."

"My suggestion would be one of the observation rooms next to the interrogation rooms, or even in an empty cell." Noting Lev's expression at his last few words, he recanted. "Okay, not a cell, but the observation rooms are only in use during the nighttime hours, and you should be safe there."

Lev still looked skeptical. "Are you sure? Just imagine what would happen if one of the interrogators walked in and found me waiting there…"

"No, like I said, interrogations usually take place at night when the prisoners are at their weakest. But I have another idea. There's a tiny hallway between the rooms that I once stumbled on during a shift down there. If you stand there quietly, nobody will notice you. I'll tell Sergei to come and get you from there once he starts his shift."

The pair left the room and hurried down a long, gloomy hallway before descending several flights of steps. After walking what seemed like miles, Boris motioned with his foot toward a narrow, dark niche in the hallway. "It gets wider deeper in," he whispered. "Try to be patient."

Lev nodded his thanks, and Boris hurried quickly away. Lev made his way deeper into the niche which revealed itself as a very long, very narrow hallway – but froze in his tracks at the sound of a muted, agonized cry. Overcoming the shock, he reminded himself that he was in close proximity to the interrogation rooms and the prisoners' cells. The cry was definitely a woman's, and it sounded very close by. For a moment, he imagined that the voice was Anya's, but he knew that his imagination was playing tricks on him. It was impossible to identify someone's cry, especially when it was so weak and choked. Of course, Anya was so close by that he could almost feel her presence beside him, but it couldn't be her…

He had almost managed to overcome the horror and convince himself that it was another woman, when another voice sounded from behind the thin wall separating him from the interrogation room, a man's voice that addressed the weeping prisoner by the name, "Anya."

CHAPTER 34

Lev kept his ear pressed against the wall, listening intently, even as part of him wanted to block his ears and pretend that this was all some dreadful nightmare.

"Anya," the voice repeated from behind the wall. "You can end the suffering easily. You know you can. Why are you torturing yourself? It hurts me to see you doing this to yourself!"

There was no reaction, and even the pitiful wailing ceased momentarily.

"Fyodorev has forbidden any of us from speaking to you. If he discovers that I'm here, I'm done for, but I couldn't help myself. Anya, please! I'm begging you. Just tell them what they want and save yourself!"

The voice trembled in reply, a voice so weak that it barely sounded like Anya's. "But I don't know where he is! I don't have the information you want. I know you don't believe me, but I insisted that he shouldn't tell me, because I was terrified all along that this would happen."

"But I'm sure you can find out if you want to! You must know who to speak to in order to get that information."

The voice steadied, and now Lev clearly recognized it as Anya's. "I promise you that I don't. I made sure that I wouldn't know. They can torture me to death, but it won't help, because there's nothing I can tell them."

"But that's exactly what they'll do! Just give them something, anything! Even if it's not significant. Whatever it is, just so they'll let you alone." The man's voice was so gentle that Anya's angry response took her husband by surprise.

"Enough of this! If you came to still your guilty conscience, then you can go already. You've done your part, and you can leave. Just leave me alone! I have nothing left to say, not to you, and not to anyone else either."

The man refused to relent. "Maybe they'll agree to release you if you agree to find him."

Anya didn't reply, and the faceless man kept insisting. "At least they'll give you a few days' respite. You'll have something to eat. You'll be strong enough to stand on your own two feet. You'll go outside, see the sun, the sky, people!"

"Vladimir, believe me – even if they released me, I'd have no way of finding him." Anya lost control again and began weeping bitterly. Lev clenched his fists tightly and pressed them furiously against the wall, barely controlling his urge to pound on the rough plaster in an effort to break through and release his wife from captivity.

"But why shouldn't you be able to find him?" the interrogator continued, his voice still smooth as silk. "I'll help you, Anya. I'll never forget what you did for me when they threatened me with demotion, and I'd go out of my way to help you, even at my own risk."

"I won't let anyone risk himself for me," Anya replied stubbornly, the despair in her tone shattering Lev's heart into millions of shards. How he longed to let her know of his presence, to reassure her, that in this world full of evil, there were still those who genuinely cared about her and were willing to endanger themselves for her sake.

"I have to go now," Lev heard the man tell Anya. "I wish you would have told me something that could help, but you still have time to think over what I've said. But before I go, Anya, let me just give you some valuable advice. You still haven't demonstrated any remorse for what you did, during any of the interrogation sessions. You know as well as I do that even an apology can help to mitigate your punishment. If you won't cooperate, at least show some regret!"

Anya exhaled loudly, and it was clear that breathing was painful for her. "Vladimir, I *don't* regret what I did. Not for an instant. And after everything I've been through here, I simply don't have the physical strength to pretend to feel anything, let alone regret."

"But Anya, if you had the opportunity here and now to save your husband from the punishment he deserves, or to smuggle him out again, would you really do it, knowing what will happen to you as a result? Think of your daughter! Don't you feel anything for her?"

Tears were coursing down Lev's cheeks, and he could only imagine that his wife was crying too – in fact, he could hear the sobs in her voice as she answered.

"Of course I feel for her. But how could I face my daughter, grown up, asking where her father is, if I knew that I had abandoned him to his fate?"

The sound of a chair being roughly pushed back echoed through the wall, and then Lev heard a heavy iron door being swung shut and bolted. A single pair of footsteps echoed down the corridor, and Lev realized that only the interrogator had left the room – Anya remained there, alone and broken.

Frantically, Lev began to review the steps of his plan in his mind. Judging from the sound of Anya's labored breathing it was more than likely that his wife would be unable to walk, let alone run. If they carried her swiftly on a stretcher, he hoped they would still make it out, but it definitely complicated matters.

There was still time to wait before Sergei was due to come and tell him to emerge from his little crevice, but Lev could no longer bear his narrow, cramped hiding place, and he also feared that another interrogator could soon arrive to further torment his wife. Silently, slowly he slipped out of the narrow space – and then stopped in his tracks. From the other end of the corridor he could hear voices, probably those of two guards, talking and joking together. Should he retreat back into the crevice, or pretend that he belonged there?

Before he even had time to make up his mind, the guards turned the corner and came face to face with him. Lev stiffened up and nodded curtly toward them, pretending to be on his way to wherever they had come from.

The guards stared at him, and one extended his hand in friendly greeting. "I don't think I've seen you around here before. Are you a new employee?"

"Right. This is my first day on the job," Lev replied, with just the perfect tinge of excitement and pride.

The other guard sized him up. "And what's your position here?"

"Security in the lower floors."

The two agents exchanged a smirk. "You're the one who came to be interviewed by Boris today?"

Word of the incident got out, Lev realized in fear. *I'd better hurry.* "That's me," he nodded quickly. "And since I'm only here on trial basis, you'll forgive me if I don't stop to talk."

He didn't even wait for their answer before sidestepping them and hurrying down the hallway. Fortunately, the door to the basement was open, as Sergei had promised, and Sasha was waiting for him on the other side of the gate that surrounded the building.

Lev scanned the area in concern. "Where's the stretcher?" he whispered frantically. "As far as I could tell, we're going to need it already in the first phase of the rescue. She's in a very bad state."

Sasha's eyes widened anxiously. "We didn't bring a stretcher. It was too risky. We hoped that her condition wasn't so bad."

Anger and anxiety flooded Lev. *Why were so many aspects of the plan going awry?* "Why did you decide on your own without consulting me? We agreed that there would be a stretcher available if we needed it!" He proceeded to fill Sasha in on the discussion that he had overheard in Anya's cell.

Sasha listened quietly, his expression serious. "If that's the case, we'll have to delay the rescue until tomorrow. If Anya's condition is as bad as you describe, then we're going to have to adapt the plan. There's no sense in endangering the whole operation."

Lev fought his temptation to yell at Sasha that *he* was the one who had endangered the whole operation, forcibly reminding himself that this, too, was from Hashem – for what reason, he couldn't fathom. Nonetheless, he couldn't fight his fear, which was mounting by the minute. Shaking his head vigorously, he told Sasha, "No – we can't delay! That's not an option. We'll get her out of here somehow, with or without a stretcher."

"But you just said that she's not even up to walking, let alone escaping!" Sasha argued.

"So we'll have to brainstorm for a better solution," Lev replied through gritted teeth. "I won't let her stay here another day! They could kill her by tomorrow!"

Sasha placed a comforting arm on his shoulder. "They won't kill her, Lev. They're still hoping that she'll cooperate with them in finding you. As long as they think there's a chance of her talking, they'll keep her alive."

Lev mopped perspiration from his brow; even the frigid Moscow weather couldn't banish the fire consuming him from the inside out. "The trouble is that she's refusing to toss them those crumbs of hope. She has no idea that we're planning her rescue. She probably assumes that she has nothing left to live for anyway, which is why she's telling the truth."

"Maybe we should send her a message?" Sasha mused. "In any case, it's a good idea to prepare her, mentally, for the escape. Boris is supposed to be guarding her floor later tonight. Maybe he can whisper something to her."

Fear of the unknown was driving Lev out of his mind. "And if they catch him? And what if we don't get this same chance tomorrow? How soon is this Pavel Bantov supposed to return? What if he discovers that one of his guards decided to start interviewing new candidates for work?"

"Pavel returns to Moscow tomorrow evening, but he won't be coming back to work until the day after. We should be able to work things out for tomorrow. I'll go over the plan again with Sergei and Boris later tonight. As for you, Lev," he cast his friend a sympathetic look, "you pray. That's your role in all of this, and probably the most important one of all."

CHAPTER 35

Lev stole back into the KGB building the following evening under the cover of darkness. This time, he didn't dare to enter via the main entrance, instead circling the building from behind and crawling through the bushes until he reached the service exit of the basement level which Sergei had left open for him. The stretcher was already there, covered in canvas and hidden beneath a layer of branches. At nine o'clock, he heard a faint whistle and noticed movement near the wall. It was Sasha, and he inched slowly over to him until he could hear the other man whisper, "The coast is clear."

Lev picked up the stretcher, which was heavier and bulkier than he had expected, and then turned to enter the building. If anyone saw him, it would all be over, but there was no choice. If Anya was strong enough to make it out of the building on her own, they would abandon the stretcher in her cell, and if not… then hopefully they would still make it out.

"Which way?" he whispered to Sasha, trying to recall the route from the day before but failing to remember.

"Turn left and then down the stairs, two flights," Sasha replied, his voice so soft that it was barely audible. "Sergei will be waiting outside the cell, unless there's someone around in which case you should go back to the crevice and wait till he calls you."

Lev nodded, and then hoisted the stretcher in his arms before heading into the building. Despite the bulk of the stretcher, he made it down the stairs in record time, and met Sergei pacing nervously back and forth in the gloomy corridor.

"I've already spoken to her," he whispered urgently to Lev. "Your estimate was right, and there's no way she can walk unassisted, so it's a good thing you brought the stretcher. I'll help you with it until the exit, and then Sasha will take over."

Silently, Sergei approached the fourth cell in the row, and slipped a key into the heavy lock. The door swung open, and the two men slipped in, closing the door behind them. Lev glanced at the woman lying on the floor – not even on a bed or mattress – and could barely disguise his horror. Was this gaunt, pale woman, dressed in dirty clothing, her hair matted and filthy – really his wife? Maybe Sergei had made a mistake and it was some other woman? But the moment she opened her eyes, all his doubts vanished. The spark of life in her eyes, even in her debilitated state, was unmistakably Anya's. They exchanged a significant look but said nothing, the silence speaking louder than any words. Bending down, Lev and Sergei maneuvered her swiftly onto the stretcher and then Sergei pushed the door open with his foot as the two of them took hold of the wooden handles at either side. After stealing a glance into the corridor, thankfully still empty, they began their hurried escape, and a minute later, they were already on their way up the two flights of stairs, back to the exit.

The fear and tension were impossible, with both of them painfully aware of the ever-present danger hovering in the air. Sergei had sent the other wardens upstairs for a few minutes, but they were liable to return at any moment. As they lifted her up the steps, Anya stifled a cry of agony with each jolting movement, but their haste was not in vain. The very moment they reached the top, they heard footsteps from below.

"Run!" Sergei whispered frantically, and suddenly the short corridor that was all that separated them from the exit seemed like an impassable ocean. They ran as quickly as they could while still trying to maintain a steady grasp on the stretcher, but from behind, they already heard loud shouts.

"Stop or we'll shoot!" Before they could reply, they heard the gunfire. Bullets whizzed past them, but they didn't slow their pace for a second.

"Crouch down!" Sergei called out to Lev, who was already bent down low over the stretcher, trying to shield Anya from the bullets as he ran.

"Just one more second and we're out of here!" he pleaded to Sergei, suddenly afraid that the other man would simply drop the stretcher and run for his life – but he didn't.

They reached the exit. Sergei was first to inhale the night air, and he dragged the stretcher after him, with Lev holding on tight. A moment before he was about to slam the door behind him and lock it, he watched Lev reel forward and his face change colors.

"Grab her!" Lev cried with his last ounce of strength, before he sank to the ground. A deep red stain began to spread over his uniform shirt, soaking it in an instant. Sergei was so shocked that he almost lost his wits, and it was Anya who suddenly jerked upright and cried, "He was shot! Lev! Lev, do you hear me?"

Lev struggled to shake his head. "Run. Go... hurry..."

"I won't leave you here!" she wept.

"You must! Otherwise... it's all for nothing," he gasped, barely able to utter the words. His strength was ebbing fast with the blood loss and he closed his eyes against the hard, cold reality.

Unable to resist, Anya felt the stretcher being lifted again as Sasha grabbed hold of the side that Lev had dropped and ran, with Sergei, toward the street where a car awaited them. Lev was abandoned in a pool of blood directly outside the building.

"Let go of me!" she screamed. "Go back for Lev!"

Sasha clapped a hand over her mouth as they scurried forward and leaped into the car. The driver tore away seconds before the entire street was awakened to the ensuing scene of chaos. Sirens screamed and wailed throughout the next hour while the vicinity swarmed with furious KGB officers who arrested any pedestrian unfortunate enough to be wandering around the neighborhood at that ill-fated hour.

And yet, apart from Lev Krasnikov, who was found bleeding and unconscious outside the building, no one who had taken part in the jailbreak was captured that night.

Anya awoke to a haze, but refused to open her eyes. During the past two weeks, she had found it easier to keep her eyes closed, in an attempt to escape her harsh reality; and now, she used the same technique to delay confronting the confusion. Her memories of the past hours were a jumble and she had no idea how to separate between imagination, hope, and desperation. It was far easier to simply refuse to think.

As she lay there, however, she slowly began to realize that something had changed. She was no longer lying on cold, hard cement, but rather on something soft – and she was warm, with something sweet-smelling covering her. In her weakened state it seemed like eons since she had felt so comfortable, but a horrible suspicion suddenly erased her pleasure. Had she capitulated to her captors? Had she given away information in return for this comfort? Had she promised them that she would help them find her husband? She couldn't recall having done so, but her mind was so fuzzy – maybe it had betrayed her?

The sound of muted voices in her vicinity finally motivated her to open her eyes, and what she saw made her blink in astonishment. She wasn't in her cell at all, but rather in a bright, warm room. It took several moments, but then the memories flooded her mind, and she felt her heart plummet. She was out of jail. Lev had rescued her, but the plan had somehow gone wrong. Lev had been left behind! The image of her husband lying prostrate on the ground, in a pool of blood, hit her forcefully.

"Lev!" she shouted. "Lev! Where is my husband?"

A pretty young woman scurried to her bedside. "Anya! You're up! I'm so happy! How are you feeling?"

"Who are you? Where am I?" The room swirled dizzyingly around her, and Anya was suddenly consumed with fear.

"It's okay, Anya. You're in good hands now. I'm Sergei's sister, and you're in a safe place. A doctor will be here soon to help you, and he'll treat your wounds. Then, we'll deal with the future."

"What about my husband? Where is he? Is he alive? We can't leave him there!"

The young woman nodded compassionately and squeezed Anya's hand.

"Stop! Why aren't you telling me more? Don't worry about me. Somebody has to go back for Lev! He's in a much worse state than I am."

"I know. I know."

"Is anybody trying to help? Has somebody gone for him?"

The woman was silent for a moment and nodded noncommittally.

"What time is it? It's light outside. It must be afternoon almost.

Are they waiting for evening?"

The woman extended a cup of tea, sweet with honey and lemon. "They'll be here soon, and they'll tell you whatever they know. Now you have to get your strength back, drink and eat something. You're terribly dehydrated. Have you had anything to eat the entire time you were there?"

Anya squeezed her eyes shut, struggling to overcome the wave of nausea that threatened to engulf her. "Food isn't what matters now… Nothing matters now, except for Lev… Where are they? Are they helping him? When he's safely out of there, I promise to eat and drink and do whatever you tell me, but I need to know that he's safe first!"

A tear glistened in the woman's eye, and Anya stared at her in fear. "Drink, Anya dear. You need to drink something to regain your strength. It'll be easier for you then. You'll see."

Anya struggled to understand what the woman was saying – and what she wasn't – but she lacked the energy to focus her thoughts long enough to figure things out or to protest at not having her questions answered properly. Instead, she allowed her to place the cup to her lips, and she sipped carefully, feeling the energy enter her body along with the steaming beverage.

A moment later, she spoke again. "Please, I want to hear every detail of your plan to rescue Lev. I know the building inside and out. I can help you."

Nina, Sergei's sister, inclined her head but said nothing. She knew that she had to take advantage of these precious hours and infuse Anya with the physical strength and stamina to cope with the bitter truth.

CHAPTER 36

Though she tried to stay awake long enough to hear some news of her husband, Anya soon succumbed to her exhaustion and fell asleep again. Meanwhile, the doctor came and went, leaving strict orders with Nina to feed Anya small quantities every hour. "For two weeks, she ate almost nothing," he noted, "and she has to be very careful what she eats, at first."

Nina apologized profusely every time she roused Anya to eat; how she wished she could just let her sleep and forget about all that she had endured. Gradually, however, the terror in Anya's eyes each time Nina woke her was replaced by a calmer expression, as she internalized the fact that she was no longer a prisoner. By evening, some of the color had returned to her face, and she was strong enough to sit up in bed.

"When are they going to get Lev?" was her first question.

"Someone will be here soon to explain," Nina replied uncomfortably

Anya treated the younger woman to a penetrating stare. "Explain what? What's there to explain?"

"He'll be here soon," Nina said soothingly.

Anya shook her head vehemently. "No! I don't like this. I don't need explanations. All I want to know is that somebody is going in to save Lev, and soon. I know it's dangerous, but we have to do it!"

When Anatoly Andrayev entered her room, all color drained from Anya's features, sure that this was the end. Andrayev was one of the highest-ranking officials in her department in the KGB, and if he was here now, it was clear that she had fallen back into their hands. All this soft treatment was merely designed to trick her, to deceive her into cooperating with them. But she would never betray her husband – never.

Andrayev read her mind as soon as he saw her clenched jaw. "There's nothing to be afraid of, Anya. It's not what you think. I was the one who helped Lev all along. You've just been exposed to one of the biggest secrets in the KGB – my real identity."

Anya narrowed her eyes suspiciously. "Why should I believe you?"

Andrayev gazed frankly at her. "Because I want to help you. And because Lev believed me too, and trusted me. My plan is to smuggle you out of the Soviet Union and to America, where you'll settle together with your daughter. Who knows? Maybe, one day, you'll even reach Israel."

Anya was silent for a long moment. "What do you want in exchange?"

"Just that you should pray for me."

Anya returned a puzzled look. "I don't even know how to pray."

"You'll learn. I'm sure of it. You have much to learn, Anya. Lev planned to study with you, to teach you. He spoke with me about this many times."

Anya stared in confusion. Lev had been learning about Judaism for two years before he had been discovered, or so he claimed, and not even once had he mentioned anything to her. If he was so eager to share his newfound knowledge with his wife, why hadn't he done so already? Yes, it would have been dangerous, but how could he have kept something so obviously central to his life a secret from her?

"When did you speak about this?"

"While we were developing your escape plan. He couldn't bear the thought that you were suffering without even knowing why, without understanding what it means to be a Jew."

Anya swallowed her tears. "I'll speak to him about it myself. How soon do you expect him to be here?"

"He won't be here in the near future." Anatoly broke the news gently and with boundless compassion.

Anya felt as if all the wind had been knocked out of her, and the little color that she had regained promptly drained from her face. "You mean… You mean, he's… gone?"

Anatoly was quick to reassure her. "Not at all. He's very much alive, but he was wounded pretty badly, and he's back in their hands and under triple guard. At this point, we have no way of breaking him out of there."

Anya's sigh very much resembled a sob. "There's no such thing as 'no way.' It might be hard, dangerous even, but we have to try!"

A door slammed somewhere in the house, interrupting the ensuing silence. Anatoly met Anya's eyes and shook his head. "It's not a matter of trying or not trying. You know that as well as I do. We would spare no effort to get him out of there safely, but right now, anything we would try is tantamount to suicide."

Anya shook her head and screwed her eyes shut as she began to weep. "I won't accept it. Lev wouldn't have accepted such an answer. Do you know what those beasts can do to a wounded man?"

"Yes, I know," Anatoly admitted, "but we can't risk ourselves for the impossible."

"We can't give up so easily either!" Anya opened her eyes again, eyes that blazed in anger and despair. "I'll help you. I'll do everything I can. We'll come up with a way to fool them. We both have friends in the building and we can find a way to get past even a triple guard!"

"Anya, by doing so, you would be condemning all those friends of yours to death. The guards they have stationed outside Lev's cell are no amateurs. They're the most professional, and they'll fire without hesitation on anyone who looks even remotely suspicious."

"Why did you agree to help Lev rescue me?" she changed the subject suddenly. "Didn't it expose both of you to danger? Didn't you suspect that it might end in failure?"

"It was dangerous, yes. And I did try to talk Lev out of it. But at least there was a chance of it succeeding. Now, however, after your escape, they're prepared for an attempted rescue, which makes it completely impossible."

Anya sank back on her pillow, but even in her weakness, she couldn't stifle the cry that issued from the innermost depths of her soul. "No! I won't hear of it! I'll recover, and I'll get him out of there myself, with or without anyone's help!"

Anatoly turned to stand by the window, and he spoke in a voice uncharacteristically heavy with pity. "Anya, life is too precious to be cast away recklessly. Lev won't gain his freedom, and you'll lose everything."

"I don't care! I can't carry on living knowing that I didn't try! I have nothing left to lose!"

"You're wrong. Life is the greatest, most precious gift we own. Even when it's hard, even when it's intolerable, even if it's spent in jail or in a labor camp in Siberia. Life is an inestimably valuable gift from G-d, and it's not even ours to cast away. You must grasp onto life with all your might and do with it as G-d wills."

Anya gazed at Andrayev in disbelief mingled with horror. Who mentioned G-d in Soviet Russia? "Since when does religion or G-d play a part in our lives?" she blurted out. "We believe in the greater good of Communism."

Andrayev's face contorted into a sardonic smile but his eyes were sad. "The greater good of Communism, Anya? What greater good? The good that landed you and your husband in jail and subjected you to torture? The Communism that forces its beliefs on us with an iron fist and oppression and dispatches all who disagree to Siberia? It's time we focused on true beliefs, Anya. It's not education or beliefs that Communism espouses, but terror, oppression and death."

"You dare to say it aloud?"

"Not in public, but in private, yes. Because life is meaningful to me. I discovered real life along with the beauty of the Jewish Torah."

It was so strange, practically inconceivable, to hear such words. "What are you talking about?" Anya struggled to sit up again, supporting herself against the wall. Since when did senior KGB agents dabble in Judaism? She closed her eyes, wondering if she would open them to emerge from this nightmare.

"I'm a Jew, Anya. Just like you. But unlike you, I've recently begun to discover all that was hidden from us for generations, just as your husband did. When you begin learning, you'll understand my feelings. You'll see why your husband was willing to risk so much to learn, and what gives his life meaning, even now, in captivity."

Anya rubbed her eyes, as if trying to emerge from a heavy slumber. "Where is my daughter?" she asked suddenly. "My daughter and my mother-in-law! Where are they?"

When Anatoly didn't immediately respond, she grew hysterical. "No! Don't tell me that the KGB has them too! I won't be able to bear it…" She began to sob pitifully.

"No, Anya – don't worry! The KGB hasn't found them!" Anatoly responded forcefully, trying to shake Anya out of her fears. "There have been attempts to find them, but nobody's succeeded yet."

"So where are they?" Anya's voice rose anxiously.

"Hiding. Somewhere. We're looking for them, but we have to do so carefully if we don't want to expose ourselves."

The door opened, and Nina entered and quietly placed a small tray on the bedside table. "Anya, it's time to eat," she said with a playful smile. "It's been an hour already."

Anya glanced at the food. It was obvious that Nina had done her best to make the bland meal appear appetizing in order to whet her appetite, but she couldn't bring herself to taste a thing. The future seemed cold and hopeless, and Anya wondered if there was any purpose in prolonging her struggle for survival.

Is there anything left for me to live for? Lev is gone, nobody knows where Karina is, and who knows if I'll ever see either of them again…

As the fatigue overcame her, the only image she could conjure up before her eyes was that of the last time she had seen her husband before his escape from prison, before she forced him to leave the building. His eyes had shone with a strange light, and although there had been no time for him to explain, somehow, she had understood that he had discovered something that had changed his life.

He had wanted her to know, to understand, to study for herself, and now he had given his freedom in order that she should be free to live and to learn. Surely it would be a betrayal of all that he had held dear if she did not at least try to follow in his footsteps.

CHAPTER 37

Natalya Kolchik sat on the bus, gazing sightlessly out the window at the row of trees lining the street. Gleaming icicles dangling from the bare branches cast an almost surreal beauty upon her city, but the winter wonderland was the farthest thing from her mind. Her thoughts were in one place, or more correctly, with one person alone.

Anya Krasnikov. Oh, Anya! Who would have believed it? Brilliant, beautiful, talented Anya Krasnikov, one of her best friends in the whole world! The girl who had progressed from being uncontested class princess into one of the few female senior KGB officers. Anya, with whom most women in the Soviet Union wouldn't have hesitated to traded places, was now languishing in a KGB dungeon, probably never to emerge again. The thought of how life could change in an instant, catapulting a person from the heights of glory to the depths of despair, sent a chill up Natalya's spine.

The truth was that while she had always loved and admired

Anya, Natalya had also envied her. Who didn't, after all? Anya's life was the realization of every woman's dream. She was rich, beautiful, intelligent, successful, and blessed with a devoted husband and adorable child. Beyond that, Anya herself was kind, generous, and renowned for her personal integrity. Only six months previously, Natalya had traveled to her friend's home in the city center and pleaded for Anya's assistance. Her request hadn't been simple, Natalya knew, but Anya had gone out of her way to accommodate her. And Natalya wasn't the only one she had helped, either – as far as she knew, Anya had frequently used her position to extend her assistance to others. It was only because of Anya that Natalya's son had received his coveted job with the KGB, and Natalya was deeply indebted to her for that. Who would believe that a woman as powerful as Anya would one day be stripped of everything and cast into the lowest pit?

In fact, she was so accustomed to viewing Anya as larger than life that it was difficult to believe what had happened. Simultaneously, she was appalled at the feeling of victory that crept into her mind, along with the horror at her friend's fate. For once in her life, Anya would know what it was to suffer, to fail. Throughout her life, Anya had progressed from one success to the next, stirring everyone's envy; now, she would experience what it felt like to be on the other side.

Recalling Anya's goodness, Natalya was instantly ashamed of herself for feeling like that. Why should she wish evil on a woman as kind and generous as Anya? Because of those first months in high school when Anya had ignored her? Since then, Anya had made a complete change in her approach. Surely she didn't deserve this treatment, regardless of what she had done.

As she alighted from the bus at the stop closest to her apartment building, Natalya wondered what news Sasha would bring home that day from work. He had shared little with her since the scandal had broken, but he looked unusually tired and anxious. Natalya hoped that this indicated that he was doing well on the job, and not the opposite.

She walked the two blocks to her home quickly, planning to use the next three hours to do some long overdue cleaning, before her husband and son returned. To her surprise, when she inserted her key into the lock, the door swung open. Someone had arrived home before her.

"Dmitri? Sasha?" she called out as she walked in. A voice called back to her from an inner room; it was her son, and she found him sitting, staring out of the window in his bedroom.

"Sasha!" she cried in surprise. "What are you doing home so early? Aren't you feeling well?"

Sasha turned his head slowly to face her. "I didn't come home early. I didn't go to work today at all."

"You didn't go to work?" The notion was virtually unheard of.

"Right."

Her son's slumped posture made Natalya's heart thump wildly. "Do you want to tell me what's going on?"

"There's not much to tell. I got myself into a bit of trouble, and I think it's best if I stay out of sight for the next few days."

Natalya dropped her pocketbook onto the floor with a thud. "Are you out of your mind, Sasha? Running away won't solve your problems! Worse yet, they could even fire you!"

"So they'll fire me."

She took a large step toward him, appall written all over her features. *"So they'll fire me?"* she repeated in disbelief.

"I can always find another job." Sasha studied his fingernails intently.

"Sasha, do you remember how hard it was to get you this job? As I'm sure you're aware, my friend isn't quite up to helping you again right now."

Sasha nodded his head. "I know."

"Sasha, I want you to tell me exactly what is going on!" Natalya demanded. "It's my right as your mother."

Sasha met his mother's gaze. "Mama, sometimes, it's better not to know."

Natalya froze in fear. "Sasha, what are you saying?"

"That it's best for you to know nothing. I called in sick to work, and I told them that it might take several days before I feel better. That's all. You don't have to know anything more than that."

Natalya struggled to swallow her anger. Turning on her heel, she stalked to the kitchen where she put up the kettle. A good, strong tea would calm her down and help both of them think logically, or at least she hoped so. She found a poppy-seed cake in the pantry and sliced several pieces. Five minutes later, she knocked on her son's door holding a tray.

"Here, Sasha," she said gently. "Let's eat something and have a talk."

The steaming tea defrosted the tension in the air. After watching her son down three slices of cake, she tried again. "Now I'd like to know what's going on."

"Mama, think good and hard if you really want to know. It won't be easy for you to handle, and once I tell you, you can't change your mind."

Natalya pierced him with a solid stare. "I want to know."

Sasha sighed. "I helped a prisoner break out of jail yesterday."

"*WHAT?*" Natalya hardly even realized that she was shouting, and she lost complete control of her senses. "Are you out of your mind? How reckless and irresponsible can you be? Do you have any idea what they could do to you now?"

A weak smile flashed across her son's handsome features. "Yes and no. But I acted with full awareness of what I was doing, and I have a clean conscience."

She stared at him in shock and disbelief. "Who? Who was worth risking your life and future like that?"

"Who do you think?"

The teacup fell out of her hand and shattered on the floor, but she was too agitated to notice. "I can't think at all right now! The only thing I can think is that my son has gone completely crazy and just destroyed his own life and future!" She burst into tears.

Sasha rose and addressed his mother sharply. "Of course you know who I'm talking about. How many people do you know imprisoned in the KGB dungeons?"

"How could you, Sasha?! How could you walk into a trap like that! Forget about being fired; they'll arrest you! You're a KGB officer and now a traitor!"

"Please calm down, Mama. They don't know who was involved. I managed to switch shifts that night, so my name doesn't even appear on the roster. I'm really hoping things will work out okay."

"Since when are you so naïve? How are things going to work out okay? You know what they'll do when they find you, and they'll find you! What were you thinking? Why did you let yourself be blinded by emotion and a little debt that you owe?"

Sasha spoke with deep conviction. "I do owe her, Mama. She went out of her way to help me because she's your friend, and the time came for me to repay her for that act of friendship."

"Not at the expense of your life!"

Sasha sighed again and returned to his perch at the window. "Mama, I didn't give up my life for this. All I did was help her break out of jail. Nobody caught me, and in the meantime, everything is fine. I think it's best that we end this conversation now and not speak about it again. Okay? Please, Mama, calm down and don't worry."

"Calm down? Don't worry? I wish! Oh, Sasha… What have you done?" Natalya shook her head, and two tears rolled down her cheek.

Three days later, four officers from the KGB banged on the door in the middle of the night and led Sasha away in handcuffs. His parents never saw him again.

Katerina waited over half an hour for Natalya's train to arrive, although she said nothing about her extended wait when her friend finally alighted at the station. They walked side by side toward Katerina's apartment, trying to keep up a lighthearted chatter reminiscent of the days of their youth, but it was pointless. Natalya's face was pale and drawn, and she couldn't contain the sighs that escaped her lips at frequent intervals.

"This must be so difficult for you," Katerina murmured sympathetically. "How are you holding up? Have you managed to meet with him yet?"

"No, and they warned us that we'd better not even try, at least in the near future, if we don't want to end up there ourselves. In any case, it won't help Sasha."

"Were you able to bribe anyone to smuggle food into his cell?"

Natalya wiped a stray tear from her eye. "After everything that's been going on there, no one is willing to take the risk. It seems like the KGB chief went ballistic after Anya's escape, and every officer, worker, and guard is quaking in his shoes. The staff is being summoned for interrogations one after the other, and anyone even suspected of doing anything wrong is being punished severely. There's nobody to talk to."

"It's probably best to wait until things settle down," Katerina said soothingly. "Right now, it's a steaming cauldron, but it'll calm down eventually. As soon as it does, you'll be able to help Sasha in ways that you can't right now."

"But my son has to survive until then!" Natalya retorted sharply.

Katerina nodded. "I know, Natalya, I know. All I want to do is show you that there is light at the end of the tunnel."

"There's no light, Katerina. None at all," Natalya replied bitterly. "And what makes me even angrier is that Anya didn't think twice before asking my son to risk his life and freedom for her. How dare she take advantage of his good heart and indebtedness to her, for her own benefit?"

"You mean she asked him to do it and arranged it herself?"

Natalya paused and thought about it. "I guess not. Her husband was the one behind it."

"So why are you angry at Anya?"

"Because she's free, and my son paid for her freedom with his own freedom, and possibly his life! The least she could do is turn herself in now in order to get Sasha out of jail."

Katerina halted mid-step and stared at her friend intently. "You know that even if she did that, they still wouldn't release Sasha. The KGB doesn't cut deals with anyone."

"So what?" Natalya spat furiously. "She doesn't deserve to enjoy her liberty when my son lost everything for her sake. I'm telling you, if I had a chance, I'd turn her in myself, even if Sasha wouldn't benefit from it! At the very least, they would give him preferential treatment if I helped them out. I can't take this any longer!"

Katerina was so appalled by what she heard that she couldn't muster a single word in reply.

CHAPTER 38

A small lamp burned on the nightstand in Anya's room, casting long shadows on the wall. It was early evening, and the doctor had just arrived to visit his patient and check up on her.

"She didn't eat supper?" the doctor gestured to the untouched supper tray on the table.

Nina shrugged. "I can't force-feed her. I try – but it doesn't help much."

"No, it is helping. She is eating something and regaining her strength, but at this rate, it's going to take a long time." The doctor frowned. "Her vital signs are all normal, but if her spirits remain so depressed, then… Well, let's hope she gets better soon," he forced himself to conclude on a more positive note.

Anya shifted in bed. "Please," she said quietly, "don't talk about me as if I'm not here."

"You are most certainly here!" the doctor replied firmly, "and you surely heard what I just said. You have to start eating in greater quantities. There's no reason not to any more, and your body needs the extra energy to build itself up again."

Anya nodded absently. "I know, I know," she murmured. "But," she turned to Nina, "it would be so different if I at least knew something about my daughter and mother-in-law. If only I knew they were safe, it would be so much easier for me to deal with everything. But I'm going out of my mind worrying about Karina!"

Nina started to reply something, but the doctor didn't even hear her words – hearing the name "Karina" had caused a red light to flicker in his mind. "Your daughter is named Karina?" he asked suddenly.

"Yes," Anya's voice caught in her throat. "But nobody knows where she's hiding, or even if she's alive."

"Is she a little blond girl who's being cared for by an older woman?"

Anya sat up in bed instantly, and her eyes sparked with fear mingled with hope. "You know something? Have you seen her?"

"Two weeks ago, I was called to attend to a little girl by the name of Karina." The doctor didn't continue, but his eyes held a huge question mark.

"Where is she? How did you find her? Who called you? And, oh no… What's wrong with her? Is she ill? Why did she need to see a doctor?" The outpouring of questions coupled with the sudden onslaught of emotion returned the color to Anya's cheeks.

"Nobody said it outright, but it looked to me like they were in hiding."

"Where are they?" Anya demanded, struggling to contain the trembling that had overtaken her.

"I promised not to tell anyone…" the doctor replied hesitantly.

"Even her mother? We've been searching the whole country for her!"

"How can you be so certain it's your daughter?" the doctor countered.

Anya forced herself to think and respond rationally; hysteria would accomplish nothing. "Nothing in life is ever certain, doctor. But a little girl named Karina who is being taken care of by an older woman and who seems to be in hiding definitely matches the daughter I'm looking for."

"Then let me double-check the facts before I answer you."

"Is she very ill?" Anya's voice caught in her throat.

The doctor chose his words carefully. "She's recuperating. She had a bad case of pneumonia, but she's getting stronger every day."

"Karina!" Anya began to cry. "It's Karina! I know it is. She's sick and she needs me! Please doctor!" she begged, her eyes brimming with tears. "You have nothing to worry about. You can tell me where they are. Even if it turns out that this little girl isn't mine, no one in the world will ever discover who she is or where she's staying. You can trust me. Believe me, I've suffered enough under their hands."

"Anya, if she is your daughter, I'll bring her with me tomorrow. Don't worry."

But Anya couldn't stop worrying.

She lay awake all night long, waiting anxiously for news. She didn't believe that if the child the doctor had treated was really her Karina they would wait until morning; they wouldn't add to her suffering for nothing. Yet the hours stretched on interminably, with no news. The first rays of dawn streaking the dark blue sky erased the final traces of Anya's hopes.

The doctor arrived for his daily visit at the regular hour, but Anya didn't even turn around to face him, unable to bear the heartbreaking answer.

"Mamochka?" a sweet little voice sounded from the doorway. Anya's heart skipped a beat. Was her distress causing her to hallucinate?

"Mamochka?" the voice sounded nearer now, and a second later, she felt familiar arms wrap around her. Anya turned around, prying the little arms off her and staring at her daughter in shock.

"Mamochka? Mamochka, where were you? I didn't know where you were! I missed you so much!" Karina cried.

Unable to contain the flood of emotion, Anya let her defenses fall and surrendered to the ocean of tears that washed over her. She grabbed Karina and pressed her tightly against her chest as if to protect her from anyone who would dare try to snatch her away.

"Karina! My Karina! My precious!" she whispered again and again, smothering the child with hugs and kisses, which the little girl returned with all her heart.

Anatoly Andrayev glanced across the room at Karina, who was curled up comfortably on the bed, sound asleep. Anya's eyes barely left her small, fragile figure.

"I'm glad that we found them," he said firmly, "because now there's no more reason to delay the next stage of the plan."

"What next stage."

"We've arranged a night flight out of here in two days that will take you to Vienna. The forged passports and other documents have been ready for a while now – we were only waiting to find Karina and your mother-in-law."

Anya jumped to her feet, scandalized at the thought. "I'm not going anywhere, Anatoly!"

Andrayev wasn't impressed by the drama. "You have to. We can't continue hiding you here forever."

"So I'll move somewhere else, but I want it to be clear that I'm not leaving the country without Lev."

"You're not helping him by staying. On the contrary, you're just adding to his worries. If he knew you were safe, it would make his suffering so much easier to bear."

Anya shook her head. "Don't tell me about suffering and what makes it harder or easier. I'm not leaving to start a new life without my husband! There's nothing to talk about!"

"Anya," Anatoly maintained a cool façade, knowing that begging Anya to see his point of view would accomplish nothing. "Please, try to think rationally. You've endured too much to let yourself get carried away with your emotions. We have to be practical if you really want to help Lev."

Anya choked back her tears and turned her head to face the wall. "I'm not up to talking about escaping right now. Please, just leave me alone."

Silently, Andrayev nodded and left the room.

The next day, he returned with a somber expression. "Anya, Lev wants you to leave. I know it – because he told me so."

Anya gaped. "You spoke to him?"

Andrayev nodded. "I bribed the guards, and although they wouldn't open the door to his cell, they opened the little hatch and we spoke through it. Anya, he wants you to leave. He was overwhelmed to hear that you were free, that the plan succeeded, and that you now have an opportunity to get out of here with Karina and his mother. And think about it, Anya. You can't live the rest of your life in hiding. It's just not possible. But, now, in any case, you have no reason to stay. Lev told me to tell you that he begs you to leave. He said that once you're out of Russia, you'll be able to learn about Judaism, just like he did, and then you'll understand what this is really all about. He had only one request." Andrayev paused and looked intently at Anya, to see how she was taking this new information.

Anya seemed shell-shocked, and she was drinking in Andrayev's words thirstily – they were the only real communication she had

had from her husband in weeks. "You really spoke to him…" she whispered, making no effort to hide her emotion. "How… how is he? Did he recover yet from the gunshot wound?"

Andrayev nodded. "He's doing okay. Still weak, but okay. Anya, he begs you to leave. For your sake, and, even more importantly, for Karina. He wants her to grow up in a country where she can be free to be a Jew. He wants his mother to live out the rest of her life in a free country, and for you to experience the beauty of a Jewish life."

Anya was silent for a long moment. Finally, she remembered to ask, "You said he had a request?"

"Yes." Andrayev's voice was soft yet persuasive. "He asks you to pray for him. To learn what prayer, real prayer means, and then to pray for him. He said that prayer is the only thing that can really help – the only thing that you can do for him. We'll still do all we can to get him released, but your role in this is over now, Anya. He wants you to leave, and with G-d's help, he'll follow after you."

Anya buried her face in her hands. "How can prayers help? The KGB is evil! Totally evil!"

"No, Anya, Lev is right," Andrayev insisted. "Prayer really is the only thing that can help, although we still have to do our best to make things happen, and we will. In any case, don't give me your answer now. Think about it, and I'll come back tomorrow and we'll talk again."

Anya nodded, her face flushed, her eyes bright with tears.

The next morning, the morning of the flight, Anya informed Andrayev that she would board the plane that evening.

The strong lighting in the airport was disorienting, turning night into day. Anya walked swiftly through the concourse, Karina at her side, her mother-in-law not far behind, reflecting that if everything went smoothly, these were the last steps she would take on Soviet soil. This was a country she now despised, and although it had been her home for all of her life, she felt no surge of emotion at the thought of leaving, other than the throbbing pain in her heart that never ceased to remind her that Lev was remaining behind.

The name in her passport read "Oksana Minchik" and Anya hoped desperately that nobody would recognize her. In truth, she hardly recognized herself; her face was still gaunt and wan from her ordeal in prison, her hair had been dyed and cut in a new style, and the collar of her fur coat partially concealed her features. Karina had stared when she first saw her mother, but somehow, she had understood enough not to ask questions.

Thankfully, their flight was not delayed, and promptly at midnight, the plane took off, first soaring high above Moscow and then rapidly covering the miles until they left Soviet airspace and entered the free world. By then, Karina was already fast asleep, as was Valeria, but Anya remained awake, staring unseeingly out of the little windowpane, her eyes dry of tears.

Lev had wanted her to leave, but how hard it was to desert him… If only she had been able to speak to him one last time, to hear for herself his words of parting. But of course, that would have been totally impossible. It was incredible enough that Andrayev had managed to speak with him. Bribing more than one guard was extremely risky, and what excuse could Andrayev possibly have conjured up in order to explain his presence in the interrogation cells? His line of work rarely, if ever, took him there.

The more she thought about it, the more she was amazed that anyone had succeeded in accessing Lev. Hadn't Andrayev himself told her that he was under triple guard, with orders to shoot at the sight of a suspicious individual? So how had he managed to get through? Suddenly, an awful suspicion shot through Anya's mind, and she started to tremble. Had Andrayev really gotten through? Had he really spoken to Lev – or had he fabricated the whole tale in order to get her to leave? Why had she believed him? The story of bribing a guard was so far-fetched – how could she have been so stupid as to fall for his trickery?

Hot tears rose to Anya's eyes, and she swiped them away furiously. He had deceived her! He had knowingly deceived her, at such a vulnerable time, and now, here she was, on an airplane to freedom – without her husband at her side. She had sworn never to leave him and now she was on her way to Vienna leaving Lev behind in the dungeons of the KGB, alone, hungry, cold, probably tortured…

Stop! Anya wanted to scream. *Stop the plane right now, and take me back! Take me to my husband! I can't leave him! I can't! I won't!* But even as the words echoed through her mind, she knew how futile was her protest, and how hopeless her cause. Even if she had stayed, she would still have been so far from Lev. And if they had found her, then what would have become of Karina?

Anya cast a sideways glance at her little girl, sleeping soundly in the seat next to her. She owed it to Karina to leave, to give her a chance of leading a normal life. Wasn't that what Lev would have wanted?

Andrayev was also a husband and father. He knew the dangers of his way of life, and still he risked everything, each and every day, for a cause he believed in, the same cause for which her own husband had forfeited his freedom. Would he have told his wife and children to leave? And, if he had been unable to tell them himself, would he not have been glad that somebody else convinced them to escape while they still could?

Although she still felt intense anger at the man who had deceived her, Anya could not avoid reaching the conclusion that, had Lev really been given the opportunity to tell her what he wanted her to do, he would have told her exactly what Andrayev had conveyed.

CHAPTER 39

The unfamiliar address in Vienna led them to a modest neighborhood in a suburb of the city. Valeria and Karina were both disoriented from the flight, and Anya still couldn't calm down completely after her shocking revelation.

They knocked on a plain wooden door and were invited to enter. A clerk sitting behind a desk handed Anya three plane tickets to the United States and explained that the flight was scheduled for one week hence, and that they would be accommodated in a quiet hotel on the banks of the Danube River for the interim. The woman, seasoned by years of life experience, studied Anya discreetly, and immediately discerned the emotional fatigue and stress that flickered in her haunted eyes.

"It'll be a good respite for you after your ordeal," she said kindly. "You'll have plenty of time to rest up, and once you're feeling up to it, you can tour the city which was once renowned as the most beautiful in all of Europe."

Anya wasn't sure why the comment riled her, but she angrily retorted, "We didn't come here on vacation."

"I know," the woman, sweet and modestly-attired, attempted to placate her, "and I'm sorry that we couldn't arrange an earlier flight for you, but we were worried that if you flew on straight away, it could attract unwanted attention."

Valeria took the tickets from Anya's hands and placed them deep inside her coat pocket. "We have no complaints at all! Only tremendous thanks," she assured the woman. "And you're right; the last few weeks have been difficult ones, and it will do us all good to spend the time together, relaxing and enjoying."

"If you need anything, please don't hesitate to ask me," the woman added.

Embarrassed by her sharp words, Anya choked out a stiff "Thank you," but couldn't bring herself to add anything else. Fortunately, Valeria took over, shaking the woman's hand warmly and expressing her thanks profusely. "We can never thank you enough for all you've done for us," she told her. "Only G-d can repay you for your kindness."

Anya whipped around, shocked at her mother-in-law's casual mention of "G-d." It was the first time she had ever heard the word escape her lips; since when did Valeria Krasnikov believe in a Higher Power – other than Communism? Too overwrought to think straight, Anya kept her thoughts to herself, saying nothing even after they left the office and took a taxi to their hotel.

Karina was the first to recover from the journey, and the following morning saw her pressed against the picture window, gaping at the majesty of the rushing Danube. Soon she was begging to be let loose beyond the confines of the small room.

"Why don't we take a walk around the city?" Valeria suggested, trying to infuse some brightness into the heavy atmosphere. "I doubt we'll ever have the opportunity to see Vienna in all its glory again!"

"You two can go out together," Anya replied listlessly. "I'm not really in the mood right now."

Valeria studied her daughter-in-law with a frown. Leaving her son behind in Russia as a prisoner of the KGB was no less agonizing for her than for Anya, but she had vowed to be strong. Anya, on the other hand, seemed completely broken, and Valeria hoped that a few hours of rest and solitude would be good for her.

Anya accompanied them as far as the street, but didn't return to her hotel room as planned. Instead, she circled the building to find herself on the banks of the Danube. Some fifty yards along the bank, she spied a wooden bench, and she walked slowly toward it, barely noticing the stunning scenery all about her.

Instead, she saw herself back in the building on Lubyanka, the place where she had worked for so many years before… before "it" happened. Despite all that she had suffered while imprisoned there, the emotional anguish of knowing her husband was a captive in one of those cells was so much worse than what she had endured. And, even worse than that was the feeling of helplessness. There was nothing, absolutely nothing, that she could do to relieve his suffering.

Nothing? Andrayev's voice echoed in her mind. He had insisted that her prayers could help – but mere words? What could they accomplish? And, prayers to whom? Did she even believe in G-d? What sort of G-d would shatter her family like this, as a reward for devotion to Him?

And yet, Andrayev was no fool. His keen intelligence, exceptional talents and professionalism had propelled him to a high position in the KGB – and despite all that, he routinely placed himself in danger because of his loyalty to his Jewish beliefs. Her very own husband had done the same. What did they know that she didn't? Why were they so certain that it was worth even to die in order to learn about Judaism and practice it?

Could it be that they were right – that Judaism was actually something so special, so precious, that it was worth more than life itself?

Lev had wanted to learn – he had wanted to teach her himself. For the meantime, that was not possible, but there, on the banks of the Danube, Anya promised her husband in faraway Moscow that she would learn even without him. Once she arrived in America, she would look for the answers he had found.

Kennedy Airport greeted them with its usual colorful rush of humanity hurrying in every direction. It seemed almost as if every world nation had sent its delegates to New York, and the massive proportions of the building along with the dizzying array of people and color was terribly disorienting for the new arrivals. Karina clung to her mother, terrified of being caught up in the ocean of people and swept away. At long last, they found their two modest pieces of luggage that Anatoly had kindly packed for them with the very basics, and they made their way hesitantly out of the terminal. Anya tried to appear calm and relatively confident in order to reassure Karina and her mother-in-law, but it was hard to do so when she herself felt so tiny and lost.

When they were safely ensconced in a cab, Karina turned to her mother with wide eyes. "Are we almost there, Mamochka?"

"I don't know," Anya replied absentmindedly. "We're all new here, and I don't know the way." She tried to focus on the passing scenery and absorb something of her surroundings, but it was all so strange and unfamiliar. *Here we are, in the West!* she reminded herself vigorously, trying to instill in herself a feeling of relief and joy. They were in the safety and luxury of the West that so many Soviet citizens could only dream of visiting. Anya had been given a wallet with American dollars – the same dollars that she could have been imprisoned in Russia for having in her possession. KGB employees were required to know English reasonably well, and Anya started practicing on the street signs and billboards, but she knew that her spoken English was halting at best and meager in vocabulary. It wouldn't be easy here, that was for sure.

The tiny, dank tenement apartment that kind people had rented for them screamed of neglect and did little to raise her spirits, yet she didn't forget the vow she had made just a few days ago, after arriving in Vienna. As soon as her mother-in-law and Karina were in bed, exhausted from the trip, Anya forced herself to cross the hallway and knock on the neighbors' door.

A woman opened and squinted at Anya from behind large, thick glasses. "You're the new neighbor?" she asked. "I was wondering who was going to move in."

"Yes. I came today, with my daughter and my mother-in-law."

The woman looked surprised, but didn't dare pry. Anya saw the questions written all over her face and realized that her words obligated some form of explanation. "My husband… he comes soon."

"I see," the neighbor nodded, though she still looked skeptical. "Well, then, can I help you?" There was a note of disdain in her voice, and Anya's heart sank to her toes. What kind of impression was she making?

"I looking for learning. A group," she stammered uncertainly, conscious of her strong Russian accent and sure that almost every word she uttered was somehow wrong.

"Learning? A group? Learning what?" the woman replied, looking completely baffled. "You want to learn English?"

Anya blushed, but refused to give up. "Learning religion," she said firmly. "Jewish religion."

The woman shrugged dismissively. "How should I know? But… you could try the Sterns upstairs. They're Jewish. Are you?"

Anya nodded quickly, wondering what that meant in America,

if anything. Judging by the way the woman wrinkled her nose, she surmised that it was no great asset here, either. The door slammed in her face, and Anya suddenly felt her exhaustion overwhelm her senses. She hurried back to her apartment and fell into bed without even bothering to change her clothes. She would pay a visit to the upstairs neighbors, the Sterns, the next day.

CHAPTER 40

The walls of the narrow cell seemed to be closing in on him in the semi-darkness, and Lev had to constantly remind himself that this was not the real world; that beyond the prison walls, the sun still shone, people walked about freely – even if freedom was only relative in the Soviet Union.

Day and night were indistinguishable in the basement floors of Lubyanka where the only source of lighting in the area of the cells was the warden's small flashlight as he moved slowly along the corridors during his rounds. Lev had long since given up trying to keep track of time, especially as much of the time between interrogations was spent only semi-aware of reality. Every one of his limbs ached, and it was far preferable to sink into unconsciousness rather than face his agonizing situation.

How long would they keep trying to get information out of him? Anya had been imprisoned for over two weeks, during which they hadn't ceased in their attempts to get her to reveal the names of others involved in his escape. He couldn't fathom how she had held out during those long days and nights, and now he wondered how long he himself would be able to hold out.

But he had to! The lives of others depended on him being strong. What was more, if he betrayed Anatoly Andrayev, not only the man himself would suffer, but also all those others whom he would no longer be able to help. It was only that knowledge that kept him focused during interrogations, when it felt like every bone in his body was being disjointed and that one more blow would shatter what was left of him. He was more or less certain that his shoulder actually was broken, and he wondered if he would ever be offered any form of medical care, or if he would be left a cripple – if he survived at all – and the pain threatened to overwhelm his thinking process entirely. There were times that he couldn't even recall what they wanted from him anymore; all he knew was that people's lives depended on him keeping his mouth shut, so he kept biting his tongue until its blood mingled with the blood of his other wounds.

Now, alone again in his cell, he tried but failed to sink back into the waves of blackness, which made him realize that time had passed since his last session. The knowledge sent tremors throughout his aching body. If time had passed, and he was already fully conscious, there was no question that they would be back for him soon.

Ribbono shel Olam! I have no more strength to withstand this! I'm not Rabbi Akiva, or even any kind of hero. I'm just a simple Jew who tried to learn Your holy Torah. Yes, I knew what I was risking, but it's so hard...

He thought back to his former life, the life of a common Soviet citizen. In his mind, the thirty years before his discovery of Judaism were colored a hazy gray and accented with fear. There were bright spots, of course: his marriage to Anya, the birth of their daughter, their respective accomplishments at work – but his life had still lacked purpose, lacked the reason behind it all, the reason that would make all the struggles worthwhile. Willing or not, he and Anya had been forced to traverse the road that others had paved for them, forced to follow orders and never question authority. Then came the dividing line in his life. The years were uneven, thirty on one side and a mere two on the other, but the meaning and joy of the last two years of his life by far outweighed everything he had experienced before then.

The only question that remained was whether that meaning and joy would now give him the strength to withstand all that he would still have to endure. The truth was that Lev was afraid to confront that question. Instead, he redirected his worries to prayer.

———༄༅———

He was tied roughly to a chair to prevent him from falling.

A glass of water was placed on the table, just tantalizingly out of reach. Lev foolishly reached for the cup, but Igor Zhiglov, the interrogator who sat opposite him, snatched it away from him. "Not yet, Lev," he smiled mirthlessly. "You'll get a drink when we finish, or if you wish, at any time. As we've told you time and again, how long this meeting takes is entirely in your hands."

Lev didn't meet the interrogator's eyes, trying hard to focus his thoughts elsewhere and distance his mind from his body. Perhaps that would give him the ability to bear the beating that would surely be coming soon.

"Look at me when I speak to you!" Zhiglov roared furiously. Lev forced himself to look up. "We have your wife, your daughter, and your mother."

The words hit him almost with a physical force, and the room spun dizzyingly around him. For a moment, the blessed darkness embraced him again, but it was only for a few seconds. Before he knew it, fetid water had been splashed on his face to revive him, and his eyes opened involuntarily.

"Do me a favor, and don't faint on us again," Zhiglov said derisively. "As I was saying, we've got all three of them, so you really have no choice but to tell us the truth. Who helped you break into this place? Who collaborated with you? Who gave you the information you needed to do what you did?"

"No one. I did it on my own," Lev replied in a voice that was faint but stubborn.

He was prepared for the physical blow, but what came next was far worse. Zhiglov leaned so close to him that Lev could feel the heat of his breath on his face. "Do you really want your daughter to pay for your refusal to cooperate with us?" he asked through narrowed eyes.

"If you really have her, let me see her!" Lev demanded boldly. He was still strong enough to doubt their words, and he wouldn't let them deceive him. The KGB interrogators were notorious for playing mind games, and it was possible that they were using empty threats. Until he saw Karina with his own eyes, he wouldn't be fooled into believing their claim.

"You'll get to see her. You'll see all three of them. After you tell us what we want to know, and after we verify that what you say is true." Zhiglov's expression made it clear that he dare not so much as consider trying to deceive them. Once again, the room swirled around him, and once again he was rudely awakened until he trembled with cold.

"I don't believe you," he attempted brazenly. "For all I know you have no better idea of where they are than I do. From my perspective, until I see them with my own eyes, they're not here."

"Are you so callous that you'd risk endangering them without purpose?" Zhiglov taunted. "You know what we can do to them. Don't you care about your family?"

Lev bit his lip forcefully, trying to subdue his feelings. He would gladly have given his life in order to save his wife, his daughter, or his mother – but there was no way he could sacrifice the lives of others in return for an empty promise from his captors.

"Let me see them," he responded hoarsely, "and then we'll talk."

"You're not the one giving orders here!" Zhiglov jumped to his feet and landed a blow square on Lev's forehead that sent him tumbling to the floor together with the chair. The blows that followed were blessed relief to Lev's tortured soul, as they clarified one thing: If any one of the three women in his life were in this building, Zhiglov wouldn't have reacted so furiously. He would have dragged one of them into the interrogation room, frightened and trembling, for Lev to glimpse. It hadn't taken much for his captors to figure out that Lev's family meant far more to him than his own life.

The relief wasn't long-lasting, however. After being shoved back into his cell, where he huddled into a corner on the freezing concrete floor, the fears began creeping into his heart like daggers. He couldn't be certain of anything; if any one of the three were in their hands, his refusal to reveal names could spell death for them, and the fear nearly sent him out of his mind. Several times that night he almost crawled to the bars on his cell to shake them and alert the guards that he had something to reveal; but at the last second, logic prevailed and preserved his sanity. Once the initial terror passed, he began reciting the prayers and Psalms that he knew by heart, struggling to recall each word and syllable until the effort exhausted his tortured mind. When he finally succumbed to sleep, there was a trace of a smile on his bruised and bloodied face.

The days passed in a jumbled mass of consciousness and unconsciousness, punctuated with increasingly vicious sessions. His only weapon was his silence, coupled with his prayers that one day soon they would tire of him and end his suffering. And then suddenly, one day, it was all over. The interrogations, threats, blows, and torture ended abruptly. He was led to an infirmary where his broken arm was set in a cast, his wounds were stitched, and he began receiving two daily meals each of which consisted of a single slice of bread with a cup of warm water.

Two days of quiet passed before he was called to trial, which began with an anonymous prosecutor reading out the list of charges against him. Lev listened almost in amusement as the man's voice droned on an on, and he wondered what sentence could possibly "atone" for his many crimes. Lev was given no permission to speak up in his defense, neither was there any defense attorney, or even a jury. Instead, the moment the prosecutor completed his recital, the judge pronounced his verdict: Ten years in a labor camp in Siberia.

The gray sky was speckled with white clouds on the day when Lev was led to the train station in chains. During the brief interval between being shoved from the jail truck into the train car, he felt a tiny shred of paper being stuffed into his hand. Lev closed his fist tightly around the scrap of paper, not daring to open it until several hours into the journey.

"Three safe in USA," were the four printed words. Lev's eyes widened and he quickly tore the scrap into even tinier shreds that dissolved in the copious tears of thanksgiving that he shed. As he reflected upon the past weeks, he couldn't fathom how he had possessed the strength to withstand the torture and remain silent rather than incriminate Anatoly and the others. All he knew was that the G-d he had learned to know and love had not abandoned him for a moment, and that He would surely accompany him into exile in faraway Siberia.

CHAPTER 41

When Anya awoke the next morning, it took her a while to remember where she was. Visions of her jail cell still punctuated her dreams by night, but the warmth of her blanket reminded her that she was free. Not only had she escaped from the dungeons of Lubyanka, but she had actually succeeded in leaving the huge prison that was the Soviet Union. Here, in America, she could build a new life for herself and her family – a family that was now missing its head, her husband.

She sat up slowly in bed, trying to get her bearings. The room was cold and drafty, but certainly not terrible by Soviet standards. In the bed next to hers, Karina lay, still asleep, but she would be up soon and wanting to eat, and as far as she knew, there was nothing in the apartment to give her. Furthermore, the little cash in her wallet that Anatoly had given her would only be sufficient for a few weeks at best. How apologetic he had been when he handed it to her, reminding her that it was forbidden to leave the country with a large amount of dollars in one's possession. Both of them had known that the first months would not be easy, and now Anya reminded herself that finding a job was an absolute priority for her.

Karina's high-pitched whine interrupted her thoughts. "Mamochka, I'm hungry!"

Anya nodded silently and headed to the kitchen, where all she found was an old, dented kettle left behind by the previous tenants. She filled it with water and placed it on the stove to warm, hoping that Karina would suffice with hot water until she had time to go shopping.

Karina stared pitifully at the cup of steaming liquid. "I'm sorry, Karina sweetie, but I didn't buy tea yet, or milk. I'll go out soon," Anya explained. To her surprise, her spoiled, pampered daughter drank the warm water silently instead of throwing a tantrum as she would have done, eons ago in their luxurious apartment in Moscow.

Twenty minutes later, Anya left the apartment to search for the nearest grocery. She found a convenience store just one block away, and the variety of products and colorfully labelled brands astonished her. She had never seen such bounty, even in the largest supermarkets in Russia, and not even in those exclusive stores that only government employees frequented. Nonetheless, Anya chose her items carefully, selecting only the very basics.

After paying, she turned hesitantly to the woman behind the checkout counter and appealed to her in her broken English. "I need to work. Maybe you can help me?"

The woman, short and dumpy, returned a quizzical stare. "What kind of accent is that?"

"I from Russia," Anya replied, trying to smile and hoping she looked friendly.

"Really!" the woman exclaimed. "I always thought that the Soviets prevented their citizens from leaving!" Now she stared in open curiosity at Anya, as if she were a queer specimen.

"It was very hard," Anya agreed, without wishing to reveal any more.

"You mean you escaped?" the woman gaped. "Wasn't that dangerous?"

"Yes," Anya replied simply, guessing that the brevity of her answer would frustrate the woman, who was clearly hoping to have stumbled upon a real live thriller. She wasn't wrong.

"Well, if you want work, you shouldn't be just hanging around here doing nothing," the woman now retorted sharply. "Go to an employment agency." And with that, she turned to her next customer.

Anya, however, wasn't about to be dismissed before receiving the information she so badly needed. "Where is that?" she persisted, as she gathered together her purchases.

"No idea." The woman had now lost interest in her entirely, and Anya nodded slowly and left the store.

The employment agency… What would she tell them there? No doubt, they would ask for references, and what experience she had – and what would she tell them? Suddenly, shockingly, she realized that her respectable position and once-sterling reputation in the KGB would not only not stand her in good stead here – it would most likely ruin any chance she had of finding employment. If people found out that she had once worked for the KGB, they could even suspect her of being a spy! The idea was on the one hand so ridiculous that she almost laughed out loud, but on the other hand, it left her as destitute as any other beggar fresh off the ship. Who was she here? She was a total nobody, with nobody to rely on, nobody to help her out…

Sighing, Anya started up the stairs to her apartment, deciding on the way up not to share any of her fears and misgivings with Valeria. For the older woman, it was surely a much harder transition than it was for her. Valeria knew very little English, and at her age, it was unlikely that anyone would be in a hurry to employ her. What would she do with herself all day long? No, Anya would not complain to her mother-in-law.

Back in the apartment, Anya boiled water for tea and was about to prepare breakfast for the three of them when Valeria stopped her.

"Anya, I think we should split the chores between us," she suggested. "You'll be working soon, hopefully, and I'll take care of the cooking and cleaning. What will I do with my time otherwise?" she argued persuasively. "At least let me make a contribution."

Already feeling despondent, Anya readily agreed. "In that case, I think I'll go out right now to this employment agency someone told me about," she replied. "And I'll also see if I can find out about a preschool for Karina, where she can learn English."

The lines at the particular employment agency she managed to find, were long. At least one thing in this country was familiar, although that turned out to be a disappointment – Anya spent hours waiting on line, and by the time her turn arrived, it was early afternoon.

"Do you have any professional training?" asked a bored-looking clerk as he handed her a printed form to fill out.

Anya looked at the form with a growing sense of panic. Although she could understand most of the questions, she knew that the replies she was capable of filling in would not impress anyone.

"Profession? Yes… office work," she replied haltingly, a flush creeping up her cheeks.

Her reply made him glance up at her suspiciously. "Where are you from?"

"Moscow," she replied, her heart sinking at the sound of her heavy accent which had never before sounded so ugly.

"And where exactly did you work? You were trained?"

"Yes, train…" Anya frowned. Why was he asking about trains? "I worked in Moscow," she repeated, hoping that the answer would satisfy him.

The clerk studied her again, trying to figure her out. "How did you get here?"

"On a plane," Anya sighed.

"Really." He couldn't disguise his skepticism. "Let me guess: On a direct flight?" he chuckled.

"Direct? No… Vienna first." Where was this conversation leading?

"So any Soviet citizen who wants to immigrate to America can get an exit visa?"

Anya sighed, and not only because it was so far from the truth. "No," she murmured. "Not everyone."

The clerk refused to let up. "So, how exactly did you get out?"

Anya felt tears pricking in her eyes, but she managed to blink them away without, she hoped, the clerk noticing. "People help me. Good people."

"And your husband?" the clerk pressed, and Anya knew he was only trying to satisfy his curiosity at her expense.

"He is in Russia," Anya replied softly. "He comes later."

The clerk nodded, finally deciding to stop his cross-examination. "So, you worked in an office? As what? For which organization?"

"For office," Anya replied, hiding behind her excuse of poor English. So the clerk would think she was a dimwit. It was still better than admitting to having worked for the KGB.

"Well, you can't work in an office here with your atrocious English," the clerk pointed out. "Nobody's going to hire you unless you learn to speak, read, and write English properly."

"No job?" Anya stared. Surely there was something she could do. There had to be something!

"No, I'm sure we can find you a job, but just not in an office," the clerk explained, his patience beginning to wear thin. "Something like cleaning, for instance." The look of shock and horror on Anya's face made him apologize, something he rarely did. "I think it's the best you can hope for in the meantime… unless you have a better idea, that is."

Anya shook her head slowly. She had no ideas, only broken hopes, and a desperate need to earn money – but cleaning? To reach America only to become a common cleaning lady? How could this be happening to her?

"Maybe. I don't know. Maybe…" she stammered, before quickly turning on her heel and exiting before the clerk could utter another word.

CHAPTER 42

At first, Valeria had trouble understanding exactly what had transpired that day at the employment agency. Anya couldn't bring herself to recount her ordeal in detail, but from the little that she did say, Valeria grasped that it had been a deeply humiliating experience. When she finally persuaded Anya to tell her exactly what sort of job she had been offered, she immediately conjured a plan of her own.

"I've got a much better idea!" she exclaimed. "You'll go to English classes, and I'll work as a cleaner. Until something better comes up," she added hastily, seeing the expression on Anya's face.

Anya looked scandalized. "You, Mama? A cleaner!?"

"Why not? It'll give me something to do, and it'll support us in the meantime, until you find something more appropriate."

"But, Mama... Do you really think you can do it?"

Valeria shrugged, oblivious to her daughter-in-law's concern. "What's the problem? To the best of my knowledge, you don't need any special degree or even good English to work as a cleaning lady!" she joked.

"But you need strength, Mama," Anya argued gently. "I think that most people would prefer to hire someone younger and more energetic."

Valeria looked insulted. "I may not be as young as you, but I'm no weakling. In fact, I could probably do a better job than you, Anya – after all, I have experience at household chores, whereas you spent all your days in a leather office chair!"

Anya chuckled uncomfortably. "You're right about that, Mama, but I still won't let you break your back on my behalf, especially not at your age. You help enough already as it is, with Karina and everything. It's my responsibility to provide for my daughter, not yours." Even as Anya spoke, she realized how irresponsible she was being. She had no right to turn down a job offer, even if it was beneath her dignity. Swallowing hard, she told Valeria, "In fact, I'm going back to the employment agency right now, to tell them I do want a cleaning job after all."

"Now? But you already spent the whole day there!" Valeria protested. "What makes you think they're still open? It's been a long day, Anya, dear. Why don't you wait until tomorrow morning?"

"Tomorrow is too late! Maybe someone else will take whatever job they have for me. I don't know how many vacancies they have." Without another word, Anya put her coat back on and left, before Valeria could talk her out of it.

Now that she knew, more or less, where she was headed, she found the employment agency far more quickly than she had done the first time, but as she entered the office, she was dismayed to find the clerk already gathering his belongings as he prepared to leave. Forcing herself to swallow her final dregs of pride, she approached him and tried to speak up clearly even though her voice was shaking.

"Sir, I am sorry. Please, give me cleaning job today."

The clerk treated her to a contemptuous gaze. "Lady, we closed here ten minutes ago."

Anya flushed deeply but forced herself to meet his eyes. "Yes, I am sorry. Please, please… There is a job?"

The clerk narrowed his eyes. "I already told you that we're closed. Read the sign. You were here, and you preferred to leave rather than accept my offer. You're welcome to return tomorrow and wait your turn."

Anya turned desperate eyes upon him. "Please, sir! I am sorry. I don't want to be cleaner—"

"Perfect," the clerk snapped his leather briefcase shut. "Then if we agree on the matter, there's no reason for you to delay me any longer."

"But I have a little girl, and a mother-in-law, and we need to eat. Please, find me cleaner job." Anya's voice cracked, and a tear slid down her cheek. Sighing, the clerk turned around and wordlessly approached a metal file cabinet. He removed a folder filled with files, and rifled through several until he found what he was looking for.

"Law Offices of Fletcher and Grant." He read off the Manhattan address, and then wrote it down for her on a slip of paper. "The law offices take up an entire floor in a large office building. They pay minimum wage." He cast a pointed stare at Anya who was too overwrought to reply. "Listen, lady, I don't have time to waste. If you're not sure—"

"No! I mean, yes! Yes! Thank you! Thank you, good sir!"

The clerk exhaled a sigh of relief. "Be there at eight-thirty sharp and ask to speak to Mr. Jameson. I'll call to let them know the position was filled."

Anya took the paper, her eyes shining with gratitude. "Thank you, sir. Thank you!"

That evening, Anya sat down with Valeria to plan for the next day. She would need to leave early in order to reach Manhattan on time. Anya washed out her best outfit by hand so she would have something respectable to wear for her first day on the job – but as she wrung out the excess water and spread it out on the radiator to dry, the thought crossed her mind that there wasn't anything respectable about the job she was going to.

No! she protested the thought. *To earn money and support oneself honestly is respectable, regardless of how other people may perceive me or what I'm used to. If this is all I can do, then that's that.*

It was late by the time she finally fell into bed, emotionally drained from the day's events, and it was only then that she recalled that she had intended to go upstairs to the Sterns that evening. How could she have forgotten her promise to her husband, her silent promise made on the banks of the Danube only a few days ago? Tears sprung to her eyes as she thought of Lev, waiting and praying for freedom, possibly having given up hope already. She owed at least that much to her husband, to do as he had asked of her – she couldn't keep pushing it off. So, it would be tomorrow night, then, and she hoped that she wouldn't arrive home too drained after her first day of work.

Exhausted, she fell asleep before she could wipe the tears from her cheeks.

Richard Jameson shot her an impatient look. "Leave your resume and recommendations on my desk. The cleaning supplies are in the utility closet at the end of the hall."

Anya froze. The clerk at the employment agency hadn't mentioned that she needed any recommendations, but she didn't dare say so to this supercilious attorney. As she hurried down the hall, anxious to prove herself, she heard Jameson's voice follow her.

"Miss! Your papers?"

She turned around slowly. "I don't have papers," she said quietly, more conscious than ever of her heavy Russian accent.

"What's the meaning of this?" he slammed an angry fist onto his expansive desk, rattling a coffee cup. "How dare those idiots send me some random wandering foreigner?"

Anya blushed furiously, tempted to pick up her feet and flee this horrid place, but her new boss was indifferent to her insulted expression. "If I had time to waste, I would pick up the phone and give those idiots at the employment agency a piece of my mind, but until I do, I'm desperate for some cleaning help, so I'll give you a chance. If you can do a decent job, I'll overlook the missing documentation."

Without another word, Anya spun around and walked quickly down the hall, hoping she would find the utility closet without having to ask anyone for help.

"And it would do you good to thank me for the gesture!" Jameson's voice pursued her down the hall. "Most self-respecting employers would have sent you packing!"

Anya didn't dare to reply, reflecting that if she had opened her mouth to speak the truth, her bold reply really would be enough to send her packing.

CHAPTER 43

Several days passed on the job, each one more humiliating than the next. In all her life Anya had never had to work so hard, but she forced herself to take pride in the fact that she was learning quickly and holding herself back from complaining to anyone. Meanwhile, she located a preschool for Karina only a few blocks from their apartment, and made arrangements for her to start right away.

Anya was disappointed that she wouldn't be able to accompany Karina to her first day of preschool, but asking her new employer for permission to arrive late that day was clearly out of the question. Instead, Valeria accompanied Karina, and Anya rushed home from work in the afternoon, eager to see Karina and hear from her how things had gone.

"How's my darling?" she greeted her, scooping her up in a big hug. "How was your first day in school in America?"

"Horrible!" Karina blurted out, her eyes blazing. "All the kids laughed at me, and I didn't understand anything!"

Anya's jaw dropped in appall. "What did the teacher say?"

"She didn't care! She told everyone that my name is Karina and then she said lots of things and I didn't understand anything..." Tears welled up in Karina's eyes.

Anya's heart sank and she hugged her little girl close. "Don't worry, darling. You'll pick up English really quickly, I promise you, and then you'll understand just like everyone else."

One month after landing in New York, Anya came home from work with a box of cookies that she had purchased specially to mark the occasion, although in her heart, she felt there was little to celebrate. The situation hadn't improved much; she was still employed in backbreaking labor, scrubbing windows and polishing floors. The one bright spot was that Karina had demonstrated a real knack for language, picking up English at an incredible speed. She still complained about being teased because of her accent, but overall, she seemed to be adjusting relatively well to the changes in their lives. As for Valeria, she had joined a free course to learn English, and she could now manage on her own in the supermarket. It was slow progress, but at least it was a beginning.

Anya entered the house, forcing herself to smile and inject a note of happiness into her voice. "Hello!" she called into the apartment. "Karina, Mama! Today is a special day! Look what I bought for us!"

Karina plodded slowly to the door, and Anya immediately noticed the disgruntled look on her face.

"What's wrong, Karina sweetie?" she asked, hoping it was nothing too drastic. "Did something happen?"

Karina promptly burst into tears. "I hate school. I hate the children in my class. I'm not going back!"

"What happened? Tell me about it," Anya replied, even as her heart lurched. How much longer was it going to take to adjust?

"Everyone is mean. They make fun of me all the time, and they ask horrible questions."

"Horrible questions?" Anya raised her eyebrows, wondering where this would lead.

Karina wiped the tears from her face. "Today, Mandy asked me where I used to go to school that I talk so weird. Then she asked me if my parents also talk weird, and where my brothers and sisters go to school. I don't even have any brothers or sisters!" she wailed.

"Well, that just proves that Mandy doesn't know what she's talking about!" Anya told Karina firmly. "You don't have to pay any attention to what she says."

"And then Mike told me that his mother is the principal, and that he's going to tell her not to let me come to kindergarten any more. So I'll stay home," Karina ended defiantly. "I hate it there anyway."

Anya exhaled slowly. "Nobody's going to tell you not to come back, Karina. I'm sure the principal really likes you, and soon enough, just like back in Moscow, you're going to be the smartest girl in class. Your English will get even better, and then you'll have lots of friends. You'll see."

"I *already* know lots of English," Karina protested. "And you know what? I told Mike that my Mama used to do important work for the KGB, even though you're just a cleaner now. That way, he won't make fun of me any more."

Anya turned as white as a sheet. "You told him what?"

"I told him you worked for the KGB! And you know what? Even Mike was scared when he heard that. He didn't laugh at me again after that."

"Karina, how could you!" In her panic, Anya didn't even realize that she had raised her voice and was now shouting at her child. "I told you a hundred times not to tell anyone that I worked for the KGB! It's a secret, and I don't even work there anymore. We live in America now, not in Russia!"

Karina burst into tears. "But they were so mean!" she sobbed.

Anya hugged her daughter, already sorry that she had shouted at her. "You know what? I'll speak to your teacher and make sure that no one ever says mean things to you again."

"You will?" The relief sounded clearly in Karina's voice, and her trusting innocence brought Anya reeling painfully back into reality. What should she say? How could she speak to the teacher? She didn't even have a telephone yet, and she didn't dare show up late to work. Jameson would fire her on the spot, and then, instead of the glowing recommendation she hoped to acquire, she would be labeled an irresponsible worker.

Anya lowered her eyes, unable to confess the truth. Sensing her dilemma, Valeria spoke up. "When I take you to school tomorrow, I'll speak to the teacher, and I'll also tell the children that they mustn't be mean," she suggested gently.

"No!" Karina shouted angrily. "I don't want you to say anything to them."

Valeria retreated, the hurt in her eyes manifest. "Why not?"

"Because they won't listen. They'll just make fun of you like they make fun of me, and then they'll laugh even more at me afterward."

Anya's heart broke for her daughter. "Karina, I think Babushka really should talk to your teacher, and then your teacher will speak to the class. Okay?"

"Okay," Karina whispered reluctantly, and Anya hoped that the teacher wouldn't disappoint them.

Karina wriggled out of her mother's grasp. "I'm hungry!" she announced. "I want the cookies."

Anya wasn't finished, however. She drew a deep breath and said in her firmest voice, "Karina, you must never *ever* again tell anyone that I worked for the KGB. Is that clear?"

"Why not?" Karina challenged her.

"Because it's a secret, that's why. Do you understand me?"

The girl nodded slowly. "But what if Mike's mother tells me that I don't belong?"

"It won't happen. If anyone ever says anything of the sort, I'll deal with it. Okay?"

"I want cookies," Karina repeated. Anya wondered if that constituted an affirmative response, but she preferred not to ask.

The bigger they are, the harder they fall, Anya mused for the millionth time as she headed down to the subway after yet another tiring day of physical labor. *But even so, why do I feel so sorry for myself? I was saved literally from hell. If I had remained behind, I'd most probably be either in jail or in Siberia for the next decade, and Karina would be in a government orphanage, where they would indoctrinate her into the joys of living in the Communist paradise. Most likely, I would never see her again, even if I got out of Siberia in one piece… I wouldn't even see Lev – they'd make sure of that.*

Yet try as she might, Anya still resented what her life had become, even more so as she could see no way out of it, no path via which she might change her circumstances. Would she be forced to work as a cleaner for the next year, the next decade – forever? Even if she perfected her command of the English language, what did she have to offer an employer? Her past in the KGB had to remain utterly secret, and therefore, her ostensible lack of experience in any profession would close many doors to her. Karina would fare better, but what of herself?

Now she reflected that it was the lack of humanity in her workplace that broke her spirit more than her back. It wasn't the fact that her talents and capabilities were ignored that hurt her as much as the fact that she, herself, was completely ignored, as if she were no more significant than the broom and mop she wielded. The office receptionist was the only person there who even acknowledged her presence, with a faint nod when she arrived each morning; the others passed by her as if she were invisible.

She spent the day passing from one room to the next in the prestigious law offices, dusting shelves, shining windows, polishing gleaming desks, and doing her best to remain quiet and unobtrusive. If she ever happened to be in someone's way, she was shooed aside like a fly. Every afternoon, she was tempted to announce that it was her last day on the job, but every day she bit her tongue and reminded herself to be grateful for what she had. She had survived far worse than this in her recent past, and she could survive this too. Whenever she pitied herself, she would think of Lev, and the humiliation she was forced to endure suddenly became insignificant in comparison.

Every evening as she climbed into bed, exhausted from her day's work, Anya reminded herself of her promise, but every evening she was simply too fatigued to climb the stairs and pay a visit to her Jewish neighbors.

Until one Sunday evening. Weekends were her blessed time off from the work she detested, and all week long she looked forward to those two days. Since they couldn't afford to spend money on any form of entertainment or leisure, Anya often took Karina to the public library as an outing, and to a park on the way home. That evening, after Karina had gone to sleep and while she was sipping tea with her mother-in-law at the tiny kitchen table, she mentioned her promise.

"Did you ever speak to the upstairs neighbors?" Valeria asked pointedly. "The lady across the hall once mentioned to you that they're Jewish, didn't she? I'm sure they can help you."

Anya nodded reluctantly. The thought of approaching strangers with her question was nerve-racking, but she couldn't think of any other way to fulfill her promise. Seeing her expression, Valeria tried to encourage her a little. "You never know, Anya. I actually think joining a study group will do you good. You'll meet other people who are also interested in learning, and it will give you a chance to relax at the end of the day too. You work so hard, Anya, and you deserve it."

Smiling gratefully at her mother-in-law, Anya drew a deep breath and trekked up the stairs. Could Valeria be right? Was this exactly what she needed right now? Surely it was a way to connect emotionally to Lev, she reflected.

She knocked hesitantly on the door which was opened by a middle-aged woman. "You're the new neighbor?" she greeted her. "I didn't even realize that the last ones moved out until I saw you leaving the building in the morning several days in a row. Well, good riddance to them! Those last tenants… they were something else! The husband smoked all day long, in the stairwell and lobby as well, and the entire building reeked of cheap cigarette smoke. Sometimes, I felt like I was wading through smoke just to get to my apartment, and it's so unhealthy! I hope *you* don't smoke," she added suspiciously.

"I don't," Anya replied.

"Good," the woman nodded, but twisted her lip as she warned her, "Just as long as you don't have any other noxious habits. We've had enough of suffering from our neighbors."

"I want to be a good neighbor," Anya hastened to reassure Mrs. Stern. "I wanted to ask if you know about faith classes," she added hopefully.

"Faith classes?" The woman blanched. "What's that?"

"Aren't you Jewish?" Anya asked, confused.

The woman's expression became guarded. "And if I am? What are these strange questions all about?"

"Strange questions?" Anya repeated, realizing that she must have said something wrong. "I don't know… I just want to find Jewish faith classes."

"Sounds awfully Christian to me," the woman muttered under her breath. "What do these faith classes have to do with me being Jewish?"

Her reply shocked Anya. "Christian? But I want classes on Judaism and Talmud!" she cried.

"Then, for heaven's sake don't call them faith classes!" the woman berated her. "Besides, I have no idea where to go for such things. What's your connection to all this?"

"Well… I'm Jewish, so of course I want to learn faith… I mean, Jewish studies," Anya stammered, before hurriedly saying goodbye and retreating back down the stairs.

CHAPTER 44

The bus stopped, and the doors opened. Anya jolted awake, and her eyes widened as she realized that she had completely missed her stop. The way home from work was long, requiring a train and then a bus from the Subway station to the stop nearest her home. It had been especially tiring that day at work, and after boarding the bus, she had closed her eyes for just a minute never imagining that she would actually fall asleep. She quickly alighted at the stop before the driver could close the doors and drive on.

Since her days were so full, she hadn't had a chance to get to know her neighborhood so well, and she wasn't sure how far she had traveled beyond her stop. Glancing at her watch, she was appalled to see that it was almost a half hour past the time she usually got home. Had she really slept for so long? She asked a woman waiting at the stop where she was, and based on the reply, Anya grasped that she was quite far from home, although she still wasn't sure exactly where she was.

Noting the one-way street, she asked where she could catch a bus in the opposite direction. The woman directed her toward the parallel street and Anya thanked her and hurried on her way. From the distance, she saw her bus arrive at the bus stop, which she reached only a moment after the bus pulled away, and so, with no choice but to wait, she settled onto the bench, hoping that Karina wouldn't be too cranky when she returned.

As she waited, Anya couldn't help but notice the interesting people passing by. Manhattan and Queens, where she lived, were an array of color, but here, everyone seemed to be dressed only in black and white. The men wore black coats and hats, and even most of the women were clad in dark, solemn colors. It was like entering a black-and-white movie, she thought in amusement, as she wondered again where she was.

Someone had dropped a local circular on the bench, and, always looking to improve her English reading skills, Anya picked it up and flipped through it. The circular contained mostly store advertisements, but there were also a few articles, none of which were written on a particularly high level, which was exactly what Anya had hoped for, as most newspaper articles were still too difficult for her to plow through. She stuffed the circular into her pocketbook, and it was then that the full-page advertisement on the back caught her eye.

The advertisement was for a lecture that would be given by one Daniel Pavlov, a Jewish refusenik who had spent eight years in a Soviet prison. The lecture would feature Pavlov's own story, of how he had secretly learned Torah in Moscow and been found out and arrested. After completing his sentence in a forced labor camp in Siberia, he had been fortunate enough to procure an exit visa, after years of rejected applications.

Anya's heart began to beat faster, and the words swam before her eyes, as the name Daniel Pavlov was replaced in her mind with that of Lev Krasnikov. Where was he now? Was Pavlov's Torah the same one for which Lev had risked his life? Did Pavlov's escape mean that her husband also stood a chance of survival?

Anya arrived home that night unusually late, but feeling more hopeful than she could remember being since fleeing Russia. Over dinner, she described her inadvertent adventure to her mother-in-law and daughter and ended by showing them the circular, which neither one of them could read.

Valeria seemed more intrigued by Anya's description of the neighborhood than the lecture. "There are a lot of Jews in New York. You must have ended up in a religious neighborhood. Religious Jews dress differently," she added knowledgeably.

Anya noted the emotional glimmer in Valeria's eyes. "How do you know?"

"My grandparents, and my great aunts and uncles were all very religious," she reminisced nostalgically. "They lived as real Jews, until Stalin came along."

Anya gazed deeply into the older woman's eyes which suddenly burned with passion. "Are you proud of Lev?" she whispered.

"Yes and no," Valeria sighed. "On one hand, I can't condone the risks he took and how he put us all in danger, but he's still my son, and I suppose I am proud of the fact that he was willing to make sacrifices in order to return to the ways of our ancestors. I remember my grandmother lamenting that we didn't fight strongly enough to preserve our Judaism. At the time, I didn't understand what she meant, but with everything that has happened, I'm beginning to understand. I think of Lev, a proud, successful husband and father; he had everything a man could want, yet he was willing to risk it all in exchange for the faith he discovered. He's a special man, Anya, and I believe that he inherited my grandparents' virtuous nature. Oh, if you'd only known them, you'd understand what I mean…"

"If it's okay with you, I'd really like to go to this lecture tomorrow," Anya said. "I feel that…" her voice cracked. "…that it will give me some way to connect to Lev. Almost like he'll be the one speaking."

Valeria nodded warmly.

The following evening, Anya entered the crowded auditorium self-consciously, searching for a place to sit. As she sank into an empty chair, she felt the exhaustion overtake her and wondered if this hadn't been a terrible mistake. Her job consumed all her energy, and by the time night fell, she had no more strength. All she wanted was to get home, eat a light supper, and collapse into bed as early as possible. What had she been thinking to commit to a two-hour event?

However, the moment Daniel Pavlov strode to the podium and began to speak, all thoughts of leaving early evaporated. She drank in thirstily every word as she listened to Pavlov so eloquently describe the fate of Soviet Jewry and how their heritage had been stolen from them by the Communists. Finally, Anya felt herself beginning to understand why her husband had risked everything – not for an intellectual pursuit, but rather for something entirely transformative. For months she had been struggling with this very issue, but now, Pavlov's story cemented her faith in her husband and she listened, riveted, as Pavlov related his own life story and how he had managed to maintain and even strengthen his faith during his exile in Siberia.

As soon as the lecture ended, Anya lost no time in hurrying to the front in order to catch the speaker before he could disappear.

"Mr. Pavlov!" she called, after he had shaken hands with the evening's hosts and several male guests. Pavlov stopped in his tracks and turned around. "Can I ask you a question?" she asked meekly, suddenly embarrassed.

Identifying her heavy Russian accent, Pavlov addressed her in fluent Russian. "Certainly. How can I help you?"

"Where can I join a faith class like you did in Russia?" she blurted out.

The man seemed shocked by the question. "New York isn't Russia, you know. The government allows people to practice their religion freely."

"I know it's not forbidden to learn here," Anya struggled to find the words, "but I don't know where to look."

He gazed at her quizzically. "You want to learn more about Judaism, and you don't know where?" he clarified.

Anya nodded, suddenly feeling very foolish, but Pavlov made an effort to sound encouraging.

"I don't live around here, but I imagine that right here, in this community center, they have Torah classes. Why don't we ask the person who invited me to speak this evening?" Without awaiting her reply, he turned around and started to look for the director.

Anya exited the community center ten minutes later equipped with a full schedule of Torah classes for women, on a wide variety of topics and for every level of proficiency. The bus ride home found her feeling happier than she had in months, and her excitement and anticipation seemed to have suddenly colored her gray life in a bright, cheerful hue.

Richard Jameson studied the two tall men who entered his office wearing dark suits and solemn expressions. "Do you have an appointment?" he asked pointedly.

The one with sandy hair flashed a badge that caused the attorney to blanch. "Derrick Fulton, CIA."

"How can I help you, gentleman?" Jameson quickly regained his bearings.

"You employ a young Soviet woman as a cleaner here?" Fulton asked bluntly.

Jameson didn't blink. "She was sent here by an agency."

"What can you tell us about her?"

Jameson scratched his bald pate. "Not much, to tell the truth."

"Describe her."

"She's blond, I think. Quiet, which is what I want. Does the job, not great, but passable. To be honest, I don't even remember her name. She's been working here for about a month, maybe two. She showed up one day and said she was sent by the employment agency, and that she didn't have references. That's really all I know, although possibly the office manager knows more."

"Please summon the office manager now." Fulton exchanged a glance with his colleague, and the two of them sat down facing Jameson, as they waited for the manager to arrive.

Charlotte Hanson entered several moments later, and Fulton asked her to close the door. The agents introduced themselves again, more politely this time, and proceeded to ask several questions, which Hanson did her best to answer.

"Are you satisfied with her work?" Fulton, who had done all the talking up until then, inquired.

Hanson deliberated. "She's clearly inexperienced, but she's a hard worker. When she started, I wasn't sure if she even knew which side of the broom was up. At one point, I was tempted to let her go, but she pleaded with me to give her another chance, saying something about needing to support a daughter and mother. I saw she was motivated, and she's learned on the job. She's all right."

"Do you know what she did previously?"

"No, but she's no dummy. Now that you mention it, she strikes me as unusually intelligent for a cleaning woman."

"And you never thought that was strange?" Fulton asked sharply.

"I never really thought about it," Hanson replied honestly, with a trace of defensiveness. "She presented herself as a cleaning woman, and I took it for granted. She wasn't very good, and I told her so, but she's improved since then… I would guess that she was probably employed in a professional capacity before she immigrated to the country."

CHAPTER 45

Anya squeezed out the mop, extracting the last droplets of dirty water. It was one of the aspects of her job that most repelled her – aside from cleaning the men's room. Dusting and shining windows was not so bad, but scrubbing sanitary units still made her gag. Worse yet was her aching back, and she hated the feeling that reminded her that she was no longer young and energetic.

Still, during the last few days, something had changed, something inside of her, and her job no longer felt quite so intolerable. That something was her evening classes; almost every night of the week found her in the community center, eagerly drinking in the information presented and trying to let its lessons permeate her life.

At first, it was jolting to her belief system, to hear her teachers speak of a Creator, who ran the world with precision and intent. In Soviet schools, the course of history was presented as being subject to the whims of humans, a story of power in the hands of the few wielded over the many, who eventually revolted and created a socialist paradise where all were supposedly equal. Anya knew all too well just how equal Soviet citizens were, but she had never consciously challenged the account of history presented to her in her youth. Now, she learned that in the Western world, history was seen largely as a random series of happenings, which actually sounded bizarre to her mind. When she learned that the Torah revealed the true course of history, one that was under the control of G-d Himself, instinctively she knew that it must be true. The natural world, with its intricacy and interconnectedness, was too perfect to be random. Surely it had been created, and therefore it followed that it had been created for a purpose. Anya was exhilarated to discover that she, as a Jew, was an integral part of that purpose, and that every deed of hers took its place in the Divine design.

So, there was G-d in history, G-d that oversaw the whole majestic sweep of the centuries – and then, there was G-d who was personal, intimately involved in every aspect of her life, guiding her, protecting her – and protecting Lev, too. During the long, dark nights, the thought that Lev was not alone, wherever he was, was her only source of comfort.

Anya finished polishing the marble hallway and had just turned to wipe down the counters in the coffee corner when she heard a voice call her name. So unaccustomed was she to being addressed that it took her a moment to realize that someone was speaking to her.

"Mrs. Krasnikov?" a deep voice repeated for the third time. She glanced up in surprise at the tall, sandy-haired man, and laid down her pail.

"Yes?"

"I apologize for interrupting you in the middle of your work. Please, would you mind joining us in the next room for a moment?"

"What?" Anya wrinkled her brow in confusion. There must be a mistake; what could this stranger want from her?

"Please join us in the next room for a moment," the dark-suited stranger repeated firmly. Anya followed obligingly.

"Derrick Fulton, CIA," the agent flashed his badge as soon as the door closed behind them. Anya's jaw dropped, and her eyes glimmered fearfully, further igniting Fulton's suspicions. "We'd like to invite you to our office for a chat."

"A chat?" she repeated guardedly. "Why?"

He nodded curtly. "We'll explain everything in my office. Now, if you'll be kind enough to collect your belongings, and join us."

"What did I do wrong?" she cried anxiously, certain that the KGB had finally tracked her down, after she had been so sure that she was safe in New York. Would they extradite her? Was she about to join Lev in Siberia? What about Karina? Did they have her in custody too?

"We'll explain everything, Mrs. Krasnikov, after you join us. We can't continue this conversation here."

"But we are in America, sir, not the Soviet Union!" she protested vigorously. "You can't arrest innocent people! I write to all newspapers! American people won't stand for KGB in New York!"

Fulton's eyebrows almost disappeared into his hairline. "KGB?" he repeated. "What does the KGB have to do with this?"

"So who are you?" she shot back. "You pretend to be American policeman! You're KGB!"

"I'm not a police officer," Fulton replied in amusement, beginning to grasp her mistake. "I'm a federal agent of the *United States of America*, and I already showed you my CIA badge, didn't I?"

His partner joined them. "Let's go. Is she ready? Mrs. Krasnikov, is there anything you need to take with you?"

Anya felt like a mouse trapped in a cage. "You can't take me away!" her voice rose desperately. "This isn't Russia. Miss Charlotte!" Her face flooded with relief upon glimpsing the office manager.

"Miss Charlotte, do you know these people? They want to arrest me! They say I have to go with them."

Charlotte Hanson gazed coldly at Anya, resenting the interrogation she had endured because of this woman. "Anya, if they're telling you to accompany them, then you have to do so. It's against the law to refuse a federal agent."

"These men are really federal agents?" Anya's heart skipped a beat, and her lips went dry. She swallowed the nausea and fear that welled up within her, hoping that she wouldn't faint. Somehow, her pocketbook found its way onto her shoulder, and the two agents escorted her into a sleek, late-model unmarked vehicle.

The ride passed in formidable silence, and Anya's mind raced in fear of what was to come. Did the CIA suspect her of espionage? But why would anyone suspect her, a simple cleaning woman? Had they found out that she had once been a high-ranking officer in the KGB before escaping Moscow?

The car pulled to a stop in front of a tall, imposing building, and Anya was taken up to a tenth floor office. She wasn't given the chance to read the inscription on the door, but a single glance at the three men sitting behind a wide desk was enough to tell her that these were no amateur agents, but rather senior officers. One gestured for her to be seated on the only empty chair in the room.

The officer sitting in the middle addressed her sternly. "Mrs. Krasnikov, I'll spare you my name and position, but I will inform you that you have been officially summoned to a federal investigation that does not grant you the right to a lawyer at this point in time. If you are ultimately charged and brought to trial, you will then be permitted legal representation."

Anya was too shocked to reply. They suspected her! They were waiting for her to admit to her crime! After all she had endured, after her miraculous escape from the shadow of lifelong imprisonment, she was now facing the same threat here on free soil.

She tried to maintain a calm demeanor, but she felt the color drain form her face and knew that her eyes revealed her terror. Did she look guilty?

"In what capacity did you serve in the KGB before arriving in the USA, under a false identity, I will add?" the officer on the right questioned her with a steely gaze.

On the spur of the moment, Anya decided to tell them the entire truth. If they didn't believe her, then her fate was sealed in any case, but maybe they would accept what she said? If, on the other hand, she was caught lying, then she would certainly be dealt with far more harshly.

Looking the questioner straight in the eye, Anya spoke up clearly, steadying her voice. "I worked in the office of Chairman Maxim Fyodorev, in Moscow. I led major operations in the three years I worked there."

The men didn't disguise their surprise. "That's not a position easily attained in the Soviet Union."

"That is true," she agreed, trying to still her pounding heart.

"And what caused you to abandon your life and position in Moscow and emigrate to the West? Judging from the terms of your current job, I imagine that you were far better off in Russia." The irony in the man's voice was heavy.

"I escaped," Anya confessed. "Three weeks before I left Russia, I was arrested and beaten. People helped me escape prison, and then I was hiding until we had documents that let us leave. Me, my daughter, and my mother-in-law. We went to Vienna, and then we came here."

"Not a bad cover story," the silver-haired officer sitting on the left smirked. He lit a cigar and blew out circles of smoke, speaking slowly throughout. "Makes for a good bedtime story, but not very convincing."

"What would you prefer me to tell you?" Anya asked pointedly.

"Why were you arrested?" the one in the middle shot at her.

"I was arrested because I helped my husband escape from prison. He was learning religion and they caught him."

"You were working for the KGB, and your husband was arrested by members of your own department?" The officer seated in the middle stared at her. "Do you really expect us to believe that, Mrs. Krasnikov?"

"I don't know," Anya replied quietly. "Please, may I have a glass of water?" she asked. To her relief, she was handed a plastic cup of water which she sipped, trying to calm herself as she did so.

"As a KGB officer, you were surely aware that what your husband was doing was illegal – and you didn't protest? You didn't stop him? You knew what would happen if he were caught!" The silver-haired officer whispered something to his colleagues and all three of them laughed.

Anya's heart sank. They clearly didn't believe her – and why should they? Her story did sound ridiculous, even she had to admit.

"I didn't know my husband was learning about Judaism. He kept it a secret, because it was dangerous for me to know. When he was arrested, I found out, when I saw his name on the list of prisoners, and then I spoke to him."

"Bravo! A stirring tale, Mrs. Krasnikov. Your next step may be Hollywood!" the officer on the right applauded her. "I see that you Russians are unbelievably creative!"

Tears rose to Anya's eyes, but she blinked them away furiously. Crying would certainly not help. Clearing her throat, she spoke in a quiet but firm voice. "If you are really CIA agents, then you can check my story with your people in Moscow. As a former KGB officer, I know that you have agents there. They can tell you that my story is true, even though the KGB probably prefers to hide the story about the escapes. But the best proof that my story is true is—" Anya's voice caught in her throat, "the fact that my husband is still there in prison. I don't even know where." She took a deep breath, trying to control her emotions. "I think that or he is still in prison, or they sent to a labor camp in Siberia."

"That certainly won't be difficult to verify," the one with the steely gaze retorted. He scribbled several lines on a sheet of stationery and strode briskly out of the room.

"Mrs. Krasnikov, there's also another way for you to demonstrate your goodwill and honesty," the silver-haired officer added. Anya turned her attention to him. "If you tell us everything you remember, especially classified information, from your years with the KGB, then we may be more inclined to believe you. But be aware that we have our ways of authenticating what you share with us, and of gauging how significant the information really is. You shouldn't be tempted to play games with us, Mrs. Krasnikov," he added menacingly.

Anya nodded slowly. She had no idea how much the Americans expected her to share with them, but she would do whatever it took to satisfy them.

CHAPTER 46

The minutes seemed to pass by interminably. Anya had been told to wait in a small anteroom, and she cringed when she heard the key turn in the lock. Not that the conditions were so terrible; she had a comfortable armchair to sit in, as well as a large window with a view of the New York skyline. However, the mere fact of being confined to a room was enough to give her flashbacks to her recent ordeal, and she struggled to remain calm and keep her breathing regular and even.

They were taking their time; apparently, the CIA wasn't quite as efficient as she had thought. It was cold outside, but the room was well heated – too well heated, in fact, and she was desperate for something to drink. Deciding that it couldn't hurt to try, she walked to the door and tried to open it, hoping that the noise would attract someone's attention.

"Sorry, ma'am, I can't let you leave yet," came a voice from the corridor outside. "Soon, okay?"

Anya sighed and sat down again, only to jump up again and start pacing the floor. What could be taking so long? Surely they could have verified her story by now? Suddenly, however, a terrifying thought flashed through her mind. What if Fyodorev had figured out a way to take revenge on her? What if he deliberately spread a rumor through the department that she was now acting as a double agent, sent to the USA to spy on the Americans from there? Nothing she could possibly say would help – Fyodorev was sly enough to outwit her every step of the way, and he was surely determined to do what he could to cause her downfall.

Anya began to tremble as the specter of being imprisoned in an American jail suddenly loomed close and threateningly. What would become of Karina? How would Valeria manage to support her at her advanced age? Would the Americans ever let her out of jail, or would she be sentenced to imprisonment for life – or worse? True, there was no Siberia in the United States, but capital punishment still existed – Anya couldn't recall in which states it was in effect.

Cold sweat ran down her back as Anya tried in vain to calm herself. What now? She was totally helpless, alone, a stranger in a strange land – nobody would come to her assistance here. There was no Anatoly Andrayev to rescue her from the claws of the American security intelligence services.

But no, I am not alone, a little voice echoed in her mind. *The same G-d who looked after me until now will surely not desert me!* With all her strength, she endeavored to recall the stirring words of her teachers, reinforcing her faith in the Al-mighty, urging her to look for His Hand in her life, in the small things as well as in the major ones.

Anya inhaled deeply and then breathed out slowly, feeling her faith infusing her with new vigor. The Anya who had fallen apart only minutes earlier was now replaced by a strong, focused woman, determined to instill within herself the belief that no one in the world had the power to harm her – only Hashem, her G-d, could control the course of her life. The agents of the CIA – or, for that matter, the KGB – may have thought that they were the ones to determine her fate, but they were wrong. Immersed as they were in the laws of nature, they were subject to them, but Anya was a Jew who lived above their rules. G-d had created her for a reason, and no man could take that away from her.

Her tears now dried, Anya walked over to the window and gazed out, watching the people in the street far below hurrying this way and that. From her perch high above, they appeared miniscule, and suddenly it occurred to her that if she could succeed in living a life of faith, all the minor events of life would be reduced in proportion as she focused on a larger, all-encompassing purpose.

As she stood there, she heard a knock at the door, and then the key turned in the lock. One of her interrogators had come to call her back into the office, where she took her seat once again.

Anya tried to read the answer on their faces, but their expressions were inscrutable. After an extended moment of silence, the silver-haired man cleared his throat and nodded curtly at her. "We received the information that we requested." Then, he fell silent, and Anya just stared, unsure what he meant. She had no idea what exactly they had requested or what she was about to hear; all she knew was that everything was in the Hands of G-d.

"We're sorry for suspecting you," the one with the steely gaze said simply.

"*What?*" Anya gasped, certain she had heard wrong.

"Our source in the KGB confirmed everything you said. We apologize if we gave you a scare."

She stared at them in utter disbelief. A minute ago, she was imagining her life in a foreign jail, and now the CIA was apologizing to her!

The men waited silently for her reaction, but all she could think of doing was shouting her thanks to her Creator. The senior officer seated between the two others addressed her again.

"Mrs. Krasnikov, may I ask you a question?"

She nodded slowly, wondering what could possibly be coming next.

"Are you looking for a job?"

"A job?"

"Something better paying than cleaning." The officer on the right cracked a smile.

Anya already guessed what they were about to suggest, but she decided to play dumb. "What do you have in mind?"

"What do you say about joining our Soviet department?"

"Your Soviet department?"

"It's a branch of Special Operations. Included in what we do is dispatching secret agents to various locations in the USSR, receiving intelligence, and deciphering codes, and so forth. We know a lot, but there's even more that we don't know. Having someone on board who once worked for them would be incredibly helpful, naturally. And, furthermore, a position with us comes along with a respectable salary, plus we'll put you through a course to improve your English and make you sound like a native. What do you say, Mrs. Krasnikov?"

"It sounds very good," Anya stammered, wondering what had happened to Anya Krasnikov, senior KGB officer, that she was suddenly bereft of all her eloquence. *They must surely be wondering how someone as seemingly dull-witted as me could possibly have been employed by Fyodorev*, she contemplated, but there wasn't much she could do about that.

Someone handed her a cup of coffee, and the sweet, hot liquid helped restore her presence of mind. The next hours passed in a blur as she carefully read the details of her contract before signing it, her eyes widening in disbelief when she saw the figure that represented her starting salary.

She returned home two hours later, practically dancing into their apartment and hugging both her astonished mother-in-law and her daughter excitedly. "I have a new job!" she sang.

"Really?" Valeria exclaimed. "So that's why you're late? What will you be doing?"

"It's a government job," was all Anya could share. Valeria nodded, knowing better than to dig for more.

"When do you start?" Valeria asked later, while Anya was busy laundering Karina's dress in the kitchen sink, a job she detested.

"The day after tomorrow. They agreed to give me tomorrow off to make arrangements." *And to recover from today's ordeal,* she added silently. A huge yawn split her face, and Valeria kindly took the sopping dress from her and wrung it out.

"This is the last time I wash something by hand!" Anya declared before falling gratefully into bed. "With my new salary, we can afford to buy a washing machine. I'm finished being a cleaning lady!"

CHAPTER 47

Anya's new job restored her lost pride. No longer was she treated as little more than an invisible speck of dust. Instead, she was a respected employee, stationed in a private office cubicle. Intelligence reports appeared on her desk at regular intervals and at first, she was stunned at the amount of data she was expected to process and interpret. However, it was clear from the outset that her presence was immensely appreciated, and her opinion was respected by all her colleagues. There was no one in the office who possessed her level of expertise in matters related to the communist states, Soviet intelligence and counterintelligence; in no time, she had proven herself as a devoted employee.

At the end of her first week, she was summoned to the accountancy department, where they explained that she would be required to open a bank account into which her salary would be deposited. When she headed to the bank to deposit her first check, her jaw dropped. The sum was almost double what she had been promised.

The following day, she returned to the accountancy department and asked if there had perhaps been a mistake or if she had just been advanced a two-month salary.

The clerk checked her file and replied, "According to the report I received, you have been executing tasks over and above those stipulated in your contact. In addition to your official duties, you have also been translating and consulting, hence the bonus."

"So this is my salary for one month?" she clarified again in disbelief.

"Yes. If you have a complaint, you can appeal to human resources. It may be negotiable," the clerk added kindly.

Anya tried to conceal her shock. The salary was more than double what she had earned in Moscow! "No, it's all right. It's fine for now. And thank you, thank you so much," she stammered.

At the time, it was still fine, but over the ensuing weeks, things began to change. Her work hours started to increase, and Anya soon found herself arguing for the right to leave work at five in order to be able to return home at a reasonable hour. Beyond her desire to spend those precious evening hours with Karina, she also refused to surrender the time needed for her Jewish studies.

Pete Stratton, her supervisor, tried persuading her to add on another two hours to her workday, late at night. "If you like, we can arrange for a driver to take you home and bring you back later," he offered. When she unequivocally refused, he compromised on one hour.

"Pete, I really can't," she apologized. "I have other things in my life aside from work."

"You'll get a significant raise," he dangled the carrot before her eyes.

"I've already gotten a significant raise," she replied calmly.

He chuckled at her reply. "That's only the beginning, Anya. The sky's the limit, you know. Besides, as a new immigrant, a raise will help you settle down comfortably."

"I'm settled and very comfortable," she replied. "We're not missing anything."

"You can always have more."

Anya rolled her eyes. "Isn't there anything you value more than your job and money?"

He didn't blink an eye as he replied. "There are many things that I value, but none as much as my job and money."

Anya couldn't hide her disgust. "I'd be willing to work for free for the rest of my life if it would only bring back my husband."

Pete immediately looked remorseful. "I'm sorry, Anya. I didn't mean it like that. Of course family means more than money, but how will hampering your progress here help your husband out of Siberia?"

"It won't help him out of Siberia, but at least I won't be hampering my own progress! Since settling in, I've begun following his path." Pete's quizzical look prompted her to explain. "My husband discovered the Judaism that was stolen from Soviet Jews for generations, and I've been investigating it myself."

"Well, *that* definitely won't get you anywhere, but to each their own," her supervisor remarked snidely, which effectively ended the conversation, as Anya was clearly not prepared to argue the point. She had already endured decades of others deciding what was best for her, and now that she was finally free to do as she pleased, this was one point she refused to surrender.

That week, the Krasnikovs moved to a nicer apartment, not lavish, but comfortable and spacious by any standards. Anya allowed herself the luxury of purchasing new electric appliances and quality furniture with a four-month payment plan. Her greatest pleasure, however, came from outfitting Karina from head to toe. From owning just two simple outfits, Karina suddenly became the best-dressed child in her class, and Anya also bought her a new coat, shoes, and toys. Karina was missing so much in life, first and foremost a father – at least now she did not have to feel physically deprived.

CHAPTER 48

Anya's job was not only prestigious; it was also intellectually stimulating and immensely satisfying. The knowledge that she was genuinely and significantly hampering the KGB's influence internationally motivated Anya to devote all of her energies to her work – but only during work hours. Once she left the office in the afternoon or early evening, she reverted to being plain Anya Krasnikov, a mother, a loyal daughter-in-law, and also a wife, even though her husband was so far away. Nonetheless, her emotional bond to her husband was such that she grasped at each and every opportunity to strengthen her attachment to him, and her Torah studies were her primary means of attachment – along with her constant prayers on his behalf.

In fact, Anya's evening classes were actually the highlight of her day. At first, she had traveled for an hour every night to the learning center in Brooklyn, but during her second week there, someone told her about a similar center right in Queens, very close to where she was living, which almost eliminated the travel time and often allowed her to remain for an extra class.

Her initial steps into the world of Judaism had been hesitant and cautious, but before long, Anya was absorbing each lesson thirstily, as if her life depended on it. She discovered a wealth of Jewish history, beginning from Creation, and was exposed for the first time to the existence of a uniquely Jewish legal system, one that governed every aspect of her life. She especially appreciated the classes on *hashkafah*, which altered her perspective on life and imbued it with meaning it had never had. Anya had no doubt that at the end of the school year, she would switch Karina out of public school into a Jewish institution.

Becoming religiously observant was certainly not a simple process, given that it entailed adopting so many new practices and routines in daily life, but Anya was long used to the idea of life being a series of challenges, and certainly, anyone who had grown up in the Soviet Union had no expectation of life being easy. However, as she learned more and more about Shabbos observance, Anya began to realize that this was one area that would be especially fraught with difficulties.

Lighting candles on Friday before dusk was the least of her problems, as by then, the days had grown longer and she had already returned from work. Local families often invited her, Karina, and Valeria to join them for the Shabbos *seudos*, and once Anya felt confident enough, she and Valeria started cooking on their own for Shabbos.

It was Shabbos day that posed the main problem. Due to the sensitive nature of their work, Anya and her colleagues worked a six-day week, which included Saturday and not Sunday. At first, once she had learned enough to understand what Shabbos meant, Anya kept only a few of the *halachos*, while intending to add to them as time passed; however, it soon became obvious that refraining from writing and answering the phone while at work was far from simple.

"What's the big idea of me pressing the buttons on the phone instead of you?" Harriet, her personal secretary, questioned, looking at Anya as if she had gone crazy. She was also annoyed at being told to type all the memos and letters that Anya usually took care of herself, and to authorize them with Anya's stamp. Instead of trying to explain, Anya chose the path of silence, doubting that Harriet would either understand or appreciate her religious sensibilities. She was fast learning that although superficially, America was the country of tolerance and freedom, in practice, many people were only tolerant of freedom itself, and had little patience or sympathy for anyone who adhered to a belief that restricted a person's freedom to do exactly as he desired whenever he pleased.

Nonetheless, Harriet was only a secretary, and she wasn't about to lose her job over her attitude to her boss' idiosyncrasies. The problem was not Harriet, however, but rather, Anya's own boss, Pete Stratton, and Anya knew that sooner or later, matters were likely to come to a head.

They did so more abruptly and extremely than she had expected.

One Saturday – one Shabbos – Anya finally decided that this week would be the last time she took the train into work, even though she was careful not to handle money. She arrived at work on time and climbed three flights of stairs to her office, smiling at Harriet as she entered, as always. The day passed slowly, with the expected friction when she tried to find ways around answering the phone or doing any form of writing, and finally, it was time for the weekly staff meeting which was held every Saturday afternoon at half past three.

The discussion was lively, as usual, but this time, Pete Stratton noticed for the first time how Anya not only wasn't taking notes, but also refrained from passing the ashtray when requested.

Before the meeting terminated, Stratton turned to her in annoyance. "Is there a problem, Anya?" All eyes turned to her.

Anya blushed crimson but forced herself to reply steadily, "Not a problem, but something I will admit. I've become Sabbath observant, which does complicate several aspects of the job. The truth is, I'd like to state now that I'm cutting down my work hours to preclude Saturdays."

A hush fell over the conference room as her colleagues stared at her in shock.

Suzanne was first to recover. "But, Anya, we can't manage a whole workday without you! You can't do that."

Stratton agreed. "Impossible, Anya. You can't just not show up to work once a week. This isn't a standard office job, and our work is too important for that."

"Of course our work is important, but as we discussed once before, there are other values in life, as well. To remind you, I had a top-notch job in Moscow too, but I left it all behind as a result of my husband's religious activities, not to mention the fact that he's now in Siberia for the very same reason. As far as I'm concerned, there's really no other option, because, well, we all see that it's not feasible for me to continue working on Saturdays and to keep the Sabbath." She didn't even mention that the next stage of her plan in furthering her observance had been to cease traveling on Shabbos altogether.

All eyes turned to Stratton to see his reaction. Aware of the import of his statement, Stratton stood up to speak, clearing his throat before he began. "Anya, I need to make one thing clear: Your contract obligates you to a six-day workweek. Skipping a day of work is not an option. If you insist on taking an extra day off, you'll have to find another job."

Anya paled, and the room spun dizzyingly around her. Perhaps it had been a grave error to announce her intention publicly before preparing Stratton earlier, but she hadn't believed things would deteriorate so quickly. Besides, they needed her. Or did they really? Could they manage without her? Had she overestimated her status in the department? They had managed fine without her before she had joined the staff, after all, and they could likely make do without her afterward, too.

"Are you threatening to fire me?" she asked in measured tones.

"I'm not threatening, just reminding you of the terms of your contract. We simply can't employ someone in your capacity who takes vacation days at will and misses a whole day once a week. It's simply not viable."

"I can come in on Sundays instead," she tried to suggest a compromise, but Stratton's expression made it clear that he had no intention of surrendering.

"There's only a bare-bones staff here on Sundays, and that's besides for the fact that you'll be missing the weekly staff meeting," Suzanne reminded her.

"I'll do what I can to make up the hours on Saturday nights," Anya promised.

"When nobody else is in the office?" Stratton retorted.

"I'll do whatever I can to make it work!" Anya's tone was becoming increasingly desperate.

"So keep things as they are!" he exploded.

"I can't! I'm sorry, and I'm sorry it came out like this," Anya said remorsefully.

"So are we."

"What would you like me to do?"

"Keep to your original schedule."

"That's impossible."

"Then you'll have to find another job."

Anya inhaled sharply and looked around the conference room for support. Other than Pete and Suzanne, nobody looked actually angry with her, but no one stepped forward on her behalf, either, knowing that it was fruitless to argue with Stratton – aside for the fact that they really did require her presence on Saturdays. Most of her colleagues dutifully avoided her gaze, and others exchanged a pained look with her, sympathetic but unwilling to stick their necks out.

Realizing that she was on her own, Anya closed her eyes for a second, summoning all the emotional and spiritual strength within her. *This is it. This is the nisayon that all my teachers have described.* Her hands were shaking, but she refused to communicate any weakness. She would overcome this challenge with confidence, grace, and faith.

"In that case, I think I'll leave now," she said quietly and walked with her head held high toward the door.

Stratton narrowed his eyes. "Don't forget to stop at the main reception desk and sign your resignation papers," he called after her spitefully.

"I can't sign on the Sabbath. If necessary, I'll come in on Monday to take care of the paperwork," Anya replied evenly.

Seeing what was happening, Suzanne tried to calm the atmosphere. "Let's not reach any hasty conclusions yet. We have the next thirty-six hours to think things through calmly. On Monday, when things have settled down, we'll discuss this again."

Anya smiled gratefully at her before turning around and leaving. Once outside the building, she stopped for a moment. Was she really about to take the train home? Although that morning, she had intended that this week would be the last one when she used public transportation, now, after her admission at the meeting, she felt it would be hypocritical to return home by train. There were still a few hours remaining until sundown, but she would wait them out in Manhattan rather than travel home on Shabbos. She now grasped how foolish it had been to try to observe Shabbos and work simultaneously. True, in Russia, there had been Jews who had done so, but only under extreme duress. It had been literally a matter of life and death, with the threat of Siberian exile hanging over their heads.

Here, in America, the worst that could happen was that she would be fired.

Fired.

The word echoed jarringly in her mind. After finally reaching a period of stability and relative security, she would once again be flung into a frightening, formidable world.

She would be unemployed once again, and most likely, she would have to return to scrubbing floors and windows in cold, impersonal surroundings where her pride would be trampled upon daily. Now, she regretted her hasty, irresponsible behavior and her shopping sprees. Had she even suspected that her period of employment at the CIA would end up being so short, she would never have moved to a more expensive apartment, nor would she have purchased furniture and appliances. Instead, she would have guarded her salary carefully, hoarding it for her uncertain future. And that future was now.

Tears welled up in her eyes as she relived the humiliation she had suffered in the law offices. After tasting the sweetness of dignity once again, she couldn't bring herself to return to such an awful existence. She found a park bench and sat down, morose thoughts accompanying her throughout the next hours as the sun made its slow descent toward the horizon. Watching the sun set and experiencing those final moments of Shabbos, she willed herself to think differently. *This is what Hashem wants from me now. This is my first real challenge as a committed Jew. Yes, I'm sacrificing something deeply precious and important to me, but it's far less than the sacrifice that Lev made and is making every minute of the day. This is the commitment that makes me proud to be a Jew.* The thought brought a smile to her lips, and as the last glimmer of sun disappeared, Anya sensed for the first time the true serenity of Shabbos. She was at peace with herself, and with her choice.

When she was certain that Shabbos had ended, she hurried

home to recite Havdalah. Valeria and Karina listened attentively as she pronounced the words carefully, and their "Amen" sounded to her like the tinkling of bells, heralding the new week, full of promise. The wine she sipped tasted sweeter than ever before, and Anya knew why. This had been her first real taste of Shabbos, the Shabbos which she had sacrificed her honor, prestige, and financial security to keep.

CHAPTER 49

Siberia

Lev marched at the end of the long row of prisoners, with the booted footsteps of the officer sounding close behind him. At the conclusion of a backbreaking day of work, it was a half hour walk back to the barracks, and at that time of year, that meant half an hour of trudging through the snow, trying to skirt the deeper patches where one fell in to one's knees and risked losing one's shoes. Today, it was snowing, and Lev walked with his head bowed against the swirling flakes. He pulled his thin coat tighter around his gaunt body, in a largely vain effort to ward off the impossible cold and warm himself with the soaked wool.

There were times when he was actually surprised to wake up in the morning and find himself still alive. He had been there in the labor camp for only five months, and he still hadn't decided which was worse: the excruciating labor, the incessant hunger, or the cruel climate. The combination of all three became more deadly with each passing day. When he had first arrived and taken stock of the living conditions, he had morosely predicted that he wouldn't survive much more than a month, but somehow, almost half a year later, his heart was still beating, although several men in his bunkhouse who had been sent there long before him had passed on since he had arrived there.

At long last, the camp gates became visible, far away on the horizon, and Lev forced his tired feet to keep on moving until he was inside the camp and standing in formation in the courtyard, ready to be counted. Not that the counting was such an eventful procedure; if anyone was missing at evening roll call, all it meant was that he had died during that day's work, as to run away was patently impossible. If the cold didn't finish a man off days before he could reach civilization further to the south, then a roaming Siberian bear surely would.

Twenty minutes later, an endless line of prisoners snaked their way from the entrance to the camp all the way to the kitchen where they received the evening meal, the second of the two meals a day they were allotted. Today, the presence of the camp commander at the food distribution did not bode well; usually he disappeared immediately after roll call, but if he had remained, it was a sure sign that something unusual was about to happen.

Lev's intuition wasn't wrong. The commander took his place at the side of the kitchen worker who was doling out the portions, and before each man's bowl was filled, he told the worker how much gruel to put in it, consulting with a chart each time – which obviously slowed the process considerably, stealing precious minutes from their nighttime hours of rest.

"From now onward," the commander explained curtly, "food will be rationed according to output. A person whose output is only, for instance, fifty percent of his quota, will receive half a regular portion. That will quickly put a stop to idleness," he predicted.

Lev knew otherwise. Half a ration today meant less output on the morrow, not more – as it was, the rations they received were barely enough to fuel them. When his turn came, half a bowl of gruel was unceremoniously dumped into his little metal container, and although he tried to protest that he had a hand injury from the previous week that hadn't yet healed, his words were ignored.

Later that night, Lev lay in bed as the hunger ate away at his intestines. The gnawing feeling was so intense that he felt almost as if it would kill him before morning. How would he fall asleep when he was so famished? And yet, he was so exhausted that just a moment later, his eyes closed of their own accord.

A moment later, however, he felt someone shake him gently awake and he glimpsed a form in the shadows. Lev trembled in fear.

"Don't be afraid," the shadow whispered in his ear. "I'm a medic, and I was sent to give you a shot of penicillin, as well as some food."

"Who sent you, and why?" Lev replied in shock. He had already witnessed prisoners collapsing and breathing their final breaths as a result of a mild infection, which he suspected had already taken root in his wounded hand. He hadn't imagined that there was anyone in the camp who offered antibiotics to those wretched prisoners.

"Haven't you learned yet not to ask questions in camp?" the medic replied. He injected the lifesaving fluid into Lev's forearm and whispered, "Boris sent me, but don't even hint that you know that."

Lev nodded; Boris was the officer in charge of his work detail, and Lev had long suspected that, unlike his fellow comrades in positions of authority, belying his rough exterior the man actually had a heart beating in his chest. Lev was immensely grateful to be working under his supervision and even more so now, seeing that his suspicion was confirmed. Once again, he saw the Hand of Hashem protecting him, even amidst the torturous conditions. Hashem had not abandoned him, and He had sent salvation that few in the labor camps merited.

"Here are several pills. Take two a day for the next three days. And here," he shoved a small package beneath Lev's pillow, "is the rest of your meal."

"Boris sent that too?" Lev whispered, in disbelief.

"No. The food is from Yiddel." And with that, the medic disappeared.

Yiddel! Lev's heart beat just a little faster. *The old, bearded Jew whose lips never stopped murmuring pesukim and Mishnayos…* Lev fingered the thin slices of bread that, to him, represented another day of life, another day of hope. He recalled his teacher's message in the basement room in the secret group in the University: "If you search for Hashem in every event of your life, you'll surely find Him there." Yes, Hashem was most certainly there in Siberia with him. Lev had no doubt of it.

A month later, the brutal Siberian winter finally relented to reveal a hint of spring. One day, Yiddel invited Lev to join a small group that was planning to secretly bake matzos for Pesach. Lev threw himself into the preparations, and during those days, he barely sensed the pangs of hunger or cold; he was too busy trying to find the right tools and build a kosher oven. It was a miracle, but by Erev Pesach, they had managed to build a semblance of an oven, and had procured two kilograms of flour which they carefully hid and guarded. Finally, when the time came, the men kindled a fire in their oven and commenced matzah baking with uncontained joy and alacrity.

As the final matzos were placed in the oven, the door to the hovel burst open to reveal the camp commander and two guards. Lev froze, and his heart plummeted to the earth. The commander looked around and required no explanation to grasp the clandestine activity taking place before his very eyes.

"Religious activity is anti-proletariat and a criminal act!" he declared. "One week of solitary confinement for each of the criminals in this room!" He turned to the guards. "And don't forget to inform the cook to reduce their meals to the minimum."

Solitary confinement in the Siberian pit was the worst imaginable punishment. As the opening was shut above him, Lev felt the walls and cold closing in on him from all sides. His heart bled, just as much from the emotional trauma as from the physical suffering. Why had Hashem deprived them of the *mitzvah* of matzah that they had sacrificed so much for? Didn't He value their desire and intense efforts to draw close to Him? The misery was so intense that it almost caused him to give up then and there and succumb.

At some point, as he hovered between consciousness and unconsciousness, the hole above him opened, and somebody was shoved inside together with him.

"Who are you?" Lev asked, since it was too dark to see.

"Me. Yiddel," the older man replied.

"What are you doing here? How did you manage to avoid solitary confinement?" Lev asked in disbelief.

"Oh, it's no problem. A little bribe goes a long way," the man smiled, a smile that Lev couldn't see, but heard clearly. He knew that Yiddel had nothing with which to bribe the guards except his meager portion of food, and he couldn't fathom what could have impelled the old Jew to sacrifice it.

"Why are you here?" he finally choked out.

"I came to tell you something important: You may think that *Hakadosh Baruch Hu* abandoned us, despite our sacrifice and yearning to fulfill His *mitzvos*, but you're wrong. Lev, the *mitzvah* we did, with such *mesirus nefesh,* definitely gives Hashem immense *nachas*."

"But after everything, we won't even merit eating *matzos mitzvah*," Lev whispered brokenly.

"We have no control over what we can eat tonight or any other night, but we put our lives on the line to fulfill Hashem's holy *mitzvos*, and that's a *zechus* that no one can ever take away from us. I would even venture to say that it's a *zechus* more precious to Hashem than eating the matzah itself. We can endeavor with all our might to keep His *mitzvos* and do His will, but at the end, we must remember that we are in His Hands alone, and the only thing we have control over is our *yiras Shamayim*."

Yiddel's final statement hit Lev like a thunderbolt, reminding him of his studies in Moscow. Then, it had all been theory; here, he was living the lessons he had learned. The knowledge that Yiddel had forfeited his meal in order to comfort him warmed his heart.

A moment later, the guard returned to drag Yiddel back to his own cell, but the man's words remained with Lev forevermore, girding him with faith. Several hours later, the door atop his dungeon opened again, and a tiny package dropped onto the ground by his side. Before he could see what it was, the door slammed shut, leaving him once again in the dark. Lev felt around until he located the package, discovering something small wrapped in thin paper.

He unwrapped the package with trembling fingers to discover a small piece of matzah inside. Tears streamed from his eyes as he recited the *brachos* fervently and bit into the poor man's bread. The taste lingered in his mouth, making him feel richer than he had felt since his exile. At that moment, he was certain that the messenger was none other than Eliyahu Hanavi. Only a month later did he learn that another group of Jews in the camp had baked matzah secretly on the very same day, without being discovered. Upon hearing the terrible news of the other group's capture, they had joined forces to ensure that their brothers in solitary confinement would receive a taste of Pesach matzah too. How they managed to do so was something that Lev never managed to figure out.

CHAPTER 50

A year passed, and the Siberian winter was once again at its peak. Temperatures plummeted as low as fifty degrees below zero, and Lev ceased believing in his chances of long-term survival; he took one day at a time, struggling to recall his previous identity as a free man, and to reaffirm his determination to maintain his spiritual freedom despite the terrible physical conditions. Whenever he felt the last of his strength faltering, he dragged himself to Yiddel's bunk where he could draw spiritual nourishment that would sustain him for another day.

"Life and death is in the Hands of Hashem alone!" Yiddel repeated constantly. "All we have to do is to preserve our holiness, to remember that we are here to serve Him and for no other reason. We have to constantly pray for the strength to overcome adversity and to praise and glorify His Holy Name!" Somehow, Yiddel's words gave Lev the sustenance he needed to face the next day of torture, to drag his exhausted body out to the woods and to do so with at least a measure of calm acceptance that this was Hashem's will for him at that time.

During those torturous hours, when the winds howled mercilessly and snow swirled about him, he could hardly remember the lessons that he had learned back in Moscow, what seemed like a lifetime ago. All he could remember was one short verse that he repeated with each strike of the axe, a verse that Yiddel repeated every day in his ear: "*Ein od milvado!*"

That morning was brighter than most, and the sun reflected blindingly off the pristine white snow, shining its glare into the prisoners' eyes. Lev began working systematically, aiming to meet his quota as early in the day as possible, before his energy was too sapped to swing the axe with sufficient force. In all that vast forest, the only sound was that of metal meeting wood. To waste one's energy on speech was unthinkable, even if it had been permitted.

A jeep maneuvered its way through the forest and felled trees, nearing the group of wretched laborers. Lev didn't give the jeep more than a cursory glance; he was working productively that day, and he knew it was foolish to slow his pace because of a momentary distraction. To his surprise, however, his labor was interrupted several minutes later when he was approached by the guard.

"Prisoner Krasnikov!" he heard his name called. Lev was astounded to learn that the jeep had been sent for him. "A visitor has arrived from Moscow who wants to speak to you!" the guard informed him. It was a strange summons, to be sure. No one visited the Siberian labor camp incidentally; the only arrivals were new prisoners, most of whom never returned. Lev wondered fearfully what was in store, but at least he knew that whatever it was, it surely couldn't be worse than what he was already enduring.

The jeep took him straight to the camp commander's bunkhouse where he found a high-ranking officer sitting comfortably in a lounge chair sipping a steaming cup of tea. Lev couldn't believe his ears when he was invited rather pleasantly to take the opposite seat.

"There's been talk of curtailing your current punishment," the officer stated laconically as he exhaled smoke from a cigarette.

Lev waited silently for the officer to continue.

"Doesn't it interest you to know who's been thinking of you in Moscow?"

"Very much, sir."

"Well, it doesn't look like it," the officer snapped. Apparently, he had expected a more animated reaction, but Lev was too astonished by the announcement to wonder who in Moscow cared enough to petition for his release.

"Our department received a special request regarding the prisoner Lev Ilyevich Krasnikov, and it was signed by a source that we cannot ignore."

Lev listened attentively, unable to believe his good fortune. Someone had petitioned on his behalf, but whom? Who would stick his neck out for a lone Jewish prisoner? The name Anatoly Andrayev sprang to mind, but he knew it couldn't be; Anatoly was too deeply engaged in the needs of the Jewish community to allow himself to take such a perilous risk. It would pose too great a danger both to him and to those he was helping.

"As I was saying," the officer interrupted his thoughts. "There's been serious discussion about releasing you. Our committee will be convening in a month, and your name is at the top of the list."

Finally Lev gave expression to his curiosity. "What did I do to deserve this?"

"Good question." The officer gave a twisted smile. "You have important information that you have been withholding. All you have to do is tell us what we want to know, and you'll be out of here."

"Information?" Lev asked, baffled. "What kind of information?"

The officer glowered at him. "Who was behind your wife's escape from prison?"

Lev couldn't prevent the color from draining from his face, but he managed to keep a steady gaze and remained silent.

"All you have to do is tell us, and you'll be free, Comrade Krasnikov."

Lev didn't reply, nor did he so much as blink an eyelash. The initial shock had dissipated quickly to be replaced by an inner tranquility. The Communists could play their game, but he would remain loyal to his principles. He shrugged slightly, and continued staring impassively at the officer.

"Our investigation is nearing its conclusion. We'll find whoever it was sooner or later in any case. If you help us, you'll buy your freedom. I can't imagine you'd be foolish enough to lose out on this golden opportunity."

"I wish I didn't have to, but I have nothing more to tell you. There was nobody involved but me."

"And you expect us to believe that?" the officer exploded angrily. "You broke into jail yourself, without a shred of assistance from anyone? Somebody showed you the plans. Somebody helped you in and out. It was *not* a one-man operation."

This time, Lev allowed himself a small smile. "I see that you underestimate me, then, because I did indeed manage to pull it off by myself."

Without warning, the guard stationed at the door suddenly approached, to beat him with a club, and the room swirled around Lev.

"You pulled it off yourself," the officer repeated in a whisper, his eyes glinting like those of a poisonous snake. "And how did you know exactly where your wife was being held? How did you distract the wardens? Who was ready with the escape vehicle, and where, exactly, did she go?"

He had been asked the same questions dozens of times already during his initial interrogations, and Lev couldn't fathom why they hadn't given up yet, or why they had suddenly remembered about him.

"I told you numerous times, and I'll tell you again," he said in measured tones. "I worked hard to think up and carry out the plan, and I was afraid to involve anyone else because I didn't know if there was anyone who could be trusted. I made my investigations until I discovered all I needed to know, and I booked a random taxi company to station a driver for when the time came. The only thing that went wrong in the whole operation was that I was shot. And once I was out of the picture, I don't know what happened to my wife or where she escaped to."

"I didn't travel all the way here to hear the same lame story you fed the interrogators back in Moscow!" the officer shouted angrily at him.

Lev shrugged helplessly. Little did these officers know that his months in the forced labor camp hadn't weakened him, but had rather fortified him immensely. At present, he had nothing left to lose but his soul, which was something he would never surrender. His life was worth nothing there in Siberia, and every hour of existence was another miracle. Yiddel constantly stressed that his greatest challenge was to sanctify the Name of Hashem in life as in death, and that was exactly what he intended to do. There in the icy forests of Siberia, there was no greater goal to which to aspire.

"I'm sorry to disappoint you, sir," he replied boldly, "but what made you think that I'd have something to add to what I already told you back in Moscow?"

"Because you had plenty to add in Moscow as well, but you foolishly kept it all to yourself. Now that you know what life is like in Siberia, none of us believed you'd be so foolish as to resign yourself to this fate in vain."

In vain? Nothing in G-d's world was in vain, but these beasts couldn't fathom such lofty concepts...

"I have nothing else to add," he repeated steadily.

The officer threw his cigarette butt onto the ground and stomped on it furiously. "You have plenty to add, and believe me, you will. Even if you don't value your life enough to aspire for freedom, you still don't want to end it in solitary confinement in the pit. And however hellish you think your life is now, it will be much, much worse if I'm forced to return to Moscow empty-handed."

"I understand, sir," Lev said quietly, his calm response serving only to infuriate the officer even more. Never before had he faced such obstinacy.

"Would you care for a demonstration to prove how serious we are?" he whispered menacingly.

"I believe that you're very serious," Lev nodded.

Finally unable to tolerate the serene expression on the face of the prisoner, the officer rose to his feet and stalked out of the room, firing furious orders at his subordinates, who hastened to execute them.

Lev was thrown back into the pit. Hitting the ground hard, he whispered his thanks to *Hakadosh Baruch Hu* for imbuing him with the strength to keep his promise and hold his tongue.

CHAPTER 51

Anya walked into the CIA office, her impassive features belying her pounding heart. She had come to tender her resignation, and it hurt. Her first stop was Suzanne's office, since she was the only one who had hinted to Anya that there might be some way for her to keep her job, and Suzanne's opinion carried a lot of weight in the department.

"Good morning, Anya," Suzanne greeted her with a reserved smile.

"Hi, Suzanne." She approached the desk and quietly asked, "Is there any way we can work this out?"

Suzanne avoided her gaze. "Depends on you. What have you decided?"

"Suzanne, I really want to continue working here. Sabbath is one point that I really can't compromise on, but there are so many ways to work around it!"

Suzanne lifted her hands in despair. "Personally, I agree, but I'm not the one authorized to negotiate on this."

"Stratton is behind this, isn't he?"

"You better believe it. He's like an angry bull."

"I hear. In that case, I guess I'll sign the papers and say goodbye."

Suzanne looked remorseful. "Anya, I feel terrible about this. Won't you reconsider?"

"Suzanne, this is a step I've been considering and reconsidering for months. All I ask is one thing from you."

"Whatever I can!" Suzanne promised.

"Would you write me a letter of recommendation?"

"With pleasure! I just wish it didn't have to be for this reason. I'll write whatever you need. You're an exceptional worker, Anya, as well as kind-hearted and honest. I'm sure you'll be an asset wherever you go, and it was a real pleasure working with you."

"Thank you." Sadly, Anya signed the documents that Suzanne handed her and turned to leave.

———

Anya was home by eleven, armed with a stack of newspapers that she had purchased at a local stand. She spent the next hours poring over the classifieds section, searching for something suitable. There were several available positions, and she lost no time faxing in her resume, each time cringing at how meager it was. Once that taken care of, she busied herself around the house and even went to pick up Karina from preschool, a pleasure she hadn't experienced since moving to America. The highlight of her day, as usual, was her night classes at the Jewish learning center.

The next two days were boring, but she filled them with household chores, shopping, and keeping her mother-in-law company. She purchased items sparingly, not knowing how long she would remain unemployed. By the fourth day, never one to be idle, Anya was sure she would lose her mind. How much longer could she do nothing all day long? After thinking it over, she decided to try one of the morning classes in the learning center, which she had never been able to attend in the past.

She walked into the center, her spirits rising the moment she entered. One of her teachers, Rebbetzin Steinberg, greeted her in the lobby. "Good morning, Anya! Nice to see you around here at this hour of the day. I don't think I've ever seen you here during the morning hours."

Anya blushed, suddenly feeling conspicuous. Until that point, she hadn't shared her fateful choice with anyone but Valeria.

"I… I…" she stammered uncomfortably, staring at the floor as she spoke. Rebbetzin Steinberg waited patiently for her to continue. "I left my job," she finally mustered the courage to admit.

"Oh?" The rebbetzin didn't press her to continue, but Anya suddenly felt an urgent need to unload her heavy burden. She needed encouragement desperately. At the time when she made her choice, everything had seemed so clear, but now she was beginning to wonder if she hadn't acted hastily. Perhaps she should have tried harder to keep her job? Who knew how quickly she would find something else?

As if reading her mind, the rebbetzin treated her to a warm smile. "I have some free time until I start teaching, and I could use some coffee. Would you like to join me?" Without awaiting a reply, she steered Anya into the tiny cubicle that she called her office and returned a minute later with two steaming cups of coffee. When they were both seated comfortably, the rebbetzin turned to Anya, understanding shining from her large brown eyes. "Would you like to tell me about it?"

The story tumbled out almost of its own accord. Until that point, Anya had been very reticent about revealing anything of her past, but there in the privacy of the rebbetzin's office, she found herself sharing everything, beginning with her life in Moscow, Lev's discovery of Judaism, his arrest followed by hers, and her subsequent escape from the KGB dungeon and flight to America. She described her demeaning job as a cleaning lady and attending her first Jewish event which had led her to the learning center in Queens. From that point, the rebbetzin was already familiar already with Anya's story and her slow steps toward observance. She was aware that Anya had begun keeping aspects of Shabbos, but she was astounded when the younger woman related the major sacrifice she had just made.

"So now, since I'm still looking for another job, I thought I'd at least occupy myself productively in the meantime," Anya concluded.

The rebbetzin had tears in her eyes. "Anya…" she said, "I'm so overcome by everything you just told me that I'm simply speechless. I can't even imagine the reward for such *mesirus nefesh*. I never met someone like you before…" She continued for several moments, imbuing Anya with the spiritual and emotional strength she so deeply craved.

By then, it was time for the rebbetzin's *shiur*, and she smiled apologetically at Anya. "I wish I didn't have to interrupt this, but I have to start teaching now. Would you like to join?" Anya followed her mentor into the library where she soon found herself absorbed in the glowing world of Torah inspiration. The *shiur* ended an hour later, and before she could leave, Rebbetzin Steinberg tapped her on the shoulder.

"I'm glad you spoke to me, Anya. I'm going to keep my ear out in case I hear of anything, plus I'll spread the word around."

"Thank you, Rebbetzin," Anya smiled gratefully.

"My pleasure, Anya. And I hope to see you here more often, at least until you get a new job!"

"Absolutely," she promised.

One week passed, and then two. Anya kept herself busy, utilizing most of her spare time to further her knowledge and make up for the gap of years in Jewish studies, but she knew that she couldn't continue like that much longer. Soon, she would have to pay the next installment on her furniture and appliances, and without a steady income, she would need that money for food.

At the beginning of her third week of unemployment, Anya finally made up her mind to head back to the employment agency. The thought made her cringe, but she hoped that this time, her now nearly-fluent English coupled with her letter of recommendation would improve her prospects.

Anya's spirits were low that morning as she gave Karina breakfast and packed her lunchbox. She was just about to leave when the phone rang. She was tempted to ignore it, knowing that the later she reached the employment agency, the longer the lines would be. Karina, however, answered the phone before she could tell her to leave it.

"Hello?" she chirped into the phone. "Mama," she said a second later, having long since dropped the Russian "Mamochka." "It's for you."

Sighing, Anya reached to answer, but her spirits soared when she heard the voice on the other end of the line. "Anya, it's Miriam Steinberg. How are you?" Without waiting to hear her reply, she forged ahead. "Listen, I just got a call from my neighbor, Mrs. Stefansky, who's a school principal. I mentioned to her a week ago that I know somebody looking for a job, and I sang your praises to the sky, but she said that she didn't have anything available just then. Anyway, not five minutes ago she called me to say that her secretary had a preemie last night, and she's desperate for a replacement because it turns out that the woman she planned to hire when her secretary gave birth has another job for this month. She said even though she's never met you, she's willing to give you a try based on my recommendation. If it works out, fantastic. If not, we'll keep on looking. Are you interested?" she concluded breathlessly.

The rebbetzin spoke so quickly and eagerly that Anya missed more than half of what was said. What she did manage to glean, however, was that there might be an available job. In a school.

"Anya? Are you there?" the rebbetzin asked again.

"I'm here," Anya said faintly.

"Would you be interested in giving it a try?"

Am I interested? Anything is better than waiting on line at that employment agency and being forced to accept one of their pathetic offers.

"Yes! Yes, definitely! Oh, Rebbetzin, thank you so much! I really hope it works out!"

Anya settled into her new job quickly, even though the school, Bnos Miriam, was so different from any of the other places where she had previously worked. The work was certainly not especially stimulating and the salary was far less than what she had been paid at the CIA, but other aspects of her job easily compensated for that, and when the previous secretary gave notice that she wouldn't be returning at least until the end of the year, Anya was happy to accept Mrs. Stefansky's invitation to stay on.

The constant bustle in the school office was exactly what she needed during that period in her life, as it helped to distract her from the thoughts and worries she preferred not to dwell upon. More than that, she enjoyed being in a frum environment where she was exposed to those living a frum life, not just learning about it. Although she divulged little of her personal life to her fellow staff members, they gleaned quickly enough that she was in need of a larger-than-usual dose of warmth, and Anya, Valeria, and Karina were often invited for Shabbos and Yom Tov to the homes of the teachers and even some of the parents of the students.

Anya loved the happy Shabbos tables and the aura of holiness that permeated the homes of her hosts. Nonetheless, it was always a bitter-sweet experience, and many times, after returning home late on Shabbos evening, she would cry into her pillow. Even though she knew it was forbidden to weep and mourn on Shabbos, it was hard for her to stem the tears once her thoughts turned to her husband and she wondered if he would ever experience the beauty of living life openly as an observant Jew.

Karina celebrated her fifth birthday as a *talmidah* at Bnos Miriam. As she gazed at her daughter, so mature and serious, Anya suddenly realized how much she had changed since they had arrived in America. Even though she was certainly not old enough to understand what had happened to them and why, the events of the past few years had left an indelible mark on her, and Anya found herself once again mourning the fact that her daughter could not grow up as a carefree little girl, nurtured by a warm, intact family.

That evening, after an afternoon spent playing with the new toys her mother and grandmother had given her, Karina suddenly turned to her mother with large, sad eyes. "Mama," she began, a little uncertainly, "do you think Papa still remembers my birthday?"

The question came so unexpectedly that Anya nearly dropped the laundry basket she was holding, and her eyes immediately filled with tears. Karina had been so happy all day long; what had prompted her sudden nostalgia?

"Of course he remembers, Karina darling! How could he forget the happiest day in his life?"

"But he didn't send me a present," Karina pointed out, with her childish logic.

Anya exhaled slowly as she tried to think up a response that would satisfy such a young child. "Karina, sweetie, Papa is very, very far away, in a place called Siberia. He can't send you a present from there, because it's too far away, but when he comes home," Anya's voice cracked, but she quickly pulled herself together, "he'll for sure bring you a present, even more than one. And in the meantime, he's *davening* for you all the time, and that's the best present of all."

Karina frowned for a moment, and then her expression relaxed and she nodded silently, accepting the confusing reality. Even as she marveled at her daughter's ability to do so, Anya herself began to wonder if she could accept the truth. Would she ever even learn her husband's fate? Anya had always been a realist, and she, better than most, knew that if Lev had been sent to Siberia, as she had reason to believe, then his chances of surviving a decade of captivity there were close to nil. There was no way of even knowing if he was still alive there a year after being imprisoned. Was he praying for Karina? Had he succeeded in clinging to his faith in such dire circumstances? If only she had the answers…

Late the following afternoon, when Anya returned home from work, she noticed that her mother-in-law looked under the weather. Valeria didn't complain, however. Supper simmered on the stovetop, and the house sparkled as always.

"Are you feeling okay?" Anya asked in concern. "Do you want to lie down until dinner?"

"I rested already," Valeria sighed, "but it doesn't help. That's what happens when you reach my age. Everything starts to creak, and I tire so easily. I never thought I'd be one to surrender to old age."

"You're not getting old, Mama!" Anya chuckled warmly. "You're as young and vibrant as ever. But maybe you do have a virus or flu? Maybe you should go to the doctor tomorrow morning."

"The doctor? Feh! For a silly little virus? I'll make a fool out of myself!" the older woman protested.

"Better to laugh that you went to the doctor for nothing than the alternative," Anya argued, but Valeria refused to hear anything of it. But later, in the middle of the night, Anya suddenly heard strange rasping noises coming from her mother-in-law's bedroom. At first, she froze in shock, but then she jumped out of bed and ran to Valeria's room, where she found the older woman gasping for air. Anya watched in horror as the woman who had accompanied her through thick and thin battled to breathe. Then, shaking herself free of her terror, she ran to the phone and dialed 911.

The ambulance came quickly, and the paramedics immediately place an oxygen mask on the old woman's face. For a full thirty minutes, they battled to stabilize her breathing before preparing to transfer her to the hospital. Automatically, Anya began following them down the stairs, but halfway down, she stopped, realizing that she had a major problem. She couldn't leave Valeria on her own in the hospital – but neither could she leave five-year-old Karina alone at home, and she didn't know any of the neighbors well enough to knock at a door in the middle of the night. Seeing no other option, Anya grabbed the phone and dialed her principal.

Mrs. Stefansky picked up the phone on the second ring, and when she heard what the problem was, she unhesitating replied, "Don't worry, Anya. I'll be right over, and I'll take Karina home with me. Tell the ambulance to go ahead, and I'll drop you off at the hospital on my way back with Karina."

Anxious and disoriented, Anya roused her daughter, explaining rather incoherently that Babushka wasn't feeling well and had to go to the doctor right then, without waiting for the morning. Somehow, she managed to find the presence of mind to pack Karina's clothing and lunch bag, and then they went down to the lobby to wait for Mrs. Stefansky, who arrived just two minutes later. Fortunately, Karina missed seeing her beloved grandmother being taken away on a stretcher, but she still craved reassurance, and, after her principal dropped Anya off at the hospital, she turned to Mrs. Stefansky, shocking her with her question.

"Did they take my grandmother to Siberia?"

"Siberia?" Mrs. Stefansky whipped around to face the little girl but immediately returned her focus to the road. "Karina, Siberia is too far away to get there by ambulance. They took your Bubby to the hospital where she will get better, *im yirtzeh Hashem*."

"Mama told her before supper that she should go to the doctor, but she didn't want to. I wonder how she got her to change her mind," Karina mused innocently.

Valeria's diagnosis was only slightly encouraging. "It was cardiac arrest," the doctor explained, "but her chances are still decent. She received the critical care in time. As far as we can tell, there was no brain damage, but her heart is still very weak." Anya felt her own heart lurch in anxiety as she waited outside the operating room while the doctors performed bypass surgery. As usual, at any time of added stress, her thoughts traveled to her husband as she wondered what he was thinking at that moment. His mother was lying on the operating table, hovering between life and death; did he sense anything? Would he pray for her? Was the terrible suffering he was surely enduring standing in their merit and safeguarding their family?

Thankfully, the operation was successful, and Valeria was transferred to the Cardiology ward. Anya waited anxiously for her to wake up from the anesthesia, but it wasn't meant to be. The following afternoon, Valeria Krasnikov went into cardiac arrest for the second time in twenty-four hours, and despite valiant efforts to restore her breathing, she passed away an hour later.

Since Valeria had only a few acquaintances, her funeral was sparsely attended, most of those present being either Bnos Miriam faculty members or people who knew Anya from the Jewish Learning Center. Mrs. Stefansky stood close to Anya who wept bitterly as if she had lost her own mother.

"I'm all alone now," she sobbed on the principal's shoulder. "She did so much for me – how will I manage without her?" Mrs. Stefansky embraced the younger woman and spoke to her soothingly but firmly.

"You're never alone, Anya. Never! *Hakadosh Baruch Hu* is with you, and now we're your family here. We'll be at your side every step of the way as you raise Karina and build a life here in America. And we'll all continue *davening* for your husband's safe return."

Her warm words made Anya cry even harder.

CHAPTER 52

Nine Years Later…

Mrs. Faigy Jakobowitz was sitting in the corner of the teachers' room, just about to take another forkful of her salad, when she heard her name being called.

"Faigy, there's a student outside who wants to speak to you," Rena Fisher, the math teacher, told her.

Mrs. Jakobowitz sighed. It was lunch break; didn't she deserve a couple of moments of peace and quiet?"

"Who is it?" she asked resignedly.

"Karina Krasnikov. In fact, I think she's been standing outside the door since the beginning of recess – I saw her there on my way to the office," Rena added.

Karina. The student who had stood out from the very first week of school. Karina was quiet and serious, smart and extremely refined. Despite her toned-down nature, she was still popular and respected among *her peers. It was so typical of Karina to wait twenty minutes rather than intrude.* Faigy rose from her chair and exited the room to speak to the girl.

"Mrs. Jakobowitz, I don't think I'm going to be able to be part of the exhibit," Karina blurted out the moment she caught sight of her.

"Why not?" Faigy's eyes widened in surprise. "The exhibit is meant for girls like you! And you were so excited when I first announced it!"

Something flitted through Karina's eyes; was it bitterness? Anger? Frustration? "I was, but the meetings are being held at night, so I won't be able come."

"Seven o'clock isn't exactly night," Mrs. Jakobowitz disagreed. "It's still evening. What's the problem, Karina? Does your mother need your help babysitting or putting the other kids to sleep then? I can speak to her, if it's a problem, and see if there's a way to work around things."

Karina shook her head. "I don't have younger siblings, and that's really the issue. I can't leave my mother home alone."

"You can't leave your mother alone?" Faigy repeated, baffled.

"No, I can't," the ninth grader replied adamantly.

Mrs. Jakobowitz was more confused than ever. "To be honest, if it were up to me, I would have made the meetings earlier, but most of the girls were happy with the time, and the teacher who's leading the project has young children, and she can't come any earlier. So…"

"So I guess there's nothing much that can be done," Karina shrugged. "It's not such a big deal, I guess, though I'm sorry that I have to drop out. Hopefully something else will work out later in the year."

Faigy Jakobowitz stared at the ninth grader in amazement. It was obvious that Karina was upset at forfeiting the project, but for whatever reason, she refused to change her schedule. She decided to try a different approach. "Why can't you leave your mother alone, Karina?"

Karina looked uncomfortable. "She's lonely, and when she's alone at home, it's much worse. We have no family in the whole country except each other, and she needs me."

Faigy tried remembering if she had heard anything specific about Karina's family, but nothing striking rose to her mind. As far as she knew, Karina was not an orphan, but perhaps her parents were divorced? She would ask the guidance counselor, but she certainly wouldn't pry any deeper than that unless Karina herself appeared to want outside help. It was obvious that this girl had more than her share of weight and responsibility on her young shoulders.

"On the other hand, I'm sure your mother wouldn't want you to miss out on this project," she suggested.

"Of course she wouldn't, which is why I won't tell her about it," Karina replied simply.

The corridor was bustling with the constant flow of students, and it was difficult to make herself heard above the din, but Faigy decided to stress one point, even though she didn't think she had much chance of convincing Karina to reconsider.

"Karina, it's almost never a good idea to keep secrets. I suggest that you tell your mother about the project and see how she reacts to the idea of you attending the meetings. Maybe she won't react the way you're expecting her to? Maybe she'll welcome the idea of giving this time to you? What do you think?"

"Oh, I know she would welcome the idea. If she hears about the project, then she'll for sure encourage me to take part in it. She always wants what's best for me, even if it's not the best for her. But that's not the point. I have to look out for her – if I don't, then who will?"

Hearing Karina's words, Faigy fell silent. Who was she, after all, to deprive this girl of what she thought was her *mitzvah*? On the other hand, maybe, for all her good intentions, Karina was going about things the wrong way? The matter required further thought, but for the moment she let it rest.

Anya finished washing the dishes and joined her daughter in the living room. Karina immediately closed her book and turned to her mother with a smile. "What day is Miss Handler's *sheva brachos*? You offered to make the rolls, right? Want to start tonight?"

Anya sank onto the couch beside her daughter. "No, not tonight. I'm too tired. Maybe we'll start tomorrow instead. I heard you have a Jewish history project," she added.

Karina's smile faded. "Who told you?" she demanded.

"Who told me?" Anya feigned innocence. "Who told me… I can't remember… Somebody, maybe a mother from the school or one of the teachers… In any case, I was so proud to hear that you were selected. It's a big honor for a ninth grader to be included in the exhibit!"

"I wasn't exactly selected," Karina said vaguely, "and I don't think I'm going to be part of it in any case. But it's okay, because I'd much rather spend time at home with you."

"Karina, I'd much prefer that you participate in this project than stay home with me. In fact, it's important for me that you're part of the exhibit."

"Why?" Karina lost the wind in her sails.

"Because you like history, and you could gain a lot from contributing to this project. Watching you learn and mature is my greatest *nachas*, Karina."

"I know," Karina nodded weakly, "but there's a problem with the scheduling, so I'd rather do something else."

"Why? What's the problem with scheduling? Are you afraid to leave me alone?"

Karina jumped off the couch. "I don't believe it! I can't believe she'd rat on me like that! Mrs. Jakobowitz told you, didn't she?"

"That's not the point."

"Yes, it is!" Tears sprang to Karina's eyes. She tried swallowing them, but they forced their way out nonetheless. "How dare she!" she cried. "I trusted her, and she abused that trust! I can't believe she'd do that to me!"

"She only wants what's best for you, Karina, and I appreciated her telling me."

"Well, I don't!" Karina said huffily. "And she didn't understand a word of what I said!"

"Just because you disagree with her reaction doesn't mean that she didn't understand you," Anya noted.

Karina held fast to her principles. "Nobody asked her to get involved. I'm not interested in being part of the exhibit, and that's it!"

But Anya wasn't willing to surrender easily; she was just as stubborn as her daughter on this matter. "Karina, Mrs. Jakobowitz told me that you were very excited about the exhibit when it was first announced, and it was only later on that you lost interest, when you heard that the meetings were going to be held in the evenings. Karina, honestly, do you think that I'm so weak and pathetic that I can't stay home on my own for a few hours once in a while?"

Karina's eyes glimmered with tears. "You're not pathetic at all, Mama. You're amazing! But… you're all that I have, and I also want to spend time with you. Is that so terrible?"

"It's not terrible at all. In fact, it gives me tremendous *nachas* to see how caring you are. But you shouldn't hide things from me, and you don't need to be so protective, either. Besides, I'll tell you a secret: The learning center just announced a new series of lectures that I'm very interested in attending, but I wasn't going to go because I didn't want to leave *you* at home on your own!"

Karina looked skeptically at her mother. "Really?"

"Really and truly."

"And you'd really like me to be part of the exhibit?"

"More than you can imagine!"

Karina wiped her tear-streaked face, feeling a great sense of relief that she didn't have to miss out on something she badly wanted to do, in order to avoid compromising her principles.

Two days later, Karina hurried home after the first meeting of the girls participating in the exhibit, eager to tell her mother all about it. She was one of only three ninth graders to have been chosen to take part, and during that first meeting, she had been too shy to state her own opinion during the discussions, leaving all the talking to the older girls.

Karina ran up the steps of the apartment building and fumbled for her key in her backpack, but when she turned the key, she realized the door was unlocked. Her mother had clearly already returned from work, which was unusual, but not unheard of. Karina dumped her backpack in the hall and headed to the kitchen to look for her mother, but, not finding her there, turned instead to her mother's room.

"Hi, Mama!" she called out cheerfully, before stopping in her tracks. Anya was lying in bed, staring blankly at the ceiling, and she didn't even respond to her daughter's greeting.

"Mama?" Karina repeated uncertainly. "Are you okay?"

Finally, Anya responded, but without even turning to look at her daughter. "Karina… please just leave me alone for now, okay. I need quiet now."

Karina retreated as if somebody had punched her in the stomach.

Her mother had never spoken to her that way before, and although she was sometimes sad or even a bit depressed, she was always happy to see her daughter, putting aside her mood swings in order to focus on her. What could have happened to make her so distant?

Karina left the room quietly, hoping that soon, her mother would emerge and respond to her normally. Meanwhile, it was already close to nine o'clock, and she hadn't eaten supper yet. Finding some leftover spaghetti in the fridge, she warmed it in a pan and then sat down to eat.

Picking up the morning's newspaper to skim through, Karina noticed that there was a letter tucked underneath it, its envelope bearing foreign-looking stamps. She turned it over to identify the sender, and then saw that it was written in Russian. Her mother had taught to read Russian years ago, and Karina now struggled to decipher the scrawl: *Katerina Nastrov.*

Forgetting that the letter wasn't addressed to her, she removed the letter from the envelope with trembling fingers and began slowly to read.

> *Dearest Anya,*
>
> *I just received a shred of information about your husband. I wish I didn't have to be the one to share this with you, but I feel that it is only right that you know the truth. A week ago, I met a mutual friend whose husband is employed by the KGB and recently visited the camps in Siberia during the course of his work. He met Lev in one of the camps, and they spoke briefly. He said that Lev seemed to be in relatively good health, physical as well as emotional.*
>
> *Oh, Anya – I wish that was all I had to tell you. But, the morning before this man left the camp, a terrible tragedy occurred. The men in Lev's labor detail left for work, as usual, but then, an hour later, one of the guards accompanying them returned with a report of an avalanche that had buried the entire group. Several groups of prisoners headed im-*

mediately to the site to try to rescue the men, but it seems that there were no survivors, and they couldn't even reach many of the men because of the dangerous conditions out there.

Anya, I'm so, so sorry to be the bearer of bad tidings and to share this heartbreaking news with you, but I couldn't withhold the truth from you either. I wept for you the whole night after hearing what happened, and I hope that somehow, you will find comfort and consolation from your sorrow.

With you in your pain,
Katerina

Karina gazed sightlessly at the letter, unable to absorb what she had just read. *It can't be! It can't! It can't be true!* She read the letter again and again, trying to find some way of interpreting the words differently, but it was hopeless. Her father was gone; all hopes of reuniting with him, of being a whole family once again, had vanished in an instant.

As she sat there, staring blankly at the tabletop, Karina tried to understand what this was supposed to mean for her. How should she feel about losing a father she barely remembered? Though she would never admit it to her mother, the truth was that she no longer recalled what her father looked like. The few memories she still clung to were vague and fuzzy; essentially, she had already lost her father nine years earlier…

CHAPTER 53

One Year Later…

Anya wandered into the teachers' room to prepare herself a cup of coffee. *The last one of the day*, she promised herself. To her surprise, she found Mindy Sirkis, a coworker, sitting there.

"Mindy! What are you doing here? I thought you finished early today."

Mindy looked up and smiled. "Actually, I was waiting for you, Anya. Want to join me for a cup of coffee? There's nobody around to disturb us now – neither teachers nor students."

Anya nodded. "Sounds good. But I can't be too long. I have a pile of work to finish before the end of the day."

"No problem." Mindy got up to make two cups of coffee and then returned, sitting down opposite her friend. After a moment of silence that for some reason, felt awkward to Anya, Mindy spoke up.

"Anya… Like I said, I was waiting for a chance to talk to you.

Because… well, you're not yourself since… since last year. We were all waiting for you to get back to yourself, but you're not, and we're really worried."

Anya lowered her eyes, but didn't reply.

"Anya, I'm sorry if I'm treading on forbidden territory, but you're one of my best friends, and I'm very worried about you," Mindy added genuinely.

Finally, Anya lifted her eyes, which were filled with unshed tears. "You're right, Mindy. I know it's been a year already, and I'm the first to admit that I haven't gotten back to myself." Mindy nodded compassionately, soundlessly urging her to continue.

"I try so hard to overcome the pain, but it never lets up, not even slightly. Sometimes I feel like I use up all my energy trying to hide my feelings from Karina so at least she will be able to grow up normal and healthy. I manage more or less when she's around, but when she's not, I sometimes feel like I'm ready to collapse. It's so stupid… I mean, I've been through harder things in the past, and… for him, at least he's not suffering any more… I wish I could be strong, but I just can't. I can't find it in myself."

Mindy nodded. "Nobody expects you to get over it completely… We're just concerned about you."

"But I learned that the more time that passes after a death, the easier it's supposed to be to deal with it," Anya protested. "Hashem lets people forget, but for some reason, He never lets me forget. I even went to speak to a frum psychologist about this, not long ago. She explained that, sometimes, there's something inside blocking the *emunah* and acceptance from being absorbed. When people don't grieve properly, they have no way to escape it, but she taught me several techniques, one of which made a big difference."

"But not enough of a difference," Mindy murmured.

"No, not enough," Anya agreed. "I don't sleep well, and I have these awful nightmares where I see him lying there, wounded in the snow, crying for help. I dream that I run in the snow, without a coat, without boots, trying to save him. There's this huge stretch of white snowy plain that I have to cross, but I run and I run, and I never get there…"

Mindy's eyes filled with tears. "Oh, Anya…"

Anya swallowed hard. "I wanted to help him, but… but I guess I didn't want enough. I let him die there, alone. I know there wasn't really any choice, but maybe if I had *davened* more, or better, or something, then there would have been a miracle and they would have released him… I don't know. I just don't know – and that's the worst of all."

Anya fell silent, and Mindy was silent too, as she tried desperately to think of the right thing to say.

"But you *do* know, Anya," she spoke up finally. "What happened is exactly what Hashem wanted to happen. Your *tefillos* for your husband were very precious and they achieved a lot, but they clearly weren't meant to bring about his release. Hashem had different plans for your husband, that involved dying *al kiddush Hashem*. But for you," Mindy paused for a moment, weighing her next words carefully, "there's a different plan. Mourning your husband forever isn't doing anything for anyone, least of all you. Anya, do you really think that Hashem wants you to stop living now, just because one chapter of your life finished? You have many good years still ahead of you, *b'ezras Hashem*."

"Good years?" Anya repeated blankly.

"Yes, good years. Anya," Mindy asked seriously, "you are still young, and maybe… maybe if you could look at things a bit differently, then you would be able to move on? To move on, and consider starting something new, with someone else." Finally, the words were out, and Mindy fell silent, waiting for Anya's reaction.

For a moment, Anya froze, but then she sprang back to life. "Someone else? Never! How could I?"

"Anya, think for a moment. Think about what this could mean. You could rebuild. You could have a normal family life, normal Shabbos *seudos*. Karina could have a father figure in her life. Do you think this is what Hashem wants from you – to be on your own forever?"

Anya sighed and shook her head. No! Mindy, happily married and a mother of seven, was simply unable to grasp exactly what she was suggesting – but she wasn't about to give up so easily.

"Anya, please! Just hear me out. In the past months, we've been hosting quite frequently a wonderful man for Shabbos. He's also a *baal teshuvah*, and he's been frum for several years already. He's a widower, and very kind, sensitive, and caring. My husband thinks very highly of him."

Anya shook her head again and got to her feet. "Look, Mindy, I appreciate the fact that you're concerned about me, but you're getting way ahead of yourself. I… I never considered anything like this before, and I don't know if I'm ready for it now, or even if I ever will be."

Mindy rose too; she had to be leaving already. "I hear you, Anya, and I'm sorry if my words hurt you, but please, do think about what I said. I have to go now, but please call me if anything changes. I just want to see you happy," she stressed. "That's all."

Anya nodded and then sat down again once her friend had left. She didn't feel ready to return to her office just yet – she needed a few more moments to herself, to try to gather her thoughts together. Mindy had thrown a curveball at her, disrupting the life she had built for herself and introducing something so unexpected that she had no idea how to react to it.

Could Mindy be, at least partially, right? It was certainly true that she didn't feel that she had recovered from the shock of the news of Lev's death last year. And yet, in truth, she had really lost him almost a decade ago – since his imprisonment, their only connection had been via their *tefillos*. She had been keeping Lev alive in her soul, but maybe that didn't have to preclude moving on, in a sense, in her physical life.

All that afternoon, and then during the evening, Anya's thoughts revolved around the issue. Moving on felt like betrayal, but logically, that made no sense. But cold logic alone could not triumph over emotions, and something so strong was still tying Anya to Lev, something that made the thought of introducing anyone else into her life unthinkable. But why? If Lev was gone, why did her heart insist on holding on to him?

Suddenly, something Anya had learned months ago resurfaced in her mind, and she gasped at its possible implications. Yaakov Avinu, too, had remained inexplicably tied to his son Yosef, even after the reports of his death – because Yosef hadn't really been dead at all. Could it be that… Anya stopped her thoughts abruptly. It was too dangerous to go down that road. The idea was crazy, ridiculous, insane. And yet…

Anya put down the skirt she had been mending and got up to start pacing the floor. Karina was at another meeting for the history exhibit, affording her the privacy she needed. But her thoughts were only going around in circles. She stopped at the telephone and dialed Mindy's number before she lost the nerve.

If her friend was surprised to hear her voice, she didn't say so.

"Mindy, you might think I'm crazy when you hear this," she began hesitantly.

"*Nu*, and if I do?" Mindy replied lightly.

"I was thinking about what you said – a lot – and…" Anya proceeded to share her thoughts with her friend, who was too shocked at first to know how to respond. "It makes a lot of sense. Maybe the time really has come to rebuild. But, I can't do it yet. Not until I know without a shadow of a doubt that my husband is really no longer alive. I know that there were claims that he perished along with the other prisoners in his group, but who knows if it's really true? What if my feelings are because Lev is actually still alive somewhere? Maybe that's what's really holding me back from moving on."

"Whoa, Anya… Slow down…" Mindy began to wish she had never raised the topic. The last thing she had intended to do was send her friend on a journey chasing illusions, one that would only end in bitter disappointment rather than a way out of her sadness. "Anya," her voice softened, "you yourself told me that he was reported dead in an avalanche. How could he still be alive?"

"I don't *know* that he's still alive, but I also don't know that he's not. From what I understand, if we had been *halachically* married, the report wouldn't necessarily be enough to render me free to remarry. So who says that he's really dead?"

Mindy felt sick to her stomach. *Poor, poor Anya…* "Who reported the death?" she tried to clarify the facts.

"My friend's husband. The morning of the avalanche, he was visiting the labor camp, and he heard about the tragedy."

"And he identified the victims?"

"Some of them. The others they couldn't reach. The conditions were too dangerous, and don't think that the Communists cared enough about mere prisoners to conduct a more thorough search during the spring, when the snow melted. They were buried there and forgotten. But… maybe Lev wasn't even there in the first place!"

"And there was no death certificate?"

"No. Like I said, they were just prisoners. Not to be treated like humans at all. That's the way things are there."

Mindy took a deep breath, feeling as if she had accidentally swum into the deep end and was now floundering. To her, it made no sense to start imagining that Anya's husband could be alive, but it was already obvious that Anya needed a real sense of closure in order to move on, and a vague "he was probably buried in the avalanche" just wasn't going to cut it.

"Anya, I hear you. We really do have to find out something concrete, despite the obstacles," she said. "Maybe you can contact the person who wrote to you? Could he or she help you check things out properly?"

"I can try," Anya offered readily. "Like you said, there are big obstacles to getting solid information out of a country like the Soviet Union, but there are a few people there who may be able to help me."

CHAPTER 54

"Mama, Mrs. Sirkis called you twice while you were out," Karina announced as soon as Anya walked in the door, her arms laden with groceries. "Actually, she called you earlier too, but I forgot to tell you. Sorry. I hope everything's okay. She sounded really anxious."

"She called three times?" Anya wrinkled her brow. "I guess I'll call her back then."

"Mama?" Karina's voice was suddenly uncertain. "Do you mind if I ask you a question?"

"Do I ever?" Anya smiled at her daughter.

"What's going on between you and Mrs. Sirkis? The two of you have been on the phone almost nonstop for the last few months. And sometimes when you get off the phone, you look so nervous. Is something wrong?"

Anya sighed. "It's nothing that you have to worry about, Karina."

"Maybe, but I wish you'd tell me what it's all about," Karina replied, her eyes fixed on her mother's features. "Like I said, it's making you really anxious."

Anya frowned. "That may be, but… whatever. Karina, this is something that just has to remain private. Okay?"

Karina shrugged. "I didn't say you had to tell me, it's just that it doesn't seem like it's so good for you. To be honest, Mama, I'm getting worried."

"You have nothing to worry about, Karina. I promise you." They faced each other, unmoving, for a long moment until Karina finally interrupted the silence.

"Aren't you going to call Mrs. Sirkis back?"

Anya gave her daughter a wry smile. "I do need to call her, but I don't want you standing behind the door and eavesdropping! Or worrying unnecessarily."

Karina couldn't hide her own smile. "So just tell me what's going on, and then I'll quit worrying!"

Anya took her daughter's hands in her own. "Please, Karina. I'm asking you to trust me on this one. Okay? As soon as I have something to share with you, if I do, I will. Believe me, I'm doing this for your own good. It could even be that it's easier for me to share it with you, but it isn't right. At least, not yet."

The ring of the telephone interrupted their conversation. Anya answered the phone and immediately hurried to her bedroom to pick up the extension. Karina was tempted to stand with her ear pressed to the door, but she overcame the impulse, forcing herself to sit down and review her *Navi* notes instead, although she knew that there was no way she would manage to concentrate until her mother ended the call.

"Anya! I'm so glad I finally caught you! I've been trying to reach you all day!" Mindy began, the moment she heard someone pick up the phone.

"Mindy? What's up?" Anya asked breathlessly. "Did your contact in Moscow find something out?"

"Anya, he found out more than any of us would have ever believed," Mindy said slowly. "Anya, are you sitting down? You know what? Forget it. Give me ten minutes, and I'll be at your place, okay?"

"What?" Anya refused to hang up so quickly. "Mindy! What's going on? Cut the theatrics and tell me what's going on!"

"I'll be over in ten minutes, Anya!"

"Stop it! Just tell me! There's no way I'll manage with the suspense for another ten minutes!" Anya protested.

"Are you sure?" Mindy sounded doubtful.

"MINDY!!"

"All right, but promise me that you're sitting down, Anya."

"I'm sitting! I'm sitting! Out with it already!"

"Anya, your husband… Lev… He wasn't killed in the avalanche. He's alive. Do you hear me? He's alive! Our contact saw him and even spoke to him. He's alive in Moscow!"

"What?" Anya's heart exploded in her chest, and the room spun so quickly around her that she nearly fell off her chair. "Mindy, what are you saying? Can you repeat that?"

"Yes, Anya! You can say '*Baruch mechayeh meisim.*' Lev is alive. Alive and well!"

"But… in Moscow?" Anya couldn't absorb it all at once.

"Yes! That's what's most incredible. He was released from the camp, a year or two earlier than expected. It's very unclear what and how this all happened; all we managed to find out was that some committee reviewed hundreds of cases and reduced the sentences on some of them."

The gasps emanating from Anya's end of the line sent Mindy into a panic. "ANYA! Anya, are you all right? Anya! I knew I shouldn't have told you over the phone. Where's Karina? Do you need help? I'm coming over as fast as I can!" Without awaiting a reply, Mindy dropped the phone and ran out of her house as if pursued, praying that she hadn't made a fatal mistake and sent her friend into shock.

The strange noises alerted Karina, as well, who uncharacteristically opened her mother's bedroom door without permission to find her weeping hysterically.

"Mama!" she cried. "Mama, what happened? Why are you crying?"

The force of her wracking sobs made it impossible for Anya to reply, and she surrendered to the powerful river of tears. The tears were purifying, cleansing, as they washed away the terror, anxiety, impossible agony and emptiness that had been her constant companion for a decade.

"MAMA!" Karina shouted, praying her mother wasn't suffering a nervous breakdown. She grabbed the phone, hoping that Mrs. Sirkis was still there, but on the other end of the line was only silence.

"Papochka," Anya finally managed to choke through her tears, which garbled the word so much that Karina wasn't sure she had heard right. Besides, why would her mother be crying now, over a year after his death? Papa was dead, Babushka was gone; who else in the family could cause her mother to drown in sorrow like this?

"I can't understand you!" Karina said frantically.

"Your father! Papa!" Anya repeated, finally controlling her sobs long enough to shout, "Your father who we left behind in Russia! He's alive and well, and he's free!"

"Papa?" Karina froze, certain that her mother was really suffering a breakdown. "Papa is gone, Mama. He died *al kiddush Hashem* in Siberia." She spoke slowly, clearly, praying that the truth would penetrate through her mother's hysteria.

"No, Karina, he didn't!" Anya said, a fresh wave of tears assailing her. "They only thought he was killed, but he wasn't. He wasn't with his work detail on the day of the avalanche, and now he's been freed! Somebody just met him in Moscow and spoke to him, face to face. Karina, your father is alive! Alive and free! I just received the news now."

"And that's why you're crying?" Karina countered in disbelief.

"I'm crying from joy, my darling. Joy and relief. Joy and thanks to Hashem! Lev... your father... he's alive!"

"Mama, are you sure about this?" Karina asked skeptically, terrified that her mother was hallucinating. "Maybe it's a mistake?"

"Why should it be a mistake?" Her mother's tears were now replaced with laughter, and her eyes sparkled like diamonds. "We sent a man to Moscow to search for proof of Papa's death, but instead, he met him alive and well! What better proof do we need?"

"He's alive..." Karina whispered, finally beginning to absorb the news and accept it. "Papa is alive?"

"Alive and well."

Anya and Karina collapsed into each other's arms, and both simultaneously began to weep. And it was into this heartrending scene that a frantic Mindy Sirkis entered several minutes later.

The following day was Friday, and the Sirkises invited Anya and Karina to join them for Shabbos. After candle-lighting, while Karina was being entertained by the Sirkis girls, Mindy and Anya sat down on the couch, and the conversation automatically turned to Lev.

"Release from Siberia doesn't equal release from the Soviet Union," Mindy sighed.

Anya looked dolefully into her friend's eyes. "After all he's suffered, I can only imagine how Lev is faring now. He's almost certainly unemployed, because as an enemy of the State, the University isn't allowed to take him back. He's probably homeless too, because the government likely seized our assets. I hope he's managing to earn a few rubles to rent some kind of room that would be a roof over his head, but I can't imagine how. Oh, Mindy! I hope he has enough to eat! I doubt he was able to turn to any of his old friends, because the authorities don't look kindly upon anyone who associates with former convicts. He's probably so lonely…"

"But, Anya, thank Hashem that he's alive! Alive and well! He survived Siberia!" Mindy was taken aback by her friend's morose reaction to these wonderful tidings. Anya's heart, however, was in a constant state of flux, her emotions alternating between fear, worry, and unadulterated joy. Mindy's remark was an important and poignant reminder that everything was so much better than it had seemed just a day ago.

"You're right, Mindy. I'm feeling ashamed already! It's so easy to get caught up in worries and fears that a person can forget to thank Hashem for the miracles He does every minute of the day."

They received the next pieces of information three days later, and Mindy hurried to call Anya and update her. The news was encouraging, but also cause for concern.

"Anya, our contact in Moscow says that there is a decent chance of your husband receiving an exit visa from the USSR," she began.

"Really?" Anya gasped, unable to believe the incredible change in fortune. The Soviets were never in a rush to authorize the emigration of any citizen, much less so a former convict.

"When your husband applied for an exit visa, he was asked if he has family abroad. When the officials discovered that he has a wife and child in America, it seems they were more disposed to approving the request. What they told us is that if you travel to Moscow and present a personal appeal to get him out of there, he'll receive the visa automatically."

Anya's joy sounded clearly through the line. "Are you sure? That's what he was told? *Chasdei Hashem!* I can't believe it! It's too good to be to true."

This was the part of the conversation that Mindy had feared. "That was my reaction too. Anya, maybe it really *is* too good to be true?"

Anya was too excited to pick up on the caution in her friend's voice. "I can't believe this… It's incredible… I have to leave as soon as possible! Do you think I should take Karina with me? Oh, Mindy, it's like a dream come true…"

"Anya," Mindy interrupted sharply, "come down to earth! This isn't as simple as it sounds. They, meaning the Soviet authorities, told our contact man that if you appear and make the appeal in person, then everything will go smoothly. But since when are the Soviets compassionate, Anya? Since when are they in a hurry to do favors to Jews? To me, it sounds like they want to get you back there, and arrest you the moment you step onto Russian soil."

But Anya was still too carried away to absorb Mindy's words. "It's been over a decade since everything happened!" she replied dismissively. "A lot of water has passed under the bridge since then. Why should anyone recognize me? Moscow is a huge city, and thousands of people pass through every day. Who would recognize one American tourist?"

"Anya, I don't think you're being rational," Mindy disagreed, drumming her fingers anxiously on the counter. "In fact, you're the one who always says that the KGB doesn't forgive or forget. What makes you think that you're not still on their Wanted list? The list doesn't grow shorter with the passage of years. All they need is your passport and fingerprints in the airport to arrest you and throw you right back into jail." Mindy's words were purposely sharp, intended to jolt her friend out of her fantasy world and back into reality.

A chill ran up Anya's spine as she finally heard what Mindy was trying to tell her, but she still refused to yield. "Mindy, tell me the truth. If our roles were reversed, wouldn't you endanger yourself to save your husband? I already left him behind once in my life, and I won't do it again. He's suffered enough, and if the time has come for me to suffer in his stead, then I'm ready."

Mindy was unimpressed by her friend's courageous statement. "And what about Karina?" she shot back. "Think about your daughter! What if this is all a ruse to draw you back into the lion's den? Then, she might lose both of you!"

"Don't say that!" Anya shouted. "It won't happen!"

"But you have to face the facts, Anya! You yourself said that it's too good to be true. What if it is?"

"I could go there undercover. Use a false passport. Change my appearance…"

"Anya, in order to submit a request to secure your husband's exit visa, you'll have to appear under your own name and real identity."

Anya fell silent. Of course Mindy was right. And, with her experience in the field, she should have seen through it all from the very beginning. She drew a deep breath and replied after a long while, "I have some friends in the CIA. I'll pay them a visit tomorrow and see what they have to say."

CHAPTER 55

When Anya opened her eyes that morning, it took her a moment to remember where she was. At first, she didn't recognize the white curtain that danced merrily in the breeze, or the cherry wood bureau across the room. She sat up in bed, staring blankly at the room, until everything came rushing back to her.

She was in Vienna, in a city she had never thought she would visit again, and if everything went according to plan, Lev would be arriving there, the next day, together with Karina. *If everything went according to plan...* The words caused a tremor to pass through her, even though, up until that point, things had gone smoothly – but at the end of the day, it didn't mean a thing. The KGB was infamous for the mind games it played with people, and the cruelest trick of all they could be planning for them now was to let everything appear simple until the last minute, when all their careful planning fell through.

Stop! Anya ordered herself harshly. *I mustn't think like that. Daven, and hope for the best. That's all.*

Initially, she had planned to travel to Moscow herself, and even her former colleagues at the CIA had agreed that there was a good chance that her visit would pass quietly, given that there were numerous documented cases of family members who had managed to secure exit visas for their relatives. She had made her travel plans with quiet confidence, encouraged by Karina's excitement, but her phone call to Katerina Nastrov had changed everything.

Katerina was her oldest and dearest friend; the two of them had grown up together, and it had been Katerina who had made the effort to maintain contact with Anya even after her escape. Certainly Katerina would be delighted to discover that Lev was not dead, as she had written – but her delight soon evaporated as she listened to Anya's plan.

"Anya, are you insane?" she exploded, the moment Anya paused to take a breath. "Don't you even so much as think of stepping foot in this country, Anya Krasnikov! Anya, pity yourself! Pity your poor child! Do you have any idea how dangerous it is?"

"But I have no other way of securing an exit visa for Lev," Anya protested. "Katerina, he's all alone, hungry, and without a proper roof over his head. He's out of Siberia, but he's not really out of jail. For him, Russia is just one huge jail, and he has to get out! I need to get him out! How can I abandon him a second time?"

Katerina banged her fist on the table. "You don't have to convince me that your husband would be best off leaving the country, but don't think for a second that there's any chance that they'll ever let him go. And even if he does receive an exit visa, what good will it be with you behind bars – this time, for good? Anya, have you forgotten so quickly what it's like here? You escaped the lion's den once, but they won't let you get away with it a second time. You deceived the KGB, and no one gets away with that. Not then, and not today either. Don't risk your life and freedom for nothing!"

"But it's been almost a decade!" Anya tried arguing the point, although she already knew what the answer would be. She had said the same thing herself numerous times.

"Ten years, twenty years, a hundred years – it makes no difference to the KGB. They'll pursue you as long as you live! You know that better than me, Anya! They have a memory as long as the train tracks to Siberia! Don't underestimate them."

Anya felt her hopes draining from her like the air from a burst balloon. Katerina was undeniably right, and burying her head in the sand to escape the truth wouldn't help anyone in her family.

"So what *should* I do?" she asked finally. "I can't just leave Lev in Moscow – I can't! After everything I've been through since I left Russia – and after everything he's been through… I can't go on like this…" Anya sank onto her bed, suddenly feeling too weak to support herself.

A long, morose silence filled the line until Katerina suddenly spoke up. "You know who might be able to help us?" she whispered excitedly. "I just had this incredible idea…"

"Who?"

"Natalya!"

"Natalya Kolchik?"

"The one and only. Her husband has moved up in the ranks over the past few years, and today, he holds a senior position in the emigration office. From what I've heard, he wields a good deal of influence, and I know of at least three people for whom he helped arrange exit visas."

"Amazing…" Anya breathed. "And, maybe you don't know this, but Natalya even owes me a favor. Years ago, it was actually only a short while before… before it all happened… I helped her son get a job with the KGB."

"I do know about that," Katerina replied, her tone suddenly dejected. "Oh. I'm sorry, Anya. I should have thought of that. Forget I suggested it."

"Forget it? Why?"

"Anya," Katerina said very gently, "many things happened as a result of your escape from prison. Some I'm sure you were aware of, but not all. How could you have been? I guess you didn't know that Sasha, Natalya's son, the one you found a job for, was actually one of the guards who helped you escape."

"Really? I didn't know that," Anya admitted.

"And Natalya hasn't forgiven you until this very day," Katerina continued softly.

"Forgiven me for what?"

"Anya, shortly after your escape, they came after Sasha. He was arrested by the KGB and thrown into jail. There, he contracted pneumonia and never received medical care. Natalya's son died in prison."

Anya inhaled sharply, tears pricking at her eyes. "Oh, Katerina! How terrible! Poor Natalya! What a tragedy! And… it was all because of me…" The thought made her feel nauseous, and she didn't need any further explanation of why Natalya would never agree to assist her now.

"Because of you?" Katerina countered. "I disagree, Anya! You weren't the one who implicated him. You didn't deny him medical treatment. Don't blame yourself for other people's cruelty!"

"Whatever. It doesn't really make much practical difference," Anya said dejectedly. "But, do you think there's any chance that Natalya would consider helping Lev, if not me?"

"No, I don't." Katerina said firmly, without elaborating. Natalya's vow of revenge still echoed in her mind, but she didn't see any reason to share it. Even prior to her son's death, Natalya had been furious at Anya, blaming her for his arrest and even considering betraying her to the KGB if she only had an opportunity to do so. "But… maybe, if she somehow doesn't know exactly who she's helping, it could still work…" Katerina was thinking out loud, hoping that her musings would lead her to something concrete. "I wonder…"

The women sank into silence, wracking their brains in search of a solution. Anya was the first to speak. "What if the person who requests the visa is somebody that Natalya would *want* to help? Like, if the person would request it on behalf of a close friend, and relay the information in writing to her husband. Do you think Natalya would bother opening up the envelope and seeing who it's for?"

"It's an idea…" Katerina said slowly. "It's certainly worth a try."

"What's your relationship with her like these days?" Anya probed hesitantly. "Are you still very close?"

Katerina deliberated. "We're friends, and we speak on occasion, but I can't say that we're very close. Sadly, Natalya is very lonely and lacking real happiness in life. She never really recovered from her son's death…" Her voice trailed off as her thoughts traveled elsewhere. A moment later, she asked suddenly, "Anya, how old is your daughter?"

"Karina? Fifteen."

"My Luba is the same age."

"So?"

"I just thought of something, and even though it's a bit farfetched, maybe we can develop it together and see if we can make it more realistic. Because if we can, it may be our best chance at winning over Natalya's heart."

"Let's hear it."

"Instead of traveling to Russia yourself, why don't you send Karina? She must be fluent in Russian, right?"

"Of course. We still speak Russian at home. But it's out of the question! I wouldn't dream of sending Karina into Russia on her own! I won't expose her to danger that I wouldn't expose myself to."

Katerina took a deep breath. "Just hear me out, Anya. My plan is something like this: Let Karina enter the country under a false identity. She'll befriend my daughter Luba. Summer vacation will be starting in another month, and then I'll send them both off to Moscow to spend some time with Natalya, who's terribly lonely. She's always complaining about her big, empty house and begging me to come visit. I'm sure she'll be thrilled to host Luba with a friend for several weeks. Actually, we discussed the possibility in theory a year or two ago, but I thought that Luba was much too young at the time. This year, she's older and in high school already. It might just work out."

"Exactly what will work out?" Anya tried to understand what Katerina was getting at.

"A close relationship between Natalya and Karina."

"Close enough that she'd be willing to arrange an exit visa for her father?"

"You got it."

"Why do you think this will work?" Anya countered. "It's so far-fetched."

"It seems like it, but I still think it has a good chance of working. Natalya craves company. Her husband is a good man, but he's rarely home, giving Luba and Karina the opening to fill Natalya's empty days."

"And once they become close, Karina can slip her an envelope, with the request, and then…"

"Right."

Anya fell silent. The idea had potential, but did she dare to risk sending Karina into Russia, even in order to save her father? On the other hand, what choice was there? Anya knew that a decade of living in America had dulled her instincts regarding the dangers of life behind the Iron Curtain, but if Katerina, still in Russia, thought the plan was reasonable, then surely she could trust her.

Ultimately, the decision was made: Karina would go, leaving

Anya behind, anxious, often fearful, feeling so helpless but trying to remind herself that her *tefillos* for the success of the mission were worth far more than all the machinations and intrigue of the spymasters. The plan was for Luba to remain in Moscow together with Karina for the first month, at which point Katerina would assess the situation and decide how to proceed. For Anya, the month seemed to drag into eternity…

CHAPTER 56

Katerina affected a raspy tone, hoping she sounded convincing enough. "Natalya, I can't thank you enough for everything. Luba's enjoyed every minute of this vacation with you, and it'll surely be a summer to remember."

Natalya was surprised by the sudden call. "Well, she's not leaving yet!" she exclaimed. "We still have another four weeks to enjoy together!"

Katerina sighed. "I know that was the original plan, and I do wish I could let her stay, but I just came down with a bad case of flu, and I really need her help at home. With Gregory away now and the boys on vacation, I can't manage alone without her. I feel guilty bringing her back after only a month when she was so looking forward to this trip, but what can I do?" she said, adding a cough to enhance the effect.

"You really don't sound good," Natalya agreed.

"I've actually spoken to Luba already, and she's disappointed but she understands. She just felt bad about telling you herself. She also felt bad about Karina."

"What about Karina?"

"Well, Karina only came along as Luba's friend…" Katerina let her voice trail off, knowing that this was a critical point in the conversation.

"I also feel bad that Luba has to leave, but Karina is still welcome to stay here with me!" Natalya hurried to interject, and her eager tone filled Katerina with relief at hearing the confirmation that her plan had succeeded. "Of course, if that's all right with her parents," she remembered to ask.

"Her parents are fine with her remaining with you. I suppose it's just up to her – and to you," Katerina coughed again.

"Well, I'd be thrilled if she'd stay, and I'll speak to her about it. After hosting her for a month, I do feel close enough to her to ask her directly. She's really such a delightful young woman!"

When Karina readily agreed to stay on as Natalya's guest, the older woman felt her heart soar. It had been a tremendous pleasure for her to host both girls, but now that it would just be Karina, she felt even more strongly that it was like a replacement for her son, and for the daughter she had never had. She pushed all thoughts of what would happen in another month to the back of her mind, and resolved to enjoy the time she had left to the fullest.

Luba took the train out of Moscow the following morning, and Natalya and Karina shared a picnic supper later that day in a park at the edge of the city. Considerate of the girl's needs, Natalya thoughtfully brought only sandwiches and fruit along with them to eat, and they spent the hours chatting pleasantly in the late afternoon breeze.

Two days later, while Natalya was at work, it was arranged that Karina would finally meet her father. Karina was still careful to call abroad only from public phones, and when Anya informed her daughter where the rendezvous would take place, tears blurred the girl's eyes. The meeting was scheduled to take place in the same park that she had visited with Natalya only two days earlier.

Karina was so tense and distracted for the remainder of the day that she could barely bring herself to respond to Natalya's overtures. When Karina murmured that she wasn't feeling too well, Natalya grew anxious and urged her to go to sleep early, adding that she wished she could take off the following day from work, but that her boss would never allow it. Karina dismissed her worries, assuring her that a good night's sleep was probably all she needed.

The following morning, Karina waited a full hour after Natalya left for work before slipping quietly out of the house. Her month in Moscow had given her a basic familiarity with the city, and she knew which bus she needed to take to reach the park. When she alighted twenty-five minutes later, Karina reflected that in a way, her entire life up until then had just been a prelude leading her to this meeting. The thought made her knees buckle slightly; if everything went well, she would be seeing her father for the first time in over a decade…

From afar, she glimpsed a middle-aged man sitting on a wooden park bench. His hair was gray, and his back was hunched over. Could that be him? Could that be her father? No! It was impossible! Her father was a tall, distinguished gentleman, with jet-black hair and intelligent, penetrating eyes – or at least that was the image that had been burned into four-year-old Karina's mind, even if she couldn't recall his features. But over a decade had passed since she had last seen her father. Could he have aged so markedly? As she watched, she saw the man's eyes flitting around as he seemed to search for something… or someone.

Could it be him? He looked old enough to be Karina's grandfather! Was this what years of imprisonment in a labor camp in Siberia could do to a person?

Karina approached warily, fearful of making a mistake. What if it wasn't her father after all? But he was sitting on the bench, as promised, and he was clearly searching for somebody. For her? The closer she advanced, the slower her steps became until she was completely seized by fear. By now, the man's eyes were glued to her features.

"Papa?" she whispered hesitantly.

"Karina…" The man's voice was low, yet so full of emotion. Karina froze, waiting for the tears she had been sure would come to redeem her from her discomfort; but the tears refused to come.

"My Karina! How you've grown and matured!" Lev Krasnikov cried, his own eyes filling with tears. "I was so worried I wouldn't recognize you, but I could never mistake you! You're the exact image of your mother! Beautiful and graceful, exactly like your mother!" He fell silent, as if the words had used up his remaining strength.

Karina couldn't help but exclaim, "Papa! What did they do to you there?"

Lev paled slightly, and his heart sank at the sight of his daughter's agonized expression. In a way, it was a moment more painful for him than years of hunger, cold, and deprivation. But just as he had done throughout the bitter years, he struggled now to lift his chin and hold his head high as he stared directly into his daughter's blue eyes.

"Karina, it's been many years, my precious. I'm sure I look different than you remember. But these are my badges of honor. They did everything they could to destroy me, to obliterate my faith and vanquish the Jewish soul inside me. Yes, they harmed my body beyond repair, but they never managed to destroy my *neshamah*. Do you understand?"

Karina was too shocked to reply. All the words that had accumulated from years of longing for her father suddenly deserted her, leaving only the simplest statement. "I'm so happy to see you, Papa! I waited for this moment for so, so long."

"Me too, Karina. Me too."

After that initial reunion, Karina couldn't bear to wait even another day, and when she called Katerina to ask her opinion, her mother's friend encouraged her to proceed as planned. When Natalya returned home from work late that afternoon, she ran to meet her.

"Hi, Natalya. How was your day? It's a good thing you didn't take a day off work for me, as I slept in late and then, when I woke up, I felt fine. I even went out to town and did some window shopping. Oh, and you'll never guess who I met in town! I hadn't seen him in several years, but it was so good to see him again."

"Who?"

"My father's best friend. And he desperately needs help!" Karina blurted out.

Natalya pierced the girl with a sharp gaze. Something about Karina's urgent expression sent warning bells pealing in her mind. "What kind of help does he need?" she asked slowly.

"That's what I'm trying to tell you!" Karina rushed to say before Natalya could ask the man's name. "When we got to talking about it, I remembered that you told me that your husband works in the emigration department. Isn't that right?"

"Yes…"

"Well, my father's friend desperately needs an exit visa out of the country. Natalya, do you think there's any hope that Dmitri could arrange an exit visa for him?" Karina's plea was so innocent and pure that Natalya felt her heart melt, as it often did when Karina grew expressive. There was something so remarkable about the girl that touched a chord deep in her heart.

"This means a lot to you, Karina, doesn't it?" Natalya asked slowly, unable to fathom why the girl was so intense that day.

"It would mean the world to me, Natalya, and I'll be grateful to you as long as I live!" she pledged earnestly. "This man is a very special person, and he did so much for my father. I have to help him. I just have to!"

Natalya hung her pocketbook in the hall closet and headed to the kitchen. "I'll speak to Dmitri about it tonight. I don't think it should be a problem, but we will need his personal details."

"I'll get them from him," Karina promised.

"As soon as you can. But aren't you hungry, Karina?" Natalya wondered out loud. "I see you didn't touch the fruit that I left out for you."

Karina spun around and blushed guiltily. "Oh, I'm sorry. I was so distracted that I didn't even notice it. To tell you the truth, I'm not really hungry."

Natalya studied the girl keenly. "You're taking this too much to heart, Karina. I admire the fact that you want to help your father's friend, but you can't let it take over your life." Karina blushed furiously; if she wasn't careful, she would expose herself.

Later that night, Karina handed Dmitri a sealed envelope containing a single sheet of paper listing her father's name and personal details. The envelope had been tightly sealed in the hope that Natalya wouldn't bother looking inside, and why should she? Karina was aware that this was the climax of Katerina's plan and could be the harbinger of either success or disaster. If Natalya discovered her now, what would she do? What would she say?

Aside from saying *Tehillim* and pleading for her safety and her father's salvation, there was nothing that could be done. And so, across the ocean and in a small room in a Moscow apartment, two people joined fervently in their prayers.

Karina couldn't believe how quickly and miraculously events unfolded. By the following evening, she had her father's exit visa in her hand, and the very next morning, she handed it to him. Meanwhile, Natalya suspected nothing, and if all went well, the following day while Natalya was at work, she would quietly board a flight with her father back to Vienna.

It was almost too good to be true, and Karina couldn't stop thanking Hashem for His constant kindness that had escorted her throughout her mission. In less than twenty-four hours, they would be taking off and leaving behind the Soviet prison once and for all. How would Natalya take her sudden disappearance? It was the one part of the plan that left Karina with a sinking heart. Natalya had been so kind and generous to her, and the thought of betraying her now pained her. She wanted so badly to convey her enormous gratitude to the woman for helping her bring her plan to fruition, but she knew that it was far too dangerous to risk.

Instead, she consoled herself with fantasizing about the emotional reunion of all three members of her family in Vienna.

CHAPTER 57

Natalya burst suddenly into her room at eleven that night, her eyes blazing with a dangerous fire and her whole body trembling uncontrollably. Karina didn't have to ask to realize she had been found out.

"Karina, who is the man whom you asked Dmitri to procure an exit visa for?" she asked in a low, menacing voice.

"Who?" Karina repeated blandly, feigning confusion and slumber, if only to gain another minute of time.

"Yes, *who*? What is his name?"

"I told you. A good friend of my father's. Of my whole family." Karina tried to stay calm, but she was aware that all the color was draining from her face.

"*What's his name, I asked you!*" Natalya's shriek rattled the windows, and Karina retreated physically in terror.

"Lev Krasnikov," she confessed quietly, knowing that it was impossible to deny the truth now when Dmitri had signed the authorization himself.

"How do you know this man? Don't tell me. I know. What I don't know is why it took me so long to figure it out myself. He's your father, isn't he? You're Anya's daughter!"

Karina forced herself to swallow her dread. "Anya?"

"Stop playing games with me! I remember now that Anya's daughter was named Karina, and I can't believe how I was so blind. You reminded me of Anya from the moment I met you! You manipulated me – all of you, Luba, Katerina, and Anya herself. How could you do this to me? What were you thinking all along?"

"Natalya, I really think you're making a terrible mistake," Karina attempted one last time. "Krasnikov is my father's good friend, but not my father—"

Natalya grabbed her furiously by the shoulders and shook her violently. "STOP LYING TO ME! If you don't tell me the truth, I'll hand you over here and now to the KGB, and they'll know exactly how to make you talk!"

Karina gasped in fear, and the tears rushed to her eyes. She was only fifteen, but she had heard enough about the KGB to know that they would care nothing about her age. It was her worst nightmare, but one she had never truly thought she would face. Horror-struck, she stared at her hostess, but the Natalya she faced now wasn't the same woman she had met a month earlier, who had taken her into her home and heart so warmly.

"WHO ARE YOU? Talk to me!" Natalya continued shaking her violently.

"I'm sorry! I'm sorry! Please, just let me go!" Karina burst into tears.

"What were you thinking? That's what I want to know! Tell me, how did you dare to try to deceive me like this? *What were you thinking?*"

"I thought we were friends, that you cared about me! I thought you would want to help me…"

Her words touched Natalya's weakest point. Natalya froze and her hands slid weakly off the girl's aching shoulders. A second later, though, she recovered, and the fire burned once again in her eyes.

"HOW DARE YOU! You exploited me and deceived me from the very beginning. You knew that I was lonely and depressed and aching for friendship. You knew that I was still yearning for my son. How dare you take advantage of my loneliness and heartbreak for your selfish, sordid purposes!"

Karina took a deep breath, trying to calm her pounding heart. "Natalya, I'm so, so sorry. You're right, and we were wrong to try to deceive you, but we never meant to hurt you. You were our only hope, and it was the only way we could think of saving my father. You're right that we exploited your situation, and I feel terrible about it, but why do you call my goal selfish or sordid? Is it selfish of me to try to rescue my father who did nothing wrong? Hasn't he suffered enough?" The tears continued to spill down Karina's face.

"You lied to me all along! You deceived me! You played with my deepest emotions!" Natalya's voice rose hysterically, and Karina wondered if the woman was suffering a nervous breakdown before her very eyes. "I trusted you from the beginning, and you let me grow attached to you. When you gave Dmitri the envelope, I didn't dream of opening it, because I *trusted* you. The only reason I even discovered your treachery was because the name rang a bell with Dmitri who asked me if I knew who Lev Krasnikov was. I couldn't believe it when he told me that he was the one you wanted a visa for!"

Karina fell silent, afraid that anything she said would only further ignite Natalya's rage. Natalya, too, was silent for a long moment as she stared at Karina with venom in her eyes.

"Don't you dare leave this room until morning, Karina *Krasnikov*," Natalya said finally. "I'm not going to wake up all the neighbors at this hour of the night, but tomorrow morning, I'm calling the KGB so they can decide what do you with you!" And with that, she stormed out of Karina's room, slamming the door behind her with such force that it rattled the windows.

Karina remain frozen in place for a long while, shocked and terrified. Her first thought was of her father and of the need to warn him of the imminent danger. When she finally managed to overcome her shock somewhat, she forced herself to take a look out of the window to see if there was any hope of escaping, but a single glance was enough to banish that thought. Natalya lived on the fourth floor of a high-rise building, and there was nothing on the exterior wall that would aid Karina in a climb down. She was trapped – there was absolutely nothing she could do to save herself from Natalya's vengeance. With the fear closing in on her from every direction, Karina did the only thing she could think of – she grabbed her *siddur* from the inner pocket of her suitcase and began to recite *Tehillim* with tears streaming down her face.

Eventually, she fell asleep, fully clothed, her tear-drenched face pressed against the stained pages of her *siddur*. At six the next morning, Natalya opened the door to her room and abruptly roused her. Karina blinked sleepily at first, and then turned to look into the woman's face. Natalya's eyes were red-rimmed from a sleepless night, but the anger in them seemed to have diminished somewhat.

"Listen well, Karina," she said sternly. "I've thought things through, and I've reached a compromise that suits me – and it will have to suit you, as well." Karina listened silently, hardly daring to hope, but praying for a miracle nonetheless. "I can bring myself to forgive you for your treachery, and I'm even willing to keep silent about your father's criminal past until he's safely out of the country. Which is what you want, isn't it?"

Natalya's words were the sweetest ones Karina had ever heard in her life, and Karina couldn't contain her gasp. Had her *tefillos* and tears stirred such a storm in the heavens that Natalya had undergone a complete change of heart? "Yes! Would you really do that? You'd let my father go... Oh, Natalya! You're the most wonderful person I've ever met! Thank you!" she exclaimed emotionally, tears of relief sparkling in her eyes.

Natalya ignored the compliment. "Yes, but there's a price to pay, Karina."

"A price? We'll give you whatever you want!" Karina promised, knowing that her mother would stand behind her pledge and pay any ransom to secure her husband's release.

"Yes. A price. You'll stay here."

Karina wrinkled her brow in confusion. "Me? Stay? Where? And for what?"

"You'll stay here, in my house. I'm lonely, and I need someone to give to and to love. I'll be completely honest with you, Karina. I would love you to be my daughter."

"*Your daughter?*" Karina repeated, astounded. The thought was simply surreal. Mere hours earlier, Natalya had threatened to hand her over to the KGB, and now she was asking to adopt her?

"Yes, my daughter," Natalya whispered softly, and her eyes glassed over with tears. "You can become the daughter I never had, the daughter I always dreamed of having. And you know what, Karina? You're the one who made me think of it!"

"I did? How?"

"Yes. You said that you thought I cared about you. And you were right, despite what I found out about you. Just as I once had a special bond with your mother, until... until what she did, so too do I have a special connection to you. That's why I can forgive your deception, because that's what mothers do, don't they? They forgive their children even when they sin."

"But Natalya..." Karina said weakly, feeling sick to her stomach. "I have parents. I have a family. I'm not a lonely orphan searching for parents."

Natalya smiled, and this time there was a trace of coldness in her eyes. "I know, but that's the price that you'll have to pay for getting your father out of Russia. Didn't you yourself say that it's a tremendously lofty purpose?"

"Of course it is! But—"

"Good. I knew you'd agree. Otherwise, you would never have dared to enter the country and my home under a false identity and play the game you played. But you'll have to make the decision quickly. I imagine that you probably have a flight scheduled for today, or tomorrow at the latest, no? You need to decide."

Karina gazed in wide-eyed terror at Natalya, hoping wildly that this was some kind of joke, that surely she didn't really mean what she was saying. But nothing in the other woman's expression lent any support to that idea. Natalya was clearly waiting for her answer, in deadly seriousness.

"I can't make such a decision on the spur of the moment," she finally replied in a choked voice. "Could I... could I at least call my mother?"

A flicker of fury ignited again in Natalya's eyes. "No, you cannot. I want an answer now. You've had long enough to prepare yourself for any eventuality – you've been staying with me for over a month, after all. And, I don't think you've even properly understood me. If you refuse, then your father will almost certainly be jailed again, for obtaining a visa under false pretenses, and you, too, risk being imprisoned for entering the country under a false identity."

Karina began to tremble. "You aren't leaving me with many options."

"No, I'm not. But you can be happy here, Karina, if you choose. When is the flight scheduled for?" she demanded.

Karina saw no purpose in hiding the truth. "One o'clock," she whispered.

"Good. Would you like me to send a message to your father from you to board the plane and say that you'll be in touch with him later? Or…" she let the unasked question dangle heavily.

Karina nodded fearfully, unsure what she was up against. She had no idea if Natalya could keep her in the country against her will, but her first instinct was to make sure that at least her father would get out. This could be his one and only opportunity to escape, and that, after all, was the sole reason for which she had traveled to Russia.

"Excellent," Natalya pronounced. "I'll be right back." She exited the room, only to return a few moments later with a pen and paper, which she handed to Karina, before proceeding to dictate a letter which Karina dutifully penned.

"I'll see that your father gets this," she said with satisfaction. "Meanwhile, you can go and eat breakfast." She shrugged in response to Karina's vehement shaking of her head. "If you don't want to eat, fine. I'll be in the living room." Despite knowing that her boss would not be pleased by her absence, Natalya remained home with Karina all morning.

"And now, we need to celebrate!" she announced festively when the clock struck one. "There's a new restaurant that just opened up downtown, and they even advertised vegetarian meal options. It will be a wonderful way to mark the beginning of our new family."

Karina swallowed her tears, determined to portray a strong veneer. "I really don't feel like going out right now."

"We'll go, and you'll find yourself enjoying," Natalya insisted.

Half an hour later, Karina found herself seated opposite her erstwhile hostess as a waiter placed two platters of food on the table. Karina felt her stomach lurch; it was time to confess the next part of her deception.

"Natalya, there's something I need to explain," she said nervously, when she noticed the woman eyeing her plate expectantly. "If I'm going to be here for a while, then you may as well know that I'm not really a vegetarian at all. I follow the Jewish dietary laws, so I can't eat anything non-Jews cooked, even if it's vegetarian." Karina steeled herself, prepared for a furious reaction, but Natalya's response was not at all what she was expecting.

"Karina, my dear," Natalya took Karina's hands in her own and squeezed them warmly. "You're living in Russia now, which means you're no longer bound by these Jewish restrictions of yours. Here in the Soviet Union, we're not restricted by any old-fashioned religious laws. You can eat and drink exactly as you please."

"What I want is to keep kosher!" Karina protested. "It's my choice – it's got nothing to do with being forced to do anything."

Natalya frowned. "You really don't understand very much about your new country, do you, my dear? There are no choices here when it comes to living an antiquated way of life. Religion plays no part in Soviet culture and you would do well to keep your private beliefs secret, while living and acting like everyone else here does."

Karina's eyes flashed rebellion. "When it comes to my religion, there are no compromises, Natalya. There's absolutely nothing to talk about."

CHAPTER 58

The sun beat down on the tarmac, and planes touched down on the runway one after the next, each one discharging long lines of passengers. Flight 153 wasn't scheduled to land for another ten minutes, but Anya had been waiting at the airport for two hours already, counting the minutes until her loved ones would finally appear. Of course, ten minutes until landing didn't mean she would actually be seeing them in ten minutes; they would still have to pass through passport control, baggage claim, and customs, but just knowing that they were in the same country, in the very same building, would make the wait more bearable.

It had been so many years… What would he look like? From their brief conversation, Anya had understood that Karina hadn't recognized her father immediately, but it wasn't surprising; the last time she had seen him, she had been only four. On the other hand, Anya wouldn't delude herself either; a decade of forced labor in Siberia didn't leave a man untouched. But the main thing was that Lev was coming home, in one piece – her dreams and her prayers had been answered.

The minutes passed by interminably as Anya's thoughts carried her back to the long, lonely years spent in America. She had raised Karina virtually on her own, returned to Judaism on her own, supported both of them, and surmounted the challenges of the West – so different from the challenges she had known in Soviet Russia – all on her own. They had been separated for so long; what awaited them now in the future? It was too overwhelming to consider, and all Anya yearned for now was to see her husband with her own two eyes. To see him alive and well.

Flight 153 from Moscow turned from red to yellow on the Arrivals screen, signaling that it had landed. Anya drew a sharp breath. Just a few more minutes…

Half an hour later, she noticed the first passenger with distinctly Slavic features exit the large double doors into the Arrivals concourse. What began with a traveler or two turned into a trickle and then a steady stream. Anya kept her eyes glued to the people like a magnet, passing her eyes over each one, terrified that she wouldn't recognize her husband when he appeared. After sixteen interminable minutes, she saw him.

It was Lev, there was no doubt about it. She recognized him instantly although his appearance had changed markedly. His back and shoulders were stooped, and his walk was slow, with a slight limp. His hair had turned almost completely gray, his cheeks were hollow, and his body was gaunt. But he was still her Lev.

Their eyes locked, and she knew that he had recognized her too. Anya longed to run toward him, but her legs refused to obey, and she remained frozen in place. He approached her slowly, their eyes never leaving one another's.

"Anya," he whispered, the emotion in his voice conveying all that he longed to express.

"Lev!"

It was all either was able to muster after a decade of separation.

Tears glistened in both of their eyes, and neither was able to speak.

Anya found her tongue first. "Lev! I can't believe I'm seeing you alive again! I was sure I'd lost you forever, and I've never forgiven myself for abandoning you there—"

"You didn't abandon me, Anya! You were wounded yourself; you weren't in control."

"How are you feeling now?" she asked, feeling foolish.

"*Baruch Hashem*," he smiled, proud to be uttering the once-forbidden words aloud. "*Baruch Hashem*, we're here together, after so long."

Something wasn't right; something was missing, and Anya couldn't put her finger on it. Suddenly, she paled as she realized that Karina wasn't there. "Where's Karina?" she cried.

Lev shook his head. "I don't know. She sent me a message saying that I should board the plane immediately, and that she would be in touch with us as soon as I arrived."

"She said *what*?" Anya couldn't believe her ears.

"I don't know myself. She didn't arrive at the airport. Instead, some stranger appeared, shoved the ticket into my hand and ordered me to board the plane or else. He had a letter from Karina saying that I must go, because if I don't leave immediately, I'll be arrested and then we'll never see each other again. I told the man that I wasn't going anywhere without my daughter, but he denied knowing anything about what was going on. All he would say was that he understood that if I didn't follow orders, I would regret it. I didn't know what to do! On one hand, I couldn't think of leaving her, but I didn't think that getting thrown back into jail would do anything to help her." Lev looked so distressed that Anya couldn't bring herself to make him feel any worse than he already did.

"So they're holding her hostage…" Anya began to tremble violently. "First me. Then you. Now Karina…" She collapsed onto a chair and began to sob.

Lev sat down beside her. "I don't think that this is the work of the KGB, Anya," he said softly. "It just doesn't fit. They never release people just in order to capture someone else."

"So who is it?" Her words emerged as a strangled cry.

"I don't know," he said sadly. "The only thing we can do now is wait to hear from Karina."

"Maybe Katerina knows something?" Anya suddenly suggested. "I'm calling her right now."

For the first five minutes, Katerina was barely able to make sense of her friend's hysterical outpouring on the telephone, but by the time she finished speaking with Anya, she was certain she knew what needed to be done. Her first call was to Natalya Kolchik, who responded coldly to her overtures but ultimately agreed to explain exactly what was going on. Poor Katerina was then faced with the uncomfortable task of breaking the news to Anya, her oldest, dearest friend…

Now it was clearer than ever that Natalya had never forgiven Anya. Holding her daughter hostage, albeit in a gilded prison, was her perverted means of getting even and simultaneously gaining a measure of solace after her own tragedy.

―――᙭―――

Karina sat on the living room sofa, leafing listlessly through a book and trying to distract herself. Classical music played in the background, intensifying the feeling of lack of substance that pervaded the atmosphere. Natalya sat on an easy chair across from her, reading the daily newspaper.

For the third time that hour, Natalya offered Karina the fruit basket. "You ate only one fruit, Karina. It's not enough. Fruit is a major part of your diet, and I don't want you to lose too much weight and get ill."

"I'm fine," Karina said, reluctantly reaching for another fruit and forcing herself to take a bite. She gazed out the window into the Moscow night. Two days had passed since her father had left Russia, and her parents hadn't ceased calling Natalya since learning of her scheme. Natalya, however, responded furiously to their attempts to cajole, plead, and even threaten, reminding her parents of the unstable ground upon which they stood. Karina had swiftly realized that her position was far from simple and that there was, apparently, no one who could help her. The whole situation was so bizarre that Karina didn't know what to make of it. On one hand, she was being held against her will in the home of a depressed, lonely woman. On the other hand, Natalya was truly making an effort to treat her well and provide her with everything she could want. But all she wanted was to go home…

"School starts in a few weeks!" Natalya announced suddenly.

Karina nodded. She hadn't forgotten the date, and she had already begun to wonder where September would find her. Had she been home in New York, she would have spent an enjoyable day with her mother stocking up on a year's worth of school supplies and looking forward to seeing her friends again. Instead, she was assailed by an overpowering wave of homesickness.

"I registered you in an excellent school, Karina. I'm sure you'll enjoy it. If you feel that you're behind because of the language or culture gap, we'll make sure to hire the best tutors for you."

Karina's lips curled into a bitter smile. "I really don't think that there are too many Jewish schools around here that are suitable for me."

"It may not be a Jewish school, but it's perfectly suited to you!" Natalya exclaimed.

"Oh yes? How so?" Karina challenged her.

"Only the best families send there, and the faculty is top-quality.

Graduating with a diploma from there practically guarantees acceptance into one of the best universities in the country."

Karina shrugged defiantly. "Natalya, I'm sorry to disappoint you, but I refuse to attend a non-Jewish school. I've spent almost my entire childhood in strictly religious Jewish institutions, and I have certain values and principles that I won't compromise."

Natalya frowned. "Karina, there are no Jewish schools here in Moscow. Surely you must know that."

A grim smile appeared on the girl's face. "Of course I know. That's what I'm trying to point out!"

"So you don't have a choice. I won't stop you from doing whatever you want to do after school hours, but you have to go to school!"

"Natalya, when are you going to understand that ten KGB policemen won't be able to drag me to a school that I refuse to attend! It's simply not up for discussion!" Karina winced at the sound of her own voice; never before had she spoken so disrespectfully to an adult.

"But… that's impossible. Schooling is compulsory!"

Karina rose from her perch on the couch and began pacing the expansive living room like a caged lion. "I'd love to tell you that the best option would be to just send me home, but I've said it so many times, it's coming out of both of our ears! So I have a better idea for you: Why don't you just hand me over to the KGB here and now? This just isn't going to work. You're right. I deceived you. I lied. I entered the country under a false identity, which means that I broke the law. But I'm going to be breaking the law constantly by continuing to observe the Torah's commandments, so what's the difference? I never wanted to hurt you, and I'm sorry that I abused your kindness. But I came here in order to rescue my father, which, in my eyes, is so much more important than anything else! You don't see it that way, so why don't we just get it over with here and now? Hand me over to the KGB. They'll stop at nothing to reeducate me, and they'll probably do a better job than any fancy private school."

Natalya glared furiously at the girl, shocked and insulted at being addressed so disrespectfully. Both knew that this wasn't the real Karina talking, and both also knew that Natalya would never hand her over to the KGB. Natalya craved Karina's company and friendship, but Karina needed to make it totally clear that she would never give it willingly.

"Don't you think you're exaggerating a bit, Karina?" Natalya suddenly softened her tone, changing tactics. "How terrible can it be to go to school and acquire an education? Am I really asking so much? I'm not forcing you to eat there or do anything else that will compromise your values. All I want you to do is learn."

"The form of education itself is in direct contradiction to my values," Karina insisted. "And so is the whole social scene. And besides, what would I do on my Sabbath? I'm not going to school here, and that's that!"

"What will you do here in the house?" Natalya challenged her.

"No idea. Climb the walls, I guess."

"But I refuse to let you deprive yourself of an education, Karina. You're young, and you have a bright future ahead of you!"

Karina turned around in disgust, tired of hearing the same refrain. Natalya was planning her future, while she was planning her escape.

CHAPTER 59

Anya sighed and sipped from the cup of cold water that Stratton had offered her. "So, that's the story. I offered her compensation, apologized a million times, begged her forgiveness, but she refuses to be reasonable. She's decided that the only form of compensation she's willing to accept is my daughter. What in the world am I supposed to do?"

Pete Stratton, her former boss and a sworn atheist, who had valued Anya's contributions to the team as much as he had disdained her religious beliefs, listened to her gravely as she outlined the situation, and when she had finished, he leaned back in his chair, his expression thoughtful.

Anya waited impatiently for his reaction, hoping desperately that he would have something constructive to offer, but his response, when it finally came, was more than disappointing.

"The problem is that our hands are tied," he said at last.

"Tied?" Anya shrieked. It was the last thing she had expected to hear from Stratton. She had expected him to either adopt her cause as his own, or to refuse outright to have anything to do with it. Surrendering quietly had never been his way.

"Yes. You see, this is not a political issue, but a private one. The USA won't enter into a diplomatic dispute with another world power because of a case like this."

"A private issue?" Anya repeated in disbelief. "This is a clear case of kidnapping! The Kolchiks are holding my daughter – a minor – in their home against her will!"

Stratton gave a twisted smile. "The Soviets have been known to do far worse. Believe me, this is one of their lesser crimes. Or actually, you don't have to believe me. You know it for yourself, Anya."

"She's a child, Mr. Stratton! She's been kidnapped."

He shook his head. "She entered the country – and this woman's home – of her own free will. It's not as simple as it appears."

"But they have no right to keep her there!" Anya shouted.

"I agree, but it's not going to be an easy battle to fight. Things are never easy with the Russians, and this case is complicated from so many different angles."

"But there has to be something we can do!" Anya was on the verge of tears. "I can't just leave her there forever."

"Anya," Pete said, the compassion evident in his voice. "I'm not trying to be cruel or apathetic, just realistic. Even if you manage to get this case to court – in Russia, of course – your chances of winning are not wonderful, let's just say. I want to help you, but my gut feeling is actually to let time do the work for us."

"What's *that* supposed to mean?" she countered in disgust. "Let time do the work? She's an American teenager. What can she possibly do there, estranged from her family and everything she knows?"

"I don't know. But possibly that's the answer. You say your friend craves company and love. If your daughter is so miserable there, it could be your friend will just let her go on her own. I can't promise anything, but what I do know is that there's no way I'll get authorization to take this on. I'm sorry, Anya." For once, Stratton genuinely did seem to care.

"But I can't rely on a vague hope, something that may never come to pass." Anya's words emerged as a strangled cry.

"So let's think of something else," Stratton suggested.

"Like what?"

"Have you contacted the media? You know what they say: 'The pen is mightier than the sword.'"

After several days of constant arguments and then cajoling and pleading, tempers finally settled somewhat. Natalya compromised on hiring a tutor to teach Karina privately, and Karina decided that it was in her best interest to cooperate. At least for now. The tutor was actually better than Karina had expected, but when she began elaborating on atheistic beliefs, Karina tuned out and protested vigorously. Natalya was forced to bribe the tutor in order to ensure that she would keep the secret of her rebellious pupil.

It wasn't long before Natalya grasped that life with Karina would be no rose garden. Before revealing her true identity, the girl had done her best to conceal her religious observance, but now that her cover was blown, she grasped onto the *mitzvos* as if for dear life. Often, Natalya suspected that Karina was flaunting her Jewish practices simply in order to goad her, but she had promised the girl that she wouldn't interfere with her religious observance, and she kept to her word.

Moreover, Natalya had no interest in resorting to threats. She wanted a friend and daughter, not a resentful, bitter prisoner.

One afternoon, she returned home from work with a broad smile. "I worked through the lunch hour every day this week in order to take tomorrow morning off and spend it together with you!" she announced brightly. "I thought we could go out shopping in the center of town. It won't be long before winter sets in, and you'll need warmer clothes, a coat, and boots. We can also get you a spare pair of shoes and a matching pocketbook. What do you say?"

"What do I say?" Karina repeated dully, deciding on the spur of the moment that it was time to stress another important point. "Natalya, I don't know if you've noticed, but I have certain standards of modesty in dress." She paused, waiting for some kind of response, but Natalya simply frowned and told her that they would leave the next morning at nine.

Not ten minutes passed after their arrival in the exclusive shopping district before the two of them clashed. Unable to fathom why Karina refused to even glance at most of the garments in the first store they entered, Natalya protested vehemently, trying to get Karina to take several stylish dresses to the dressing room and go try them on.

"But your wardrobe is so dull, Karina! It needs freshening up, a bit of color and flair!" she coaxed.

"I like my wardrobe. My clothes are modest and respectable," Karina argued.

"Respectable? What's that supposed to mean? Why do you insist on hiding under all that material?" Natalya persisted. "You could look amazing."

"I don't want to look amazing. I want people to judge me based on my character, not my body."

"Who's talking about judging? Come on, Karina. Everyone wants to be attractive."

"Maybe, but not *attracting*." Karina calmly placed the hangers back on the rack. "You're not going to get me to change, Natalya, so you may as well give up now."

"But Dmitri's office is hosting a party next week," Natalya pleaded. "You can't go there dressed like you do!"

"I don't want to go to any party, whether or not I look the part."

If Natalya hoped that they would strike gold in any of the next stores, she was sorely mistaken. They returned several hours later with empty hands and bitter spirits. When he arrived home that evening, Dmitri did his best to calm the stormy feelings.

"Let her be," he attempted to soothe his frustrated wife. "You need to give her time. She'll come around eventually, but she'll do it on her own, without coercion. It's probably the pressure that's making her so defiant."

Karina, overhearing their discussion from the next room, started to panic. Would she begin to yield over time, even against her will? How long would she be able to keep up her resistance? Natalya, in her desperation, would certainly devise more devious methods of trying to make her conform – and therefore it was imperative for her to escape as soon as possible…

Several weeks passed before she managed to contact Katerina Nastrov, who promised to make arrangements to purchase an airline ticket that would await Karina at check-in. To allay any suspicion, Karina began responding more kindly to Natalya's overtures and trying to avoid conflict, thus forging a greater level of trust between them. They often spoke late into the night and even managed to find a new outfit that satisfied both of their tastes.

Finally, the last evening before her flight arrived, and Karina couldn't shake the formidable feeling of *déjà vu*. Would Natalya discover her again, or was she finally on her way to freedom? Once again she wished she could part amicably from Natalya and thank her for everything, but of course it was still impossible. When she wished Natalya goodnight, she added a mental goodbye, hoping and praying that this would be her final night in the country that had become her prison.

Natalya left to work early every morning, usually before Karina got up. That gray morning, Karina leaped out of bed as soon as she heard the front door close, dressed quickly, and *davened* a fervent *Shacharis*, beseeching Hashem to lead her safely out of the country. She quickly packed her suitcase, something she hadn't dared to do the night before, and was ready to leave within the hour. Once outside, she flagged a taxi, sighing in relief when nobody stopped her. She knew it was still early to rejoice, but at least she had passed the first stage.

She arrived in the airport approximately forty minutes later, her lips constantly mumbling the chapters of *Tehillim* that she knew by heart. At the check-in counter, she received her ticket and boarding pass and again exhaled a sigh of relief. Phase two accomplished.

Dragging her suitcase over to security, she mentally calculated the hours until she would land in Vienna, accounting for the time difference. Absorbed in her thoughts, she failed to notice two uniformed officers holding a photograph and scanning the crowd. By the time she saw them, their eyes had locked on her and they were advancing quickly toward her.

A second later, they were at her side. "Karina, come with us without making a scene."

Karina, still holding onto her suitcase, began to tremble violently and the color drained from her face. Had Natalya sent the KGB after her? She could barely force herself to drag her feet after them. Seeing her hesitation, one of the officers took her heavy suitcase from her and began walking faster, urging her to hurry. Together, they marched out of the terminal toward a familiar-looking car where a grim-faced Natalya Kolchik awaited her, Dmitri at her side. Ironically, the sight of their familiar faces was an inordinate relief. She may not have succeeded at her plan that day, but at least she wasn't being arrested.

Natalya didn't deign to even look at her. As soon as Karina was seated, Dmitri turned the key, and they drove back in silence toward the city. The ride passed in heavy, awkward silence with no one saying a word. Finally, when Dmitri pulled into the underground parking lot, Karina could tolerate the silence no longer. "How did you know I was leaving?" she dared to ask.

"Perhaps it's time we told you that the doorman stationed in the front of the building reports to us any time you leave the building unaccompanied," Natalya replied coldly.

"You can't hold me here against my will forever!" Karina exploded, bursting into tears.

"You'll remain here as long as I wish," Natalya replied harshly. Suddenly, the veneer of love and companionship disappeared completely, to be replaced by cold estrangement and an endless tunnel of time to which Karina saw no end.

CHAPTER 60

Anya dropped the receiver and sank tearfully onto the couch.

"What happened?" Lev asked anxiously.

"They caught her!" she choked out through her tears.

Lev went deathly white. "The KGB?" his voice was barely heard.

"No. Natalya. Dmitri. Katerina just called. They have somebody stationed at the entrance of their building. She'll never manage to escape. We were so stupid to think they'd trust her enough that she'd manage to break free."

A heat wave had settled upon the city, and the two fans circulating nonstop in the room did little to banish the impossible heat, yet Lev shivered. "We have to contact the media!" he announced, clenching his fists together. "It's not the ideal way to act, but it's our only hope."

Anya forced herself to swallow her tears; this was not time to weep, but to act. "Maybe we could let the Kolchiks know our intent before we actually publicize the story?" she suggested. "Maybe if Natalya hears what we're about to do, she'll reconsider?"

"Especially if she is acting on her own, without legal backing," Lev added in agreement.

Anya wiped a stray tear from her eye. "We know she's acting on her own. The KGB doesn't work like this."

Lev straightened his yarmulke, which had become a nervous habit. "You'll call her now?"

"I see no reason to wait."

As Anya dialed the number that she had long since committed to memory, she breathed in deeply and exhaled slowly, determined not to betray her true feelings of desperation and helplessness. Once, during her years of work for the KGB, portraying a cold, calm exterior had been almost effortless for her, but light years had passed since, transforming her radically. Now, however, she had to call upon her innermost reserves in her struggle to rescue her daughter.

Static filled her ear as her call was transferred across international lines, and then she heard Natalya's familiar voice answer.

"Hello, Natalya. This is Anya Krasnikov," she spoke crisply into the phone, amazed at her poise. "I just wanted to inform you that we're giving you exactly twenty-four hours before we contact the media. We'll begin with the American newspapers, but it won't take even a day for the story to hit the international press."

"Enough of your empty threats," Natalya reacted with barely-contained fury.

"These are not empty threats," Anya replied coolly. "We are perfectly serious, but out of respect for you, and for old time's sake, we decided to give you advance warning. You can save yourself the embarrassment that will surely result from this, or you can let it unfold of its own accord. It's completely up to you. And to your husband."

Natalya felt her blood boil. If they were pushing her against the wall, then she could respond in kind and take action in a way that she personally eschewed – but she would have no choice. "Listen well, Anya. Once the story breaks, I realize that I will have lost my hold on Karina, but don't delude yourself. You'll never get her back, because as soon as I see the first hint of the story in the papers, I hand her straight to the KGB. And this is not an empty threat, either. You called me to inform me of your intentions, and I'm reciprocating in kind. Goodbye."

Anya heard the click on the line, and she turned, stricken, to her husband.

"What did she say?" Lev forced himself to ask, although judging from his wife's expression, he thought he probably preferred not to know.

"That they'll hand her over to the KGB."

The silence that fell between them was thick and heavy. "The international community won't let them get away with it!" Anya tried to protest. "She's an American. The Soviets wouldn't dare!"

Lev wasn't so sure. "Would you bet on that?"

Anya was a pale as a ghost. "I would never bet on my daughter's life."

"So we'll steer clear of the media, Anya."

The impossible silence continued, escorting them throughout the day, and Anya knew that beneath the silence, Lev's heart was being gradually eaten away by his guilty conscience – the same guilty conscience that she had suffered with for almost a decade.

The announcement came not unexpectedly later that night when they both picked at their dinner, pretending to eat.

"Anya, I'm going back to Moscow. My freedom is worth nothing if Karina is being held hostage there. I would never have agreed to board the plane if I'd had any idea what was going on."

Anya felt too desperate even to argue. All she knew was that, once again, she would be saying goodbye to her husband, probably never to see him again. She buried her face in her hands and broke down in tears.

"I know it's excruciating," Lev continued softly, "but there's no other choice. We did our best to reunite as a family, but we failed. Karina put herself in danger in order to save me, but I'm her father. I won't let her sacrifice her youth and future like this. We can't know what Natalya has in store."

"Lev, you know that if you go, you'll never get out of there alive!" Anya attempted a single weak protest, the despair stealing her very breath away.

"Maybe, and maybe not," Lev replied, a sparkle of hope glimmering in his eyes. "Anya, we both thought that you'd never escape the KGB, and that I'd never leave Siberia. And yet we both came out of there alive and well. *Im yirtzeh Hashem*, Karina will return to you… and one day, so will I. It's no secret that new winds are blowing in the Soviet Union. People are beginning to dare to speak out, and all kinds of wild predictions are being made. Who knows what another year or two, or even less, will bring? We must never give up hope, Anya."

"Lev, I know what you're trying to do, but we both know that it could be another century before the Iron Curtain lifts, and by then, it will be too late for us."

"And for Karina?"

She stared quizzically at him. "What do you mean?"

"It'll be too late for Karina then too. She's young and impressionable; as her parents, we must fight to help her preserve her heritage. We can't leave her there all alone!"

"Are you sure there isn't some other way?" she begged desperately, suddenly terrified to let him go.

"Haven't we thought of everything already? Can you think of anything?"

Anya dropped her eyes; there was nothing left to say.

This time, Lev called the Kolchiks himself. "I'm returning to Moscow," he informed Natalya flatly. "I should be arriving within seventy-two hours. On the day that I land, my daughter returns to Vienna."

A moment of silence stretched across the line, and Lev felt an inordinate sense of relief, certain that this episode was finally reaching its conclusion. But it was not meant to be.

"I'm sure you understand the implications of your return to Moscow," Natalya replied coolly.

"I do, and it's a price I'm willing to pay for my daughter's release."

"I'm sorry, Mr. Krasnikov, but you're too late. Karina will remain here. You can do as you please, but nothing will change as far as I'm concerned."

An icy cold hand wrapped its fingers around Lev's heart. "Where's the logic in this game you're playing?" he challenged her.

"It's Soviet logic," she replied lightly. "Perhaps you've forgotten, but in the Soviet Union, logic isn't necessarily the supreme ruler. Your daughter entered the country under a false identity, and she'll pay the price for her crime. If you wish to return to our marvelous Communist state, you're welcome to do so!"

"You let me leave, conditioning my freedom on Karina remaining!" he protested, even though he knew it was pointless.

"I said what I said to soften the blow. However, the fact is that the moment I discovered her treachery, she forfeited her right to leave. It's time you faced the facts."

The call ended on this unpleasant note, and the Krasnikovs stared helplessly at each other, wondering if they had really exhausted all possibilities.

"I wonder if this is Hashem's way of reminding us that everything is in His Hands?" Anya whispered tearfully. "We can do everything we possibly can – even sacrificing what's most precious to us – but the only One with the power to change things is *Hakadosh Baruch Hu*."

Lev nodded slowly, but the joy and inspiration that usually sparkled in his eyes upon discussing concepts of *emunah* and *bitachon* was noticeably absent. He still blamed himself for leaving his daughter behind.

"I never should have let her place herself in such danger," he continued to berate himself. "The whole plan was doomed to failure from the very beginning. I was just so lonely and tired and weak that I didn't think things through clearly. How could I have been such a fool? How did I sacrifice my own daughter?" His voice cracked, and Lev broke down in intense sobs for the first time since he had regained his freedom. Many tears had been shed since they had reunited, but never had Lev lost himself so completely. Anya watched her husband in shock and fear, unable to bear seeing his weakness.

"Stop it! It's not true, Lev! It's not your fault!" she pleaded. "This is just another *nisayon* from Hashem! Hashem has tested you in so many ways, and you always prevailed. You can't let this break your spirits now!"

"Anya, there are some tests that are simply too great to bear."

"We'll get past this one, as well. You'll see!" she promised. "Don't give up now, Lev!"

His next question threw her off guard. He lifted his red eyes and gazed directly into her own. "What makes you think I never lost hope?" he asked quietly, with a trace of disbelief.

She thought a moment before replying. "You yourself described the impossible days – the cold, the hunger, the humiliation. But you never gave up. Did you?"

He lowered his eyes again. "That doesn't mean that I didn't suffer moments of weakness either. There were days when I wished death would come and finish me off. There were months when I didn't believe I would live to see the next hour, let alone the next day or month. I don't like to speak of it, but I was there. Believe me, I was there many times, and I almost didn't survive with my faith intact."

"But you did, Lev. You did in the end! And we still have a way to go! Our journey isn't over yet. Yes, we've reached 'safe shores' in

America, but we can't know what awaits us. One thing I do know, though, is that Hashem is with us, guiding us and supporting us. If He's carried us so far, He won't abandon us now. He won't abandon Karina either. Don't you feel the same?" she begged. Anya knew that her words weren't as compelling as she wished; the desperation still sounded so clearly in her voice, and she hated the weakness she radiated, when she knew that what her husband needed was for her to transmit strength and belief.

Lev heard her plea, and he couldn't bring himself to disappoint her. "I do feel it," he replied after an elongated silence, "but I still feel the need to act, as well."

They spent the whole night talking, discussing their options and trying to think of what they could do as a *zechus* to rescue their daughter from the lion's den. It was Lev who thought of the idea first, and they lost no time in putting their plan into action.

Three weeks later, they held the grand opening of a small, Jewish learning center geared especially toward Russian immigrants. The first classes attracted only a handful of participants, but the Krasnikovs refused to allow the low numbers to disappoint them. This was their gift to Hashem, their effort to find favor in Hashem's Eyes and inspire Divine help for Karina in Moscow. Indeed, within just a few months, the center was bursting at the seams with newly-arrived Russian immigrants all thirsting for the Judaism they had been denied for three generations.

CHAPTER 61

Karina gazed out of her bedroom window at the scenery, which although familiar, was still not beloved. Moscow was a beautiful city, but a city without a soul. A city that was stealing her life from her, along with the lives of so many others.

It was summer once again, two years since she had first arrived to stay with Natalya, and she was still imprisoned there, a hostage in a gilded jail. Her pillow was often saturated with tears; her heart in shreds from longing for her parents; and she was still battling constantly, remaining steadfast to her faith. There were certainly days when she asked herself "Why?" wondering if there was any purpose to her seemingly never-ending struggle, but as the days passed, she began to sense ever more strongly that Hashem's Hand was still guiding her and sustaining her throughout her trials.

She could never understand why Hashem had placed her in this position, and perhaps she never would. At first, the question had haunted her mercilessly, leaving her angry and restless, but eventually she had learned to accept her fate and ceased questioning the ways of Heaven. Who was she to grasp Hashem's master plan? She knew that despite the myriad challenges her parents had faced, they had never questioned His ways. One thing was eminently clear: Hashem loved her deeply, and it was during these two years that she had truly learned to appreciate this love. Hashem was her Father and Mother, supporting her and loving her constantly, granting her the strength to carry on.

As they often did, images of the past two years passed before her eyes as if in a movie. Lonely Friday nights singing *zemiros* alone. Lighting Chanukah candles in the privacy of her bedroom. On her first Pesach, when Natalya had realized that Karina would eat virtually nothing, Dmitri had actually made inquiries for her and managed to procure several kosher matzos. She was repeatedly amazed by the irony of the Kolchiks harboring her in their home despite the peril she placed them in by insisting on her *mitzvah* observance. Natalya's longing to adopt her legally impelled her to compromise on issues that she would never have agreed to otherwise. Her relationship with Karina was terribly complex, and Karina herself could never quite figure out how she felt toward the woman. On one hand, Natalya had stolen her from her family and was holding her hostage in her home; on the other hand, she was a loving and compassionate hostess who strived to act as a mother. Natalya had caused Karina unbearable pain and emotional suffering, yet she didn't hate her. Sometimes, Karina even pitied her; she was so desperate for a child, for someone to love, that she was willing to cross all lines in order to achieve her goal.

Karina's communication with her parents had also increased throughout the years. Karina didn't believe that Natalya could be so oblivious as not to know that she spoke to them several times a week on the telephone, but apparently, she preferred to turn a blind eye to the issue. During their conversations, Karina rarely spoke of her challenges or the despair that sometimes overcame her. With maturity that far surpassed her years, she understood that her parents' emotional torment was as great as, or even surpassed her own. She was thankful that they were able to speak frequently, and their voices imbued her with sanity and strength, even from the other end of the world. Somehow, she felt better every time she hung up the phone with them, more convinced that the day would come when she would return to them for good.

In the last week, though, she had begun wondering, hoping against hope, that freedom was imminent. Gorbachev's *glasnost* was gaining momentum at an astonishing pace, and talk of a new era in Russia had progressed from frightened whispers to brazen public speeches. For the first time in over half a century, Russian citizens were expressing their opinions – and criticism – of the Soviet state aloud, and surviving to tell the tale! Many frustrated Russians exploited this new, wondrous period of liberalization. Travel had also become much simpler, and exit visas were being approved frequently and quickly. Yesterday evening, over dinner, Dmitri had been telling his wife about the mass emigration expected in the near future; and Karina was certain that if Natalya hadn't silenced him with one of her looks, he would have had more to share…

Could salvation be on the horizon?

It was a bright summer's day, and Karina waited at the crosswalk for the light to turn green. A friendly wave drew her attention, and she waved back politely at Svetlana, a girl whom she had befriended slightly during the past year. Svetlana was her age and lived at the other end of Natalya's block. Karina wouldn't describe her exactly as a friend, but she was perhaps the closest thing she had to a friend in Moscow. She studied in an exclusive high school in central Moscow, and when Karina had once confided that she was Jewish, Svetlana had mentioned that, to the best of her knowledge, she was too – but what was the difference, anyway?

"Karina!" Svetlana called, running to catch up with her. "I'm so glad I bumped into you! You won't believe it, but we're leaving Russia! In a month! For good! Can you believe it?" The girl's eyes shone with excitement.

"You are?" Karina gaped at her in disbelief.

"Yes! My whole family is going! Even my grandmother is coming along!" Svetlana exclaimed.

"I don't believe it," Karina whispered, her eyes filling with tears.

"What's wrong? You're not going to miss me *that* much, are you?" Svetlana teased.

"No. I mean, of course I'll miss you!" Karina covered for her blunder. "I just don't believe it. You mean people are really getting out as easily as they want – even Jews?"

"Why not?" Svetlana retorted, tossing her hair. "From the way my parents talk, it sounds like Jews are trying to leave by the masses! We're going to Canada because we have distant relatives there, but tons of others are leaving to the United States, or even Israel. It sounds like a dream, doesn't it?"

Karina nodded in shock. The dream was so close, she could nearly touch it. And it hurt. It hurt so, so much. Would she be forced to watch as her brethren left one after the other, while she remained?

That very night, she dropped the bombshell. As usual, she joined Dmitri and Natalya for dinner, picking at her food and listening to them chat quietly.

"You seem very distracted tonight, Karina," Natalya observed.

"I want to go home," she replied quietly yet firmly, refusing to allow a hint of emotion to cause her voice to waver. It was time that they absorbed that she was serious about her intentions.

"This is your home, Karina," Natalya responded automatically.

"No, it's not. It never was, and it never will be." Karina looked Natalya straight in the eye. "You know it, and I know it. Even the Soviet authorities have finally grasped that Russia is not a home for Jews. And I – I have parents waiting at home for me. Parents who love me and are waiting for me to come home."

"Oh, Karina, we've discussed this so many times already! What prompted you to bring it up again?" Natalya said dismissively. "I thought you'd finally grown up and gotten over this nonsense. I have no desire to return to those early days when every conversation was an argument."

"I *have* grown up, Natalya, and that's why I will no longer be held here against my will. You know as well as I do that you can't keep me here any longer. Russia has changed; times have changed; and you can't threaten me anymore."

The Kolchiks gazed at her in shock mingled with fear, secretly knowing the truth.

"And you didn't even threaten that you'll hand me over to the KGB!" Karina added snidely. She was sick and tired of this game.

Natalya, however, decided to keep up the pretense, hoping that the rules that had applied until that day would continue to serve her. "I don't have to threaten you, Karina, for you to know what I'll do," she replied coldly.

Her plane ticket arrived at Svetlana's house two weeks later, arranged by her parents, and Karina began preparing for her departure. She debated whether to conceal her plans, fearing that the Kolchiks would do something to sabotage them, but ultimately decided to be open with them. There was no point in hiding what they were bound to discover anyway.

Natalya burst into bitter tears as soon as Karina shared the news. "You can't leave me, Karina! I need you! You're the daughter I never had! The daughter I've always wanted."

"I was never yours," Karina answered simply. "Natalya, I've always felt your pain, and even after all this time, it still it hurts me to see you suffer. But it's time you absorbed that my mother was never responsible for your son's death. I never knew him, but he was obviously a good man, a wonderful human being who didn't want another person to suffer needlessly. Nobody ever forced him to do what he did; he helped my mother escape of his own free will and out of the goodness of his heart. I don't believe that any person in my mother's position would have refused such help. The ones responsible for his imprisonment, the ones who denied him the medical care he deserved – they are the ones accountable for his death, the KGB! It was the cruelty of the Soviet authorities that brought about Sasha's death, as they did to so many others. You were always powerless to blame them, so it was easier for you to blame my mother who at the time wasn't even aware of who exactly helped her escape. You could never fight the KGB, but it was easy for you to take revenge against my mother who never intended you any harm." Karina fell silent, breathing heavily.

A long silence passed between them until Natalya replied. "You're right, Karina. I admit that there's truth to what you say. But still, why won't you stay? The anti-religion laws are practically non-existent now. You can finally observe your faith as you wish, without fear. We've done everything we can to pave your way and be kind to you."

"You have been kind to me, but what about my parents? You won't forgive my mother for taking away your son, and yet you ruthlessly steal me away from them! Natalya, do you realize that except for during two brief meetings here in Moscow, I haven't seen my father since I was four?!"

Dmitri surprised them both by interrupting the tearful conversation. "I agree with Karina. It's time for her to go home."

"WHAT?" Natalya whipped around in shock.

"Yes, Natalya. We've enjoyed her presence for two years, and now it's time to send her back to where she really belongs."

"She belongs here!"

"No, she doesn't. She belongs with her parents."

"How can you say that? How can you deny me a daughter?" Natalya lashed out brokenheartedly at her husband.

"Natalya, I'm only being realistic. Karina is not your daughter, and we can't legally keep her here against her will. I say that it's best that we part from her as friends."

Five days later, the Kolchiks drove Karina to the airport. With mixed feelings, Karina embraced Natalya and nodded respectfully to Dmitri.

"Thank you for hosting me all this time," she said quietly. "I'll never forget you." She didn't say anything more, knowing that it was pointless. With a final wave, she passed through the security check and left Moscow behind forever.

The Arrivals concourse at JFK was hardly the place for an emotional reunion, but there was no way that they could wait another moment. They stood there, all three of them together, for the first time in twelve years. People surged around them, moving in all directions, but they were oblivious to it all, oblivious to everything but each other.

The tears came in a deluge, while mother and daughter embraced tightly, weeping for all the lost time. As soon as Anya released her, Lev gathered his daughter in his arms.

"I'm home! I'm finally home!" Karina whispered joyfully. "We're finally together again."

Anya grabbed her tightly again, hugging her as if she would never let her go. Feeling her mother's wracking sobs against her body,

Karina began to grasp what her parents had endured; the emotional torture they had suffered far outweighed the physical torture at the hands of the KGB. Would this anguish accompany them forever? Would they ever overcome these traumas and enjoy true peace and happiness?

"We never stopped *davening*, Karina. Never for a moment," her father whispered tremulously. "We knew what they could do to you, even to you, a sweet, young, innocent girl. "So many times, I was prepared to board a plane and switch places with you, return to Siberia or anywhere else…"

"Papa!" Karina exclaimed. "I wasn't in Siberia or in prison. Nobody ever laid a finger on me. I won't deny that I faced challenges, fear, and loneliness, but whenever I felt on the verge of despair, I would remember what you were willing to pay to preserve your Judaism. You sacrificed everything for Torah, despite having learned so little; and this only proved how incredibly precious it is! It reinforced my commitment to follow in your path and risk sacrificing myself to keep it. Once Natalya understood that, she stopped standing in my way."

They walked toward the exit with Lev carrying Karina's little suitcase, while the girl continued, "From early on she grasped that I wouldn't allow fear of the KGB to keep me from observing the Torah. Both of you had been there, and neither of you yielded, and I was determined not to let you down. I kept whatever *mitzvos* I was able to keep, and I kept them with love. Natalya was never able to shake my beliefs. Do you believe me?" Her tone was pleading.

"Of course we believe you!" Anya replied, swallowing her tears. "I so much hoped to be able to raise you in America, in a free country, far away from the fear and repression. But Hashem had other plans, and we may never understand why. The main thing is that you're back with us, and that you never left our path."

They were outside on line waiting for a taxi. Lev spoke now:

"I remember the day I was caught and thrown into prison. I was certain my life was over – after all, how many people survive what I did – what we all did? Who would believe that we're all here together now?"

Karina reached for her mother's hand and grasped it tightly. "We were the strong ones," Anya whispered emotionally. "They ruled over us with an iron fist, but we believe and follow the Torah of the One Who rules over them and the entire world!"